DECISIVE ENDGAME

MIKAEL CARLSON

WARRINGTON
PUBLISHING

Danbury, Connecticut

Decisive Endgame
Copyright © 2023 by Mikael Carlson
Warrington Publishing

All rights reserved. No part of this publication may be reproduced, stored in a retrieval system, or transmitted by any means – electronic, mechanical, photographic (photocopying), recording, or otherwise – without prior permission in writing from the author. For such requests, contact the author at www.mikaelcarlson.com/contact.

Printed in the United States of America
First Edition
ISBN: 978-1-944972-30-1 (paperback)
         978-1-944972-29-5 (ebook)
         978-1-944972-31-8 (hardcover)

Book cover designed by JD&J
Editing by Michael Waitz of Sticks and Stones

This book is a work of fiction. Names, characters, places, and incidents are products of the author's imagination or used fictitiously. Any resemblance to actual persons, living or dead, events, or locales is entirely coincidental.

Also by Mikael Carlson:

– The Michael Bennit Series –
The iCandidate
The iCongressman
The iSpeaker
The iAmerican

– Tierra Campos Thrillers –
Justifiable Deceit
Devious Measures
Vital Targets
Revealed Secrets
Decisive Endgame

– Watchtower Thrillers –
The Eyes of Others
The Eyes of Innocents
The Eyes of Victims

– The America, Inc. Saga –
The Black Swan Event
Bounded Rationality
Boiling the Ocean

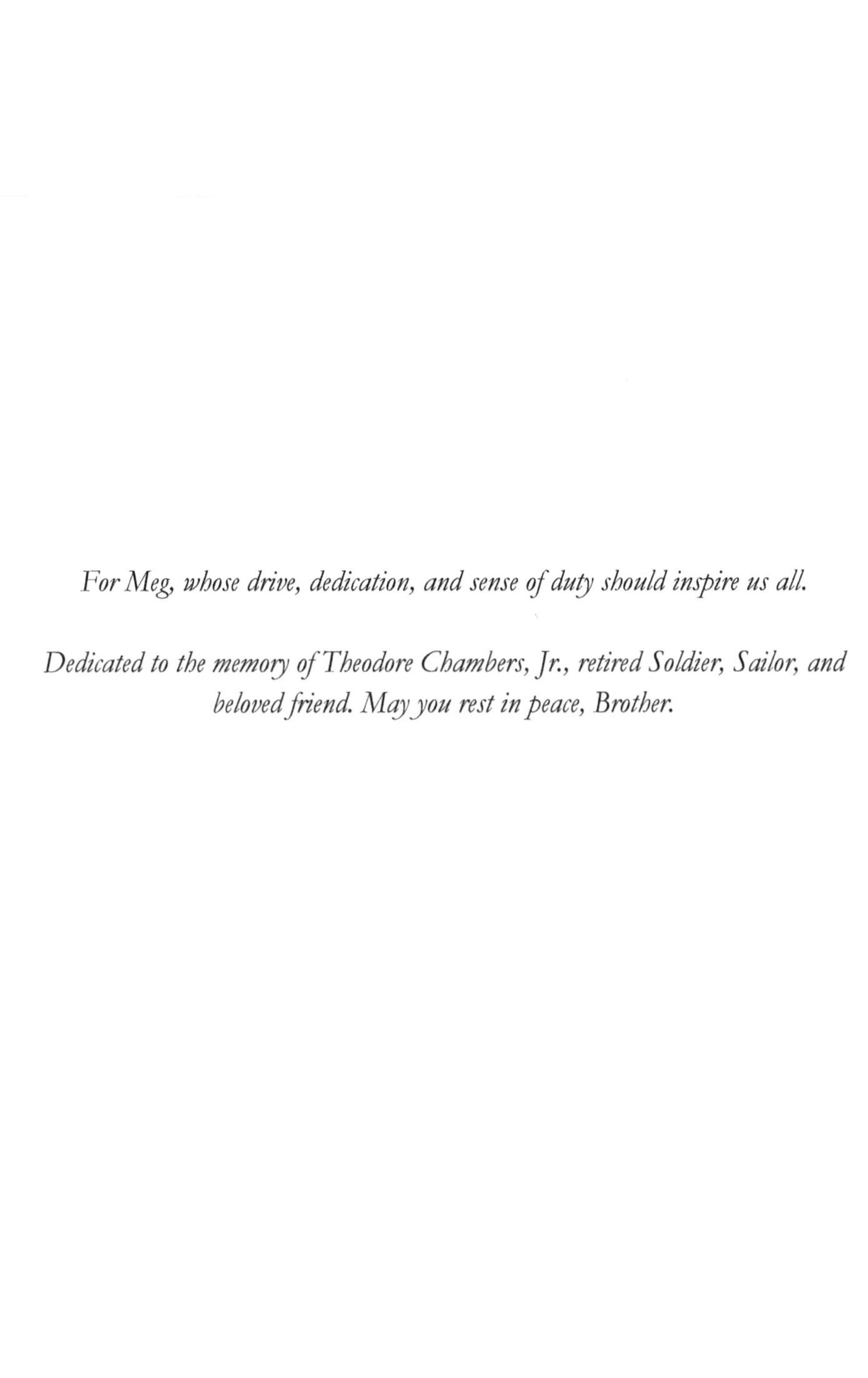

For Meg, whose drive, dedication, and sense of duty should inspire us all.

Dedicated to the memory of Theodore Chambers, Jr., retired Soldier, Sailor, and beloved friend. May you rest in peace, Brother.

PROLOGUE

VICTORIA LARSEN

Hogan's Alley FBI Training Grounds
Quantico, Virginia

Victoria stares out the window at the target building. Surveillance work is boring, and this is no exception. They've been sitting here for over two hours without noticeable movement in or around the structure. But this is Hogan's Alley, America's most dangerous ZIP code. Something will definitely happen, so she can't afford to lose her focus.

In 1987, the FBI consulted Hollywood set designers to create an authentic mock town complete with a bank, barbershop, pool hall, post office, hotel, jewelry shop, and houses. The ten-acre training complex was called Hogan's Alley after an 1890s comic strip featuring a boy living in a crime-infested New York City tenement. The fake town was designed to provide trainees with realistic scenarios, complete with local actors playing the town's citizens. So far, Victoria has found the experience brutally realistic.

"I'll give you a hundred bucks if you go kick the door in," Daniel Murphy moans from the driver's seat.

"The mission is to observe and report," Victoria says, continuing to stare out the passenger window.

"I know. I'm not an idiot. I'm just bored out of my skull. We need some action."

Victoria rolls her eyes. She would rather be teamed up with anyone other than this guy for this exercise. Audie would have been the perfect choice since she's become close friends with him during her time here. Instead, she got her nemesis. The instructors must have done this on purpose. Bastards.

All special agents begin their careers at the FBI Academy in Quantico, Virginia. For twenty weeks, trainees live on campus and adhere to a grueling schedule of training activities, firearms instruction, physical conditioning, and classroom study covering a wide array of academic and investigative subjects. Victoria is already becoming well-versed in behavioral and forensic science, basic and advanced investigative techniques, and interviewing tactics.

Her assigned partner, Daniel Murphy, excels at the classroom stuff. He absorbs information like nobody she's ever met. He's also a hypercompetitive pain in the ass. Most of her class failed the "Legal II" exam covering advanced criminal procedure and constitutional law. It's not uncommon for attorneys to fail that exam. He was top of the class and let everybody know it.

Victoria cocks her head at the attempted deflection. She's about to snap back at him but bites her tongue. By the look on the instructors' faces, the attempt has already backfired.

"Your little rivalry is cute, Trainee Murphy. Go ahead and get sarcastic. You may be a rockstar in the classroom, but know this: Trainee Larsen just saved your ass in Hogan's Alley today. Sleep well tonight, knowing that."

Murphy's jaw tenses, but he wisely stays silent.

"Everyone report to the classroom for debriefing. Maybe you and your fellow trainees can learn something from today's dumpster fires."

The instructors move off as Victoria holsters her weapon. Murphy walks over and stands next to her.

"Do you expect me to thank you?"

Victoria scoffs. "I know better."

"Then wipe the smug smile off your face. You win this round, Larsen, but your actions will catch up with you sooner or later. I only hope I'm there to see it."

EIGHT YEARS LATER

CHAPTER TWO

PRESIDENT-ELECT ALICIA STANDISH

Standish Temporary Presidential Transition Headquarters
Hay-Adams Hotel, Washington, D.C.

The presidential transition in the United States begins after Election Day. Unofficially, it starts much sooner. Both candidates prepare teams well in advance of the voting that are charged with drafting the necessary plans to take over the Executive Branch from the outgoing president. Once the victor is determined, the winning team goes to work while the losing side updates their resumes.

Unfortunately, the reality is much messier. The transition formally starts when the General Services Administration declares an election's apparent winner and releases the funds appropriated by Congress. That process ends on Inauguration Day when the president-elect raises a hand and takes the oath of office, at which point the powers, immunities, and responsibilities of the presidency are legally transferred.

"I'm sorry, Herbert, but this is ridiculous," Andrew complains, displaying the best fake outrage Alicia has seen in a long time. He should have been a congressman.

"I understand your feelings, but you have to look at the situation from our perspective."

"Alicia Standish is the president-elect. Period."

"The events in Pennsylvania have cast doubt on that," the bureaucrat argues. "The GSA has withheld ascertainment letters for far less egregious accusations of voter fraud. The Pennsylvania secretary of state needs to weigh in. Until then, my hands are tied."

Herbert Waller is a minor functionary. This isn't exclusively his call. He's the one who most likely lost a spirited game of rock-paper-scissors to report to the Hay-Adams Hotel to deliver Alicia bad news.

The ascertainment letter formally declares an apparent winner and authorizes the release of $9.9 million in transition funds, secure office space at the Presidential Transition Headquarters in downtown Washington, and agency access to the transition team. Following the 2016 presidential election, the acting GSA administrator issued the ascertainment letter the next day. Recent elections have seen considerable delays, and this one appears to follow that trend.

"Thank you for the update, Mr. Waller," the president-elect says, rising from the sofa and extending her hand. "We look forward to Pennsylvania's secretary of state making a final determination and the GSA's issuance of the letter."

"We all hope it happens quickly," Herbert says. "Transitions are difficult enough with the full amount of time allocated."

Andrew shows him to the door and closes it behind him. He retreats into the modified conference room and pours a cup of coffee.

"It will be okay," Andrew says after ushering the bureaucrat out. "We'll continue using the Hay-Adams until they name you the apparent winner. I have already arranged for campaign funds and the party to cover the costs."

Alicia has been forced to start the transition from the Hay-Adams Hotel, located across Lafayette Square from the White House. It's a magnificent yet extremely costly space. She doesn't need to conduct meetings and interviews in rooms with brass chandeliers, ornamental fireplaces, and silk-covered walls. She needs her people to get to work so they can hit the ground running after the last songs are played at the inaugural balls.

"How long will that be?"

Andrew shakes his head. "I don't run the GSA."

"What makes you think that the secretary of state in Pennsylvania will even certify the election there?"

"Brian has dirt on him. Apparently, he's a sexual deviant in ways that makes Caligula look like a candidate for the Papacy."

Alicia rubs her chin. Among the many depravities attributed to Caligula is sex with his sisters and ordering guests' wives to accompany him to his bedroom. After having intercourse with them, he would return to the party and rate their performance in front of their husbands. Whatever the secretary of state was into must be bad.

"Blackmail."

"Extortion, technically."

"You played a good game with Herbert Waller, but you put us in this position. I think you want it this way. You don't want an official winner named yet."

Andrew smirks and takes a seat on the sofa. "Consider this a probationary period for you, Alicia. It's time to demonstrate that you'll play nice in the sandbox with us."

The president-elect bristles at the use of her first name. It's beyond disrespectful. Upon assuming the highest office in the land, the use of a president's first name is reserved for family and the very closest of friends. People who serve in an administration would never use it in public and often won't in private.

"Are you *really* willing to blow this up if I don't? I've heard your threats to go to the media. You're risking prison or worse. Maybe you are, but is Brian Cooper willing to throw his life away? How about the rest of your cabal, or whatever you call it?"

"Call the bluff."

"Maybe I will."

"The media is right out there. We understand the risk. The question is, do you? I can make you a pariah with one statement to the press corps, or you can do it yourself. It's your choice, as it's been since the day after the election. You are on the precipice of realizing your dream of becoming the president of the United States. If you want to throw that away, I won't stop you."

This should be the happiest moment of Alicia's life. After a career in public service and two years of hard work on the campaign trail, she achieved her ultimate goal. She's about to become the president of the United States. It's one of the most awesome responsibilities a person can have. Instead, she's dreading the specter of life as an indentured servant to a man she once considered an ally. There is no easy way out of this mess.

"You haven't given me your list of demands," the former senator mumbles.

"This isn't going to work that way. As we said, you are the president and get to call the shots. You'll only get input from us when it suits our needs. At that point, you will be expected to do as we ask. Everything else in your purview is yours."

"What about cabinet appointments?"

"You already know about the obvious ones. Conrad will be your AG. We will likely have a few other…suggestions. You may fill the rest of the cabinet positions with whichever candidate you select, assuming you can get them through the Senate. I wouldn't expect them to be too cooperative after this election, so choose wisely."

"Is that your advice as my chief of staff or Machiavelli?"

"Is there a difference?"

"You make that deal sound so rosy. Like your interference will be limited."

Andrew smirks. "It's a bargain when you consider the alternatives. I would have thought you'd be more grateful, Alicia. We *made* you president. We could have just as easily chosen Bradford to win. We still can, if it comes to that. I'm willing to bet he'd take our deal."

Brian Cooper picked the members of the coup well. With Conrad Williams as attorney general, he has full control of the investigative arm of the government. Congress could investigate, but nothing holds a candle to the Department of Justice's power. DeAnna Van Herten is a media giant. She has positioned the VHM empire as a dominant force in news reporting and has significant cultural influence. And then there is Andrew Li. A chief of staff is perhaps the most important job in the White House besides the president. All roads lead through him. He's the perfect babysitter.

"I don't respond to threats, Andrew."

"It's not one. It's just how it is. You get to make the choices, Madam President-Elect. I'm only appealing to you to choose wisely. Enjoy your flight back to Boston. We'll talk again when you return on Monday. We have a lot of work to do before January."

CHAPTER THREE

SSA DANIEL MURPHY

"The Forge" Militia Compound
Liberty, Pennsylvania

"The Forge" comprises a dozen buildings on the grounds of the Liberty Lumber Company. The Keystone Militia was remarkably well-funded by the proceeds from their day jobs. They were almost all mill employees, and the property doubled as a paramilitary base hiding in plain sight. They had an armory, barracks, bunker, planning center, and a rifle range that was inconspicuously set among storage sheds, loading docks, an office, and a fully automated sawmill. Despite their anti-government leanings, they were dedicated to their cause.

Special Agent Daniel Murphy has taken his time walking around the grounds. The place is crawling with men and women in FBI windbreakers collecting every piece of evidence they can find. There was almost a bloodbath here. The men on the assault team could have been decimated as they made their way up the plateau. If not for the lights and a premature detonation of the mines protecting that flank, it may have been the deadliest day in the FBI's history.

The bunker on the southern part of the property is cordoned off. It's where Ian Drucker's body was found and is marked with yellow crime scene tape. Murphy ducks under it and enters the concrete and steel structure.

A blood stain on the floor marks where Drucker took his last breaths. The old cliché of the tape or chalk silhouette is a visual crutch for detective shows, but police don't outline murder victims because it contaminates the crime scene. Instead, hundreds of digital photographs of the body and its surroundings are taken to document the scene.

Drucker didn't spend his final days in comfort. There's a worn bedroll in the corner and almost no airflow in this tomb. A map on the wall outlines the militia's extensive defensive positions. Murphy shakes his head and moves to the hatch that led to the tunnel Larsen must have used to leave the grounds. The experts say it must have taken years to dig by hand.

The desk in the middle of the room contains a map of Pennsylvania with no markings. A series of chess pieces off to the side was probably used to identify key places, but for what exactly likely died with the man known as "Engels." More curious are the cords left behind. One leads to a power supply. The other is a CAT-5 cable for a network connection. Whatever device they connected to is long gone.

"Hey, Murph?" DeAndre asks from the bunker's entrance.

"Yeah?"

"You should come and see this."

"All right," Murphy says, taking one last look around before following his agent back up the dirt road toward the main facility. "Am I going to like this?"

"That depends on what you think about Victoria Larsen."

"I think she's become a domestic terrorist intent on overthrowing the government."

"Has she?"

He already knows Special Agent DeAndre Wright's opinion. He's a fan, and it isn't because Victoria looks great in a bikini. She became a superstar after the Brockhampton investigation. Her reputation was gold-plated after teaming up with Tierra Campos to stop the interference in the New Hampshire Primary. Murphy's fellow agents spoke of her exploits with awe and reverence, much to his chagrin. With every line of praise for his Quantico classmate, he had to privately stew and hold his tongue. His feelings about her weren't popular.

"What do you see?" Wright asks after they arrive in the small control room in the mill's main facility.

"Uh, a control panel. So?"

"The technicians dusted everything. These buttons all have Larsen's prints on them. She activated the mill, which caused the tactical team to halt their movement into the facility, as confirmed by Special Agent Burns. She also activated the floodlights on the grounds."

Murphy rubs his chin but remains silent. Those are interesting developments that are not easily explained away. If Larsen was working with Drucker and the militia, it would make no sense for her to take those actions even to cover her escape. A prolonged firefight would have been better for that.

"There's more. Come on."

Murphy follows the agent out of the automated sawmill building and up a ladder welded to the side of the adjacent lumber storage structure. An observation platform is built on the roof with a line of sight to the command area. While the position doesn't have a commanding view, it's enough to track the movements of anyone approaching from the north or west.

"One militiaman was posted up here. We believe he was in charge of blowing the claymores. They were remotely detonated and probably couldn't get a signal directly from the command building."

"They blew early before anyone was in range," Murphy says, recalling the operation report. "They should have assigned someone more competent. The guy screwed up."

"Unless he didn't. The detonator also has Larsen's prints on it."

Murphy can't hide his surprise. "What are you trying to say, DeAndre?"

"Look, I know what the Bureau is saying. Larsen was working with Ian Drucker all along."

"Yeah, and she needed to exfil before we moved in."

"Which she could have done quietly. Instead, she activated the lights and equipment to get the assault team to stop, and then triggered the mines before they wandered into the kill zone and got ripped apart."

A pit forms in Murphy's stomach. His assumptions are starting to look increasingly shaky. "Unless she made it look that way to throw us off."

"You know better, Murph. You know *her.*"

"I *used* to know her. It's been a long time since our days at Quantico. She has always been a maverick who doesn't like rules. Would you bet against someone like that getting radicalized?"

People change. It's a fundamental part of the human condition. Larsen played hard and fast with the rules during her time in Boston. It's who she is. The FBI can be a stifling bureaucracy, and Victoria would be among the first he would expect to tire of it. There is nothing that leads him to believe she isn't capable of turning to the dark side with the proper motivation.

"Or you're being played. Listen, you got a promotion, a team, and a blanket mandate from the FBI director and deputy attorney general to track Victoria Larsen down. Do you think that maybe it's coloring your judgment? Because from what I've seen, Victoria Larsen saved countless lives here."

"I appreciate your frank assessment, Special Agent Wright, but it's misplaced. This is bigger than you or me. The FBI brass and bigwigs at the DOJ say she's gone bad. I'm not about to doubt them, and you shouldn't either. It's a career-limiting move. Larsen is a terrorist. Our job is to find her, bring her in, or put her down. That's the end of the discussion."

Murphy pats the junior agent on the shoulder and climbs down the ladder to continue his walking tour of the lumber mill turned militia base. Larsen's takedown of Ethan Harrington made her the highest-profile agent currently serving in the FBI. They wouldn't lie about this. Now it's his turn to take that mantle by catching her.

CHAPTER FOUR

BRIAN COOPER

Wolfwood Estate
Vienna, Virginia

The stately European-style home of DeAnna Van Herten is impressive not because of its overwhelming size but its presentation. The grounds are immaculate, the mansion is ornate without being gaudy, and the entire property reeks of class and wealth. Not that Brian would want to live here. It's too ostentatious for his liking.

He parks in the circular drive behind the other vehicles and rings the bell, admiring the marble statues in the fountain that has been winterized to protect it from the impending cold weather. The butler arrives at the door to escort him through a grand foyer, past the formal sitting room and living area, to a staircase that leads to the subfloor.

The utility bills for this place must be outrageous. DeAnna should be grateful that this mansion is in Virginia instead of a harsher climate like Arizona's heat or Minnesota's cold. Not that money matters to the heiress of her father's media empire. She could have a dozen homes like this and still have extra money for a yacht or two.

DeAnna has no need for multiple homes. She isn't a world traveler nor a regular in the country's elite social scene. She rarely leaves Wolfwood Estate, even to run her empire. That can be done remotely via videoconference. If the media maven attends an in-person meeting, it's only because someone royally screwed up.

Brian's conspirators in this endeavor have already gathered in the basement living room – or maybe it's a rumpus room. There are so many rooms in this house. Who knows what DeAnna calls it. The space has a generously stocked bar, an elegant red fabric pool table that has likely never been used, and furniture that looks like it was boosted from Versailles. Everything is cream-colored except the red accents, making the room feel like something plucked out of a dream. Or nightmare, depending on one's perspective.

"Nice of you to finally join us, Brian," Andrew says, finding a seat on one of the sofas with a tumbler of whisky in his hand.

"Leave it to the unemployed guy to be the last to arrive," Conrad piles on.

"Not having a steady income or official job title doesn't mean I'm not working," Brian argues, moving to the bar to pour himself a drink. "It looks like you're all starting the celebration early."

"It's been a long couple of years. We deserve to drink the good stuff."

Brian checks the bottle. The Macallan in Lalique Crystal comes in a luxurious French crystal decanter and easily costs more than a hundred thousand dollars. DeAnna may be a diva, but she has a taste for the finer things in life and a willingness to share.

"It's premature."

"Since when did you become such a pessimist?" their hostess asks.

"If I were a pessimist, I wouldn't have brought all of you into this endeavor. We've had great success and met our primary objective. Alicia Standish is set to become president, and we have the control we need over her. Or do we?"

Brian stares at Machiavelli from the bar. The others all turn to him to await a response. If there's a problem, they haven't heard it yet.

"She is still getting used to the idea," Andrew admits.

"How likely is she to challenge us?" DeAnna asks nervously.

"We may need to slap her hand to show how far we're willing to take this."

"I've known Alicia Standish forever," Conrad says. "That woman would have sold her kids into slavery for the presidency. She won't sacrifice her chance to sit in the Oval Office to expose us."

"That's a big assumption, Conrad," Brian says. "Cornered animals are unpredictable. They could just act threatening, or they could fight."

"You all said that she wouldn't," DeAnna says, growing concerned at the direction of this conversation.

"It was always a risk," Andrew reminds her.

"Then mitigate it. You are going to be her chief of staff. Make her see the light by any means necessary."

"There's no reason to panic, DeAnna. I worked with Alicia for years. Brute force is not how you handle her. Andrew's approach will work. We can box her in, but it must be her decision. Once she relents, she'll be ours."

DeAnna shakes her head, annoyed. She owns a media empire that will spend night and day spinning the coverage of any scandal that erupts. Her superpower is her ability to set a narrative and amplify it until her competitors report it as truth. While the heiress may have the most to lose, at least financially, she's the least exposed of anybody in this room.

"Then we have nothing to worry about."

"That's not exactly true. Victoria Larsen is still a threat."

Conrad narrows his eyes at Brian. "She's being handled."

"She should be dead," Andrew says with a sneer. "Your man Vassyl didn't get it done."

"Neither did Drucker. Do you know how many headaches he and his militia are causing me right now?"

"The claim that Victoria Larsen was working with them won't hold up to prolonged scrutiny, Conrad," Brian says. "DeAnna can shield the story from the public, but the truth will come out unless it's buried with her. She needs to be taken off the board before the inauguration."

"I said it's being *handled*," Conrad seethes. "The director put one of his best men on it. Daniel Murphy was Victoria's classmate and rival at Quantico. He still despises her. He'll be motivated to find Larsen just for the name recognition and laurels it will earn him. It's only a matter of time."

Brian nods. "Let's hope he's as good as you say."

"What about Tierra Campos?" Conrad fires back.

"What about her?"

"You have been telling us since New Hampshire that you'd take care of her. Instead, she's back at *Front Burner* and knows too much about us, courtesy of Isiah Burgess."

"She knows *everything* about us," Brian deadpans. "I confirmed it all with her."

The consultant suppresses an amused smile as mouths around the room hang open. This is not an easy group to surprise. Like him, they are purveyors of information and pride themselves in being well-informed. They also don't like surprises, especially when it's news about a meeting they consider reckless. That's why he met with Tierra in the first place.

"Are you stupid?" DeAnna asks.

"I wouldn't characterize myself that way, no."

"She's going to expose us!" Andrew almost shrieks.

"If Tierra publishes anything about this, *Front Burner* will bury themselves. They are only now gaining minimal traction on their rebuild. An article about a grand conspiracy will make them sound desperate and unhinged. It'll be their death knell."

"And if she doesn't care or is reckless enough to roll the dice? Or if she keeps circling now that she has the scent of blood?" DeAnna asks.

"Or starts working with Standish to reveal the truth?" Andrew adds.

"Are you serious? Were you both asleep during the Brockhampton investigation? Campos may have thrown her a bone in New Hampshire, but Standish still despises her. That gun control bill Ethan was pushing meant everything to her. Given their history, Standish would choose to work with Satan before agreeing to have coffee with Tierra Campos."

"Who's making the assumptions now?" Andrew asks.

"It's time to take her off the board as well," Conrad concludes.

"You're playing with fire, Brian," DeAnna adds. "You might like the thrill, but we don't. Don't force us to make a choice for you."

Brian rubs the three-day-old stubble on his chin. He doesn't like threats, especially coming from this crew. There is no way he can let them think that he'll do what they want. It doesn't work that way.

"I have methods to ensure that Campos stays in check. She'll be removed from the game when it best serves our purposes."

Everyone stares at Brian awaiting more details. They don't get any. Conrad is the first to break eye contact and look at the others.

"It has to happen soon."

"No, Conrad, it has to happen *right*. The timing isn't as important as the result."

"Then get us some results," their host demands.

"You know, you're all awful bossy considering the circumstances. DeAnna, VHN landed Oliver Jahn as its flagship show and is positioned to be the country's foremost news authority with the access you have. Andrew, you're the White House chief of staff. Conrad, you're about to become the next attorney general of the United States. You all got exactly what you wanted from this, and none of it would have happened without me. Remember that."

"What did *you* get out of this, Brian?" Conrad asks.

The political operative grins as he brings his glass of expensive scotch to his lips.

"Satisfaction."

CHAPTER FIVE

VICTORIA LARSEN

Benitez Family Rowhouse
Upper Fells Point, Baltimore, Maryland

Rigo's father knows how to make a good cup of java. She shouldn't be surprised. First, the coffee in any FBI office in America is horrible, so any brew that doesn't taste like turpentine is a treat. Second, he's Latino. It may be a stereotype, but Victoria has always viewed that culture as one that takes coffee seriously.

"You look troubled, *Hija*," Rigo's father says, sitting in his easy chair with his own porcelain mug full of steaming nirvana.

Hija. Daughter. Victoria smiles every time he uses that as a term of endearment. Or maybe he's hoping that she'll marry his son. Either way, it makes her feel warm inside to hear it. He's a good man.

"I can't stay here, Guillermo," Victoria concludes, still awkward about using his given name. She would much rather stick to *Señor Benitez*. "I'm putting you in danger."

"And I told you not to worry about it. *Me importa un pimiento.*"

"You're an important pepper?" Victoria asks, cocking her head as she tries translating that into English. She missed something.

Rigo's father smiles. "It means something with no value. In English, it's...I couldn't care less."

Victoria stares at her mug. "I need you to care. I'm a fugitive, and the harboring charge will be the first chapter of the book they throw at you. They will lock you up and throw away the key when they learn I'm here."

"*If* they learn."

"The FBI is the world's premier organization for finding people. It's not if but when they find me. Even if your home is the last place on Earth they check, and it isn't even close to the last, they'll come eventually."

"You are a hero," the man says with a dismissive wave.

"I'm a pariah. A traitor, at least in their eyes. My FBI career is over. That much you can be sure of. When they catch me, the best I can hope for is a long prison stay."

"You sound like you're quitting," Guillermo says, frowning.

Victoria closes her eyes. Hearing that word hurts. She has never been a quitter and rarely uses the word "can't" because it's so defeatist.

"Federal agents who get arrested for anything, especially DUI, usually means they're done. The unofficial motto of the FBI is 'Never Embarrass the Bureau.' The people in charge protect themselves at all costs. They think I was working with the Keystone Militia. There's no way to come back from that."

"You shared your amazing stories with me. You've never shied away from confronting dangerous men who protect themselves," Guillermo argues.

"This is different. I work for these people."

"Is it different, *Hija*? Is your enemy what's bothering you, or is it something else? You carry a heavy burden."

Victoria lowers her eyes. This feels like a confession.

"I killed Ian Drucker."

Guillermo shrugs. "He needed to die. *Vaya con Dios, cabron.*"

"No, you don't understand," Victoria says, wiping away the tear starting to form in the corner of her eye. "I *murdered* him. He wasn't armed and wasn't resisting. I should have arrested him but shot him in the head instead."

"You faced a difficult choice. What would have happened had you arrested this Ian Drucker? These men in this *junta* that control your bosses…they are powerful, *si*? Would they have locked him up? Or would they have released him and locked you up instead?"

Victoria sighs loudly. That's a couple of good questions she doesn't know the answer to. Then again, she didn't put herself in a position to find out.

She didn't know how she would react to ending Ian Drucker. Killing is never easy, even when it's necessary. He deserved to meet his maker like Marx and Vassyl before him. They were not good men, and this world is a better place without them in it.

That justification doesn't console Victoria or alleviate her guilt. She believes in the rule of law, and she violated it. While Ian's death may be justice, it doesn't bring Takara Nishimoto back. It won't breathe life into Lance Fuller and his family. Ending Drucker's life wasn't as satisfying as she imagined.

"It doesn't—"

"It does matter, *Hija*. You did what you needed to do. *No le busques tres pies al gato.*"

"Don't look…for a cat with three feet?"

"Don't complicate matters. If you hadn't done what you did, you'd be *una prisonera* and have no chance to defeat this cabal you speak of."

"I don't think there's much chance of stopping them, unfortunately."

"Low odds are better than no odds. I put my money on you. And Tierra Campos," Guillermo says, wagging a finger. "Never underestimate a pissed-off Latina. Rigo's *madre*, whooo…. *Ella esta como una cabra.*"

These idioms are killing Victoria. "She's like a goat?"

Her host laughs after he nearly snorts his sip of coffee. He's having a lot of fun using these expressions with her. They were never taught in any of her language courses.

"In English, it's…mad as a hornet or crazy…like a batshit."

"You mean batshit crazy," Victoria says with a slight laugh and a smile.

"Ah, *si*. She was *loco* when she was *enojada conmigo.*"

Victoria smirks. She understood that one. "Most women are crazy when they get mad at their spouses."

"You need to let go of what happened with Ian. You may not be proud of it, but it was necessary. Deal with it later. Focus on what's next. What do you need to do to defeat this *junta*?"

"I don't know."

"I think you do. Do not let your fears control you, *Hija*. The world is a scary place. Those who overcome them go on to do great things. What are you waiting for? *Camarón que se duerme se lo lleva la corriente.*"

"Uh…the shrimp that sleeps is taken by the current? That can't be right. What's the English meaning?"

Guillermo smiles. "You snooze, you lose."

Victoria lets out a chuckle. He's right. She's been the guest of honor at her personal pity party since Rigo plucked her out of the stolen truck in Pennsylvania. She needs to accept what happened with Ian, but that's for another day. Guillermo's bilingual pep talk is exactly what she needed to move past what happened – at least for now. It's time to act before it's too late.

"Thank you for this. You must have been a great father. Rigo is very lucky."

"Ah, *gracias*. Keep telling my son that. He should be reminded often," he says, leaning forward in his chair. "I will do whatever I can to help you."

"You've already done enough. I do need one more favor, though. I need you to call your son."

CHAPTER SIX

TIERRA CAMPOS

Front Burner Washington Office
Washington, D.C.

I walk through the turnstiles after swiping my badge, not that I need to. There are still no security guards here to enforce that particular rule. Or any rules, for that matter. The front desk staff was among the first to go when *Front Burner* hit financial turbulence. The way things are going, they won't be rehired anytime soon.

The elevator takes me to the floor with the conference area we coined the "war room." There's no point in going to my desk yet. Nobody else will be here this early on a Saturday. Or so I thought.

Austin began collecting information on the cabal and sticking it to the whiteboard in his office. We were tracking down the S.O.F. when they were monkeying around with the New Hampshire Democratic Primary. When it became too much information to post and more people needed to be involved, it was moved to the empty conference room on this floor.

Before the election, Austin tasked me to track down Isiah's files, hoping they were a solid lead. That's the reason this room has become sentimental for me. I've spent an insane amount of time here. Rarely does anybody beat me into the office. The last time it happened was when Dial Pirate showed up to surprise me. Now, it looks like it may have happened again.

I creep over to the door, careful not to bump anything that would give away my presence. I peek in after I hear a playful giggle. Olivia is sitting at the table alongside DP. Everyone still calls him Dial Pirate or the abbreviated DP despite his physical presence and knowing his given name is Brian. They all think his handle is cooler.

The information I had on the hackers who doxxed me during the Brockhampton investigation into Ethan Harrington was gold to the FBI. Too bad for them that I never shared it. Even Victoria didn't press me for details. The others have long since gone to ground, but DP rewarded my loyalty by becoming an invaluable resource in getting Isiah's files. We'd be lost without him.

Brian isn't a bad-looking guy, assuming you like pasty-white men with little to no muscle tone. But Olivia is into him. I haven't seen her this happy since I started at *Front Burner*. The first time, not the second.

The two banter back and forth as Dial Pirate works a laptop. I have no idea what he's doing, even as he methodically explains it to Olivia. She's hanging on his every word like he's reciting French poetry over a bottle of wine in a pastoral, sun-drenched meadow. Sensing my presence, he finally glances up and spots me spying on them.

"Tierra? How long have you been standing there?"

"Long enough. What are you two…." I stop when I notice that the whiteboards are erased and the pages of information taped to them removed.

"Don't worry. We saved everything," Olivia says, following my eyes to the blank board behind her. "We took pictures of the whiteboards and scanned all the documents before uploading them."

My heart sinks back into its rightful spot in my chest. "Thank God. Uploading them to where?"

Dial Pirate offers me a mischievous grin. "The Vault."

I'm not sure what to think about that. Isiah sent me a cryptic note leading me to the information he gathered on the cabal. It was to be delivered in the event that something happened to him, and unfortunately, something did. Thinking I like puzzles following my investigation into Ethan Harrington, I had to travel down the rabbit hole and solve a series of clues with the help of Josh and Dial Pirate. It was the hacker who was able to retrieve the files from a darknet data store called The Vault.

"He's been teaching me how to navigate the dark web," Olivia says, her tone a couple of octaves higher. "I thought it made sense to secure all our information. Just in case."

"I thought storing it there had a nice symmetry to it."

"Are you expecting something to happen, DP?"

"No, but that doesn't mean it won't. I'm a hacker and am naturally cautious with data. In this case, it's prudent."

"The cabal knows you have Isiah's files," Olivia says. "Now that their candidate won the election, how long do you think it will be before they come for them?"

I wish I could argue with that. It's unnerving to think Brian Cooper has been protecting me and terrifying to know he could change his mind at any time. We are a threat, and powerful people often find ways to eliminate those who endanger them.

"Fair point. If the feds do come, DP, you shouldn't be here."

"They don't know who I am."

"Are you willing to bet your freedom on that? You've done so much for us. I'd hate to see you end up in prison because of me."

"They have a name and had a location. Maybe the feds have a rough sketch of what I look like from the neighbors who bump into me occasionally. That's it. I appreciate your concern," he says, looking at Olivia, "but I should be thanking you. Interacting with real people is…different than I thought it would be."

"I suppose that depends on the company you keep. Show me how to access this data," I say, taking a seat on the other side of Dial Pirate.

Olivia doesn't seem annoyed by my intrusion. She knows it's time to work and seems energized at the prospect of doing her part. I wish I could say the same.

CHAPTER SEVEN

PRESIDENT-ELECT ALICIA STANDISH

Standish Residence
West Cambridge, Massachusetts

There is no place like home. While Alicia spends considerable time at her Foggy Bottom apartment when Congress is in session, it isn't Cambridge. This is where she is most comfortable. It's where she moved with her husband and raised her kids. It's familiar and comforting. She doubts the White House will be either once she moves in.

Alicia clutches the framed picture of her parents. It got her through the Safe America Act debacle and the mess in New Hampshire. It has always given her strength, and she needs some right now.

Saturday morning used to be for cartoons. Now, it's for catching up on what the political shows are saying. She has no time during the week to watch them, so they are recorded and watched during her rare moments of downtime. Time is one of her most precious commodities in this job, and choices must be made about how it's spent.

"Mark, what are your initial thoughts of the new president-elect?" the host asks.

"Well, Tom, she's more timid than I thought she'd be, for starters. Senator Standish had the reputation of being a pit bull in the Senate. She was ruthless about promoting her vision of America on the campaign trail. People can agree or disagree with that vision, but she promoted it passionately. I don't see that now that she won the election."

"But she hasn't technically won, and not because the Electoral College hasn't met. Colin Bradford hasn't conceded the race, and Pennsylvania hasn't certified the election. They have no slate of electors, and neither candidate wins without them."

"No, he hasn't conceded, although he should. America is ready to move past the election."

Alicia frowns. Half of it is. The other half is hyperventilating about voter fraud and election interference. Rightfully so. If the roles were reversed, the Democrats would do the same thing. It's the new reality in modern elections.

"Even after what happened in Pennsylvania?" the host presses. "I mean, allegations of voter fraud over the past few presidential elections have almost become cliché. In this case, Republicans have a legitimate argument, don't they?"

"The investigation needs to run its course. What happened in Pennsylvania was ugly, but I don't think it makes a difference."

"Is that perhaps why she's toning down her messaging?"

"I would have thought it was the opposite. Standish declared victory in Boston despite what happened. The media declared her the winner, knowing about the fake ballots and Election Day bombings. Her margin of victory in the Keystone State makes it unlikely the outcome will be overturned."

"Could this reluctance be something else? Some other factor?"

Alicia sits a little more upright on the sofa.

"She may realize for the first time that the job is too big for her. The responsibilities of that office are immeasurable. It's easy to say what you would do or not do as an outsider. The view is different once you're the president-elect and begin to prepare for the inauguration."

Alicia finds the power button on the remote and presses it hard. If they only knew the truth. Instead, she has to endure listening to clueless pundits offer their idiot opinions and armchair psychological analysis. It makes her want to throw the clicker at the television.

"They're wrong," Brendan says, rubbing Alicia's shoulders when he comes up behind her. "It's not too big for you. No president has ever had to assume office wearing the lead weights Brian Cooper chained to your ankles."

"I can't exactly run to the press and admit that, can I?"

"No, I guess not," her husband acknowledges as he moves around the sofa and sits beside her.

"I've wanted this for so long…."

"I know. I think you mentioned it on our first date. Now you have it. You reached your goal."

"At what price? Am I going to be the president or a marionette? I don't know if I can do the job with someone pulling my strings."

"Maybe they won't. They could be bluffing, thinking you aren't strong enough to call it. Nobody wants to go to prison. Even if Brian Cooper or Andrew Li is willing to spend their days in a cell, could you imagine DeAnna Van Herten risking jail time?"

"I learned something the day I got sworn into the Senate. Power is meaningless unless you're willing to wield it. This cabal, or whatever we want to call it, wouldn't have embarked on something this reckless unless the gains outweighed the risks."

"Do you think they're just telling you what you want to hear?"

"It makes sense. Transfers of power between administrations in this country are always unnerving. Out with the old, in with the new."

"And the riskiest moment for Cooper and his cabal."

"It will be harder for me to say anything after the Electoral College casts their ballots. It'll be harder still after the Senate certifies the results. After the inauguration, it'll be impossible. I have a short window to do something about this."

Not that there is anything she can do other than go public. Alicia knows she has no ally in this cause outside of Brendan. Nobody will stand next to her at that podium. Her only possible support would come from her "frenemy," Tierra Campos. That thought sends a shiver down her spine.

"You could always resign. Claim a health emergency and hand the reins to the vice president."

"And I'll lose everything I've worked for…maybe I already have."

"Then we fight. We find a way to take them down."

Tears roll down Alicia's cheeks. "How?"

"You're going to be president, Alicia. There has to be something that you can do."

She wipes away the streaks on her cheeks with her sleeve. "The powers of the presidency are misunderstood. We don't live in a monarchy. I can't just issue a decree and make things happen. Even if I did, when people find out the election was rigged and I knew about it, my presidency is over."

The couple remains silent for a long time. Alicia knows Brendan wants to help. He has never been able to stand watching her suffer. He was tied in knots watching her deal with the fallout of Ethan Harrington's arrest. This is no different.

"You know that I support you, whatever you decide to do."

"What do you think I should do?"

"Alicia, you're a beautiful, brilliant woman with integrity and an unbreakable spirit. I don't see how you will let yourself live under the yoke of a lesser man. I think you need to do what you feel is right."

She gives her husband a hug and holds it for a long time. She loves him as much as she did the day they got married. His advice has always been rock solid. In this case, he may be wrong. Brian Cooper is a snake, but whether he's a lesser man remains to be seen.

CHAPTER EIGHT

BRIAN COOPER

Union Square Park
New York, New York

The easiest way to navigate the urban jungle of Manhattan is by subway. Rideshares and taxis will get you where you want to go, but the cost is often exorbitant, and the ride is stressful for anyone not used to the hectic nature of New York City traffic. Fortunately, the Broadway Express N train had a convenient stop for Brian to reach his next meeting.

New York has an energy that makes it unique, but he prefers the white marble of Washington to the gleaming glass skyscrapers of Manhattan. Brian climbed the stairs out of the station and into the former burial ground that became Union Square Park. Some of the best chess masters in the city ply their trade here. Hustlers play from sunup to sundown, bilking tourists brazen enough to challenge them out of their vacation money by destroying them at a game they thought they could play well.

Brian turns his nose into the wind as a delightful aroma fills his nostrils. Food trucks are all the rage in the Pacific Northwest. In Manhattan, it's food carts. All manner of fare is available on nearly every street in the city. In this case, some good Italian sausage is causing his mouth to water.

"Say it, and a doctor will need mining equipment to remove that queen you're holding from your rectum."

Brian smiles and bites his tongue. One of his late father's oldest friends calls this park home. Given his chess skills, Abe probably has a fatter retirement fund than Brian does. He drops in from time to time when he's in the city to play a game with the old man. Abe's last name happens to be Froman, "The Sausage King of Chicago" in the movie *Ferris Bueller's Day Off*.

"I was only going to say that I'm getting hungry," Brian says, lying.

"No, you weren't. Eat after you lose."

"That's an optimistic assessment of the board, Abe."

"Are you ever going to move? I'm not getting any younger here."

"You've been playing speed chess for so long that you forgot that the best strategies sometimes take time to develop," Brian says as he moves a piece.

"Are we talking about chess or life?"

Abe immediately counters the move and leans back impatiently.

"Is there a difference? Both involve moving different pieces that work together toward achieving a goal."

"People as pieces. Interesting. That cesspool of a city you work in has jaded you."

"It was metaphorical," Brian muses.

"You're in politics. You work with the largest gathering of assholes in the country. There was nothing metaphorical about it."

"Touché."

Brian is acutely aware that his late father's long-time friend despises the political class. In that way, he's representative of most Americans. Politics has engrained itself in culture over the past decade, but most people would rather spit on a politician than vote for one. Some do.

"And people never work toward the same goal," Abe says, continuing his masterclass in machinations of life. "They look after their own interests. Chess is different. For example, that rook you are about to lose doesn't have a mind of its own. You are manipulating it into doing what you want it to do. In this case, needlessly getting it killed."

"I'm not going to lose it. I'm thinking about sacrificing it for the greater good."

"Now you really sound like a politician," Abe says with a chuckle. "You should run for office."

That will never happen. Brian once ran for student body president in college and got trounced. From then on, he knew his political career would be backstage, not headlining on the campaign trail. It's better suited to his "particular set of skills," as Liam Neeson once professed in *Taken*.

"I like to be behind the scenes."

"Behind them as in watching, or behind them as in at the table moving the pieces around the board?"

Brian smirks as Abe takes three consecutive pieces following his moves. He stops and studies the board and laments the dumpster fire this attack is turning into.

"Give it up, son. You're toast."

"I believe in fighting until the bitter end."

"Ah, yes, the most romantic of all notions. The captain going down with his ship. It's also a foolish one. I know you were taught that every battle is won before it's ever fought."

Brian loves that line. There is a lot of truth to it. The trick is recognizing whether you are on the winning or losing side.

"Sometimes those battles come down to the last bullet fired," Brian argues.

"Oh, yeah? Name one."

"Abe, are you telling me that you give in to tourists who get the upper hand on you? I find that hard to believe."

"Then you aren't paying attention," Abe says, leaning forward in his flimsy plastic chair to look Brian in the eyes. "My goal isn't to win every game. It's to make money. There is no point in dragging a game out if defeat is inevitable. This game has taught me a great many things about life. The key to being a chess master is knowing when the game is over. True freedom is laying your king down before someone does it for you."

The distraction paid off. Brian's attack failed miserably, but it wasn't meant to succeed. He learned long ago that beating superior enemies is easier when they're preoccupied with other thoughts or events. Abe must not have learned that lesson.

"You should have thought of that ten moves ago," he says, moving his knight to clear a path for the bishop he had waiting for this moment. "Discovered check and, as it turns out, mate."

A discovered check is when a piece moves out of another piece's line of attack and creates a clear path to the opponent's king. In this case, moving the knight also negated Abe's only escape. He could have used his remaining knight to stop it, but his father's old friend was so busy offering pearls of wisdom that he focused on the diversion instead of sniffing out Brian's strategy.

Abe scans the board, his face looking like a toddler trying to figure out how his grandfather got his nose in his hand.

"I want a rematch."

"Not this time, Abe," Brian says, getting up from the table and putting on his jacket. "Some of us have honest work to do."

"Does anyone actually call what you do honest?" the man calls out at Brian, who is already fifteen feet away.

He looks over his shoulder before responding. "Don't be a sore loser, Abe. I'll see you again soon."

CHAPTER NINE

SSA DANIEL MURPHY

Upper Fells Point Neighborhood
Baltimore, Maryland

This came together faster than any operation Daniel has ever planned. The FBI, at its heart, is still a slow-moving government bureaucracy with all the red tape large organizations generate. Not this time. When the director and deputy attorney general are involved, things happen quickly.

The number of men descending on this house is overkill. They could take Paris with a force half this size. But too many is better than too few. The men have been briefed and know what to do without instruction. There are eyes already on the target, ready to feed them intelligence on any changes to the situation. He isn't about to fall into the same trap Rigoberto and Victoria did up in Loughborough. Not that he expects Larsen to be armed with a pair of heavy machine guns.

The convoy rolls up, lights on, and men exit their vehicles and get in position. The tactical team, dressed in full body armor and armed with high-powered rifles, takes the lead. The agents in windbreakers take up positions around the Baltimore townhouse. There is no escape.

"Alpha team ready."

"Bravo team ready."

"Breach," Murphy orders.

A heavy battering ram is slammed against the front door. The residential lock and deadbolt give immediately, and the men rush in. Murphy can hear the helicopter circling overhead, providing an eye in the sky if Larsen manages to slip out and tries to escape on foot. He hopes it isn't needed.

There is shouting on the radio and then nothing. No gunfire is exchanged, and no harried calls come over the radio for assistance. Maybe Victoria was sleeping. That's the point of conducting a raid at one in the morning.

"All clear," Murphy hears over his walkie-talkie. "One male in custody."

"One male?" DeAndre asks, turning to his boss.

"Shit."

The two men jog across the street and step inside past the severely damaged front door. The house is modest and impeccably tidy. Nothing appears out of place, and there is no clutter that one might expect in a small townhouse.

"Where is he?"

"Secured in the bedroom," an agent on the tactical team reports.

"Okay. Search every inch of this place from top to bottom. When you're done, search it again. Don't assume Larsen isn't here."

"Yes, sir."

Murphy walks to the master bedroom, where a cuffed man dressed only in his underwear is lying face-down on the floor. The lights in the townhouse have all been turned on. Like the living area, the bedroom is neat and clean.

"Go to the closet and find a robe or something. Stand him up. Mr. Benitez, I'm Supervisory Special Agent Daniel Murphy," the agent says as the older gentleman is hoisted upright. "We are executing a search warrant for Victoria Larsen. Is she here?"

"*No hablo Ingles.*"

"I know you speak English very well, sir. I'm going to ask you again. Is Victoria Larsen here?"

"I don't know who you're talking about."

"Do you know where she went?"

The man cocks his head and grins. "Who?"

"Where is your son, Mr. Benitez?"

"Rigoberto is working. He's an FBI agent like you."

Murphy doesn't know much about Supervisory Special Agent Benitez besides what he read in a file. He's well-respected and has had a productive career in the Bureau. That doesn't say much about the man. He only knows that if he's helping Larsen, he's a traitor, just like she is.

"He may be an agent, sir, but he's *not* like me."

An agent in a windbreaker signals Murphy, and the senior agent takes several steps over to him.

"Sir, Guillermo Benitez has a white 1997 Cadillac DeVille registered in his name. We can't find it. It's not on this street or any of the side streets in the area."

"Mr. Benitez, where is your car?" He gets no response. "Sir, if you don't cooperate, you'll be charged with obstruction of justice. If Victoria Larsen was here and you don't tell us before I find out, I will charge you with harboring a fugitive."

"She is not here. You will not find her. *No tengo pelos en la lengua.*"

"*No tengo…?* Gomez! Translate '*no tengo pelos en la lengua.*"

The agent smiles. "Literally? He has no hairs on his tongue. It means he tells it how it is."

Daniel nods and smirks at Rigoberto's father. "Cute. You're going to tell us everything we want to know, Mr. Benitez. Trust me. Take him to the field office."

DeAndre comes in and taps Murphy on the shoulder. A second agent behind him reports her findings.

"The guest bedroom is made up. If Larsen was here, she didn't leave anything behind."

"Oh, she was here," the senior agent says, watching as they escort Guillermo out the door. "Rigoberto Benitez's father is a terrible liar. Have an agent grab some clothes for him. He can change at the field office. Get a BOLO out on the car. Focus on the Washington metro area and the I-95 corridor between here and Boston."

"Right away, sir."

"This is a perfect neighborhood to hide in," Agent Wright says. "It won't have cameras, and Larsen could play in the street with the children all day without anyone ratting her out. Spanish Town is a tight-knit community."

"Yeah, it is. I need to check in with the boss. Make sure the windbreakers turn this place inside-out."

Murphy exits the townhouse and walks onto the dimly lit sidewalk that's awash in the pulses of red strobe lights. There is a growing crowd of neighbors gathering outside the yellow police tape going up, and most don't look happy. It could be the disturbance that roused them from their slumber. It's more likely that this neighborhood doesn't like the idea of one of its residents being hauled off by the government.

It is time to break the bad news. Daniel pulls out his cell, selects the appropriate number, and places the call. He hopes the man isn't sleeping.

"Williams."

"Mr. Deputy Attorney General, it's Special Agent Murphy."

"Is Victoria Larsen in custody?"

"No, sir. She wasn't here."

Conrad Williams sighs but doesn't lash out at the failure. "Find her, and quickly. That woman is capable of doing enormous damage. You have every resource you need at your disposal."

"Thank you, sir. I'll find her."

The call disconnects. Murphy slides the phone back into his pocket as he watches the activity on the street. He may have just lied to the number two man at the DOJ. He has no idea if he can find Victoria Larsen or where he should even start looking.

CHAPTER TEN

TIERRA CAMPOS

Front Burner Washington Office
Washington, D.C.

There isn't much need for office space at *Front Burner* these days. We're growing again but are still a hollow shell of what we once were in terms of manpower. Most of the key staff have procured desks in the old investigative area. Legal and accounting, what few people there are for each, sit in a different part of the floor.

Not today. The manhunt for Victoria has dominated cable news broadcasts since the election. Reporters have filed more stories about her than the president-elect. As soon as they learned that the raid in Charm City may have been related, satellite trucks screamed up the Baltimore-Washington Expressway to cover it. We have our choice of networks to watch as almost everyone has gathered to watch the developments from our office.

Wilson walks in with Mi Sun hot on his heels. He left to get away from the din and make some calls. He isn't using his excited walk, which I learned he had when *Capitol Beat* was a part of DeAnna Van Herten's media empire.

"Any news from your sources?"

"The Bureau is being uncharacteristically tight-lipped."

"That's a good thing," I conclude. "If Victoria was in custody, they would have perp walked her right past the cameras."

"Have you heard from her?" Mi Sun asks.

"No. That's what has me worried. It's not like her to be incommunicado for this long, especially after this," I say, gesturing at the television on the wall.

I catch the motion out of the corner of my eye. A man in a suit waltzes in like he owns the building. Then another arrives behind him. They are the spearhead of an army of men and women wearing FBI windbreakers. They flood into the office, moving to the desks and standing beside them.

"This can't be good," Wilson moans.

"What the hell is this?" Naomi screeches as she jumps out of her chair and charges over to the lead agent.

"Are you Naomi Merritt?"

"Who's asking?"

"My name is Special Agent Rodger Brownback of the Washington, D.C. Field Office for the Federal Bureau of Investigation," the burly man says, holding up a folded piece of paper. "This is a warrant to search the premises for written records pertaining to Isiah Burgess, Ian Drucker, and Victoria Larsen, and seize all computer storage currently used by *Front Burner.*"

"What gives you the authority to do that?" she demands.

He unfolds the paper and holds it in front of her face. "A federal judge."

Naomi rips the warrant out of his hand and studies it. "On what grounds?"

"Suspected possession of information critical to an ongoing investigation, assisting in subversive activities directed against the United States government, and providing material support for a federal fugitive."

This is a bold move. Maybe Cooper is more scared of us publishing what we have than he let on at our meeting. That's the only way he would risk having Conrad Williams send federal agents here. Americans around the country will be screaming about freedom of the press and the blatant violation of the First Amendment. If they learn about it at all. The media has a jaded way of determining what is news in this country and what isn't.

"Williams?" Austin leans in and asks me in a whisper. I fold my arms and nod.

"I need everyone to step away from their computers. Give my agents space. Your cooperation is appreciated. Step away," Rodger says, directing our staff.

"Everyone, do as he says," Naomi orders.

It's probably good that the boss gave that order because Tyler and Logan look ready to throw down. While jumping a federal agent may satisfy the primal male need to show dominance, it will also land them in prison. This is nothing worth incarceration. None of the information on these machines will get them in trouble. Dial Pirate saw to that.

Jerome is a late-comer to the party. He walks in and bumps into an agent. I'm not sure if it was intentional, but the man in the windbreaker spins and grabs Jerome, and shoves him up against a wall.

"Whoa!"

The room erupts. Agents back into the center of the room for protection as Tyler and Logan take several steps toward them. Naomi is going ballistic. Even Dial Pirate, who is trying to keep a low profile to avoid attention, gets in on the verbal assaults.

"Everybody, calm down! Calm down!" Brownback barks. "Stand down, Agent. Release him."

Jerome yanks his arm away after he's released. "What the hell is this?"

"A raid on an American newsroom," Naomi says, detest dripping from her tongue.

Agent Brownback looks around. "It doesn't look like one to me."

"How dare you—"

"Shut up, Austin," I warn. "Keep your mouth shut."

"Why?"

The senior agent spots me and walks over. I stand a little straighter.

"Because Agent Brownback here is itching to arrest someone. Don't give him an excuse."

The man smiles. "You're Tierra Campos, right?"

"Unless you live under a rock, you already know that."

He gestures to the door. "Do you mind stepping into a conference room so we can ask you a few questions?"

"Yes, I do mind."

The hint of a smile on his face disappears. "Don't make this hard on yourself, Miss Campos."

"I'm making it hard for you. If you have questions, ask them here."

"Fine. Let's start with a simple one. Do you know the whereabouts of Victoria Larsen?"

I stay silent.

"Answer my question."

My top lip remains welded to my bottom one.

"Miss Campos, would you rather have this conversation here or at the field office? Where is Victoria Larsen?"

"You don't get to ask that question!"

"Oh, he can ask it, Austin. I just don't have to answer, and I won't until I have the opportunity to consult with an attorney, as is my right."

"Ah, another journalist who thinks she can masquerade as a legal expert during a national crisis. Would you like me to arrest you?"

"Do you have an arrest warrant for me? You'll need one, as I have committed no crime during your presence here. Then again, once you arrest me, I'm covered by my Miranda rights, so I still won't be answering your questions. The last I checked, Constitutional rights apply even in times of national crisis. Unless you treat our founding document with the same brazen disregard you're treating me with."

Wilson beams like a proud father. My response was polite yet firm and chippy without being blatantly disrespectful. Even Agent Brownback smiles a little.

"I have a feeling we're going to meet again, and soon, Miss Campos," he says before walking away. "Search every space in this office. I want every computer found. The information may be stowed away."

Tyler walks over with Logan right behind him. We all watch helplessly as the agents begin seizing laptops and searching desks.

"They're going to rip this office apart."

"Yeah," I say, watching them work, "but cleaning this place after they leave is going to be the least of our problems."

CHAPTER ELEVEN

VICTORIA LARSEN

Boston College
Boston, Massachusetts

Rigo pulls his father's car into the parking garage, finds a spot on the second deck, and kills the engine. They had to stay off the interstates to make it this far. Victoria is surprised they did. They knew something was up when his father didn't answer his phone, and media reports confirmed their suspicions an hour later.

It wouldn't take a genius to figure out that Boston is a likely destination. A BOLO, or "Be on the Lookout" request, would have gone out to departments along the route. A late-model white Cadillac with Maryland plates is going to stand out. There was no point in tempting fate by using heavily patrolled roads like I-95.

Victoria arranged for alternate transportation before they reached Massachusetts. That's what brings them to Boston College and the workplace of someone she hasn't seen in a long time. She would have called Seth Chambers, but he's on duty and is likely a surveillance target. The FBI wouldn't ignore their history, so her involving him will need to be an emergency measure she hopes not to need.

"How reliable is your friend?" Rigo asks, staring out the windshield.

"Denise is more of an acquaintance than a friend."

"Great," he moans. "We're going to get turned in for sure."

"Not likely. Denise owes me a life debt. Of course, she doesn't necessarily know the men who fired at us were aiming at me."

Victoria got a text from her friend at the beginning of the Brockhampton investigation after she was unceremoniously dumped by her commitmentphobe boyfriend. Needing to drown her tears with copious amounts of red wine, they arranged to meet at a hot spot called Veni Vidi Vino. Upon leaving the bar, some MS-13 thugs opened fire at them. Victoria pulled Denise down, sending her to the hospital with cuts and bruises instead of entry and exit wounds.

"I remember reading that in your file. I didn't realize it was *that* Denise. Either way, this is a stupid idea."

"If you have a different one, I'm all ears."

"We could go catch a Patriots game."

"They play in Foxboro. It's a half-hour from here. Plus, they're away this week."

"Of course you know that," Rigo says, shaking his head.

A campus police squad car crawls past them. Rigo and Victoria slide down in their seats and stare intently into their rearview mirrors. The car stops and backs up slowly, blocking them in the parking spot. They can see the driver reading their license plate and then typing on a computer mounted to the dash.

"Oh…shit."

"What are the odds? Any ideas?" Victoria asks.

"We could make out like a couple of horny co-eds and hope he leaves," Rigo says, using the same playful grin desperate men use in bars with pretty women when they know the answer will be no.

"Keep dreaming, Benitez."

The officer got the information he was looking for. The car's lightbar pulses to life with red and blue strobes. The car door opens, and the man draws his weapon, using his vehicle as cover.

"Boston College Police! Get out of the car! Slowly!"

"If we get busted by a college cop, I will kill you at our trial," Rigo deadpans. "How do you want to play this?"

"We comply until I give you the signal," she says, checking to ensure a round is chambered in her weapon. "Then move fast."

"Vic, he's a cop," Rigo warns.

"I know."

Rigo and Victoria do as instructed. They open their doors slowly, and Rigo shows his hands as his partner in crime holsters her weapon and pulls her sweatshirt down over it. They ease out of their seats and stand behind the Cadillac with their hands held at shoulder level.

"You're…you're Victoria Larsen."

"It's nice to make your acquaintance, Officer…?"

"Don't move!"

Victoria isn't going to get an answer to her question.

"Dispatch, this is Unit Thirty-Two requesting backup—"

"Now, Rigo!"

Rigo bolts around the front of the car to their right. It was the only alternative he had besides rushing the cop and getting shot for his trouble. The nervous officer sees the movement and is distracted just long enough.

Victoria yanks up her sweatshirt with her left hand and draws her Glock with her right. She develops a hasty sight picture and squeezes the trigger. At this distance, she doesn't need to spend much time aiming. The flashing blue strobe next to the officer's head explodes. He ducks behind the car, waiting for additional shots that never come.

"Shots fired! Commonwealth Avenue Garage! Shots fired!"

He pops up from behind the engine and shoots where Victoria was standing. She's gone, and there is no sign of Rigo, either. He catches movement behind the car that the man fled around and crouches low, waiting for him to reveal himself. He raises his weapon and tries to hold it steady.

"Pull that trigger, and I'll drop you," Victoria says from behind the officer. "Set your weapon on the hood."

The man immediately does as instructed. Now she knows what it's like to be on the other side of that Hogan's Alley scenario, although the odds were different then.

"Move to the Caddy. Rigo, clear!"

"Backup is on the way. I already called it in."

Victoria relieves him of his radio as Rigo moves to the squad car and secures his weapon. "I know. Get in the car."

She pulls the officer's cuffs from his belt and slaps one around his left wrist. The other gets attached to the steering wheel. Victoria turns to see Rigo eject the magazine and work the action of his weapon, then he puts it all on the front seat.

"I can't believe you got the drop on me," the cop laments.

"It was two-on-one. That's not a fair fight. Don't be too hard on yourself."

"You shot at me!"

"I shot *near* you. If I had shot at you, you'd be conversing with Saint Peter instead of me right now."

"Vic, we need to go," Rigo shouts as the distant sirens grow louder.

"You won't be here long, Officer…Antonelli. But if you get thirsty, the water in the center console is still cold. Tell your captain I said hello. He's a good guy."

The cop gives her a quizzical look before she meets Rigo and they head for the stairs.

"Now what?" Rigo asks.

"We hope Denise is waiting for us."

"Is she punctual?"

Victoria purses her lips as they begin walking faster. "I don't remember her ever being on time for anything."

"Wonderful. What do we do if your *acquaintance* doesn't show up before Officer Antonelli's friends do?

"Make a break for the metro station and hope for the best."

They reach the bottom of the stairs and exit the garage onto Campanella Way. There's no sign of Denise, and the sirens are getting louder. They can't be more than a minute away. Probably less.

"They'll shut down the metro if they think we're on it. This campus will be locked down for an active shooter any minute now."

"Yeah, that's where the hoping for the best part comes in."

"I'm going to need therapy after this. How are you still alive?"

It's a good question that she doesn't immediately need to answer when she spots Denise swinging around a corner and pulling up outside Maloney Hall.

"You read my file. You tell me," Victoria says as Denise rolls down the passenger window. "Hey, stranger."

"Hi, Vic! Get in."

Victoria climbs into the passenger seat as Rigo scurries into the back seat.

"I'll thank you later for this, but I need you to drive right now. Fast."

CHAPTER TWELVE

SSA DANIEL MURPHY

FBI Baltimore Field Office
Baltimore, Maryland

Murphy took a break from the interrogation hours ago to let DeAndre have a crack at it. He wasn't getting anywhere and wanted to coordinate the manhunt with the team. Tired and under-caffeinated, he retreats to the breakroom for a cup of something that resembles coffee.

He takes a seat and lets his mind wander. Taking the leash off his thoughts allows him to focus when a situation demands it. The exercise is interrupted when DeAndre appears in the room and pours a coffee for himself.

"Guillermo is sticking to his story, or so the interpreter says. He doesn't know where Victoria and his son went."

"Still sticking to Spanish?"

The man was speaking decent English after the raid. Guillermo Benitez may be more comfortable in his native tongue but didn't forget the language in the past twelve hours.

"Yeah. Are you going to charge him with obstruction?"

Murphy plays with his almost empty coffee cup. "For what it's worth, I think he's telling the truth. It makes sense that Victoria didn't tell him in case he was taken into custody. There's no reason for him to know."

"Do you think Larsen knew we would raid the house?"

"It's not that far down the list of possibilities. She worked for Rigo and knew we would check his place the moment he didn't report to work. After extracting her from Pennsylvania, it wouldn't take a genius to figure he stashed her with his closest relative."

"So, Benitez is in on this, too?"

That is almost as shocking as Larsen. Murphy reread the man's personnel file from cover to cover. Benitez is a model agent, and his actions make no sense. He could be sleeping with her. That's the only reason he can find to explain Rigo's involvement. Still, it's flimsy. The more he dives into this assignment, the more questions he has.

An agent from his team bursts through the door. "There you are! We just got a report from the Boston Field Office. BC Police confronted Larsen and Benitez in a campus parking garage. Shots were fired."

Rigo moves so fast that he almost loses balance when he springs from his chair. "What? Who fired?"

"Larsen fired first and hit the lightbar. The cop returned a single shot. Then they got the jump on him."

"Is he dead?"

The agent shakes his head. "They disarmed him and handcuffed him to the Cadillac's steering wheel. The campus is on lockdown, and they're searching for them. Metro stops on that branch are shut down. Boston FBI is assisting in the search."

"They won't get far on foot. Have Boston assign every available agent to assist local police. Have the plane ready for us at BWI. We need a lift up to Massachusetts."

The agent scurries out of the breakroom to make the necessary arrangements, including transportation to the Baltimore-Washington International Airport. Working directly for the director of the FBI has its perks. Every Bureau resource is at his disposal, including helicopters and their fleet of Gulfstreams. He could get used to this.

"How did she miss from that distance? What is it? Ten feet? Fifteen? I thought Larsen was a good shot."

"She's one of the best, DeAndre," Murphy says, shaking his head. "Larsen doesn't miss at that range. If she shot the lightbar, it's because that's where she was aiming. She didn't want to kill a cop."

"Not for nothin', that doesn't sound like any terrorist profile I've ever heard of."

Murphy presses his lips together. He can't argue with that. If Victoria was working with Ian Drucker, who made killing people a sport, she wouldn't have hesitated to waste a campus police officer. She didn't. That behavior can't be reconciled. That will be yet another question he'll ask when he catches her.

"All right, Vic, what's your play?" Murphy mumbles as he stares at a wall print of Fort McHenry duking it out with the British fleet during the War of 1812.

"Maybe she's going there to hide."

Murphy shakes his head. "No way. The city's too big, too obvious, and has way too many cameras. She went there for a reason."

"Except it could have gone to hell now that we know she's there."

It's an interesting observation. Murphy hangs his head as he paces around the room. DeAndre watches him, unwilling to break his supervisor's train of thought.

"Larsen was a great trainee. I beat her in the classroom, but she excelled on the shooting range and during practical exercises. It was infuriating. It wasn't until I graduated from Quantico and got to my first field office that I figured out how she did it."

"Let me guess. She cheated like Captain Kirk in the Kobayashi Maru?"

Murphy didn't peg DeAndre as a Trekkie. In the fourth year of Starfleet Academy, cadets take the Kobayashi Maru test before graduating. It's a simulation of a no-win scenario where the ship responds to a distress call from a heavily damaged freighter in the neutral zone near Klingon space. The attempted rescue in restricted space is an act of war, and the Klingons attack, destroying the ship and killing the entire crew.

It is used to test a cadet's character and morals. Any candidate who ignores the distress call might not make a suitable captain. James Kirk beat the Kobayashi Maru by reprogramming the test's conditions so that when the Klingon battle cruisers attacked, they'd stop firing after recognizing his name and assist in the ship's rescue.

"Nothing like that. Larsen was always a step ahead because she was a planner. But when the plan went to hell, she relied on her instincts. She could evaluate an action plan and dismiss or adopt it as effortlessly as the rest of us breathe. She never panicked."

"Okay, she's a superstar. Got it. What's she planning in Boston?"

Murphy's eyes grow wide. "Alert the Secret Service of a possible threat to the president-elect. Standish is in Cambridge this weekend. Do we have a friends and family list for her?"

"Yeah. It's most of the Boston FBI, for starters."

DeAndre hands him several sheets of paper with columns of names on them. He recognizes some of them. The idea of another colleague helping her is nauseating. But if she turned Benitez, anything is possible.

"Have the team check the personnel records. See if any of these agents have ever engaged in questionable activities or received reprimands for flouting procedures. Get a couple of agents to scour camera footage on campus to see if one of them caught something. She'll need help in Boston—transportation and a place to lie low. If we're going to find Larsen, we need to figure out who's helping her."

"And then what?"

"We're gonna do something unexpected that she can't plan for and is too late to react against."

CHAPTER THIRTEEN

PRESIDENT-ELECT ALICIA STANDISH

Standish Residence
West Cambridge, Massachusetts

Sunday mornings have always been reserved for family time. After breakfast, Brendan and Alicia would load the family into the car for church and then take them on a drive through the rural areas of Massachusetts. It was a routine that they stuck with until her kids reached high school. Now that they are off at college, it's just her and Brendan.

Of course, that's if you don't count the two dozen Secret Service agents in and around the house. One of the sacrifices a president makes is privacy. There is precious little. Schedules are maintained, journals document meetings and events in meticulous detail, and there is never a moment when a guard is less than fifteen feet away. The idea of a Sunday drive now would entail a convoy of no fewer than five vehicles and possibly a helicopter hovering overhead.

Retreats to a private residence are no exception, even as the president-elect. Given the near impossibility of securing this house, it's one of the few remaining times she will visit in the next four to eight years. Her trips out of the nation's capital will be to a private estate or Camp David.

That's a worry for another day. Tonight is a moment for Brendan and her to appreciate what they have. The wine is open, the candles are lit, and dinner is in the oven. It's a perfect evening.

Alicia stares out the window at the darkening street. It will be Thanksgiving soon – one of her favorite holidays. She is not much of a cook, so she turned preparation into a group effort. Some of her best times were around their dining room table. She is going to miss that. Her next Thanksgiving will likely be at the Hay-Adams.

"Ma'am! I need you to step away from the window," an agent orders.

Three other men burst into the living room as Brendan emerges from the kitchen to investigate the ruckus. One of the men draws the curtains as another hustles into the kitchen to close the blinds.

"What's going on?"

"Crimson is secure," the head agent barks into her sleeve microphone.

Alicia frowns at the code name. The Secret Service picks it, but it's not what she would have preferred. She may live near Harvard but didn't go to the university.

"We have a credible threat from the FBI and increased our defensive posture. A car just aggressively pulled up to the checkpoint, so we are locking things down until the situation is resolved."

"What kind of threat?" Brendan asks.

"Why didn't you tell me?" Alicia demands.

"Madam President-Elect, understand that we will never brief you on every measure taken to ensure your safety. You have to trust us to do our jobs. Yes," the agent says, pressing her fingers to her ear as she listens.

Brendan slides over next to his wife. "Are the Secret Service always this jumpy?"

"I don't know. I've never had a detail before."

"Roger," her lead agent says. "Confirm the credentials and search the vehicle."

"What's going on?" Alicia asks, getting no response.

"She doesn't have an appointment...okay, let her through." The agent turns to her charges. "Victoria Larsen was spotted in Boston. She got confronted by a campus police officer at Boston College, and shots were fired. Nobody was hurt, and Larsen managed to flee the area. The FBI gave us a heads-up that you are a possible target."

Alicia glances at the three other agents in the room. "Unlikely. Who's at the gate?"

"The attorney general."

Alicia nods. This can't be good. Brendan knows this will be an uncomfortable conversation and excuses himself to the kitchen. Alicia paces until her old friend is escorted into the house.

"Give us the room, please."

The agents leave but will stay close by. Lisa doesn't track their movements. Her eyes are welded on the future president.

"I apologize for my detail. They're a little spooked right now. Would you like a glass of wine?"

"I'm not staying long. I only want to look you in the eyes while you tell me why Conrad Williams is about to be named the new attorney general."

Alicia stops pouring. That leaked fast. She is going to need something stronger than a Malbec after this conversation.

"Hard decisions had to be made."

"And what part of my job performance made the decision for you? Have I not supported you enough? Have you not been someone I've called a friend since you joined the Senate? Did I forget your birthday or something?"

Alicia turns to face her friend. "It's complicated."

"Simplify it. Were you planning on telling me or just making the announcement and finding out that way?"

"It was never my intention to—"

"Then why? Huh? You aren't close to Williams and have never particularly trusted him. Why would you make him the government's top lawyer?"

Alicia clenches her jaw. The truth is elusive, especially when you can't tell it. "I felt a change needed to be made."

Lisa looks wounded. Her face fills with sorrow before it changes into something else. She is a no-nonsense AG with a reputation for being tough but fair. Ehler isn't afraid to speak her mind, even if the opinion she offers is unpopular. That makes her services invaluable to anyone who sits in the Oval Office.

"What happened to you, Alicia? You've always been ambitious. Everyone elected to Washington is. But I never thought you would betray your friends once you achieved your goal. It's a shame. You aren't the person I thought you were."

"Lisa—"

"No," the attorney general says, raising her hand. "I get it. I guess you and I value different things. Good luck to you, Madam President-Elect. With Williams running the DOJ, you're going to need it."

Lisa turns and leaves without another word. Alicia hangs her head. The damage is done. A woman she has considered a friend and ally is no longer either, all because of Brian Cooper and his despicable cabal.

Alicia promised Lisa her position would be safe if she won the election. Now, one of her first acts as president-elect is to renege on that promise. Lisa will spread that word. Nobody is going to trust her after this. Unfortunately, betraying a friend is the least damaging thing Brian Cooper is capable of.

"You okay?" Brendan asks, emerging from the kitchen.

Alicia shakes her head. "Nothing about this is turning out to be okay."

CHAPTER FOURTEEN

BRIAN COOPER

Actyv Private Equity
Midtown Manhattan, New York

One Vanderbilt is Midtown Manhattan's tallest building and stands as the city's fourth-tallest. Brian marveled at its modern beauty the first time he was here. He's no less impressed on this occasion as he checks in at the security desk and rides the express elevator up to the 55th floor.

The Actyv Private Equity office is the single most stunningly beautiful workspace he has ever seen. The spectacular view of Manhattan out the floor-to-ceiling windows is worth every dime of the astronomical rent they pay. Not that the three men running the firm worry about such things. Actyv is basically a printing press for money. The revenue they make in an hour covers their monthly fee to the landlord.

No buxom receptionist greets Brian as he steps off the elevator. That's too bad but not completely unexpected for a Sunday. Instead, Xinming Qi is waiting patiently for him.

"It's good to see you again, Brian," the man says, gesturing him into the office.

"I appreciate the invite."

The first time Brian was here, he had to act like he had never had a conversation with the three men joining him in the conference room. Nothing is further from the truth. He has been in contact with one or more of them almost weekly for nearly three years. This is only the second time they have ever met in person.

Actyv funded the legal challenges that the Republican and Democrat parties have launched in the aftermath of the Pennsylvania debacle. Their involvement in challenging the election is by design. He knows this whole effort is only part of their master plan, one Brian was happy to play a key part in. They haven't told him their endgame, and he hasn't bothered asking. He's getting what he wants out of this arrangement.

Roman Muratova and Garrett Brewer are hard at work on laptops in the conference room. Both men rise to greet their guest. These men are all wealthy beyond imagination but are still cordial.

"I didn't expect to meet at your office," Brian announces following the greetings.

"Our apologies, but there is much work to be done," Roman says.

"The office is mostly empty on Sundays, so we can speak freely," Garrett informs him. "There is no need to keep up the appearances like last time."

Brian doesn't hide his disappointment. "That's unfortunate. You guys know how to enjoy life."

"Perhaps we can arrange something special for your next visit," Qi says. "After the inauguration?"

"On that note, congratulations on your success with Alicia Standish. You and the others have done a remarkable job."

"You sound surprised, Garrett."

"Let's be honest, shall we? For as brilliant as your plan was, there were a great many things that could have gone wrong."

Roman steeples his hands, and Qi folds his arms while waiting for Brian's answer. Everything is a challenge with these three. They are results-driven to a fault and expect transparency. Brian has no issue with that but resents them testing his willingness to provide an honest analysis.

"Yes, there were."

"Has the president-elect been told about her new reality?"

"We handled that right after the election. Alicia Standish has realized that she has no suitable alternative to working with us if she wants to sit behind the Resolute desk. We're taking preventive measures to limit her ability to do something…reckless."

"Excellent."

Brian smirks. They are smart enough not to ask for the details. They see the big picture and have farmed out the tactical elements of their plan to men like Brian. How many others are involved in their master scheme is a mystery, although the political operative does have some idea.

"What about Tierra Campos and Victoria Larsen?"

"I'm sure you're keeping up with current events," Brian says, leaning back in his obscenely comfortable chair. "What is it you're really asking me?"

"Okay," Roman says, leaning forward. "Why is either still breathing?"

That was spoken like a true Russian. "Larsen was underestimated," Brian admits. "The assets who had orders to neutralize her both failed."

"And Campos? I'm sure killing a reporter wouldn't be difficult," Qi says.

"The decision to delete her was deferred until she has no utility."

The three barons exchange glances and shift uncomfortably. Brian has made a career out of studying people. He learns more from body language than from words escaping their mouth. These men don't like that answer, and he knows why.

"You can understand why we seem uneasy about that."

"Of course. You view Tierra Campos as a risk. I see her as an asset. She has a role in this that she isn't finished with," Brian says, expecting that response. "She will be dealt with when the time is right."

"She will be dealt with as we see fit."

"What Qi is trying to say is that we've made a sizable investment in you, Brian," Garrett clarifies. "One of several high-risk, high-reward endeavors we expect will pay huge rewards in the coming world. We cannot allow our work to be undone."

"It's my judgment that has brought us this far. Mine. I have already demonstrated that you can trust that."

Roman and Qi remain impassive as Garrett rubs his chin. "Of course. We do trust it. You are an invaluable asset to Actyv and the world we seek to create. Even if you had failed, we would have whisked you away on a jet to ensure your safety. That is how much we value you."

"I'm thrilled that it wasn't needed."

"As are we, but you also understand why we aren't celebrating prematurely. Standish won the election, but she is not *yet* president."

"I concur with Garrett," Roman says. "Tierra Campos and Victoria Larsen are threats that we expect you to deal with. It only takes one poison pill to sour a deal."

"I'm aware. You should leave me to be concerned with that. I'm sure you have better things to do."

Roman looks like he's about to lash out at Brian but holds his tongue. Out of the three, he's the man of action. Qi remains silent but is the planner of this triad. He's likely architecting eight different contingencies for Brian's "accidental" death. Garrett is the diplomat. He's the interface with the world and the one who moves the pieces around the chessboard. The trio makes an effective team, especially when they're on the same page. In Brian's experience, they usually are.

"Then it's settled," Garrett says, rolling his chair away from the table and slapping a knee. "Are you interested in an early dinner? We haven't eaten lunch and can order from an amazing steak restaurant down the street."

"That sounds good."

"Consider it done."

Qi excuses himself to make the arrangements.

"Now, regale us with your stories. We lead dull lives by comparison," Garrett says.

"Yes," Roman agrees, leaning forward. "We want to know everything you know about what happened in Pennsylvania."

CHAPTER FIFTEEN

TIERRA CAMPOS

Front Burner Washington Office
Washington, D.C.

The conference room at *Front Burner* has all the life of a morgue. I wonder if this is how Germany's generals and field marshals felt when they realized they would lose World War II. That was then, and they were the bad guys. They were supposed to lose. This is now, and the team assembled around the table needs to be the winners. The fate of the country may be at stake.

Naomi Merritt walks in and sits at the head of the table. The normally level-headed and stoic head of *Front Burner* doesn't have her usual air of confidence. Instead, she rests her chin on her hands. Whatever news she has isn't good.

"The government froze our bank accounts pending the results of an investigation. No transactions are allowed in or out, meaning there's no place for advertisers to pay their invoices. At least the advertisers we have left. Most have already canceled their buys. The mainstream media saw to that when they wasted no time taking to the airwaves to claim we are anti-American."

"How is that even legal?" Olivia asks.

"A judge said so," Tyler moans. "One Williams probably plays golf with."

Naomi stands abruptly and shuffles over to the door. The usual determination we're used to has vanished, and her demeanor reflects something else: defeat.

"I'm sorry, everyone. It's over."

"What now?" Tyler asks after she leaves.

"Dial Pirate, is the information you stored on the dark web still secure?" Austin asks, still searching for some angle we can exploit.

"Yeah, they'll need more than a court order to get to that."

"Then we publish."

"How, Austin?" Tyler asks. "How do we post it to our website when they seized our computers?"

"The hosting company took the site offline," Logan informs him. "We have no platform."

"Then we get our affiliates to do it."

"Yeah, that's not going to happen," Jerome moans. "I've been on the phone with them all afternoon. Tom Swim, Alétheia, and Radio Free America are taking a wait-and-see approach, but the rest are out. Even bloggers and podcasters who support us won't run into the fire to save us. There's too much at stake for them."

"Then we leak it to the mainstream."

"Austin, there isn't a reporter on Earth who will touch this after what just happened," Olivia argues. "Even if you found someone looking to make a name for him or herself, their editors would never approve it."

I close my eyes. Olivia's right. Even if we could get the mainstream media to listen to us, which is unlikely, the story would never see the light of day. They are corporate interests, not news organizations. For them, money drives reporting, and none of them would take a chance on this and risk alienating their advertisers.

"Tierra? What do you think?"

"That the war is over," I say in a near whisper. "We lost."

"I refuse to believe that."

"It's over, Austin! The FBI raid isn't meant to stop us from going public. It's to manage the response when we do. If we publish Isiah's files now, we'll look desperate."

"We *are* desperate," Logan muses.

"No!" Austin spins and punches the whiteboard. His reaction is immediate. "Aw, damn it."

"That was dumb," Olivia says as Austin flexes his hand in pain.

"Tierra, I need you to be with me on this. You can't give up."

This isn't the first time I've faced a situation like this. I would have thought that Brockhampton or New Hampshire would have prepared me for the battles ahead. They didn't. The lesson I've drawn is that sometimes you need to quit while you're ahead. If this can be called being ahead.

"What choice do we have? This was a warning. How long before we start getting arrested, or worse? What will it feel like if we're mourning more than the death of *Front Burner*? This cabal has already killed people. What if it's one of us? Will any of you be able to look in the mirror again? I know I wouldn't be able to."

Silence blankets the room. Austin takes turns staring at our faces, looking for any hint of fight left in any of us. He isn't going to find any. Everyone here has drawn the same conclusion I have. We fought a good fight, but there is no point in struggling onward.

"Well, guys, I don't know about you, but I'm going to go and get drunk," Tyler says.

"I'll join you," Logan adds, standing and following him out.

"What do you think, DP? Want to go drown yourself in tequila?"

He turns to Olivia. "I prefer vodka and Red Bull."

"Naturally."

Jerome nods at us before leaving. Austin sits and rubs his eyes. Part of me wants to say something, but the words don't come. I'm too numb to speak, let alone move.

"You're taking this better than I thought you would."

I lower my eyes, not wanting to see the hurt in his. "I've already come to terms with the inevitability of this. Once I learned that Brian Cooper was Rasputin, I knew it was only a matter of time. He's a brilliant strategist, and he thought this through."

"Then why are you still sitting here?"

I look around the empty conference room. "I don't know. Looking for an answer, I guess."

"What's the question?"

"Cooper just ordered Williams to raid an American newsroom. The cabal could have shut us down at any time. Brian could have had me killed when he suspected I had Isiah's files. He didn't. Why is he keeping me around?"

"What did he say when you spoke to him? Did you ask?"

"I did. Brian said he had his reasons, but I still don't see them."

"Then let's find out," Austin says, slapping the table.

I shake my head. "You know, after the Summerville shooting, I had a question that was left unanswered. I wanted to know why a classmate, a kid I had known since kindergarten, one day decided to come to school with a rifle and open fire in a library full of his peers. To this day, not knowing why someone would do that haunts me. But I learned to live with that nagging question because I had no choice. The reason Brian chose to keep me in the loop may bother me, but I will learn to live with that question, too."

"You don't have to. You can get the answer."

I press my lips together. I'm not going to like the flavor of the words about to come out of my mouth. "It's not worth it. This cabal is someone else's problem now."

I exit the conference room, leaving Austin alone in a place he might as well call home, given the time he spends here. *Front Burner* wasn't his creation, but he cherishes it like a child. We will all mourn the loss, but its demise will hit him the hardest.

CHAPTER SIXTEEN

VICTORIA LARSEN

Water Street
Danvers, Massachusetts

Darkness comes early in New England this time of year. The winter solstice is only a little more than a month away. Normally, Victoria relishes the longer days of the summer months. Now, the encroaching darkness serves their purposes. People are indoors with their families, making this sleepy little bedroom town nice and quiet.

Danvers is near the renowned beaches of Gloucester and Revere, about a half hour north of the Boston Field Office in Chelsea. It was originally known as Salem Village, part of the town widely known for a famous religious hysteria in 1692. Most of the accused women in the Salem witch trials actually lived in Salem Village, with a smattering coming from nearby hamlets.

"I think this is it," Denise observes, pulling her car alongside the curb in front of a small ranch-style house.

"Thanks, Denise. For everything," Victoria says, holding her hands.

Her old acquaintance watches the news. She knows this simple act of help could land her in trouble and chose to do it anyway. Rigo was wrong. She didn't turn them in. Victoria may have to consider her life debt paid.

"It's the least I can do. Good luck."

Denise drives away as the pair walks up the sidewalk to the front door. Victoria can feel Rigo's eyes on her and steals a glance.

"What are you grinning at?"

"Nothing. Nothing at all."

Victoria rings the doorbell. There is shuffling inside and a couple of shouts before a child, about seven or eight years old, meekly answers.

"Hi there. Is your mom home?"

"Mom! Black Widow is at the door."

Victoria strokes her hair and checks her clothes. Yeah, she can see the resemblance. One of the stops on the way here was at a convenience store. Victoria asked Rigo to grab black hair coloring to make her less conspicuous. He grabbed red. The second stop was a thrift store for new clothing. She was looking for something to help her blend in, and he selected dark jeans and a black leather jacket. The ensemble makes her think he's living out some childhood fantasy.

Miranda shows up to see what her young son is talking about. Her mouth hangs open as she stands in the doorway.

"Queen V?"

"Hi, Miranda. We're sorry to bother you, but we need your help. You know I wouldn't have come otherwise."

"I…uh…come in, come in. What do you have?"

Victoria holds up a laptop after stepping into the house. "It belonged to Ian Drucker, and it's encrypted."

Victoria tried to break it herself while she was stashed away at Guillermo's. Encryption encodes plaintext data into ciphertext that people cannot read until it's decrypted with a key only authorized users possess. Victoria thought she could figure it out but never got close.

"Honey, who is it?" Miranda's husband shouts from the other room.

"Some people from work. I'll be down in the workshop."

Miranda waves them over to a door, and they proceed downstairs to the basement level. It's full of old toys, cribs, and seasonal décor like most cellars are. In the corner is something Victoria doesn't see every day. Miranda erected a metal mesh around her workspace as a Faraday cage to block unwanted wireless signals. The setup reminds her of what Brill used in *Enemy of the State*.

"Welcome to my fortress of solitude. You've been busy, girl. Every agent in Boston is searching for you."

"I know. This is the last place I wanted to come. Please believe that. I don't want to endanger you or your family."

"You know, I was hit with a bout of regret and self-loathing after we met on the Esplanade. Here you are, trying to save the country, and I'm acting selfish. I'm glad you are giving me the chance to do my part. Red hair works for you, by the way."

"Miranda, you should know, if they find out—"

She holds her hand up, stopping Rigo. "No warning is necessary. I know how the game is played. Let's see what my favorite Avenger managed to get."

Miranda powers up the device. The woman is far too dedicated and woefully underpaid for her work at the New England Regional Computer Forensics Laboratory. Her discoveries have helped Victoria multiple times and assisted federal agents and state police detectives in four states in solving countless crimes. If anyone is the superhero, it's her.

"Can you defeat the encryption?" Rigo asks. "I know the Bureau makes a fuss about what's commercially available."

"It depends on what Ian used. The Advanced Encryption Standard is a secure symmetric encryption algorithm. The chosen key bit encrypts and decrypts blocks in 128 bits, 192 bits, and so on. 3DES is a current block cipher standard, like the older Data Encryption Standard, which uses 56-bit keys. However, 3DES encrypts data three times using three individual 56-bit keys. So, your 56-bit key becomes a 168-bit key. It's just slow."

"Okay, that's all over my head. What would a guy like Drucker use?"

"BitLocker Drive Encryption," Miranda says without hesitation as she stares intently at the screen. "It's easy to use and native to Windows. Let's hope he didn't. I can't brute force anything 256-bit or higher. If he…ah. Bitshield. Well, that changes things."

"In what way?"

"It makes life way easier, Queen V."

"What do you mean?" Rigo asks after sharing a confused look with Victoria.

Miranda spins her chair around to face them. "It's a myth that the geeks bested the feds in the crypto wars of the 1990s. The government wanted to prevent the sale and export of advanced encryption products. The cyber community fought them every step of the way and was deluded into thinking they had won.

"Instead, the government changed tactics. They worked with…well, more like extorted companies to build in backdoors that law enforcement can use to access the data they want."

"Is that legal?"

"Where did you find this guy?" Miranda asks Victoria before staring up at Rigo. "You're in the FBI, man. You should know better. Since when does the government play by its own rules?"

She spins and goes to work on the laptop. Victoria can barely suppress her smirk as Rigo smarts from being so viciously owned. A couple of minutes later, the drive is unencrypted.

"Okay, we're in. Let's see what secrets Mr. Drucker has been…whoa… he's been a busy boy."

Miranda starts opening files. There are notes, a journal, operations plans, dossiers, and dozens of jpeg screenshots. She clicks on one of the images, and the screen capture from a game fills the screen.

"What the hell kind of game is Knights of the Crusade?"

"It looks like an MMORPG. An early one. Drucker was using the chat feature."

"An MM…what?" Rigo asks.

"Massively multiplayer online role-playing game," Miranda clarifies. "It's a story-driven online video game in which a player takes on a persona and interacts with other real players in a fantasy world. Drucker went by the name…TavernWench."

"Look at the names of the players he was talking to," Victoria says as Miranda chuckles.

"Machiavelli and Robespierre," Rigo says, glancing at Victoria. "This was how he communicated with the cabal."

"I think we just hit the motherlode."

CHAPTER SEVENTEEN

BRIAN COOPER

Carolina Cookin'
Washington, D.C

Andrew peers in the large picture window from the street and sees Cooper demolishing a rack of ribs. The sign may read "closed," but he swings open the eatery's unlocked door and steps inside. Other than Brian, the place is completely empty. The cooks have finished for the day and are all cleaning up the stainless steel pans and serving trays in the back.

Brian thinks that few things in life approach the heavenly smell of good barbecue. The thing that first drew him to Carolina Cookin' was the smell emanating into the street. The aroma of barbecue sauce and brown sugar inside makes Andrew ill.

"Seriously? I haven't been this nauseated since watching Luther and Isiah Burgess chow down fried chicken at a greasy spoon in New Hampshire."

"That sounds…stereotypical," Brian manages to say between bites.

"That's what I thought. Are you even taking time to breathe as you eat?"

"It's a secondary consideration right now. These are the best ribs north of the Mason-Dixon."

Andrew looks around the joint. "My God, I just walked into an episode of *House of Cards*."

Any fan of the hit political drama series knows about Freddy's BBQ Joint. The too-good-to-be-true fictional spot was where Frank Underwood went at odd hours to enjoy his famous ribs. The eatery also served as a covert meeting place for Frank, Raymond Tusk, and Remy Danton, making the reference relevant.

"We're here for the same wonderful anonymity. Even if one of the guys in the kitchen recognizes you, nobody gives a shit that you're about to become the White House chief of staff."

"I find this country's apathy occasionally refreshing. Why am I here?"

Brian leans back and wipes his face with a paper napkin. "I'm worried about Standish."

"I told you," Machiavelli says with a scowl. "I have her under control."

"Nobody controls Alicia Standish. You can influence her and maybe even extort her. But she won't willingly live under anyone's thumb. Don't let her make you think otherwise."

"If she's that much of a problem, we should have made Bradford president."

"He's as bad, but for different reasons. Standish wants the title. Bradford wants to serve the people. He's a shield away from being Captain America. The risk was higher of him exposing us."

"Then you're going to have to trust me. Alicia doesn't so much as have a phone conversation that I'm not privy to. She can't hurt us without me knowing it."

Brian tosses the napkin aside and picks up three more. "I know. But knowing it and stopping it are two different things. It's time to limit her options as well. You need to execute Order Sixty-Six."

Order Sixty-Six comes from the *Star Wars* prequels. It was a top-secret order identifying all Jedi as traitors to the Galactic Republic and subject to summary execution. The order was programmed into the clone troopers through behavioral modification biochips, making it impossible for them to disobey the command. It was a contingency protocol the Sith intended to bring about the long-awaited fall of the Jedi Order. Brian picked the title because Andrew despises the franchise.

"It's premature."

"I don't think it is. Even if I'm wrong, it's a win-win. You know that."

Machiavelli is the one who came up with the scheme, if not the name. Andrew Li may not have Cooper's connections or panache, but he's an effective manipulator worthy of his Florentine namesake. The plot is a stroke of brilliance, even if Brian won't admit it to his face.

"Okay. I'll set it up. Have you told the others?"

"Robespierre will find out tomorrow. Nietzsche can learn about it when the news leaks and her network breaks it on air."

"She's going to love that," Andrew moans. "When is our other announcement going to be made?"

"Tomorrow morning, if all goes according to plan. Stay tuned."

Andrew nods before getting up from his chair. He isn't about to stay in this dive any longer than necessary.

"Are you sure you don't want some ribs for the road?"

"Quite sure."

"There is one more thing, Andrew. Standish is going to start getting desperate. Don't let her out of your sight."

"Don't worry about me. Worry about what those things are doing to your stomach."

Brian smiles as Andrew disappears out the door. He goes back to cleaning the remaining deliciousness from his plate. The pieces are falling into place. All the hard work of getting to this point is over. This late in the fourth quarter, all he needs to do now is keep someone from throwing the game because they did something stupid.

CHAPTER EIGHTEEN

PRESIDENT-ELECT ALICIA STANDISH

Standish Temporary Presidential Transition Headquarters
Hay-Adams Hotel, Washington, D.C.

People inherently don't like change. Still hungover from the election, there is anxiety among the population about what the next four years will bring. Add to that a genuine disgust for what happened in Pennsylvania and half of the nation brewing with anger over the result, and it's even more complicated. Despite those distractions, there is work to be done.

Transition is a set of complex tasks the incoming and outgoing administrations take to ensure a smooth transfer of federal governance. Alicia needs to focus on selecting the White House staff and the key cabinet posts. She will appoint four thousand people to positions across the government in the next few months, with more than a quarter requiring Senate confirmation to assume their duties.

Many of these cabinet positions must be filled by people who can help her turn campaign promises into federal policy. Some actions she can take unilaterally, like rolling back executive orders issued by the previous president or signing new ones. The sooner these key positions are filled, the sooner her new cabinet can prepare for their new roles.

The day's first meeting is with a woman Alicia is eyeing to take over the Department of Education. They aim to promote student achievement and preparation for global competitiveness by fostering educational excellence and ensuring equal access. The department was created in 1980 by combining several federal agencies, and is much maligned by the Republican party. They level accusations of waste at them, and in some regards, they're right. That's one thing Alicia plans to fix.

The meeting concludes, and the future secretary of education leaves the room. It's one of the cabinet positions that Cooper and friends didn't show interest in making demands on. Alicia shows her out and sees Robert Ackerman waiting patiently. It's only 8:30 in the morning, and she's already behind schedule, but it's not a good idea to blow off the outgoing White House chief of staff.

"Good morning, Robert. Please, come in," Alicia says, inviting him into the meeting room she's using as an office.

"How's the transition going?"

"It's still early in the journey. Honestly, it would be much easier if the GSA declared a winner and released funds and office space."

"I understand," Robert says, nodding. "We're working on that and believe the Pennsylvania secretary of state is close to certifying the election. Once that happens, the GSA letter will come quickly."

"What brings you to this side of Lafayette Park?" Alicia asks, changing the subject.

"I had an early meeting with Andrew to plan your meeting with the president."

Alicia cocks her head. "I thought that was off until after the Electoral College meets."

Robert grins. "The president had a change of heart."

"Ah. He's feeling the heat over not having a declared winner a week following the election. He thinks what happened in Pennsylvania jeopardizes his legacy and hopes a meeting with me will help move things along."

"Your political skills are above reproach, Madam President-Elect."

Alicia smiles at the compliment. He's not a man who offers many of them. "Tell the president that I look forward to meeting him."

"I will. I have to head over to the DOJ."

"Why?"

"Press briefing. They are about to name Victoria Larsen as a domestic terrorist."

A shiver runs up Alicia's spine. "Seriously?"

"Director Krekstein presented compelling evidence about her involvement with the S.O.F. in New Hampshire. Her taking them down was smoke and mirrors. She was helping Ian Drucker every step of the way, including during their time at the militia compound."

"That's…unbelievable."

Because it is unbelievable. The question now is whether the FBI director is involved with Cooper and William or just their stooge. Scarier still is that they could fabricate evidence that convinces the president and his chief of staff that the woman who took down the Sword of Freedom and saved the New Hampshire Democratic Primary was working with them.

"I thought so, too, but the evidence is there, and it matches her actions. That's why Larsen fled the lumber mill that night. She couldn't be seen with Drucker. It's also why she killed him."

Anyone who believes that is delusional. Alicia only forces a smile. "Thank you for the heads-up."

Robert leaves, and a staffer ushers in another candidate for a federal appointment. Alicia greets the man and smiles, but her head is elsewhere. Williams is getting desperate to find Larsen. They are making another move to close the walls in on her. If they succeed, there will be no stopping them.

CHAPTER NINETEEN

SSA DANIEL MURPHY

Federal Bureau of Investigation Boston Field Office
Chelsea, Massachusetts

The team assembled in this room is doing its thing. There weren't many leads following the shootout at Boston College. Murphy assumes they either found a ride with someone or managed to otherwise procure one. Larsen had no known friends or acquaintances at that school, but that doesn't mean she didn't know someone there. And that's the problem – Boston is a big city, and she could be anywhere in it.

A female agent is given an assignment by Special Agent Wright and quickly disconnects her laptop, leaving the cords splayed on the table. Murphy stares at them for a long time. His mind drifts back to that bunker in Pennsylvania and the desk in the center of it. The cords were left because the device was hastily removed, likely by Victoria before she used the tunnel to escape. Murphy curses his carelessness. He's been so focused on hunting Larsen down that he missed anticipating her most obvious play.

"DeAndre, are there any computer experts on the list of Larsen's known acquaintances?"

The junior agent gives his boss a quizzical look before shuffling some papers around the table to find the one he's looking for. He scans the names, most of which have locations and employment information.

"Uh…yeah, a Miranda Ramirez."

"Where does she work? Tell me it's here in Boston."

DeAndre's finger traces across the page. "The New England Regional Computer Forensics Laboratory…it's in this building."

"Of course it is. Let's go."

The pair navigates the Chelsea Field Office and find their way to the NERCFL. Computer forensics has become increasingly important in building federal cases against modern criminals. Murphy has relied on them in the past but has never had the pleasure of working with this unit.

They find the supervisor and explain the situation. He agrees to let them interview his employee, and he points them to a desk. She isn't making it obvious but has been watching them since they walked in.

"Can I help you, Loki?"

"The name's Supervisory Special Agent Daniel Murphy. Are you Miranda Ramirez?"

She taps the nameplate on her desk. "Not very observant for a federal agent, are you?"

"It never hurts to confirm," Murphy says with a grin. "Come with us, please."

There was little about the tone of his voice that made that sound like a request instead of an order. Miranda accompanies them to a conference room and is asked to sit. Murphy pulls up a chair across from her as DeAndre leans against a wall.

"What's this about?"

"Do you know Victoria Larsen?"

"Are you going to waste my time asking questions you already know the answer to? I know her well. We've worked several cases together, which is why my name was on a list that black Robin here is probably toting around."

"Pssh. If I'm anyone, it's Black Panther."

"Can you even spell T'Challa, boy wonder?"

"Have you seen Victoria Larsen?" Murphy demands, raising his voice to end the banter.

"Lots of times."

He clenches his jaw. "Recently?"

"No."

Murphy studies her face and cocks his head. "You're a terrible liar, Ms. Ramirez. Did she bring a laptop to you? Something that was either damaged or encrypted?"

"No."

"Okay, that's another lie. That device belonged to Ian Drucker and is evidence in a federal investigation. I don't need to remind you of the penalties for obstruction. That's the first in a long list of charges I could bring against you. So, I will ask you again…did Victoria Larsen seek your help to gain access to that laptop?"

Miranda crosses her arms and keeps her mouth shut. She can't be accused of lying if she doesn't speak. The lack of response is enough confirmation for Murphy.

"That's what I thought. DeAndre, Larsen is probably still in the city. We need to find her before she knows we're onto her. Start with that police detective she's chummy with. She'll turn to friends she can trust, which rules out most of this building."

Murphy exits the conference room and stops in the hallway to dial the director. He takes a deep breath as it's picked up on the third ring.

"Krekstein. This had better be important."

"Director, it's Agent Murphy. We have a development. The laptop that went missing from the Keystone Militia base?"

"Have you recovered it?"

"No. We believe Larsen had help accessing its contents. It's a safe bet she knows everything that's on it."

The FBI director curses under his breath. "Okay. I'll handle briefing the deputy attorney general. I need you to find Victoria Larsen…at all costs."

It wasn't an order up for discussion. The head of the FBI severs the call without waiting for an acknowledgment.

"That sounded tense," DeAndre says, getting a grimace in return. "What do you want to do with Ms. Ramirez?"

"Have the guys search every inch of her house and check every computer they find. If Larsen left the laptop there, or Miranda downloaded the data, we need it found. I want you to go back in there see if you can talk some sense into her. Use some MCU references. You both seem to be into the Marvel Cinematic Universe. I want her singing like a canary in the next thirty minutes. It'll make our job a lot easier."

"And if she doesn't?"

"Arrest her."

CHAPTER TWENTY

VICTORIA LARSEN

Detective Chambers' Family Residence
Revere, Massachusetts

Revere is a city of around sixty thousand located approximately five miles from downtown Boston. Originally called North Chelsea, it was subsequently renamed after Revolutionary War patriot Paul Revere. Its population swelled with Italian immigrants in the first half of the 20th century, and their influence is hard to miss with all the Italian markets, restaurants, pizzerias, and bakeries.

Seth lives in a cute white house on the corner of a decidedly quiet, middle-class neighborhood. His home has two floors and a small front lawn with a larger back yard, and was clearly decorated by his wife.

The trio are congregated around the dining room table. Shauna is out of town, so he decided to play chef for the evening. Victoria wouldn't have expected a hard-boiled Boston detective to be an avid watcher of the Food Network. The meal he prepared was shockingly delicious.

"Seth, if you ever decide to retire from the state police, you have a future as an Iron Chef," Rigo says, wiping his mouth.

The big man laughs. "I'm better with a grill or a smoker. You should come back in the summertime. I make a brisket that could convince you to change your religion."

"Well, if this meal was any indication, I'll take you up on that."

"I'm glad you liked it. What about you, Vic?"

"Dinner was amazing. I appreciate you sticking your neck out for us, Seth. I really didn't want to involve you. I figured that the FBI was keeping an eye on you."

"If they check with the state police, I'm at a conference in Las Vegas. My guys are covering for me. And, for accuracy, I'm sticking my neck out for you…*again*," the detective points out with a wink. "Happy to do it. I'm getting used to living dangerously when Black Widow here is involved."

"Oh, don't you start with that crap, too! I get enough of it from Miranda."

Seth and Rigo laugh before their host collects the plates and enters the kitchen. Victoria catches a message that pops up on his cell. First, it's the alert from the front lawn camera. Then another announces movement at his kitchen door.

"Seth, are you expecting visitors or an Amazon delivery tonight?"

"What do you—"

The door is violently kicked open. Victoria hears the glass shatter all the way from the small dining room. She looks at Rigo in disbelief. The FBI found them. Then gunfire erupts. A single belch from a submachine gun rattles the house's walls. Seth screams as they hear him collapse to the floor.

Rigo and Victoria have the same idea. This isn't an FBI team serving a warrant. Needing cover, they flip the dining room table on its side, causing the remnants of dinner to crash to the floor. Rigo draws his weapon and huddles behind the makeshift cover. Victoria has a different thought and moves to the wall between the dining room and the kitchen.

She can hear a man say something that sounds like it's in Russian. Then the weapon goes full auto. She expects the wall she's hiding behind to get turned into Swiss cheese, but the fusillade is unleashed on the cabinetry along the wall that separates the kitchen from the den.

 Rigo peeks over the table and sees a figure move into his field of vision opposite the entryway. He fires three rounds and ducks as the man's weapon opens up. The dining room table splinters, but the heavy oak prevents the rounds from penetrating.

He slides into Victoria's line of sight and tugs at the top of his shirt. The men have body armor. That's why the man Rigo shot at is still standing. He lies prone as the gunman fires another burst that shreds the table.

Victoria backs up and raises her weapon. The man charges through the entry, and she trains her sights on his head. She pulls the trigger, and the gunman lurches to the side after her shot passes through his neck below his right ear.

She walks up and taps a round into his forehead as she crouches. His buddy shouts something in Russian and unleashes a volley that stitches the wall she was hiding behind until his weapon runs dry.

An experienced soldier can reload a rifle in a matter of seconds. Ammunition pouches are located on the front of body armor for quick access to reduce the movement necessary to complete the task. Unfortunately, in a firefight, seconds can feel like hours.

Victoria pops up and immediately trains her weapon on his head as he slaps a fresh magazine into his weapon. Her shot punches right through his forehead, and he pitches backward like a fallen gunslinger in a Hollywood Western.

Rigo is already moving. He checks the first guy as Victoria checks the second. Both are dead.

"Clear," Victoria says, keeping her eye on the door. Where there are two, there could be three or four.

"MP5s and tactical gear," Rigo observes. "These aren't gangland thugs."

"They were speaking Russian. Check Seth."

She doesn't have much hope that her friend survived the initial salvo. The first thing the commandos would have done before rocking and rolling on the décor was double-tap him in the head.

"He has a pulse…three shots, through and through. He's losing a lot of blood. Find his first aid kit."

Victoria doesn't question the information or bother wasting time overcoming her surprise. She leaps into action. Seth is a cop, meaning he's prepared for almost anything. He'll have a well-stocked kit around in case of a riot or zombie apocalypse. She finds it in the bathroom and rushes back to the kitchen. Rigo pulls out a bandage as approaching sirens from outside grow increasingly louder.

"Vic, you need to go," Rigo says as he feverishly tries to stop the bleeding while Victoria tears open another bandage.

"I can't."

"You have to. I'll tend to Seth. You have to get out of here before the cavalry arrives."

"I'm not leaving him, Rigo!"

He grabs her hand. "Yes, you are. You're no good to anyone in a jail cell, and that's where you'll be if you stay. You have Ian's information. Use it. I got this. Go. Go now!"

Rigo's not going to pull rank. He doesn't need to because he's right. She doesn't want to admit it, but he is.

Victoria kisses her fingers and places them against Seth's forehead. "Take care of him, Rigo. And yourself."

"Count on it."

Victoria gives the detective one long look before retrieving the backpack with Ian's laptop and leaving the house via the back door. Neighbors gather around the property, curious as to why it sounded like a warzone in the house. She slings the backpack's straps over her shoulders and makes it down the street before the first squad car arrives. Several more are only seconds behind it.

She has no idea what to do next but needs a plan. She just can't force herself to think of one. Her mind drifts back to the detective lying almost dead on his kitchen floor. She never should have involved him in this. Her rising anger forces her to begin to run. Her gait becomes faster and faster until her lungs burn and her back begins bruising from being slammed by the computer.

Spent, physically and emotionally, Victoria collapses on a lawn and tucks herself into a ball. She has always prided herself on controlling her emotions. She was raised to be tough and chose a profession that calls for that kind of discipline. Not tonight. For the first time in recent memory, she can't stop herself from crying.

CHAPTER TWENTY-ONE

TIERRA CAMPOS

Josh's Apartment
Georgetown, Washington, D.C.

The raid on *Front Burner* has left us all at a loss for what to do. Locked out of our office because the DOJ leaned on the landlord, returning to our homes was the only real alternative. Of course, I don't have one. I have Josh's couch. Again.

Naomi immediately began to seek outside counsel willing to make a case against the illegal search and seizure of our office. We haven't heard anything yet, so it can't be going well. The government never would have attempted this against *The Wall Street Journal* or *The New York Times*. We're not that old, that rich, or that established. We're also digital. That seems to make a difference these days.

"If you keep staring intently at the phone, you'll subject yourself to Higgins' Razor."

I turn and look at Josh, wondering what language he's speaking. "*What?*"

"Higgins' Razor," he says, sipping his beer. "You've heard of Occam's Razor, right?"

"Yeah…essentially, when faced with competing explanations, the simplest is likely the correct one."

"Uh…basically, yeah. Somehow, I'm surprised you know that. Anyway, Higgins' Razor states that the time spent staring at a cell phone is inversely relational to the time it will take to ring."

"You're insane and possibly a classic egotist."

"Ouch. Not true."

"The fact that you named a philosophical principle after yourself would convince most people otherwise," I argue as the phone rings. "You're also apparently wrong."

"Not really," he says with a smile as I pick it up. "You stopped looking at it."

"Ass. I'm taking this in your bedroom. Hi, Naomi."

I hear a knock at the door and don't think much of it as the head of Front Burner launches into a monologue about how no law firm in the city will help us. I'm not surprised. It might be different if we had financial resources, which we don't, but few firms would be eager to aid a media outlet the government considers treasonous.

A series of thuds causes me to pull the phone from my ear. Then I hear a crashing sound and shouting. That gets my attention.

"Something's going on, Naomi. I'll call you back."

I end the call and move to the door. I'm about to open it when I hear two men talking, and neither is Josh. It's also a foreign language. Polish…maybe Russian. I can't be sure. I move my hand off the knob.

Josh isn't saying anything. There's no announcement that friends or co-workers are here. He isn't talking at all.

My fight-or-flight instinct kicks in. With a dearth of good options, I shimmy on my stomach to get underneath Josh's full-size bed. There isn't much clearance between the cheap wall-to-wall carpet and the bottom of the frame. Content I can't be seen, I hold my breath.

Then the bedroom door opens. Black combat boots glide into the room…slowly, carefully. The man moves to check the bathroom. If he peeks under the bed, it's over. It feels like that kidnapping scene from *Taken*, but it's much more terrifying in real life.

Satisfied that I'm not in here, the man leaves, leaving the door slightly ajar. I exhale slowly…quietly.

"Where is Tierra Campos?" a heavily accented voice asks.

"Who?"

I can hear the fear in Josh's voice. He's trying to be brave, but his tone betrays him. The men are speaking in that same foreign language. It definitely sounds like Russian. One of them chuckles.

"You are Josh Higgins. You are her friend. Where is she?"

"I don't know."

"I don't believe you. You will tell me, or I will shoot you."

"I don't know. I swear."

A single gunshot rattles the basement apartment. Josh yelps in pain. The sound of his anguish causes tears to pour down my face. I'm not letting this happen. I won't stay under the bed while Josh dies trying to protect me. He risked his life for me once. It's time to return the favor.

I quietly slide out from under the bed and open the nightstand drawer. The gun Victoria gave me is still in its holster. I haven't touched it since she gave it to me in that Philadelphia hospital.

I adjust my grip like she taught me and do a press check. I didn't know what that was until I met Victoria. Now she's got me acting like James Bond. Satisfied that the weapon is ready for action, I move to the door. I can hear Josh grunting on the other side.

"If you do not talk, you are no good to us. Answer me, or the next shot is between your eyes. Where is Campos?"

I won't put Josh in a position to make that choice. He would likely sacrifice himself, and they'd find me anyway. The hell with flight. It's time to fight.

I push the door open and raise the gun. The men are standing side-by-side, so I point and start shooting. I keep pulling the trigger, leveling the gun after each shot like Victoria taught me. I keep shooting until no bullets are left in the magazine, and the slide locks to the rear.

Blood is pouring from the men's heads onto Josh's carpet. They aren't moving. They aren't even twitching. Ignoring them, I rush over to Josh, who's bleeding from his shoulder.

"Oh, my God! Are you okay?"

"Uh, yeah," he says, leaning against the wall. "Other than being shot, I'm just ducky. When did you learn to be Annie Oakley?"

I don't answer, focusing instead on dialing the three digits on my cell and getting help. Josh is bleeding, and I just killed two people. There's nothing funny about this moment of distress.

"9-1-1, where is your emergency?"

"Georgetown. Two men came in with guns. I think I killed them. My friend has been shot! He's bleeding! Please, hurry!"

CHAPTER TWENTY-TWO

BRIAN COOPER

Cooper Residence
Bethesda, Maryland

One doorbell ring is sufficient to let him know someone is there. Five consecutive rings are excessive. As he walks from the study into the foyer, the incessant knocking has gone from urgent to panicked. He's waiting for someone to belt out, "FBI! We have a warrant!"

Instead, he peeks out the window to see an angry deputy attorney general bruising his fist against the sturdy oak door. Brian violently pulls the door open, causing Conrad's fist to hit nothing but air on the next knock. It was enough to throw the big man slightly off-balance.

"What the hell do you think you're doing?" he asks after recovering.

Brian smirks. "It's good to see you too, Conrad."

The bureaucrat brushes past him into the foyer without an invitation. The gesture is a power move, and it's also rude. Brian closes and locks the door behind him. The tongue-lashing over the impropriety can wait until he finds out what the problem is this time. He'll settle for the passive-aggressive approach.

"Come in and make yourself at home."

"I'm not staying."

"Good, because I was being sarcastic. What do you want?"

"An explanation," Conrad demands. "What the hell happened at Seth Chambers' house? And why was Tierra Campos attacked?"

Brian gives him a faux puzzled look. "I thought you said at DeAnna's soiree that you *wanted* her removed."

"I do! But there are less conspicuous and more successful ways of doing that. The men were ex-Spetznaz, for crying out loud. Nothing screams 'I want you dead' louder than that. And do you want to know what the irony is? They failed."

Brian tucks his hands into his pockets. "Is this where I get to joke about Russian efficiency?"

"You can, but it won't be funny. You took a shot at Larsen and Campos and failed."

"That's where you're wrong. I wasn't involved in either attack."

"Bullshit. You're working behind our backs. Don't deny it."

There it is. Brian's mind races ahead. The "cabal" has always been a marriage of convenience. He likes to think of their quartet like the Clintons – a power couple with more love for power than each other. He doesn't know if that's true, but it admittedly looks that way.

Now that they've achieved their goal, the paranoia amps up. They shared a common objective and common enemies. As one is reached and the others neutralized, suspicions that they would turn on each other are only natural.

"Deny what? Your ridiculous accusations? If you're playing a game of Clue, I promise I'm not Colonel Mustard in the conservatory with the candlestick. I had nothing to do with those attacks and have no reason to lie."

"You have every reason to lie if you're trying to undercut the rest of us to consolidate power."

Brian hangs his head theatrically. "I see. Mmm, no, I don't. Explain why you think I need to do that."

Conrad widens his stance and crosses his arms. "Andrew is about to become the White House chief of staff. I'm going to be the AG. DeAnna is…DeAnna. We're all about to assume powerful positions that can wield enormous influence. What do you have?"

The corner of Brian's mouth curls. "The presidency."

The smug response has the desired effect. Conrad drops his guard and has to think about that for a moment. The other cabal members wanted something specific – for Andrew and Conrad, it was a position. DeAnna wanted more access to supercharge VHN's ratings and catapult her media empire to the next level. Brian thought bigger. He wanted control, and that's what he earned.

"You really think it'll be that easy, don't you? That Standish will be wrapped around your finger?"

"I know Alicia Standish far better than you do. I worked for her for years. I watched her and learned everything there was to know. So, yeah, I do think it will be that easy because we gave her the gift she always wanted, complete with ribbons and bows."

"And there is no way she's going to let the man she despises most control her."

Brian is amused. Conrad is acting like the mastermind of this plot hasn't thought about the most obvious objection. Alicia despises Brian and has since relieved him of his duties as her chief of staff. One of the first orders of business was to create a situation where that didn't matter.

"So long as we don't overdo it and let her think she has a modicum of control, she won't make waves. Once she's sworn in, it won't matter. If something like this goes public after she moves into the White House, she'll be ushered out as fast as Congress can assemble for the impeachment."

That means everyone will go down with her, which is the point. Brian reimagined the old Cold War concept of mutually assured destruction. Moving forward, each member, even the president-elect, is vested in each other's success. They only need to get through the transition and inauguration to realize the benefits of that symbiotic relationship.

"We all took a lot of risks to get to this point. If you think you can undermine us, you have another thing coming."

"Conrad, I'm not undermining anyone. I told you. I had nothing to do with those attacks."

Conrad sticks his beefy finger in the consultant's face. "Don't let me find out otherwise."

The deputy AG storms out, slamming the door behind him. Brian shakes his head and locks the door. All that bluster and so little to back it up.

The attacks were a mistake. Even if the one in Boston wasn't gunning for Larsen herself, his friends at Actyv seriously miscalculated. Larsen will redouble her efforts after what happened to Seth Chambers. Brian's attempts at silencing and cowing Tierra into submission are now compromised.

He returns to the study to check the news sites for information about the attacks. DeAnna will squelch the story nationally, but it will still be reported, especially on the local news in Boston. If there is a saving grace in the timing, it's that there is a new, more devastating storm on the horizon.

CHAPTER TWENTY-THREE

PRESIDENT-ELECT ALICIA STANDISH

Standish's Hay-Adams Hotel Suite
Washington, D.C.

"Religion is the opiate of the masses." That is Karl Marx's most frequently paraphrased statement. The actual line is "religion is the opium of the people," and when taken into context, he argued that religion was a construct to calm humanity's uncertainty over their role in the universe. Cable news can be viewed the same way. On the surface, it is meant to inform, but it is really a construct to force people to adopt a narrative. As a politician, Alicia uses it. As a private citizen, she'd rather read a book.

Tonight is no different. Although her mind is swimming, Alicia has no mental energy to read. She turns on the television and is greeted by Oliver Jahn delivering his opening monologue. She is about to change the channel when she notices the difference in his delivery. It's stale and unenthusiastic…very un-Oliver-like.

"A week has passed since the most controversial election in American history ended, and already news of another scandal is rocking the country. This network earlier reported that a whistleblower came forward and accused Vice President-Elect Everett Kerrigan of offering bribes to election officials in several key swing states.

"Shocker. It sounds like something The Queen of Pretenders would gin up to discredit President-Elect Standish," Oliver says, his high-pitched obnoxiousness toned considerably down. "We have now learned that several others have also come forward to validate that account. These additional whistleblowers, whose names are not being released to protect their privacy and physical safety, have provided this network with detailed accounts and damning evidence of misuse of campaign funds to secure support for the desired outcome in this hotly contested election. These payoffs were made to several off-shore accounts belonging to campaign officials in Arizona, Nevada, Virginia, Michigan, and Wisconsin.

"Coincidentally or not, these were all states in which the now vice president-elect held numerous campaign events leading up to Election Day while Alicia Standish focused on Pennsylvania."

Her cell phone rings, and she checks the caller ID before connecting. She doesn't bother with a greeting. She knows why he's calling.

"Are you watching *TNT*?"

"Unfortunately."

"There's no way that Everett did this, right?" her husband asks.

"Not a chance. This is Brian Cooper making sure I don't do something rash like step down."

"What do you mean?"

Alicia sighs. "If I decide not to do the cabal's bidding and resign before the Electoral College meets, they will choose the next president. The slate of electors will be Democrat, and their next choice will likely be the vice president-elect to preserve and maintain the integrity of the election."

"And if the VP is embroiled in scandal…." Brendan's voice trails off as the implication of the tactic hits him. "Have you spoken to Everett today?"

"We had a conversation when the reports of the first whistleblower hit the news cycle. He denied everything."

"You didn't tell him about Cooper, did you?"

Alicia closes her eyes. She could use an ally, but she isn't particularly close to Everett. He was chosen by the party because it would seal her win in the swing rust belt states. Everything at this level is about electoral math. Running mates are chosen by geography over capability. He would see this as a red carpet guiding his way into the Oval Office. Every vice president dreams of someday dropping the first four letters from the title.

"I can't tell anyone, Brendan. Brian made it clear what happens if I do."

"So, what now?"

Alicia leaves the question unanswered as she tunes back in to Oliver Jahn.

"The first hundred days of any presidency are the most important. With the midterms two years away and another presidential race following that, it's the best chance to make a real legislative impact. How will Standish govern if half the country thinks she stole the election and her VP helped?

"I mean, if what happened in Pennsylvania isn't bad enough, this could make matters worse. Bradford hasn't conceded, meaning it will be up to the Electoral College to decide. Pennsylvania needs to make the result official for their electors to be chosen, but what happens if that embattled state ends up on this pay-for-play list? What would happen if President-Elect Standish was also doling out bribes when she was campaigning in Pennsylvania?

"There is no proof of that, but additional whistleblowers could come forward. My loyal audience, where there's smoke, there's fire. One whistleblower could be someone with an ax to grind. Multiple people with the same story… complicates things. I, for one, need to see what evidence they have, if any."

Alicia mutes the television and tosses the remote on the other side of the sofa. She leans her head back and massages her temples after setting the cell phone to use the speaker function.

"Will they release proof?" Brendan asks.

"That's act two. The cabal needs to create it first, which they can and will do. If I toe the line, I'm betting Oliver Jahn reports a few weeks from now that all these mysterious whistleblowers were discredited due to the excellent investigative reporting by VHN. DeAnna Van Herten will be honored for her contribution to America by discrediting the scandal."

"And you can't exactly have the FBI investigate."

Alicia shakes her head. "You have to give Cooper credit. He thought this through."

"Honey, you are much better on offense than defense. You need to turn this around somehow."

It's a Captain Obvious statement, but that's because what needs to happen is obvious. She can't go four years like this. They will likely force her into running for re-election and rigging that race so that she wins. Eight years. If the past week has felt like a month, she can only imagine what toll this would take over the better part of a decade.

"I know what I need to do…I just don't know how."

CHAPTER TWENTY-FOUR

SSA DANIEL MURPHY

Detective Chambers' Family Residence
Revere, Massachusetts

It is a little white house on the corner of a peaceful street. Or it was. Now it's a scene of unadulterated chaos filled with frantic cops, flashing strobes, police tape, and curious neighbors. Woburn police officers and Massachusetts state troopers scurry everywhere. Seth Chambers was one of theirs. They are invested in understanding everything they can about the men who tore apart his house with gunfire.

Murphy makes his way up the driveway to the shattered side door. They breached it with a battering ram, and the deadbolt didn't stand a chance against the heavy steel cylinder.

"Jesus. Is this suburban Boston or Fallujah?" DeAndre asks as they stand in the entry that leads to the kitchen.

Photographers document every inch of the scene. They have a lot they need to capture. Bullet holes have destroyed the once nice kitchen, and brass casings litter the floor. Each man must have gone through a couple of magazines.

"Who are you?" a Woburn Police detective asks.

"I'm Supervisory Special Agent Daniel Murphy with the FBI. This is Special Agent DeAndre Wright. What can you tell us?"

"Welcome to hell," the detective muses. "Two shooters breached the door, clad in body armor and armed with MP-5s. Detective Chambers was closest to the kitchen and caught the first couple of rounds."

The Maschinenpistole 5 might be Heckler and Koch's most popular weapon. It's the Mercedes-Benz of submachine guns and is a favorite among elite police and military forces. The lightweight, accurate, and reliable firearm rapidly spread across the globe and seeped into pop culture. The weapon was ubiquitous in everyone's favorite Christmas movie, *Die Hard*, leading to the famous "Now I have a machine gun, ho, ho, ho," line.

"Is the detective alive?"

"Somehow. He was rushed into surgery the minute he got to the ER. He's in critical condition, but your man kept him alive long enough to get him to a hospital."

"My man?"

The detective refers to his notepad. "Supervisory Special Agent Rigoberto Benitez. He was administering aid when we arrived. Once we established his identity and learned about the federal warrant for his arrest, he was detained, and you were called."

"DeAndre, get on your phone and start the process of having him remanded into our custody."

"You got it."

"What about Victoria Larsen? She was likely your other shooter."

"Gone. There's no trace of her anywhere. We're canvassing the neighborhood, but nobody saw anything. We're searching the area and setting up checkpoints leading out of town, but I wouldn't be optimistic."

"I'm not," Murphy concurs, knowing Victoria is too smart for that. "Any word on the two shooters?"

"No. Your people have the prints. You'll get an answer faster than we will."

"Thanks, Detective. One more thing…did you find a laptop anywhere?"

"We haven't completed the search but only found a desktop computer upstairs."

"Okay, thanks. Has the detective's wife been notified?"

"We took care of it," the detective says, starting to step away before stopping. "Agent Murphy, there's one more thing. If Benitez and Larsen are domestic terrorists, why did he stay behind to save the life of a police detective? I may not be a fancy agent trained at Quantico, but that doesn't make any sense."

"Keep me informed," Daniel says, ignoring the observation.

There are bullet holes everywhere. These men intended to send a message, not just kill. Both attackers were dropped in the kitchen, and it looks like they were caught by surprise. They wouldn't have wasted ammunition shooting up the house if they knew others were here. Regardless of how this played out, they broke a cardinal rule: Never go up against Larsen in a gunfight. If he learned anything from watching her in Hogan's Alley, it's that.

Murphy squats next to one of the bodies and pulls back the white covering. The man is muscular, is dressed in black fatigues, and has short hair with Eastern European facial features. A soldier, not a thug. This wasn't a revenge attack from well-equipped gang-bangers. Muephy'a phone rings, and he pulls it from his pocket.

"Hey, boss," one of his team says on the other end. "We got a line on the two shooters in Woburn."

"Let me guess. Mercenaries working for a PMC."

"Ex-Spetznaz to be exact. They're employed by a private military company called Voin. It's the English pronunciation of the Russian word for—"

"Warrior. I've heard of them."

Many soldiers are lost when they leave the military. The civilian world is a different place, and many want to continue excelling at the jobs they performed while on active duty. The camaraderie with fellow soldiers is intoxicating and the thing most veterans miss most. Private military companies offer all that with a nice bump in pay.

PMCs have existed for decades but became better known during the wars in Iraq and Afghanistan. At the height of the Iraq war, tens of thousands of private contractors hired by companies such as Blackwater were conducting armed convoy protection missions. That company became notorious after several high-profile incidents, including the murder of fourteen civilians in Baghdad in 2007. Daniel is sure the Russian PMCs are far worse.

"They're no joke. Why would someone send them after Seth Chambers? He's a Massachusetts State Police detective."

"I don't know. See what you can find out."

Murphy takes one more look around and heads out of the house to find Agent Wright. Unless Chambers had somehow tangled with the Russian mob, a professional hit on him doesn't make sense. Unless Larsen was the target. Unfortunately, that makes even less sense. He can't shake the feeling that something else is going on. Something he hasn't learned, or worse, isn't being told.

CHAPTER TWENTY-FIVE

TIERRA CAMPOS

Georgetown University Hospital
Washington, D.C.

Bullets negatively affect the human body regardless of where they hit. There is no part of your anatomy where it's good to be shot, but there are a few contenders to choose from over other options. After my close call in the Summerville High School shooting, I spent an unhealthy amount of time studying wound ballistics while contemplating what could have been. I know too much about the destructive power of projectiles on human tissue, bones, and organs.

The mass of a projectile isn't what makes gunshot wounds deadly. A bullet is a carrier of force designed to transfer that energy within the body. This kinetic energy causes injuries, and the combination of the weight, velocity, and gravitational trajectory determines how much damage a bullet causes.

As a bullet enters the body, it causes lacerations and crushing wounds as it punctures tissue and bone. The cavity created can be thirty times wider than its track and closes behind the bullet less than a second later. This cavitation damages nearby tissue, organs, and bones.

That's where location comes into play. The type and amount of injury depend on what a bullet encounters as it travels through the body. Soft tissue carries shockwaves easier than denser bones, which splinter and cause further damage as the fragments travel through the body.

If someone is lucky, like Josh was, the bullet passes straight through. It's why soldiers, cops, or EMTs check for exit wounds on gunshot victims on television and in movies. A bullet that stays in the body transfers all of its kinetic energy, thus ensuring maximum tissue damage. Jacketed bullets fragment after impact, dividing their destructive power. Hollow-point and soft bullets are designed to flatten and spread, creating a wider area for their tracks and increasing the damage.

A doctor enters the waiting area and heads toward a family in the corner. I lower my head. I know Josh is still in surgery, and I won't hear any news for some time. That's the rational thought. The irrational part of me will intently watch every white lab coat that walks through the door, hoping it is a doctor delivering the news I want.

My thoughts drift back to Josh. The arms and legs seem the best place to take a bullet, but feature femoral and brachial arteries. If a bullet severs either one, the blood loss causes death within a few minutes. Josh was shot just to the left of his right armpit. A lot of nerves run through that area, and that's why he's in surgery. He wasn't shot by a pea shooter. An MP-5 packs a punch with its nine-millimeter rounds.

I hear footsteps approaching and expect another doctor to enter the waiting area. Instead, a man in a suit with a badge hanging around his neck enters, flanked by two uniformed D.C. officers. I stand, expecting they want to take my statement about what happened at the apartment.

"Miss Campos?"

"Yes."

The detective nods at the officer to his right before staring at me. "You are under arrest for violation of District of Columbia code 22–4512, alteration of identifying marks of weapons."

"Are you kidding me with this?"

"No, ma'am. I'm afraid we're dead serious. You have the right to remain silent. Anything you say can and will be used against you in a court of law. You have the right to an attorney. If you cannot afford an attorney, one will be provided for you. Do you understand the rights I have just read to you?"

Everyone in the waiting room watches the show. A mother is holding her young son tightly. I want to be indignant and irrational and lash out at these ass clowns who will hide behind the shield as they utter, "I'm just upholding the law."

But I remain silent. I will not let my words be used against me in court. They aren't here to listen to my pleadings about a friend I owe my life to lying on an operating room table. They don't care that my actions were in self-defense or that the two men came in with submachine guns to kill me. So, instead, they get a one-word answer.

"Yes."

My anger will need to be vented another day. Cooper is getting what he wants in this round, and I hold my head high as they lead me out of the hospital to a waiting squad car. I will be booked and arraigned for the crime of defending myself. Brian must want me out of the way very badly to pull a stunt like this.

CHAPTER TWENTY-SIX

VICTORIA LARSEN

Cobbs Creek East Rowhouse
West Philadelphia, Pennsylvania

Victoria pulls her Eagles cap down to hide her face. She's glad she's agnostic when it comes to sports. Wearing the colors of a hated rival would be problematic. Fortunately, she blends in on SEPTA's Market-Frankford Line. She exits at 56th Street in West Philadelphia and walks south down the familiar street lined with rowhouses.

She hurries up the stairs to the door of Imani's grandfather's house and knocks. The young agent opens the door quickly. Even in a neighborhood like this, it's best if she doesn't spend too much time out in the open.

"You made it. Thank God. I've been worried sick."

Imani steps aside, looking up and down the street before closing the door behind them. It took Victoria a while to recover from the trauma of the attack and formulate some semblance of a plan. After making her way back into the city, calling the Philadelphia agent was the last thing she did before boarding a southbound Acela train. It's a risk, but her options are getting scarcer. It is one worth taking.

"Any problems?"

"Other than that being the longest train ride of my life? No. Any news?"

"Lots. You'd better sit down." Victoria doesn't move. "Okay, first, Seth Chambers is out of surgery but still in intensive care. His prognosis isn't good, Vic. The bullets ripped through his intestines, and he lost a lot of blood. He's lucky to be alive."

Victoria lowers her eyes. She's kicking herself for calling Seth after seeing Miranda. It was too obvious.

"Who were they?"

"I don't know. The details aren't being released. That's not all. Chambers has a pair of agents waiting outside his door in the ICU to arrest him for aiding and abetting a fugitive if he makes it."

"What about Rigo?"

"Physically, he's fine. He was arrested by the Boston Police and remanded to Bureau custody."

"Okay."

Rigo has his demons. Seeing Seth clutching his abdomen on the floor was traumatic for Victoria but rattled Rigo to his core. He lost his whole team in Loughborough. She feels responsible for what happened, but Rigo *was* responsible for them as their supervisory agent. He could have done nothing to save them, but he could save Seth. He made that choice knowing the consequences.

"There's more," Imani says with a grave look. "Tierra Campos was attacked in her D.C. apartment with her boyfriend around the same time you were in Boston."

"Boyfriend? You mean Josh Higgins? They aren't together…attacked by whom?"

"That part is being kept quiet, too. Josh was shot in the shoulder, but he'll recover. Tierra was arrested at the hospital on a gun charge. The weapon didn't have a serial number, nor did she have a permit to own one."

Victoria hangs her head. "It was your grandfather's Glock. I gave it to her just in case."

"It's a good thing you did. It saved Tierra's life. My grandfather would be proud as hell."

"I need to go."

"Where?" Imani asks, grabbing Victoria's arm as she tries to brush past her.

"Anywhere but here. Williams is coming after me, Imani, and anyone they catch working with me. All I've done is leave a trail of bodies in my wake. The lucky ones are only arrested and will likely spend the next two decades behind bars. I can't subject you to that. I'm sorry."

Imani rushes ahead of her to block the door. She throws her weight against it like a barbarian horde is trying to break it down.

"Get out of my way."

"Make me."

"Imani—"

"No, you need to listen, Victoria. Do you know why your friends stick with you? It's because they believe in you. You aren't a superstar agent because of the skills you learned at Quantico. It's because of who *you* are. You didn't ask for any of this. It was thrust upon you and Tierra, and now you need to end it. Like it or not, I'm with you until the bitter end. To hell with the risks."

"I'm the angel of death, Imani. I'm a *murderer*. You don't—"

"Do you really expect me to weep for Ian Drucker? You did what any of us would have done under those circumstances. It's not like there were better alternatives. If you had turned him in, you'd probably be at Gitmo by now."

Victoria covers her face with her hands and begins to weep. She isn't a crier. For the second time in twenty-four hours, the stress has gotten the better of her and caused her to break down.

"I can't do this anymore."

Imani places her hands on her shoulders. "You can because you have to. If you and Tierra Campos don't do this, who will?"

Victoria eases herself back into a chair at the kitchen table. She pulls her ballcap off and runs her fingers through her hair. Imani joins her at the table, staying between her and the door, just in case.

"We're going to lose, Imani. It's a war of attrition; they have the firepower and numbers. I can't compete with that."

"Then stop trying. Do you know why I admire you so much? It's not just because of what happened in Brockhampton and New Hampshire – it's because you're always willing to do what you need to. Most people aren't like that. They take the easy way out. Quitting is the easy way out."

"It doesn't matter this time."

"It does matter, more than ever. If you can't beat Cooper and the cabal the conventional way, start fighting unconventionally. Stop playing defense and start playing offense."

"I don't know how to do that."

Imani lowers her head slightly to look Victoria in the eyes. "I'm willing to bet my career on you figuring that out. But I can't convince you of that. You have to know it in your heart."

Victoria has always thought she could overcome anything. There was no mountain too tall or sea too vast for her. But everybody has a limit. She realizes now that she's reached hers.

"I'm about out of fight."

"Okay. If you want to leave, leave. But they'll catch you, and your greatest fears will become a self-fulfilling prophecy. You will be arrested or worse. Tierra will be imprisoned. *Front Burner* will fold. Americans will pay the price of dark forces running the country without their knowledge. If you think you're upset now, wait until you see what happens if you give up."

Imani rises and pats Victoria gently on the shoulder before moving into the living room. There is only one person who can make this decision. Imani said what she needed to. That's the extent of the pep talk.

Victoria buries her head in her arms. She needs to overcome this, but the emotional toll is draining her. Most of all, she needs a plan. Drastic times call for drastic measures. If the end is near, it might as well be on her terms.

CHAPTER TWENTY-SEVEN

BRIAN COOPER

Correctional Treatment Facility
Washington, D.C.

The Central Detention Facility in Southeast D.C. is the last place Brian wants to hang out. It's bad karma, especially considering he's at the heart of a coup. Females are imprisoned at the Correctional Treatment Facility, while most male inmates awaiting adjudication of cases are locked up next door.

Defendants arrested in Washington are taken to this set of buildings known as "DC Jail." This is where things get stupid. Unless arrested for a serious felony or in cases where a defendant is considered dangerous, almost ninety percent are released without paying a monetary bond after completing the booking process.

The mainstream media hasn't covered Tierra's arrest, partly thanks to DeAnna quashing the story at her network. There is enough going on to command VHN's attention elsewhere. That left the court free to require a cash bail for her release – one eagerly paid by Brian as a co-signer.

He has been waiting outside the entrance for almost an hour, watching hundreds of people come and go. Despite being the campaign manager for the Republican nominee for president and the subject of countless news articles and interviews, not a single person recognizes him. Well, one person does.

Tierra storms up to him after leaving the CTF. He's almost grateful this place is crawling with cops. She looks pissed.

"Josh is going to be okay," Brian says, trying to de-escalate the coming confrontation.

"So I was told. I figure you probably arranged that as well."

Brian nods. "I knew you would want to know but wasn't sure if word made it to you."

"Is bailing me out your idea of a sick joke? Or was it Conrad Williams's?"

Brian lets out an amused laugh. "Please. He's going to be livid when he finds out. I know you don't have the cash, so you're welcome."

"Cut the shit, Cooper. I wouldn't have been in there if it wasn't for you."

He rubs his chin. "Funny, I don't remember handing you an unregistered and untraceable handgun."

"You're a piece of work. What did you think would happen to me? You know, I honestly never thought you would send thug assassins after me. It's so not you."

Brian pulls her away from the entrance. She yanks her arm away but continues to walk with him.

"I didn't send them, Tierra."

"Yeah, right. So much for protecting me."

"I *am* protecting you. I told you that others wanted you dead."

"They stopped listening to you."

"That's the way it works. I don't expect you to understand. You're too far behind to catch up now. Just know that other forces are at play here. Ones more powerful than you can imagine."

"Someone in Actyv Private Equity?"

Brian frowns and shakes his head. "Tierra, for as much as you think you know, you're only scratching the surface. You can't win. You were never going to."

"So you keep saying. I've already surrendered, Brian. What more do you want from me?"

Brian turns and surveys the construction happening across the street. "It's not what I want. This isn't about me and never has been. You aren't safe now, Tierra."

"Clearly."

"Let me give a dollar's worth of free advice. Take some time off until after the inauguration. Get away from *Front Burner* and steer clear of Victoria Larsen. Hell, leave Washington, and don't ever come back. The best thing you can do now is to make yourself invisible."

Tierra feels like she was hit by a bolt of lightning. Three hundred million volts of electricity ride up and down her spine. She has spent a lifetime wanting to be invisible. It wasn't until Brockhampton that she realized hiding in a cocoon she built for herself after the Summerville shooting wasn't the way to go through life. Now, her nemesis is saying that it's the only way to see her next birthday.

"I assume you can get a ride to where you're going. I hope this is goodbye, Tierra. If we ever have cause to see each other again, it won't end well for you. Good luck to you."

"Will disappearing guarantee the safety of my friends and me?" Tierra calls out as Brian starts to walk away.

He stops and looks around before turning back to her.

"It's the best chance you have."

CHAPTER TWENTY-EIGHT

PRESIDENT-ELECT ALICIA STANDISH

Standish Temporary Presidential Transition Headquarters
Hay-Adams Hotel, Washington, D.C.

It's a typical run-of-the-mill hump day nightmare. On their best day, the media horde are like vultures picking at a carcass. On their worst, like today, they are hungry red-bellied piranhas taking bites while their prey is still alive.

The phones have been ringing off the hook for statements and interview requests. Anyone who dares come to the temporary transition headquarters is mobbed outside the doors. There is enormous pressure on Alicia to hold a press conference to address the budding scandal. The staff is working on putting one together, but what can they say? Deny everything?

The story has legs, and it's being championed by every news outlet in the country. So much for Republican insinuations that the mainstream media protects Democrats. Even reliably liberal networks are devoting significant time to analyzing the whistleblowers' accusations and hypothesizing about the impact on her upcoming presidency.

Alicia leans back in her executive chair when Andrew enters her office, his face buried in a tablet computer. He has a smug look that starkly contrasts with the rest of her harried staff. The asshole is enjoying the chaos.

"Did you cook these charges up?"

"Excuse me?"

"You heard me, Andrew."

He glances out the open door before moving closer to the desk. "I suggest you keep your voice low."

"I am going to fight this tooth and nail. Everett Kerrigan is a good man and a faithful public servant. He doesn't deserve to have this hung around his neck."

Andrew grins. "I admire your loyalty, Madam President-Elect. I would expect you to fight for your running mate. After all, he will be a whisper from the presidency himself."

"Good. Then we have an understanding."

"Of course, that could also pose a problem," Andrew says, causing a surge of nervous energy that makes Alicia's skin crawl. "A full-throated defense from Everett's boss is expected in this political climate had the opposing party leveled the accusations, but they didn't, did they? You know, a thought just occurred to me. It isn't inconceivable that the VP-elect actually *did* what they accused him of."

"He would never—"

"Are you certain? Would you be willing to risk your presidency on it? Because politics is perception, and you are already off to a rocky start. If evidence were to surface that he was involved…phew, that would be an impeachment worth watching."

"Everett assured me that he didn't try to buy anyone."

Andrew shrugs. "Yes, of course. And the people will believe him over the preponderance of the evidence because trust in politicians is at an all-time high, and honorable public servants never get caught in their lies."

"I will not let you drag him through the mud," the president-elect says through clenched teeth.

"Bring him to Washington for a chat. I'll set it up. We can make decisions following that."

"I'm serious, Andrew. I'm not going to ditch my vice president."

Andrew nods in understanding. "That is your choice, ma'am. Just know that there are other options. I already have a list of potential replacements should it need to come to that."

"You're a son of a bitch, Andrew."

Her chief of staff moves back to the desk and leans over. "And then some. The sooner you realize that you have no play but to accept the terms we offered, the sooner you get to govern. It's simple math that even an arrogant politician like you doesn't need fingers for."

Alicia is about to say something snarky when one of her aides quickly knocks on the door jamb three times. "Ma'am, I'm sorry to interrupt, but Robert Ackerman is on the line for you. He says it's urgent."

"Thank you, Jennifer."

"You're going to want to take that. The chief of staff is about to tell you that the president is canceling your meeting at the White House until this scandal sorts itself out," Andrew says with a gloating smirk that Alicia wants to smack off his face. "But that's just an educated guess."

CHAPTER TWENTY-NINE

SSA DANIEL MURPHY

40,000 Feet
Somewhere over Long Island Sound

Like all other government agencies, the FBI has access to government aviation transport ranging from small prop aircraft to business jets. However, use is severely restricted for reasons including cost, public perception, and fear of abuse. That's why he always smiles when reruns of *Criminal Minds* air and he sees them climbing into a jet that happens to be waiting for them.

It's not realistic. Fuel and crew costs, landing fees, and other incidental expenses make it less expensive to fly a team first-class than using a government jet would ever be. Teams could be transported that way in an extreme emergency, but nothing ever seen on that program would qualify.

This does, at least in the minds of the Bureau leadership. The FBI has two Gulfstream G550s with the primary mission of carrying Director Krekstein. It's not an ego thing. By law, the Federal Bureau of Investigation director is forbidden to fly using commercial aviation. So, he offered Murphy and his team one of the jets in the manhunt for Victoria Larsen. That's how high this ranks.

What he can't figure out is why. None of this makes sense. Recent events have only muddied the waters. How did a hit team know where Larsen was when the FBI didn't? Unless she wasn't the target. And, if that's true, why go after a Massachusetts State Police detective? Was it a warning or something else? Murphy knows he's missing something important, and the search for what is eating him up.

"You look bothered," DeAndre says, holding a can of Coke and a tablet as he sits in the chair across from Murphy.

"Everything about this operation is bothering me. What do you have?"

"SIOC has been busy," the junior agent says, setting down the drink and powering up the device.

The Strategic Information and Operations Center is the Bureau's global command and communications center tasked with collecting, processing, and promptly disseminating information. The goal is to get pertinent information into the hands of decision-makers in a timely manner. At least, that's how it's supposed to work. Most agents would disagree with the "timely" part.

"Ballistics came back on the gun Tierra Campos used to kill those Spetznaz guys...and seriously, what does that say about Russian special operators? They got offed by a one hundred ten pound journalist with no training and—"

"Get to the point, DeAndre."

"Sorry. The gun matches a weapon belonging to an Amos Bangura of West Philadelphia. He was a retired Philly cop who received it as a gift before he passed away a few years ago."

"That's random."

"Yeah, not really. Amos is the grandfather of Special Agent Imani Bangura. Wanna guess where she works?"

"The Philadelphia field office," Murphy says, exhaling.

"Give the man a prize. There's more. You know how we were all wondering how Victoria Larsen avoided capture so easily the night of the Liberty raid? Bangura was working support for the tactical team moving in on the Keystone Militia. She knew the composition, tactics, positions of air assets…she could have relayed it all to Larsen."

Murphy takes iPad and opens Bangura's personnel file. His eyebrows go up when he sees an attractive woman's picture. Match her with Victoria Larsen, and there isn't a head in the room that wouldn't turn, women included.

"Have some agents check her apartment to see if she's harboring Larsen there."

"I can do one better," DeAndre adds. "Agent Bangura maintains her grandfather's old rowhouse in West Philly."

Murphy rubs the stubble growing on his face. Larsen could hide out there, but there are a million other possibilities. Since they are looking for a needle, they might as well start with this haystack. Philadelphia is on the Amtrak line running from Boston to Florida. If she had hopped on an Acela at North Station, she could have made it to William H. Gray 30th St. Station in five hours. Murphy sends word of the change of destination up to the cockpit.

"Besides craving a cheesesteak, why would Larsen bother going there?"

"Convenience. She's running out of friends and may have another target in mind. Conrad Williams is in the city."

"Would she go after him?" DeAndre asks.

Murphy stares out the window and ponders that question. "He just went on television and announced to the country that she's a domestic terrorist. I think she may have an ax to grind, and if you want to make a splash on the news, why not take out the guy leading your manhunt?"

CHAPTER THIRTY

VICTORIA LARSEN

Cobbs Creek East Rowhouse
West Philadelphia, Pennsylvania

This call is long overdue. The longer Victoria waited to pick up her cell and dial, the harder it got. It's not fear driving her apprehension. It's regret.

"Hello?" Tierra's voice asks on the other end of the line. There was no expectation that she would recognize this number.

"Hey. It's me."

"Oh, my God, Vic. Are you okay? Are you safe? I was worried. I haven't heard from you forever."

"I'm sorry. Things are…chaotic. I'm fine. Safe is another matter. I heard what happened to you in Georgetown. How's Josh doing?"

"He's all right. I think he likes the attention the nurses give him. He thinks chicks dig scars, and they'll make him look more manly or something. He should be discharged any time now."

"He's not wrong. About women liking scars, I mean."

"He's an idiot, so please don't say that in front of him. He could have been killed."

"But he wasn't, Tierra. That's what you have to focus on."

An awkward silence grows between them. Her friend should be focusing on that, but she isn't. She's dwelling on the negatives. "What ifs" can be a dangerous exercise after something traumatic happens.

"Vic, how many close calls will we have before our number finally comes up?"

"I heard you were arrested. I'm sorry," Victoria says, not wanting to answer that question.

"Well, I met a nice woman in lock-up who offered to be my drug connection in the district. Oh, and another wanted to kick my ass because, apparently, I was sitting on her part of the bench in the holding cell. But that isn't the worst of it. Brian Cooper was nice enough to post my bail. He's such a sweetheart. I mean, if you ignore the fact that I shouldn't have been ordered to pay bail to begin with."

Victoria closes her eyes. "What did he say?"

"Uh, the short of it was, leave town and never come back before something bad happens to you."

"Tierra, I need you to be strong. Don't let him get into your head. I need you—"

"You don't understand, Vic! I can't do this anymore. I just killed two people!"

"Yeah, two men who were there to kill you. What were you supposed to do? Ask if they wanted coffee?"

Tierra's voice comes down a few octaves as she catches her breath. "It's easy for you. You're a trained agent. I'm a school shooting survivor."

"Hon, it's not easy for anyone. I killed Ian Drucker. He got what he deserved, but I still feel guilty despite despising the man. He surrendered and was unarmed when I pulled the trigger."

"How do you cope with it?" Tierra asks in a whisper.

Victoria stares out the window. There is no easy answer to that question. She doesn't cope with it, at least in ways a psychologist would consider healthy. She internalizes it and makes it a part of her. That's something she doesn't want her friend to do again. Enough damage was done to Tierra after her high school was shot up.

"The hardest part for both of us since New Hampshire is doing things we don't want to. What's the alternative?"

"We quit," Tierra decrees. "Is this really our fight?"

"They made it our fight. Tierra, everything that is happening is designed to make us quit. They need us to stop and are scared that we won't."

"Is the sacrifice worth it? The country will tear itself apart. For what? I almost lost the man that...."

"You're in love with. I get it."

"I didn't say that," Tierra snaps.

She doth protest too much. Tierra has always been cagey with Victoria whenever the subject of Josh comes up. They have a long history, and the desire to keep him in the friend zone is strong. Nothing alienates friends faster than becoming lovers who don't find a way to make the relationship work.

Victoria stares at the phone and smirks. "You didn't have to. I profiled you ages ago. You've been in love with him since high school and were too scared to admit it. You're not the frightened victim you once were, and those emotions are bubbling to the surface. Stop fighting it."

"Pot, meet kettle," she says with a sneer.

Victoria stands a little straighter. She has long said she is the least-equipped woman on the planet to give relationship advice. Nothing has changed that, her fledgling possible relationship with Austin included.

"Yeah, no argument from me. Our baggage is on the same flight, but mine is in a different container. Tell Josh how you feel, Tierra."

"What if he...what if he doesn't feel the same way?"

Victoria scoffs. "He does. Trust me."

"I can't put him through what we are going through."

"Something tells me he would volunteer. Look, I told you that I need you. I may be in prison or dead by this time tomorrow if things go wrong. I've accepted that. Now it's your turn to make a choice. In or out? Left or right? The time for half measures is over. I need you to decide."

"Victoria, what are you talking about? What are you planning?"

The agent eyes the freshly cleaned and oiled Glock resting on the bed. "It's time to end this. That means risks need to be taken."

"You're not planning on doing something stupid, are you?"

Stupid is a relative conclusion. Most people would think it is. She wants to tell her friend the plan, but Tierra is already on the fence. There is nothing about this information that will help the cause.

"I had Miranda upload the contents of Drucker's laptop to the dark web vault DP set up. You know what to do with them if this goes wrong. Take care, Tierra. I wish you the best of luck."

"Victoria, wait—"

The former agent ends the call and quickly powers down the phone. There is no need for more conversation or discussion. This whole sordid affair will end, so it might as well be on her terms. Cooper, Li, and Williams have forced her into being the prey for too long. It's time to become the predator and bring the fight to them.

CHAPTER THIRTY-ONE

TIERRA CAMPOS

Georgetown University Hospital
Washington, D.C.

I take a moment to compose myself. That conversation was harder than I thought it would be. It's not that Victoria was taking me on an epic cross-country guilt trip. She has every right to do that, considering the bind that she's in. It's just that I'm conflicted. And scared.

I don't want Josh to see any of that. He was shot and has bigger things to worry about, like healing up. I try to paste a smile on and concoct a plausible reason I stepped out that doesn't include former Special Agent Victoria Larsen. I swing into his room, content that I conjured something workable.

"On the phone with Vic, huh?"

I stop cold and stare at him as he sits in the plastic visitor's chair, awaiting discharge paperwork. He sleuthed that out in record speed.

"What makes you ask that?"

"She's the only person you'd leave the room for and give me five minutes of peace. My own mother didn't dote on me this much when I was a toddler."

"Haha. Yes, that was Victoria, if you must know."

"How's she doing?"

I bite my lower lip. I'm not about to tell Josh she plans to do something rash. We already have enough drama in our lives. If we lose Victoria, things will get a lot worse. And I'll lose a dear friend.

"Okay…under the circumstances. Vic is afraid I'm going to bail on her."

"Ah," Josh says with a nod. "You told her about Cooper's ultimatum. So, are you going to bail?"

"I…I don't know."

"Yes, you do."

"What's that supposed to mean?" I ask, feeling a tinge of anger. I've never liked it when people make my decisions for me or assume they know what I'll do before I've even decided.

"It means you know what you want to do. You're only afraid to tell me because I got shot over this, and you think I'll be angry."

"Slow your roll, buddy. You think you know me that well?"

Josh looks up from the chair. He has no playful grin or little squint like when he's about to launch a witty or sarcastic remark. It's a serious look...or as serious as Josh can muster.

"I know I do. You have that look in your eyes, Tierra. You had the same one during the Ethan Harrington interview and again when you were grilling Isiah Burgess. You're only pretending to be indecisive because you think you should be. You won't let this go."

"More people could get hurt," I whisper.

"Yeah, maybe. More people *will* get hurt if you let Cooper win. He didn't hijack the presidency to bring world peace. He has an agenda, and whatever it is, it's bad news for the rest of us."

There's no arguing that point. Brian absolutely didn't embark on this to better America. He has a plan, because he always has one. Whatever the desired outcome, Josh is right: It won't be good for the country.

"Josh, this isn't a game. It's life and death. Two men came into your apartment and almost killed you because of me."

"They shot me. They didn't almost kill me."

"They could have!"

Tears start pouring down my cheeks. I haven't had much time to process what happened at the apartment. I killed two people and almost lost Josh. Then I got arrested and bailed out by the man responsible for all of it. It's too much to bear, and I can't keep my emotions in check anymore.

Josh stands and hugs me with his good arm. I bury my face in his chest and sob. He doesn't try to stop me or offer hollow expressions like, "It will be okay." He just lets me cry until I run out of tears.

"I'm sorry," I whisper, finally pulling away from him.

"You don't need to apologize. You need to get angry."

"What?"

"Remember when you asked me how I found the strength and courage to pull you off the library floor and drag you to the closet at Summerville High? I'll answer your question now. It's because I was angry, Angry that one of our classmates was doing that. Angry that there wasn't anything I could do about it."

"I didn't know that."

"Yeah, well, it took me a long time to discover it myself. I blocked out a lot from that day."

I hang my head and stare at the floor tiles. "You didn't kill anyone at Summerville."

"No, but I didn't have to. I needed to keep you safe. That was my job then. You did the same thing at my apartment, except we had no closet to hide in. You did what you had to do. Just like you need to now."

"Josh, more of my friends may get hurt...or worse. You could be killed next time they come after us."

"We get to make that choice for ourselves. Speaking for me, I'm invested. Cooper needs to go straight to hell and take his miserable cabal with him. I'll do whatever it takes to make that happen because that's what you do for someone you love."

My body freezes. I don't even blink. Did he...? Was that...?

"What did you say?"

"I...I love you, Tierra. I always have. I've always wanted to tell you, but I could never find the—"

I grab Josh by his shirt and move my lips up to meet his. It's the perfect kiss – not too rough, but still filled with energy and pent-up passion. My whole body tingles. For a moment, we aren't in a hospital room. There is no cabal threatening the country or assassins trying to kill us. The world falls away.

I always wondered what it would be like to kiss Josh. The experience isn't disappointing. If this kiss lasted an hour, it would still end too soon. When our lips finally part, I stare into his blue eyes.

"About time you said it."

"Sometimes it takes a brush with death to realize what's important in life. For me, that's you."

I smile and hug him, squeezing as hard as I can. He has always meant the world to me. I owe him my life. He owes me his. After admitting that he became suicidal after the school shooting, my phone call stopped him from taking a handful of pills to end the anguish. We are two souls bound together. Now, we are a couple.

"Uh, Tierra?" Josh asks with a slight gasp.

"Yeah?" I ask without letting go.

"I was just shot in the shoulder. It's a little tender."

"Oh, I'm so sorry," I say, letting him go and gently caressing his bandages.

"So, what's the plan? What do you need me to do to help you take down this cabal?"

I frown. "I wish I had an answer. I don't know what to do."

Josh nods and holds out his hand with his good arm. "Let's get this discharge paperwork done and dusted and start figuring it out together."

I feel good for the first time in...forever. I know it won't last. A thousand things can go wrong between now and the inauguration. At least it feels like I don't need to walk the path alone. I have Wilson and Austin, the rest of the *Front Burner* team, Victoria, and now Josh. Whatever happens, it will be to all of us.

CHAPTER THIRTY-TWO

BRIAN COOPER

Standish's Hay-Adams Hotel Suite
Washington, D.C.

It's been a day. The damage control effort downstairs must be soul-consuming following the allegations against Vice President-Elect Kerrigan. The president didn't make Alicia's job any easier when he canceled their meeting at the last minute. She's on the defensive and forced to delay work on a transition already behind schedule due to the GSA's decision not to declare a winner.

With the staff still feverishly working downstairs, he knew she would come to her suite for a breather. It's too early to call it a night, but Alicia is a creature of habit. She'll want to escape the insanity unfolding downstairs.

The Secret Service agent monitoring Brian puts his fingers to his ear and heads for the door. He opens it just as his charge arrives. The agent departs, leaving him alone with Alicia, who circles the sitting area after spotting the back of his head.

"Crimson is in the nest," he says into his sleeve microphone before leaving the room.

"How did you get in here?"

"Andrew cleared it with the Secret Service," Brian says. "I was smuggled in through the service entrance. The nice thing about your protective detail is they don't question meetings like this. Most people would find it odd that you'd meet with the chief of staff of the man you vanquished."

She doesn't take the bait. Alicia knows she didn't vanquish anyone in an election manipulated by outside forces. "Should I expect consistent visits to where I sleep?"

"I certainly hope not. I don't want to be here any more than you want me here."

"Then why are you sitting on a sofa in my suite?"

Brian turns to look at her for the first time. "Because we can't exactly meet downstairs, can we?"

Alicia would love to see that. Brian knows he'd awkwardly stand there, bathing in the looks on her staff's faces as she explains that he's the man running the country. She always thought shadow governments were a myth. The reality that they aren't must be terrifying for her.

"What do you want, Brian?"

"To meet you face-to-face."

"Why?"

"I want to look you in the eyes and see if you plan on doing something stupid. You have a lousy poker face."

Alicia scoffs. "Like what? What avenue have you left me? Even if I was determined to not play your game, what recourse do I have? The future VP is tainted. Larsen is a fugitive. Campos was just assaulted in her apartment, and *Front Burner* is gone. Ehler has been neutralized, and you have Andrew installed downstairs playing Mary Poppins."

Brian presses his lips together and crinkles his brow. "That's a fairly accurate summary. Congratulations. You get the point. You have no recourse if you want to sit behind the Resolute Desk."

"Which I do. That's why you chose me, right? So, what do you want this time?"

Brian withdraws a tri-folded piece of paper from his suit jacket and hands it to Alicia. "A few addendums to our previous list of demands. Don't worry, it's nothing serious. Just minor appointments and a couple of policy proposals."

Alicia scans the list of names. None of them stand out to her. Even the policy proposals at the bottom aren't radical or indefensible. He tracks her eyes as she checks the next column to see what positions Brian wants her to fill.

"The Department of Agriculture? Why do you care about who the secretary for that is?" Alicia asks, causing Brian to shrug. "I thought I was able to name the other cabinet positions."

"You are, except this one. You don't even have someone in mind for that position yet. It shouldn't be a big deal."

Alicia rereads the list. The rest of the names are for deputies or undersecretaries in the Department of Defense, Interior, Commerce, Energy, and Transportation.

"What are you up to, Brian?"

"Nothing of importance," her nemesis replies.

"I don't believe you. You've always been a planner, Brian. I don't think you're content stopping at hijacking the presidency. There is something bigger going on."

"Hijacking is such a nasty word. Ours is a cooperative alliance. Outside of our choice for attorney general and White House chief of staff, have we made any demands that you're losing sleep over?"

"No."

"See? There's no reason we can't work together, Madam President-Elect."

Alicia winces at the sound of her title. It wasn't the words themselves but the tone used to utter them. They were ominous and foreboding. He owns her and knows it.

"I never thought I'd hear that title come out of your mouth."

"I'm warming up to it. Especially since we're seeing eye-to-eye."

"What about the VP? Will Kerrigan's name be cleared, or do you plan on selecting a new one?"

Brian smiles and slaps his knee emphatically. "Let's see how things play out. Good to see you again, Alicia. Oh," he says, standing. "You're starting to get bags under your eyes. Make sure you're getting enough sleep."

CHAPTER THIRTY-THREE

PRESIDENT-ELECT ALICIA STANDISH

Standish's Hay-Adams Hotel Suite
Washington, D.C.

Brian wasn't even at the elevator when Alicia fired up her laptop. She doesn't recognize any of these names and wonders why Brian wants them elevated to positions in her administration. There has to be a catch – something in their background that is a red flag.

After two hours of searching the names on this list utilizing various databases and public-source information, there are no warning signs. Each name on the list is someone with an honest government or private sector career. They are honorable individuals who are qualified for the positions they seek. Some of them might even be considered overqualified.

Alicia tries a different approach and does a series of searches, including their names and Brian Cooper. Nothing comes up. She redoubles her efforts with a series of searches that link the names with other members of Cooper's cabal. Still nothing. Just by the law of averages, she would have expected one hit to come up. A photo at a fundraiser or a group shot at a D.C. cocktail party. Instead, she gets nonsense in each of the search returns.

Frustrated, the president-elect rubs her eyes and tilts her head back. The headache she's been nursing is now pounding like a boxer working over a heavy bag. She took a couple of Advil an hour ago. She needs more but elects to wait until it's time to crash.

Something must make these people valuable to Brian in these positions. Alicia just can't find it. With no other leads to follow, she closes the laptop and sets it aside. She stands, stretches, and moves over to the windows with their magnificent view of the north side of the White House.

Alicia has always been fond of the building's south façade. It combines Palladian and neoclassical architectural styles in a projected bow of three bay windows and a ground-floor double staircase leading to an Ionic colonnaded loggia and the Truman Balcony. The north façade she's staring at is nice, but the south is iconic and majestic.

Her thoughts linger back to the list Brian handed her. It doesn't make sense. If Angela Mays were still alive and handed her those names, she would have appointed any of them without a second thought. Does the cabal run far deeper than she thinks it does? There is no evidence to show that, but it doesn't mean that there isn't a connection just because she can't find it.

And then there are the positions. Defense is an understandable choice, but then why not dictate who the secretary for that department is? It's an incredibly important and high-profile position that ranks high in the line of succession. Or State? The secretary of state is the president's representative to the world. Brian's not pushing to exert his influence there makes no sense.

Another list could be forthcoming. This is the second round of names Alicia has been handed. They could be presenting this to her like an intravenous drip to not scare her this early in the transition. The real heavy hitters could come later, but Andrew hasn't said anything about the shortlist for the key cabinet posts.

The policy proposals are another matter. The ones Cooper outlined aren't anything special. Most can be done via executive order, and the others would enjoy broad bipartisan legislative support, especially in a friendly Congress. Democrats would support it enthusiastically, and Republicans wouldn't find it abhorrent enough to spend political capital defeating. They may even embrace them in the name of bipartisanship to not look like obstructionists while looking forward to the midterms in two years.

It's all mystifying, and then another thought pops into Alicia's head. Maybe this is something she can live with. So far, Brian has been true to his word. After the election, he said they only wanted to make a few key appointments and weigh in on policy measures when appropriate. The cabal stated unequivocally that the presidency was hers outside of those wishes. Alicia doubted that, but is it possible they mean it?

The specter of intervention is daunting, but what choice does she have? A public acknowledgment now would damage her reputation forever. It would, beyond the shadow of a doubt, cost her the presidency. Even a Democratic congress would vote for impeachment and removal. She doesn't want to be the fourth president impeached by the House and the first president to ever be removed from office by the Senate. She doesn't want that asterisk next to her name in the history books.

Sleep isn't going to come any time soon. Alicia decides to head back downstairs and get her mind off this for a while. She has another, more pressing matter to worry about. She may need to find a new vice president if this scandal worsens.

CHAPTER THIRTY-FOUR

SSA DANIEL MURPHY

FBI Philadelphia Field Office
Philadelphia, Pennsylvania

The Philadelphia field office is located on the eighth floor of the William J. Green Jr. Building on Arch Street, near the downtown. They are responsible for eight resident agencies in Pennsylvania and New Jersey and keep busy, like those in other major cities.

DeAndre sets off to procure them a conference room after talking to the special agent in charge. Murphy takes the opportunity to check in with his team in Washington. They have no information on Larsen or her whereabouts but are still sifting through CCTV footage at the train station. Unfortunately, there are dozens of cameras, and even an army of agents will need time to meticulously sift through dozens of hours of footage. He isn't expecting results anytime soon.

This is going to be an awkward conversation. Bangura is a fellow agent, and he doesn't have much evidence that she's involved. It's worth the conversation. How Larsen managed to slip out of the Keystone Militia camp has always bothered him. She appears to be the answer to that question.

Imani comes in, and he's immediately struck by her looks. She has flawless mocha skin and bright, intelligent eyes, and she carries herself with confidence. She and Larsen would make a devastating duo.

"Agent Bangura. Sit down, please. I'm—"

"Supervisory Special Agent Daniel Murphy. I know who you are."

He cocks his head as Imani sits in the chair and leans back. An agent who thinks she's wrongly suspected of illegal activities should be a bundle of nerves. Agent Bangura is confident and relaxed.

"Did Victoria Larsen tell you to expect me?"

Imani grins. "I watch the news. Your handsome face is memorable."

"What is your relationship with Victoria Larsen?"

"I don't have one."

Murphy narrows his eyes. "I don't believe you."

"I don't care if you do or don't."

Murphy nods before folding his hands on the table. "I read that your family has a law enforcement background."

"My grandfather was a cop. He lived in—"

"Cobbs Creek East. A rowhouse belonging to one Amos Bangura of the Philadelphia Police Department. I already have a team searching the residence," Murphy informs her, studying her reaction. "You look surprised."

"Yeah, I am. I haven't heard about any rioting in the city. That neighborhood is known for its warm relationships with law enforcement and tends to react negatively to things like that."

"Your grandfather lived there in that residence until his death, and you visit it frequently. They must not be too fussed about cops and federal agents."

"His neighbors knew him. They know me. They don't know the pasty white boys in windbreakers searching through my spare underwear drawer."

"What are we going to find there, Imani?" Murphy asks, changing to a graver tone.

"In my underwear drawer? A few lacy bras from—"

"In the house," Murphy says, correcting the question before he gets an itemized list of her unmentionables. "What will they find in your grandfather's rowhouse?"

"Dirty dishes, a house in desperate need of dusting, and a small stack of unpaid bills on the counter. Feel free to take care of those for inconveniencing me."

Murphy cracks a smile. As frustrated as he is with her sarcastic responses, she has grit. That's admirable, even if it's misplaced.

"I know Larsen came to Philly. I suspect you're either harboring her or know where she is."

"And you'd be wrong on both accounts."

"Time will tell. You were working here the night of the raid at the Liberty Lumber Company, yes?"

"I was."

"Were you in contact with Agent Larsen that evening?"

"I was a little too busy to dig up her number and introduce myself. From the reports, she wouldn't have been able to take the call anyway. Rumor has it that she saved that tactical team from annihilation. Instead, you want us to believe she was helping Ian Drucker. Tell me, Agent Murphy, do you bother looking at evidence, or do you just mindlessly follow orders?"

The comment smarts. Murphy has always been by-the-book. He prides himself on following procedure but has been occasionally criticized for relying on it. He wonders if she spoke to Larsen about it. Her observation is too on-the-nose after just meeting.

"Agent Bangura, you have a promising career ahead of you. Victoria Larsen is a master manipulator. If you helped her, the reason can be easily understood. That will only help you if you help me catch her. Don't make me dig into your life and destroy you."

Imani straightens in her chair and leans slightly across the table.

"That's an interesting threat, Agent Murphy. You've already arrested most of her friends, or so I've read. Are you moving on to everyone else who has heard of her now?"

"Everyone in custody has helped a domestic terrorist who's threatening the country. Do you know what the penalty for helping her is?"

"I know what the law says, if that's what you're asking. I don't see how it applies to me. You brought me in here to shake me up. Agent MC Hammer here made a spectacle of walking me here in full view of my colleagues to embarrass me."

"I prefer to be called Tupac, thank you very much," DeAndre says, his face contorting at the slight.

"You don't have proof I'm involved in anything. This conversation would be entirely different if you did. You're at a dead end and are grasping at straws because Larsen has stayed three steps ahead of you."

"So far. The outcome is inevitable. Victoria Larsen will be caught."

"You look tired, Agent Murphy. Go to your hotel and get some rest. Or we can sit here and dreamily stare into each other's eyes. Either way, I'm done talking."

Murphy stands and signals DeAndre to the corridor. He stops before leaving the room in one of the most clichéd television cop show moves ever drafted by a screenwriter.

"Tierra Campos was arrested in Washington for possession of an altered firearm. There was no serial number, but ballistics matched it to a weapon you bought for your grandfather. You don't know Campos, Imani. I'm certain of that. But you both know Victoria Larsen. I'm going to give you a chance to reconsider this conversation. Then I want the truth from you."

"MC Hammer, my ass," DeAndre mumbles once they leave the conference room and the door is closed behind them.

"She knows something. We just need proof so we can leverage it with her."

"I'll have her work area searched," DeAndre says, looking back toward her desk. "They may find something at her apartment or grandfather's house."

"I doubt it. Imani's as smart as she is beautiful. You need to get her talking. Spend some quality time with her and see if you can build trust. Sing 'You Can't Touch This' if you have to."

"Haha. What are you going to do?"

"She's right. I need to crash for a few hours. My fatigue is slowing me down. Victoria is planning something. We need to figure out what before she can execute it."

CHAPTER THIRTY-FIVE

TIERRA CAMPOS

Wilson Newman's House
Falls Church, Virginia

Everything is harder after I run. Breathing, walking, opening a door, and even thinking are difficult. And that's largely the point. Taking a break from the happenings in my head helps with stress. Unfortunately, my jaunt through the neighborhoods of Falls Church was more exertion than anticipated, and I'm woefully out of shape.

I force my jelly legs to carry me into the kitchen and I manage to refill my insulated bottle with filtered water from the fridge. I collapse against the counter and have sucked about half of it down when Mi Sun rounds the corner. I scowl, but it's more because of my slow physical recovery than anything she did.

"I'm sorry, I didn't know you were in here, Tierra. I'll come back."

"No need, Mi Sun. You aren't bothering me."

"How was your run?" she asks, pulling an apple from the bowl on the counter.

"Enlightening."

"How so?"

"I concluded that I need to exercise more than once a month to not feel like I want to die. How are you doing?"

Mi Sun pulls a knife from the drawer and slices off a small chunk of the fruit.

"I'm going a little stir-crazy. I've been working since I was twelve. I don't cope well with idle time. If I don't do something productive soon, I'm going to find another use for this knife."

"You've been working since you were twelve?"

Mi Sun shrugs. "My mother and father are immigrants. Hard work comes with the territory, and nobody is more demanding than parents who came here to provide lives for their children. Can I…."

"What is it?"

She stares down at the floor. "I'm worried about Wilson. He isn't eating right, and I don't think he's sleeping well. It's taking a toll on him."

"The stress is getting to all of us."

Mi Sun puts the apple down. "Yeah, but I think it's more than that. He looks worse since you were assaulted at Josh's and then arrested. He didn't handle that news well."

"No, I didn't think he would," I admit.

"Does it bother you that Wilson and I are…were…working so closely? I don't want to interfere…I know you two are very close."

"Honestly, it did…at first."

"Not anymore?"

I shake my head. "Can I ask you a question, Mi Sun? Why did you really leave Oliver Jahn?"

She sighs and sits on the stool. "Because Oliver changed. No, that's not quite right. The circumstances changed him."

"What do you mean?"

"You never got to see the real Oliver Jahn. What you saw was his posturing. The old version – the one from our podcast days – never would have done what he did to you. He started doing the news because he hated the agendas and the hit pieces. Then he became the thing he despised most. It got worse when he went over to VHN."

Mi Sun has said multiple times that Oliver isn't happy there. His misery contributed to her discontent, leading her to seek employment at *Front Burner*. That's not looking like such a good move now, but I understand the need for a change of scenery. That's why I left the desert Southwest after high school.

"Well, you're right about one thing. Whether it was the circumstances that changed Oliver or something else, he absolutely changed."

"That's what was so weird. Oliver admired you. He would never admit it, but he was mesmerized by the Brockhampton investigation. I remember him saying what guts it took to go after Ethan Harrington. Part of him was jealous because he wanted to conduct investigations, uncover the truth…."

"And instead, he became an entertainer."

"Yeah, that's partly my fault," Mi Sun admits. "Oliver was always funny. It was how he delivered the news, and he's a natural at it. I pushed him to do more, and then he went overboard."

"That's an understatement," I moan. "Do you miss working for *TNT*?"

"I miss the old version. Wilson is great, but Oliver…well, he's like a first love. You never completely get over it."

"Ew."

Mi Sun smiles, and I let out a laugh. The more I interact with her, the more I like her. I think Wilson knew I would, and that's why he wanted to see her hired. I hate it when he's right.

"I hope Oliver finds his way back to the light," Mi Sun says. "I pray that he does. It's really a shame there's bad blood between you two. Under different circumstances, I could imagine you being close friends. You have a lot in common."

I should be more uncomfortable hearing that than I am. "I think there is a better chance of seeing a leprechaun riding a unicorn through Times Square than my ever being in a room with him, let alone friends."

Mi Sun nods and starts to leave. She stops at the door and looks back.

"Thank you, Tierra."

"For what?"

"Accepting me. You didn't have to give me a chance at *Front Burner*. Anyone else in your position wouldn't have. It means a lot to me."

I still want to be angry at her. Under her guiding hand, Oliver Jahn made my life miserable. But that is dissipating. I'm learning to trust her and her judgment.

Mi Sun is a good person who got caught up in a bad situation. I can't stomach the thought that Oliver was, too. I'm not ready to deal with that right now. There is already enough stress in my life.

CHAPTER THIRTY-SIX

VICTORIA LARSEN

Independence Square
Philadelphia, Pennsylvania

Independence Square is the perfect place to loiter if you want to get lost in a mob of tourists. Three buildings here are connected by arcades: Independence Hall in the center is flanked on the left by Old City Hall and on the right by Congress Hall. It's an area steeped in American history, and there are still hundreds of tourists milling about despite the mid-November chill.

Victoria appreciates the historical value of this city. The Second Continental Congress met here. This small area witnessed the drafting of the Declaration of Independence from the British and the ratification of the Constitution. Until the Centennial Bell replaced it, citizens could hear the Liberty Bell ring out from the bell tower.

From 1790 to 1800, Philadelphia was the seat of the federal government. The United States Supreme Court, Congress, and the president governed from these buildings. It's breathtaking to imagine the decisions made on behalf of the young nation in this spot. It's also a bad place for her to be.

The area is covered with cameras, which is why she chose it to fake her aneurysm during a chat with Tierra. The ruse was necessary, but her closest friend is still traumatized and will be scarred for life because of it. Tierra is a true friend. She found out just how true that day.

Victoria meanders around the square, taking pictures. As long as she stays low-key, the Philadelphia Police won't pay her any attention. The FBI certainly isn't looking for her mere blocks from their field office. Her only concern is facial recognition technology. One good look at her face and a computer running the image through the right database could spell disaster. That's the modern danger of trying to hide in plain sight.

She grows impatient waiting for the call and pulls out her phone to help things along. She has a long history at the Bureau with Audric LeClair. They were best friends at Quantico, and he betrayed her during the Brockhampton investigation. They've managed to patch things up since then. Sort of. It will never be like it once was, and he owes her. Now, it's time to cash in.

"LeClair."

"Hi Audie, it's me."

"Vic…you're going to be the death of me!"

"Probably. Did you find the information I need?"

"It's only been two hours."

Victoria stares up to check the time on Independence Hall's clock tower. It's been less than two hours, but that's irrelevant. Not finding the information isn't the problem. She knows Audie all too well.

"You found the info in five minutes and have spent every second since debating whether to tell me."

Audie breathes sharply. "Do you know what they will do to me if I get caught talking to you, let alone find out I provided you with *that* information?"

"Absolutely. Agents will call their buddies in the CIA and take you into the basement. They'll chain you to a chair and start yanking your fingernails off until you talk. And then they'll start breaking bones one at a time until—"

"That's not funny."

"Audie, all I need is *one* piece of information. They will never know how I got it. The faster you give it to me, the faster this call ends."

There is a long pause. Victoria knows the line is still active. Audie can be a pain in the ass, but he wouldn't dare disconnect her.

"Are you going to kill him?"

"Audie, just tell me. The less you know, the better."

He sighs. "Whynnspar Historic District Hotel, room 302."

"See how easy that was?"

"Vic? Please be careful. I don't want to attend your funeral or sit in the back of a courtroom when they lock you up for life."

"I don't want you to have to. Thank you, Audie. Take care of yourself."

Victoria hangs up. The hotel isn't far away, and she starts walking without looking like she's in a hurry. The key to this working is her looking the part. She ducks into the ladies' room in the hotel lobby and peels off her sweatshirt. It figures that the one time she's dressed like a civilian, she needs to look like an agent.

She pulls her jacket from the backpack and slides the gun into a holster that she secures to her hip. Once her hair is properly tied back in a bun, she checks herself in the mirror. That's the best she can muster, but it ought to do.

Victoria grabs the backpack and passes through the lobby before taking the stairs to the third floor. Housekeeping is there making rounds. Perfect. That's the only way this is going to work.

"Hi. I'm sorry to bother you," Victoria says, pointing at the door. "I locked myself out of my room. Could you…"

The woman gives her a bewildered look.

"*Por favor. Está bien,*" Victoria says, producing her gold FBI badge. "*Soy un agente del FBI. No te meterás en problemas.*"

The woman smiles and swipes a card to unlock the door. Victoria exhales, happy that her Google translate version of Spanish did the trick.

"*Gracias, señora.*"

"De nada."

Victoria slides her Glock from the holster and extends her arms as she enters the room. After a quick sweep, she knows he's not here yet. The room is tidy, with shoes lined up and clothing neatly hung in the closet. His one redeeming quality may be that he's not a slob.

She gets comfortable in the chair beside the bed and props her feet up on a hassock. She pulls Ian's laptop from the backpack. Investigative work has always come easy to her. Time loses all meaning when she begins digging into something.

The next couple of hours are spent perusing Ian's journals, then there's a scuffling sound in the hallway. The telltale click of the door's magnetic lock announces it's showtime. Victoria closes the laptop cover and leans the device against the chair. The next few moments will define the rest of her life.

The door opens, and a light flips on in the entry. Victoria hears the lock twist and the screech of the chrome arm door guard being moved into place. Shadows bounce in the small hallway with the bathroom and a closet.

The man finally emerges, taking two steps toward the bed before freezing in his tracks. His eyes grow as big as saucers. Victoria knows the last thing he expected was to see her sitting in the upholstered chair beside his bed with her feet up.

"It's about time you got here. I was close to ordering room service."

CHAPTER THIRTY-SEVEN

BRIAN COOPER

Il Diplomatico Infuriata Ristorante
Washington, D.C.

The Furious Diplomat is a popular destination for the who's who in Washington. Politicians, lobbyists, and celebrities frequently dine here, drawing throngs of tourists with funds to absorb prices that sear your retinas when reading the menu. That's not to say the food isn't worth every penny. Plenty of overpriced restaurants serve mediocre cuisine in the capital, but this isn't one of them.

Brian's guest was punctual, and the pair was seated right at their reservation time. Besides a greeting, the two men don't speak until after the waiter reads the specials, drinks are ordered and delivered, and an appetizer is selected.

"I didn't think you would want to meet in a public place, especially one as popular in our circles as the Diplomat," Brian says, adjusting the linen napkin resting in his lap.

"I was in the mood for Italian," Garrett Brewer says, admiring the restaurant's decor. "I heard they have a steak that's to die for."

"Mmm, the Bistecca Fiorentina. It's an enormous T-bone steak that people have recurring dreams about after eating. Still, this is risky."

"Brian, you aren't Deep Throat. There's no need for the two of us to meet in a Rosslyn parking garage."

Deep Throat became engrained in the nation's collective memory when reporters Bob Woodward and Carl Bernstein introduced him in *All the President's Men*. The mysterious figure was a key source in a series of articles that introduced the Nixon administration's misdeeds to the general public, ultimately leading to the president's resignation. Deep Throat's identity remained one of the great mysteries in American political and journalism circles for decades. It wasn't until 2005 that the world learned the pornographic moniker belonged to former Federal Bureau of Investigation Associate Director Mark Felt.

He would meet the reporters at an underground parking garage in the Oakhill Office Building located at 1401 Wilson Boulevard. Brian has been to the spot, which has been demolished and is now a residential apartment building. The historical marker commemorating the Watergate scandal is still there, though.

"I'm sure your visit to D.C. isn't a social call. What can I do for you, Garrett?"

The financial baron steeples his fingers. "My associates tell me you are displeased with the actions taken in Boston and Washington."

Brian looks around to see if anyone is paying attention to them. "You should be, too. They failed."

"Not entirely. The message was sent as designed. It would have been better had Campos been eliminated, but things happen. As for Larsen, we didn't even know she was there. Killing Chambers was meant to be a warning. I'm certain she received it."

Brian is suddenly glad he is using his toy from the NSA. The jammer disrupts voice recordings by messing with the microphone. The din in the room will obscure their voices from anyone nearby. They should be able to talk freely, not that there's much of a chance that anyone is listening in on them anyway.

"And the hired guns could be traced back to you."

Garrett smirks. "That's unlikely."

"But possible. It was reckless, and I would have explained that if you had asked me. Why didn't you?"

Garrett raises an eyebrow. "Are you under the impression we need your permission?"

"No, but a heads-up is warranted. You entrusted me with this operation. It could have been out of courtesy."

"Roman felt that was untenable. You have a relationship with Miss Campos, and there was a risk of you warning her. That's why you were left out of the loop, Brian. As for your operation, we were defending our interests. I'm sure you understand that."

"I do because I'm defending your interests, too. You jeopardized everything we have worked for."

"Hardly," Garrett says with a scoff. "This is only a part of our overall operation, albeit a critical and ambitious part. We understand the risks and are willing to accommodate various degrees of success. I believe we explained this to you once before."

"Yes, you mentioned it without providing any details."

"Because you don't need to know them."

Brian leans back in his chair. He can't tamp down the feeling he's being kept in the dark. He knows more is happening, but he also assumed that Actyv's owners would include him in future endeavors. It's starting to not look like it, making him expendable. There is another name for that: a loose end.

"Fair enough, but I'm entitled to know the details when it affects my responsibilities. You mentioned Deep Throat. The Watergate scandal made Woodward and Bernstein's career just as Ethan Harrington made Campos's. She has since then added the S.O.F. and their shenanigans in the New Hampshire Primary to her resume. There cannot be a third success."

Garrett leans forward. "Thus, we did what you were apparently unwilling to. We are not adversaries, Brian. You would have been removed from the equation long ago if we were. You do as you see fit. We will do the same when the occasion calls for it."

The waiter comes with their appetizers and offers to refresh their drinks, which both men pass on for now. The interruption gives Brian a moment to gather his thoughts. He knew this could happen. Mission completion can be as perilous as a mission failure. He only hoped it would go differently. It's clear who is calling the shots versus taking the orders. If there was any chance of forging a more collaborative relationship, the moment has passed. He knows he needs to start taking preventive measures.

"With that unpleasantness dispensed with, tell me what you have in store for Standish's presidency. When you're done, I will tell you what we need from it."

CHAPTER THIRTY-EIGHT

PRESIDENT-ELECT ALICIA STANDISH

Hay-Adams Hotel
Washington, D.C.

The interview is a pleasant one. Hotel management let them use a corner of the Hay-Adams Room for it. The space is one of Washington's signature event venues, featuring a warm ambiance, rich woodwork, and two working gas fireplaces. The network's producers set up near one of them, hoping to capture the audience's imagination in a literal version of FDR's fireside chats.

Moira Kinsella sits opposite her and Brendan with a notepad in her hand. The middle-aged reporter is a stalwart in political circles. She has made no qualms about wanting to be the next Barbara Walters, and while Moira has a long way to go to reach the status of that iconic journalist, she's on the path.

In her late thirties, she has already made a name for herself by landing interviews with some of the world's most prominent celebrities, thought leaders, and heads of state. She no longer needs to beg for interviews — most are honored to get the request, the new president-elect included.

Andrew Li is hovering nearby. Alicia set this interview up, so he's on high alert. Moira isn't under his thumb and doesn't belong to DeAnna Van Herten's expansive media empire. His window to conduct damage control is limited, and his ability to shape the questions or direction of the interview is nonexistent.

Andrew's vigilance over a friendly interview with someone he didn't approve of further proves that Alicia can't live like this. What she is about to do is a massive risk. It's also one that needs to be taken. Despite being on the precipice of becoming the world's most powerful leader, she has little control over her destiny. She's isolated and bound, and there is no way to escape the shackles Brian Cooper slapped on her without help.

Moira begins to wrap things up. They have already covered a bevy of questions, ranging from the primaries, the campaign trail, debates, the election, and the issues in Pennsylvania. She tried to remain complimentary to Colin Bradford, decreeing that under the circumstances, she wouldn't have conceded either if the roles were reversed. The final questions are likely to be about the path forward.

"Brendan, there are people out there who say you're emasculated by calling yourself the First Gentleman. That you are taking a back seat to your wife. How do you respond to that?"

"I'm not sure how to. My wife is a strong, intelligent woman who was just elected as the next president of the United States. Do they want me to try to upstage her? Because that isn't ever going to happen."

"So, you aren't feeling any pressure about being a man in a supportive role?"

"We have been supporting each other since long before we married. If people consider that somehow emasculating, they have a warped view of relationships. I have a career in finance, and Alicia has a successful one in politics. We have always been there for each other, and I have no doubt that the trend will continue. She earned this. She put in the work, not me."

"What are you looking forward to most?"

"The easy answer is riding on Air Force One, but I look forward to making a difference. There are a host of causes I would like to work on, starting with educating children about finance – how credit works, investing, saving, budgeting…. We can do a lot to help set this generation up for financial success."

Moira wraps up the interview. The cameras stop recording, and the lighting is switched off. The journalist stands and thanks them for the interview. Alicia slides her hand into her pants pocket to ensure the note she drafted earlier is still there. She knows it is. Still, the feel of it is reassuring.

Alicia nods, and Brendan excuses himself and walks over to Andrew Li. Machiavelli is still off to the side, content to watch the interaction without interference. That doesn't mean he isn't poised to strike like a cobra at the first hint of trouble. That's why this moment of interference is necessary.

"Did that meet your requirements?" Alicia hears Brendan ask.

This is not a conversation her chief of staff wants to have in earshot of a reporter. He pulls Brendan farther away from Alicia and Moira. This is her chance.

"I appreciate the tenor and tone of the interview. I sincerely hope we can do this again."

Alicia palms the note in her pocket and extends her hand to her interviewer. A quizzical look pops on Moira's face. If she opens that note here, the game is up. Alicia narrows her eyes and glances over to Andrew.

"We have no secrets here except the ones we *need* to keep. Sometimes, discretion is *everything*."

Moira nods. "I understand, Madam President-Elect. I hope we can speak again soon."

Alicia smiles warmly as her husband returns under the watchful eyes of the devious Machiavelli.

"I'm counting on it."

CHAPTER THIRTY-NINE

SSA DANIEL MURPHY

Whynnspar Historic District Hotel
Philadelphia, Pennsylvania

Murphy drops his laptop bag and draws his weapon. His finger instinctively moves to the trigger and stops only when his brain processes what his eyes see. Victoria Larsen is sitting there with her hands folded in her lap. She's unarmed. With that realization, he returns his index finger to its resting position along the slide and takes a breath.

"Relax, Murph. My weapon is sitting over there on the desk. I'm not armed."

He glances at the workspace to see a Glock lying there, the magazine ejected, and the slide locked to the rear to show no round is chambered. She could have a backup piece, so he isn't about to lower his sidearm.

"Victoria Larsen, you're under arrest for—"

"Save it," she says, raising a hand before returning it to her lap. "You may have a reputation for being by the book, but the subject of a manhunt turning up in your hotel room must be a first. You won't arrest me until you find out why I'm here."

"To kill me?"

Victoria chuckles. "If that were the case, you wouldn't have made it past the entry."

Murphy's eyes narrow. She still isn't moving aggressively, and there is no obvious weapon. He takes three steps backward and glances into the bathroom. It's empty.

"I'm alone. You've arrested all of my friends."

"Not all of them. I wasn't involved in the Campos arrest. That was the D.C. Police on orders from someone above my pay grade."

"Let me guess. Conrad Williams. I assume that's who you and Director Krekstein are taking orders from."

Murphy tries to play it cool, but the surprise still flashes on his face. "How did you know that?"

Victoria smirks. "You know, I admired you when we were at Quantico."

He lowers his weapon slightly to relax his arms and reduce fatigue. "Do you think buttering me up will make this end well for you?"

"No. I'm beyond thinking this will end well at all for me. I'm telling you the truth because you need to hear it."

"I didn't know that," Murphy says, playing along.

"That's because you were too busy despising me to notice."

"You were my competition."

"Mmm, not really. We were both going to become agents. The difference is you always *needed* to be the top dog. I wanted results."

"And then you got both after Brockhampton."

The tone in his voice had a sharper edge than he meant it to. Victoria picks up on it and smirks. He was jealous of her, not that he wanted to admit it.

"And Williams knew that. Have you ever wondered why you were chosen for this assignment? You're good…I mean, really good…but a dozen different agents could fill your role. Why you?"

"I'm better than they are."

Victoria shakes her head. "You're not enough of a narcissist to believe that's true. It's your history of following orders without question. You have a reputation for setting aside your gut instinct and deferring to procedure and protocol. You're ambitious, want glory, and are motivated because it means getting the better of me. That's why Williams and Krekstein wanted you."

"Gee, Victoria, flattery will get you nowhere," Murphy says sarcastically. "Enough of the armchair psyche profile. You have ten seconds to explain what you're doing here before I make a call, and you find yourself in the deepest hole this country can throw you in."

Victoria lowers her feet and leans forward in the chair. Daniel brings his gun back to level and trains it center mass. His finger twitches.

"You've been chasing me for a couple of weeks now. In that time, you can't tell me you haven't noticed the inconsistencies between the official narrative and reality. A little voice in your head is warning you that something isn't right."

"You'd like to believe that."

"I do believe it, Murph. You're too good not to hear it barking in your subconscious. The evidence and actions…just don't match what you're being told. In the next ten seconds, you'll decide what kind of agent you are: The one who lives by the book or the one who respects that voice and listens to his instincts."

"I'm not playing this game with you, Victoria."

"It's not a game, trust me," she says with a scoff. "I'm giving you a choice. You can arrest me and reap the accolades for bringing a dangerous domestic terrorist to justice because that's what they expect you to do. Or, you can holster your weapon and let me show you what's really happening behind the curtain. The decision is yours."

CHAPTER FORTY

TIERRA CAMPOS

Wilson Newman's House
Falls Church, Virginia

Falls Church is a unique and historic city conveniently located just miles from Washington, D.C. The nine miles to the Capitol area can be traveled in under twenty minutes on most days and is accessible on the metro's Orange Line. It's a quaint community with great restaurants and shops that reflect the city's ethnic and cultural diversity.

Wilson's house is large and beautiful but still modest for a man who has earned as much money as he has. The upstairs is on the formal side, so he spends much of his time in his finished basement lounge. It's a man cave if the man in question has been in journalism for decades.

The esteemed anchor is reserved and modest in public but enormously proud of his accomplishments in private. The basement walls are covered in pictures of him posing with politicians, world leaders, diplomats, and celebrities. There is military paraphernalia from his war corresponding days, gifts from heads of state, and signed sports memorabilia.

In the center of the room that covers most of the first floor's footprint is an L-shaped leather sectional that faces the massive flat-screen television. The large sofa is flanked by a matching easy chair on which Wilson is currently seated under a blanket. The lighting is turned down to a warm level, and a gas fireplace adds to the ambiance. It's a very comfortable room despite its size.

"Thank you for letting us crash here, Wilson," I say. "I'm sorry to inconvenience you."

"Are you kidding? You are never an inconvenience. It's nice having someone here to talk to other than my cat," he says, earning a look from the mound of fur cuddled in his lap. I didn't peg him as a cat person.

"Too bad we have to watch the History Channel," I moan, getting a grin from Josh, who's riveted to the television.

"Would you rather watch the news?"

"No," Wilson and I both say.

"What is this, anyway?"

Josh still doesn't look at me. I won't get a glance until the next commercial.

"It's a documentary about Napoleon's military tactics during his European campaigns."

"Big excitement and very relevant to today, I'm sure."

"Don't knock it, Wilson. The past is the key to the present."

"True, in some respects. I'm not sure it can be said for nineteenth-century warfare, but if you say so."

"Don't mind him, Wilson. Josh is the dorkiest of dorks. The History Channel will be his mistress in this relationship."

"Hey! Remember that I took a bullet for you."

"I look forward to you holding that over for me forever," I say, snuggling into his chest. It's a new feeling, but a good one.

"Ugh. You guys are too cute. It's sickening."

New love is like that. I remember seeing kids in high school and college when they were all lovey-dovey at the beginning of a relationship. It was nauseating, especially when you knew it wouldn't last.

I have higher hopes for Josh. We've been friends forever. We know and accept each other for who we are. That's always the hard part – getting through someone's façade. Josh and I have never erected one for each other.

I let the thought fade as I tune in to the narrator. So far as documentaries go, this one isn't horrible. The graphics are excellent, the acting prudent, and the narrator's voice isn't grating. I guess I should plan on getting used to this.

"Napoleon had intelligence and cleverness, but he was methodical and paid close attention to the details of his adversaries. He believed that victory was achieved by utilizing superior maneuverability, morale, staff officers, and, where possible, manpower. He studied the strategies of past generals like Alexander, Hannibal, and Frederick the Great to improve their ideas and eliminate their mistakes. Military commanders of today's modern armies study his tactics because of his tenacity and battlefield experience in dealing with suboptimal circumstances."

"There you go, Wilson. Not so outdated after all."

"I can slug him for you if you want me to," I say.

"From 1796 to 1809, Napoleon displayed near-invincibility on the battlefield, propelling him from a lowly officer to the self-crowned Emperor of France. His strategy of excellent maneuvering, flanking, and isolating the enemy left his opponents battered and broken. When faced with superior numbers or a more powerful force, he would divide the enemy army and defeat each section individually by skillfully deploying his reserves at the right time and place."

An alarm klaxon sounds in my head as the narrator's words rattle around my ears. I feel a jolt of electricity in my spine and shoot off the sofa. I'm shaking as I stand nervously in the middle of Wilson's basement lounge.

"Tierra! What's wrong?" Josh urgently asks.

"That's it!" I scream as the meaning of the epiphany becomes clearer.

"What's it?"

"It was in front of me the whole time. I'm such a moron. That's why he kept me around when I should have been dead. It's so obvious!"

"Wilson, do you know what she's talking about?"

The aging journalist shakes his head as he leans forward, disturbing his sleeping cat. "Not this time."

I place my hands on Josh's cheek and kiss him hard on the lips. "I will never complain about your ridiculous History Channel shows again."

"Well, I'm grateful for that, but can you tell us why you're freaking out?"

I look at Josh and then at Wilson. "I think I know how to beat Brian Cooper."

CHAPTER FORTY-ONE

SSA DANIEL MURPHY

Whynnspar Historic District Hotel Room
Philadelphia, Pennsylvania

The moment grows tenser after the ultimatum. Murphy knows that it's his duty to arrest her. A federal warrant was issued for her arrest, and it falls on the FBI to execute that warrant. A judge wouldn't have issued one without cause unless someone gave him one under false pretenses.

Victoria is right when she says he's always been by the book. She knows that, so why would she risk coming here? It'd be a hell of a bluff, and that's the problem. Special Agent Victoria Larsen doesn't bluff.

Murphy's phone rings, causing him to jump. Victoria doesn't flinch. He takes his right hand off his weapon and fishes his cell out of his jacket pocket, not taking his eyes off her for even a split second.

"Murphy," he says, answering the call.

"Hey, boss," DeAndre says. "I know you're ready to crash, but I wanted to let you know that Imani Bangura hasn't given us anything. It's looking like a dead end. What do you want to do?"

This is the moment of truth. Murphy takes a cleansing breath.

"Cut her loose. We'll talk in the morning."

"Copy that," DeAndre says before ending the call.

Murphy lowers his weapon. "Okay, Victoria. I'll play your game, but you need to understand something. If I think you're lying or manipulating me, I will slap the cuffs on you, and our next conversation will be in an interrogation room."

Victoria nods. "I would expect nothing less."

"Where do you want to start?"

Victoria reaches alongside the chair and hefts a laptop. "From the beginning."

They hook Drucker's system up with a new power supply she probably procured from Miranda Ramirez. Victoria accesses a site on the dark web and walks him through the Isiah files first. It's compelling but not concrete. Then she shows him the files on the laptop's hard drive.

They don't get a quarter through before Murphy holsters his weapon. She isn't lying. This is no joke, and the information is damning. That's when they get to the part about Conrad Williams. He reads, not believing his eyes. Murphy abruptly stands and stomps from the desk, running his fingers through his hair.

"You okay?"

"No, I'm not okay. You must think I'm an idiot."

Victoria leans back in her chair. "I would have if any of this was predictable or apparent. It's neither. Conrad has almost everyone fooled."

Murphy's hands clench into fists. "They've been manipulating me, and I didn't see it. I didn't even *consider* it."

"You did, at least at some level. Otherwise, I'd already be chained to a desk at the field office while you give Williams the good news."

"What are you going to do with this, Victoria?" Murphy asks, pointing to the laptop. "This is nothing short of a coup."

She shrugs. "I don't know."

"What do you mean you don't know?"

"I mean, short of marching into the DOJ and shooting Williams in the head, I have no idea how to stop him."

"What does Campos say?"

"Not much. I haven't talked to her since yesterday. Her entire world is turning like a washing machine's spin cycle. *Front Burner* is gone. She was just attacked by Russian commandos, and her closest friend was shot. Then she was arrested. She's not in a good place."

"All right," Murphy says, retrieving the chair and pulling it back to the small hotel room desk. "Walk me through the rest of this, and then we'll devise a plan. If I'm going to go to prison for helping you, it won't be without a fight."

He picks her weapon up from the desk, inserts the magazine, and racks a round. Murphy hands her the gun, holding it by the barrel. He notices the appreciative look on her face as she takes the weapon. For the first time in their lives, they are allies. He has to admit that feels good.

CHAPTER FORTY-TWO

BRIAN COOPER

Republican National Committee Headquarters
Washington, D.C.

He never expected an invitation to come here. Despite running Colin Bradford's campaign, Brian's still an outsider who spent most of his career working with Democrats. He once served as their opponent's chief of staff. His promotion to national campaign chairman was controversial and led to no shortage of grumbling in conservative circles that he threw the election on purpose. Brevin Hawkins is no doubt leading that charge.

The truth is inconvenient. Republicans lose because they aren't bold. They try to placate voters instead of appealing to them. There is nothing inspirational in calling the opposition the enemy and their plans dangerous when you don't offer alternatives. Democrats act similarly, too, which is why so many Americans hate politics.

Standish was different. While the race between her and Bradford got testy at times, it was largely run on the issues. Bradford might have won if he had started appealing to voters sooner than Brian forced him to. Instead, it was a struggle to keep the race close to make interference plausible enough to extort Alicia Standish.

Brian knows he doesn't belong at this meeting with Republican National Committee strategists. The first half hour has been insufferable. Yet, here he sits, in the corner, minding his own business while Monica Stengel and her counterparts talk about the lawsuit in Pennsylvania and discuss press strategies. It's a bore until Brevin Hawkins stands and points in Brian's direction.

"Monica, I have to ask, why is he here?"

Everyone in the room turns their heads to watch the consultant's reaction. "That's a good question, Brevin. I figured it was your idea."

"Oh, believe me, it wasn't. I don't suffer losers."

Brian smiles deviously. "You must have a hard time looking in the mirror."

"Enough! Both of you," Monica snaps.

Monica Stengel is in hot water with her party. She *needed* to win this election. Brian believes Monica blessed the decision to replace Brevin as campaign chair to line up a patsy when it was clear they wouldn't. Part of him still feels that way despite her not casting any blame in Brian's direction in the weeks since the election.

"He quit," Brevin says, with a sneer, "like the quitter he is."

"Eloquently put, as usual, Brevin. I didn't quit. I left because I offer nothing in a legal fight. I explained that to the candidate down in North Carolina, and he agreed."

"You didn't have anything to offer in the campaign either."

"Brevin, he outperformed you by a country mile," Monica says, defending Brian. "He single-handedly saved the convention and the campaign. That's water under the bridge. I asked him here because of what comes next. The Pennsylvania lawsuit aside, the scandal with the vice president-elect is an opportunity. Brian is a top-notch strategist, and I want to hear if he has any ideas on exploiting it."

Brian scans the room. Some actually look interested in hearing his perspective. Most offer little more than hostile glares of contempt. That's the thing with political parties – they are so blinded by ideology that they don't see the obvious path in front of them. His experiences with the Democrats were much of the same, if not worse.

"Simple. You don't."

"Yeah, that makes sense," Brevin moans.

"It makes perfect sense for anyone staring at the chessboard. There's an investigation forthcoming, and Republicans need to ensure that it's fair and thorough. You own the high ground if Kerrigan did what he's accused of. If you start making accusations and are wrong, you lose the confidence of the political middle – moderate Republicans, libertarians, and right-leaning independents. You'll look like political opportunists who will do and say anything to gain power in this city. In the process, you'll alienate people you can't afford to. Angry, they'll abandon you during the midterm election and next presidential race."

"That's ridiculous. The midterms are two years away, and the presidential election is four. American attention spans aren't that long."

"They are when the media plays it on an endless loop. Scandals are fleeting, but the Internet is forever."

"We can't pass on this opportunity. Anybody who thinks otherwise is a fool."

Hawkins has the political IQ of a houseplant. Not only can he not play the great game, he doesn't understand the rules and only has a tenuous grasp of the objective. In a world where the unqualified manage to fail upward into more prestigious positions, he is the undisputed king.

"Brevin, do you want to know why you sucked as a campaign manager? You don't know which pitches to swing at. You hack at the ones in the dirt and let the ones right down the middle pass. It's why Republicans can't win elections these days."

"You have some nerve!"

"Settle down, Brevin. Brian, do you think this could be a trap?"

"It's possible these whistleblowers are full of shit, yes."

"Based on what evidence?"

"None. Look at the situation. These so-called whistleblowers are anonymous Democrats. There is protection there, and, likely, we'll never know who they are. Can their word be trusted? Second, the media is going out of its way to report on the VP-elect's accusations. When was the last time any misdeed on the left was reported with such gusto?"

"Never," someone in the room says.

"Exactly. You wouldn't hear a peep if there was real juice in this scandal. The media would bury it to protect the party they helped win the White House. So, why do they breathlessly report it like an asteroid hurtling toward Earth? Do you think it's suddenly because they worship at the altar of fairness and factual reporting?"

"Not likely," another person says.

"Then maybe they believe there's nothing to it and are trying to lure us into stoking the partisan divide."

"And make us look like clowns when the world finds out the whistleblowers were lying and no laws were broken."

Brian taps his nose before pointing to Monica.

"You could be wrong!" Brevin shouts.

"Yes, I could. Monica asked for my professional opinion. I gave it. I advise you to sit tight, let this play out in the courts, and see what the Democrats do with the VP. If Everett Kerrigan is forced to resign or evidence becomes public, you have the opening you need to go on the attack."

Brian stands and buttons his suit jacket.

"Where are you going?" Monica asks.

He presses his lips together and looks around the room. "I'm not wanted here. I'm the guy who lost the election. Everyone in the room is looking at me that way, and some wonder if I did it intentionally. I know Brevin thinks that."

"Damn straight," the pompous ass mutters.

"You need a scapegoat for the loss. That's fine. I accept responsibility, so long as you remember the truth. The media wrote off Bradford's campaign before he was even nominated. He was down fifteen points after the Democratic convention and was gaining no ground during ours. I made this a race, and I did it by addressing problems and listening to the people."

"You still failed."

"I did," Brian says with a nod. "We lost because there was too much ground to make up in too little time. Can you imagine what the shellacking would have been had Brevin remained in charge?"

"Hey, I resent—"

"Winning elections isn't about destroying your opponent. It's about weakening their support while bolstering your own. Go after the VP-elect if you want to. Just understand that if you swing and miss, and Pennsylvania certifies this vote, which they will, you will make Standish unbeatable four years from now because you've offered nothing to the country except baseless accusations and sour grapes. Nobody votes for that."

Brian leaves, having made his point. He did the song and dance for the party. Now, it's time to get back to ensuring Standish takes office and doesn't leave for the next eight years.

CHAPTER FORTY-THREE

TIERRA CAMPOS

Wilson Newman's House
Falls Church, Virginia

The doorbell rings, and I check the camera on the app Wilson configured for me. After what happened at Josh's, any sound outside puts me on high alert. I see a lone woman standing there. She doesn't look like a fed, so that's a good sign.

I answer the door and immediately cross my arms. Out of all the people who could be standing there, she isn't the last one on the list. She's near the bottom, though.

"Hi, Tierra. I'm—"

"Moira Kinsella. I know who you are."

"Yes, I suspect you would."

"Considering how you gushed about me in your articles, are you here for an autograph or something?"

Her articles were anything but complimentary. She joined the ranks of Oliver Jahn and followed his lead in doling out daily beatdowns. Moira is an agent of the system and secures access by catering to the prevailing political and cultural winds. There isn't a career politician she doesn't rub noses with unless a transgression gets them canceled on social media. The sarcasm of my comment isn't lost on her.

"Not quite. May I come in?"

I want to say no. I want to tell this mindless automaton to pound sand. Instead, I gesture Moira in and let her pass by me.

"How did you find me?" I ask after closing the door and locking it.

"You may not think much of my skills, but I am still a reporter. It's what we do."

"Fair enough. What do you want, Moira?"

"I don't want anything. I'm here out of morbid curiosity."

"Okay...."

"I interviewed the president-elect yesterday."

I grimace at the sound of those words. "I'm not sure she's officially earned that title yet, but how is Alicia Standish holding up these days?"

"Fine, I guess. The interview was...vanilla. She said all the right things, but it felt off...forced, even."

"And you traipsed to Wilson's door because you wondered why and think we know something?"

"Even I wouldn't be that brazen. I'm here because the president-elect handed me this at the end of the interview."

Moira dips her fingers into her jacket pocket and pulls a folded paper from a memo pad. I unfold it, immediately noticing the Hay-Adams logo and information at the top.

Tell Tierra Campos she was right. I need to speak with her.
Ask her to explain everything, and then come back to see me.
-Alicia Standish

I take a deep breath. The missive is signed by Alicia Standish, and I've seen enough documents from her to know it's her handwriting and signature, at least to my untrained eye. If this is a forgery, it's a damn good one. I refold the note and hand it back to her.

"Do you want to tell me what this is about?"

"Not really," I say, brushing past Moira and walking into the kitchen.

"Tierra," she says, following me. "You have absolutely no reason to trust me. I understand that our history is only slightly better than what you have with Oliver Jahn."

"All true," I announce.

"But the next president of the United States handed me a note on the down low because she couldn't say something in front of her chief of staff. I don't need an abacus to do the math that something is terribly wrong, and you apparently have the answers."

"You're not entitled to hear them," I argue.

"No, I'm not. I'm asking."

I walk to the range and start the burner before plucking the kettle off it to fill it with water. I think back to a maxim I read once: The only thing worse than yearning for something you don't have is actually getting it. Most people want fame until they realize the sacrifices required when you're a household name. Moira thinks this is a story. Standish wants her involved. Is she prepared to learn that it's much more than that?

"Moira, you need to understand something. If I tell you, your life will be in danger. That's not a threat or a warning. It's a fact. There is no going back once you're told, and you may find yourself looking over your shoulder for the rest of your life. I don't think you're ready for that. Take my advice. Walk away, and forget you ever saw that note."

Moira stares at the ground for a moment before shaking her head. "I can't do that. I've known Alicia Standish since before she was a senator. I consider her a friend. Could you walk away from this?"

No, I couldn't. I might not think highly of Moira, but she is a good journalist. She has the gene. She may toss softball questions and has probably sandbagged her fair share of stories, but that doesn't mean she lacks an inquisitive mind. Since she's Standish's friend, I may have found a conduit to exchange communications. It's worth the risk.

"Do you want a cup of tea? We'll need to save the wine for after I'm done."

"Sure."

I retrieve a second cup from the cupboard. "Only twelve people alive know what I'm about to tell you. Some of them are already in federal custody. Everyone else who knew is already dead. This is your last chance to walk away before becoming the thirteenth."

Moira nods. "I appreciate the warning. What kind of tea do you have?"

CHAPTER FORTY-FOUR

PRESIDENT-ELECT ALICIA STANDISH

Standish Temporary Presidential Transition Headquarters
Hay-Adams Hotel, Washington, D.C.

Alicia tapped her foot anxiously for a half hour before this meeting. It was an uncharacteristic sign of nervousness from a woman not known for exhibiting any. When her guest was shown in, the initial discussion was frosty. Now it's arctic cold. This man isn't here to devise a strategy or continue his denials. He's pissed and isn't shy about showing it.

Andrew has remained observant but quiet during the tense discourse. He is standing along the wall, ready to crash into the conversation like a WWE wrestler jumping off the top rope. It will raise an eyebrow. This isn't *The West Wing*, and he is not Leo McGarry. This conversation would normally have nothing to do with a chief of staff.

"You asked if the accusations were true," Everett Kerrigan says. "I told you they weren't, and I was one hundred percent honest in that answer. I had hoped that would be enough to earn your support. Instead, you stabbed me in the back."

Alicia stares at her future vice president. She has known the man for years, but he isn't a friend. He's an ally who helped deliver the rust belt during the election. They share similar, although not identical, policy views.

"Give us the room, please," the president-elect commands.

Andrew Li stays behind as the staff files out of the room. Everett scowls when he notices that the future chief of staff hasn't budged.

"The president-elect asked for the room, Mr. Li. That means you as well."

"I'm staying, Mr. Vice President-Elect. You don't dismiss me, as I don't work for you."

Everett appeals to Alicia, who turns to Machiavelli and is met with a warning in his eyes. She will not be permitted to be alone in the room with her running mate. Not until after the inauguration, at the earliest.

"He can stay."

Kerrigan leans back. "So, that's how it is."

"Everett, Andrew was my campaign manager and is my closest advisor. He needs to be present for this conversation."

"I see. Are you making any decisions for yourself these days, Alicia?"

The comment was meant to provoke her. Under any other circumstances, it would. She has always considered herself a free-thinker and capable of independent decision-making. Unfortunately, it isn't true with Brian Cooper's boot on her throat. With Andrew in the room, she can't say that, so she opts for a direct rebuke to benefit the unwanted audience in the room.

"I've been in politics for a long time and can abide a lot. But some lines shouldn't be crossed."

"Did I cross a line?"

"Look behind you."

"Well, excuse me for offending you," Everett says with a flourish of his hands.

Alicia takes a cleansing breath. "These accusations—"

"Are nothing else but accusations!" Everett screeches. "They're hollow words with not a shred of evidence behind them. How do I know? Because my accusers haven't provided any. You know how else I know? Because I didn't do the things these so-called whistleblowers said I did."

Alicia leans back and folds her hands. "Politics is perception, Everett."

"Yes, it is. You used that line when you asked me to be your running mate. I guaranteed you a win in Michigan and made a Boston liberal competitive in the rust belt. There were others you could have chosen. Luther Burgess would have helped you immensely with the black vote. Even after his disastrous interview with Tierra Campos, Senator Veach remained viable. You still chose me."

"I did."

"And we both know why. I helped deliver you this election, but not by cheating."

"You are a partner on the ticket," Alicia confirms. "I don't doubt your denials."

"Then what's the problem?"

"Politics is perception," Andrew chimes in, parroting the line. "You were an asset on the campaign trail. Now, you're a liability that we can ill afford."

"Is he speaking for you now, too?"

"The president-elect has a great amount of loyalty to you, sir. I do not. Sometimes it's left to me to deliver the messages and do the things she doesn't want to."

Alicia glares at her chief of staff in waiting. That was uncalled for, not that Andrew cares. His delivery was acidic and hostile, and his demeanor matches his tone. That's what catches Everett's attention.

"And what is that?"

"Ask for your resignation."

Everett's jaw drops. "What?"

"Did I stutter? You need to tender your resignation as vice president-elect."

"Is he serious?" Everett asks Alicia.

"I don't have to accept it, but you must offer it," she says. "If we can clear you of wrongdoing, it goes away."

"I see. Guilty until proven innocent. I guess everything is backward in the country," Everett says, standing. "When I hand you my resignation, you will accept it. I don't want to serve as your vice president under these circumstances. You can spin your narrative to the people, but everyone will find my story more compelling."

"I doubt that," Andrew says, moving in front of the man elected to be a heartbeat away from the presidency when he assumes office. "You will tender it on the Friday after Thanksgiving. Not before and not after."

The VP-elect stares at Alicia, waiting for any objection or show of support. She can't offer any. Going against Andrew would have ramifications, and she can't face those consequences right now. There is too much at stake.

Realizing that there won't be any encouraging words or stay of execution, Everett stands and straightens his jacket. "Very well. Good day, Madam President-Elect."

Alicia turns to Machiavelli after her running mate leaves the room. "You said that he would be allowed to stay on."

Andrew shrugs and smiles. "Things change, Alicia. You should get used to it."

CHAPTER FORTY-FIVE

BRIAN COOPER

U.S. Marine Corps War Memorial
Arlington, Virginia

Twilight hours are Mother Nature's recurring light show. It may not be the dancing spectacle of the Northern Lights, but dawn and dusk are among the most striking sights to behold. Some locations highlight the experience more than others. Places like Angkor Wat, the Taj Mahal, Grand Canyon, and Mount Batur in Indonesia are just a few. While Washington may never make the top ten list for any photography enthusiasts, the sun rising behind this monument is worth getting up early to witness.

On the morning of February 23, 1945, Marines of Company E, 2nd Battalion, started the tortuous climb up the rough terrain to the top of Mount Suribachi. Men all over the island were thrilled by the sight of a small American flag flying from the peak. When all signs of enemy resistance were neutralized, a second, larger flag was raised in the same location and captured on film by Joe Rosenthal of the Associated Press. That moment earned him a Pulitzer Prize and was commemorated in bronze on a hill overlooking the Theodore Roosevelt and Arlington Memorial Bridges and the classic silhouette of the U.S. Capitol Building in the background.

Although it is colloquially called the "Iwo Jima Memorial," the monument is officially known as "The United States Marine Corps War Memorial." The inscription is dedicated to all Marines and reads, "In honor and in memory of the men of the United States Marine Corps who have given their lives to their country since November 10, 1775."

"You're a son of a bitch, Cooper," a woman's voice says from behind him.

The diminutive and highly eccentric Adika Patel stands there with her arms crossed. Wearing a long wool jacket and heeled boots, she almost looks normal. Of course, Brian isn't sure she's wearing anything under the coat. The biggest difference since their last meeting is her hair. Instead of blue and purple streaks, she colored it in autumnal gold and red hues.

Adika is one of the best opposition researchers in the country. Her rate is obscene, and politicians, special interest groups, and corporations happily foot the bill since no information escapes her probing. The downside is she is a prodigious flirt, an inappropriate dresser, and likely a sexual deviant that would distract any heterosexual coworker.

"Good morning to you, too."

She walks up and slaps him across the face. "What the hell are you getting me into?"

"What are you talking about?" Brian asks, rubbing his cheek.

"The information on the Pennsylvania secretary of state. You're using it to delay the outcome of the election."

"I'm doing no such thing. There is an investigation—"

"Stow it, Cooper. I'm not stupid."

"No, but you're acting naïve. Opposition research is *meant* to be used. Only I'm not using it to delay anything. It's to safeguard the process and ensure Bradford gets a fair shake. That's it."

Adika folds her arms and pouts. "I don't believe you."

"I don't give a damn. It's the truth. Whether you accept it is your problem."

"And this?" She holds up a thumb drive she retrieves from her pocket. "What is this for?"

"Life insurance."

In all reality, this isn't much of a policy. Isiah Burgess learned that the hard way. Information needs to be safeguarded, and dead men tell no tales. Even when you possess damaging information, it doesn't make you untouchable. In some cases, it places you in more jeopardy.

"I don't know what that means."

"You aren't meant to. What did you find?"

"Rabbit holes. Lots of rabbit holes. Most of them lead to dark places. What's your interest in this group?"

"They're funding the legal challenges of both campaigns in the election. I want to know why."

"Yeah, well, that's not on this," Adika says, wagging the drive with her fingers.

Brian smiles. "I didn't expect it to be. They would never leave a paper trail that leads to that particular holy grail. What is?"

"Corporate holdings, non-governmental organizations, suspicious charities, shell corporations, cutouts, shady deals, questionable investments, unethical business practices, political influencing operations...."

"In the U.S.?" Brian asks, not at all surprised about the list.

Adika snickers. "Everywhere. You need to start thinking globally when it comes to this group. The only continent they aren't involved in is Antarctica, and I bet I can find them extorting a raft of penguins if I dig deeper."

"Raft? I thought it was a colony of penguins."

The researcher rolls her eyes. "It depends on what they're doing. The most common collective nouns for penguins are colonies, rookeries, or huddles, but swimming penguins are called a raft, and walking penguins are called a waddle."

Brian crinkles his brow as he thinks that over. "You're a fountain of useless knowledge."

"It's what happens when you spend fourteen hours a day in front of a computer."

Adika holds the drive in front of him, and he takes it. She rubs her hands together like she's washing them. The metaphor isn't lost on Brian, but he doesn't say anything. Whatever Adika found has her spooked.

"This is where our road ends, Cooper."

"What do you mean?"

"I mean that the exorbitant fee I charge you is no longer worth the risk. These guys are dangerous. I don't plan on getting on their bad side by digging holes in their lawn."

"Adika—"

"The decision is final. It's also non-negotiable."

Brian smirks. "I was just going to say that I'm disappointed that I never got to see you naked."

"Most men are," the normally flirtatious Adika deadpans. "Goodbye, Brian. I expect my final payment in my account once you verify what's on that thumb drive. Don't make me hunt you down for it. You have no idea what skeletons I will unleash from your closet."

"You did research on me?"

She flips her hand in the air as she walks toward the access road that loops around the site. "I check everyone."

Brian stares at the thumb drive in his hand. If the founders of Actyv Private Equity knew he was holding this, ex-Spetsnaz commandos would be breaking down his door. It's a universal rule that people with secrets don't want them exposed. He needs to store this someplace safe, like Switzerland.

CHAPTER FORTY-SIX

SSA DANIEL MURPHY

The National Archives Museum
Washington, D.C.

Conrad Williams is a tough man to track down. He's often barricaded in his office and rarely sees visitors. Not that Murphy wants to meet there - it's his home turf. This meeting requires a neutral field, so he asked to meet here.

Entry to the National Archives Museum is free, and reservations aren't required for anyone entering through the general public entrance. It's not peak tourism season in the nation's capital, so there are no long lines outside or a crush of groups wandering around the museum.

The National Archives is home to over three billion records, including the three most important documents in American history: the Declaration of Independence, the Constitution, and the Bill of Rights. All three are housed in the Rotunda for the Charters of Freedom – a room reeking of the freedom and democracy inherent in the philosophy of the nation's founders.

Murphy is early, so he lets his mind wander as he gazes at the Constitution. He's torn about Victoria. Everything she's said since ambushing him is against everything he believes. She has the evidence, but he needs more – he needs to know that she's right. The senior agent knows that he's getting played. The only question is whether it's by Larsen or Williams. If it's the former, he'll make a call, and this saga will be over by the end of the day. He hopes it's the latter, even if it costs him his career.

He slides over and stops in front of the Declaration of Independence after a family moves off. This parchment has been proudly displayed for decades, including being exposed to thirty-five years of sunlight opposite a Patent Office Building window. No wonder it's faded. Today, it is sealed in the most scientifically advanced housing that modern preservation technology can provide.

"Why am I here?"

Murphy glances to his right to see Conrad standing there impatiently. "I didn't think it was a good idea to be seen in the DOJ. It's a short walk. Would you rather us continue this conversation in your office, sir?"

"You should be searching for Victoria Larsen instead of talking to me, so let's get on with it. What do you want?"

"Information."

"What kind of information?"

Murphy nods, and the duo moves to a quieter part of the Rotunda. There is anonymity in a crowd. To bystanders, they look like two men talking. The museum's guests could never know that the subject of their conversation may profoundly affect their lives.

"Why did commandos try to kill Detective Seth Chambers and Tierra Campos?"

That's not the question Williams expected, which is precisely why Murphy asked. Shock registers on the big man's face for a split second before he recovers.

"How the hell would I know? The better question is, why are you asking?"

"There's no evidence linking Larsen to Ian Drucker or the Keystone Militia. If anything, the opposite is true. Then a PMC tries to take out Chambers and Campos. It appears there is a lot more going on here."

"I think you're misreading the situation in Pennsylvania, and what a private military corporation is doing on American soil is someone else's concern. Your job is to find and neutralize Victoria Larsen. Those are your orders. That's all you should be focused on."

Murphy studies the deputy attorney general's face. He meant exactly what he said and didn't suffer from a poor choice of words. He wants an American citizen killed. J Edgar Hoover would be proud.

"Neutralize?"

"Yes, as in taking Larsen into custody by any means necessary. She's a threat to this country and needs to be apprehended before she can do more damage."

It's a nice recovery, but Murphy isn't buying it. "What damage? What is she planning?"

Conrad stands a little more erect as he tightens his jaw. "You don't need to know."

"As the lead investigator, I should be the *first* person who needs to know. If you want me to find someone as skilled as Larsen, I need every advantage I can get. Knowledge of her plans could be the key to finding her."

Williams starts to say something and stops. Instead, he offers a weak smile. "I was told by Krekstein that you're a hotshot agent. You shouldn't need my help. Quit wasting my time and do your damn job, Agent Murphy. If you spent more time searching for her instead of questioning what you're told, maybe she'd already be in custody."

He starts to walk away. There's one last card for Murphy to play.

"She's in Washington, sir. We're sure of it. If there's a target here you know about, you need to arrange to protect it."

Conrad stops and turns. "Find her, Agent Murphy. If you can't or won't, I'll have your director find someone who will."

With that parting shot, he heads for the exit. Murphy nods slowly. He got his answer – the manhunt is bullshit. They want Larsen dead, and it isn't because of any threat to the country. She's a threat to him, which means the evidence she revealed in Philadelphia was legitimate. Good. At least Murphy knows he can trust her.

He also knows what comes next. Conversations will be had, and pressure will be applied. If he's right, his life is about to get even more complicated.

CHAPTER FORTY-SEVEN

TIERRA CAMPOS

Wilson Newman's House
Falls Church, Virginia

The doorbell rings, and I look toward the front door like Death himself is waiting on the other side. I'm not sure why I agreed to this. I have been on the losing side of too many confrontations lately, and this is one that I don't want to add to that tally.

Mi Sun's argument for this was compelling but not that persuasive. I almost said no. I almost questioned her sanity. Ultimately, I capitulated and agreed to meet my nemesis, and now I'm questioning *my* sanity.

"It'll be okay, Tierra. It's a meeting, not a marriage. All I'm asking you to do is listen and give this a fair chance."

She might as well be asking me to relocate Mt. Everest to North America with only a wheelbarrow and a rowboat. She rises from the sofa to answer the door when the bell chimes again. Austin is still out of town and won't return until later tonight. Josh is resting in one of the bedrooms, and Wilson is hiding. He wants no part of this meeting.

Oliver Jahn enters the foyer and looks around before settling his eyes on me. Mi Sun stands off to the side as we face each other like a pair of Western gunslingers outside a saloon. One minute elapses. Then another. Even Mi Sun shows little interest in opening the conversation.

"Sadly, this isn't the most awkward moment I've had with a woman," Oliver finally says.

I don't want to smile. I just can't help it. It was funny.

"Why don't we sit?"

We make our way into the sitting room and take seats. I don't offer him a beverage. I'm not in the mood to be hospitable to a man I consider one of the most despicable human beings I have ever encountered. We descend into another uncomfortable silence.

"Well, I'll let you two talk," Mi Sun says, pointing to the other room. "And be ready with bandages just in case."

"Her optimism is infectious, isn't it?"

"Is everything a joke to you, Oliver?"

"No," he says, lowering his eyes. "I was bullied relentlessly when I was a kid. I know, shocking, right? Humor was my way of coping with it. There are times when people find it inappropriate. But I also learned that people like other people when they're funny. So, I guess it worked out okay."

"Thanks for the after-school special. So, instead of doing stand-up in L.A., you decided to do the news instead?"

"It's a strange life choice, I know."

"'Unfortunate' is a better term. You don't do the news and stopped being funny when you signed your cable deal. You're nothing more than a well-paid pundit with an ax to grind."

Oliver presses his palms together and grimaces. "I'm happy you didn't write that in my Rotten Tomatoes review. You know, you're not at all like I envisioned."

My eyes narrow. "Were you expecting me to wear a tiara?"

"No, queens wear crowns. Princesses wear tiaras."

"We're done here," I say, waving my hand and jolting up from my seat.

If he calls me the "Queen of the Pretenders" to my face, I will likely stab him with Wilson's fireplace poker. I'm under enough stress. I am not about to sit here and listen to this arrogant ass. This was a bad idea. I knew I should have refused to see him.

"It's still better than the dunce cap I'm wearing."

I stop at the entry to the sitting area but don't turn to face him.

"Tierra, I should have done my homework on you before making your life miserable to advance myself. I would have realized that we aren't that different."

I turn on my heels and storm over to him, pointing my index finger inches from his face. "We are different in every way imaginable!"

Oliver shakes his head. "No, we aren't. We both suffered trauma growing up. For you, it was a school shooting that you barely survived, and for me, it was an awkward phase that I barely outgrew. You climbed into a shell after what happened in Summerville. I became obnoxious because I was bullied. We used those tools as coping mechanisms."

"That...that's a surprising level of self-reflection coming from you," I say, removing my finger and standing straighter.

"I wish I could take the credit. Most of it came from a small, angry Asian woman. One whose opinion I respect above everyone's, including my own."

"Do you realize that you became the bully? That you tormenting me is manifestly the same as what happened to you?"

Oliver nods and presses his lips together before speaking. "You have to appreciate the irony. I became the thing I despised to make you weaker, only it made you stronger. And I did it because you became what I always wanted to be."

"What's that?"

"Relevant."

Against my better judgment, I return to the sofa and lower myself onto a cushion.

"I realized after Mi Sun left how much of a joke I'd become. The contract I signed with VHN had stipulations...and the executives ignored them. Whenever I complain, they remind me how much money I'm making. I realized I was just another instrument in the DeAnna Van Herten Orchestra. She gives us the music and has us play it nightly, and people follow like children to the Pied Piper of Hamelin. Only the music has gotten worse and worse."

I shrug. "It's what you signed up for."

"Money is blinding, Tierra, and I chased it hard. That's why it's the root of all evil."

"Words can also be dangerous, Oliver. You weren't under DeAnna's thumb when your broadcasts compelled your supporters to chase me down a boardwalk or beat me on a sidewalk."

Oliver lowers his head. "I never wanted you harmed. If you take anything away from this meeting, I need you to understand that. I wanted them to stop watching you, not physically attack you. I just thought…I didn't think. I guess that's the problem."

That's as close to an apology as I expect I will ever get from Oliver. Still, it's something, and that's progress. It will in no way mend our relationship. We will never be friends. But it might help me let go of my hatred for him, just as Wilson said it would if I accepted Mi Sun.

"What are you really doing here, Oliver? Is this a ploy to get Mi Sun to return to work for you?"

"Yes, I want to work with her again. I'm a better man when she stands behind me, rolling her eyes. No, it's not a ploy. She said you could use my help. More importantly, she also said it would be a real chance to be what I want."

"Relevant?" Oliver forces a smile and nods. Not that it changes anything. "I can't trust you."

"I know. That ship has sailed…and probably even sank off the coast. Do you trust Mi Sun? Because, I'll tell you, she likes *Front Burner* and loves Wilson. She wouldn't have let me in that door unless I was truly willing to help. And I'm only here to face the prospect of your wrath because I am."

Damn, he's making this hard. I'm fighting to convince myself that he's telling me what I want to hear. The real Oliver Jahn could never be this magnanimous.

"That's not going to be enough."

Oliver nods and stands, looking dejected. "Okay. I honestly never thought I would step foot in Wilson Newman's house. After what happened, I thought any meeting with you would start with your swinging a fire extinguisher at my head. Instead, we had an honest and civil conversation. It's a day of firsts. Thank you for meeting me, Tierra. I know you didn't want to."

He turns and leaves the sitting room. I close my eyes, and a thousand things flood into my head. Waves of different emotions wash over me. One of them sticks out more than the other: fear of regret. We don't have many allies in this fight. Can I afford to let one of the most prominent news personalities walk out the door? Should I trust him enough to let him into our circle?

"Aw, screw it," I mumble, standing and moving to the sitting room entrance as he reaches the door. "Oliver?"

"Yeah?"

"Be here at nine tomorrow morning."

He smiles and nods before heading out to his car. Mi Sun slides into the foyer from the living room, her hands behind her back. She has a stupid grin on her face.

"Bandages?"

"Better," she says, revealing a much-needed bottle of wine and two glasses. "Tomorrow's a big day, and it's five o'clock somewhere."

CHAPTER FORTY-EIGHT

VICTORIA LARSEN

Wilson Newman's House
Falls Church, Virginia

Victoria stares out the windshield as Oliver leaves the house via the front door. She slides down in the seat, hoping he doesn't notice her sitting there before it's too late. It's not a primary concern. The man displays no situational awareness as he heads for his car.

Oliver opens the door and climbs into the driver's seat. He reaches back and slams it shut before noticing Victoria sitting beside him. He jumps and clutches his chest as his body presses against the door.

"Holy Jesus!"

"No, I'm just plain Victoria."

He takes a couple of deep breaths. "Are you here to kill me?"

Victoria stares at the house. "If Tierra hasn't already, you get a stay of execution from me. Unless you're telling me that I have a reason to kill you? Do I, Oliver?"

"Well…I almost got your best friend killed, so you probably do."

"She seems to have moved on from that, so why shouldn't I?"

"Some people hold grudges about things like that," Oliver says, holding his defensive posture. "Especially angry blonde fugitives. Well, red-headed ones, now."

Victoria strokes her red hair. The look is growing on her, but it's not something she's likely to keep. As a blonde, she always feels underestimated because of societal perceptions. She can turn their mistake to her advantage.

"Has anyone told you that you look like Black Widow?" Oliver asks, relaxing a little.

"It's been mentioned. How was your meeting?"

Now it's Oliver's turn to stare out the windshield. He eases his body around so that his back is in the seat instead of the door.

"Strange."

"I bet. Why did you take it? Do you miss Mi Sun that much?"

"Tierra asked essentially the same question. Yes…but that's not the whole story. She's happy. Maybe not with the current situation, but…she likes working with Tierra and Wilson. I wanted to see why."

"What did you learn?"

Oliver looks at Victoria. "That I'm an ass."

"What did you learn other than the obvious?"

He cocks his head. "Are you always this blunt?"

"I don't have the time or patience for games."

"That's not comforting, considering you're a fugitive who still found both to climb into my car and scare the shit out of me."

"It should be a little comforting. I'm risking your getting on the phone and turning me in when I leave this car. I'm sure that will make for great television."

"Agent Larsen, I know you don't think highly of me, but I do of you. I've followed you since the Ethan Harrington scandal. There's a better chance you're an alien than a domestic terrorist. Why are you here talking to me?"

"Because I have a warning. Tierra took a big step in deciding to meet you. She's a strong woman, but she's already been burned too many times. If you cross her, I will do a Riverdance on your face before I go to prison. Understood?"

Oliver swallows hard. "Yes."

"Good. Drive safely."

Victoria slaps him on the knee and exits his vehicle. She walks to the house as he starts the car and pulls out of Wilson's driveway. Under different circumstances, she would be paranoid coming here. There is little doubt the FBI would have a surveillance team watching the house. That's one thing she doesn't need to worry about now.

Tierra opens the door, and the two women hug. It's a genuine embrace that lasts for longer than most. They have been through a lot together, and Tierra has grown into the closest friend she has ever had. She would not have expected it when they first met in a Massachusetts hotel room and shared information. Life is like that sometimes.

"I see you had a cozy chat with Oliver. What did you say to him?"

"Not much," Victoria says with a shrug. "I'm just ensuring we're on the same page. Are you okay? How did it go?"

"Better than expected. Let's leave it at that."

"Okay. How's Josh?"

"On the mend. He's upstairs napping. Thank you for giving me that gun, Vic. It saved my life."

It also landed her in DC Jail, but at least she's alive to go to a hearing. She was hoping that her friend would never have to use it. Giving Tierra the means to defend herself was a sensible precaution, but Victoria didn't expect her to have to shoot two Russian Spetznaz commandos with it. That's next-level stuff.

"Tierra, do you ever feel we're living charmed lives? After everything that's happened…now we both survive armed assassins showing up with MP-5s within hours of each other. And that isn't the strangest thing that's happened to us this week," Victoria says, cocking her thumb over her shoulder toward the driveway.

"I like to think our survival is plot armor from the sadistic author writing our life stories. Unfortunately, that epic is about to get weirder. Sit down, and I'll give you the latest update on what's coming next."

CHAPTER FORTY-NINE

PRESIDENT-ELECT ALICIA STANDISH

Standish's Hay-Adams Hotel Suite
Washington, D.C.

Date night is taking on a whole new meaning now. Romantic dinners in Boston or at their Cambridge home are now a thing of the past. Alicia isn't eager to indulge in any event that requires a convoy and a Secret Service advance team to sweep, and this suite isn't equipped with a gourmet kitchen.

Brendan will have to make do with room service. He flew down from Boston so they could spend some time together that wasn't through a screen or over a telephone. He will be a full-time resident of the White House after the inauguration but has a lot to settle with his job back home until then.

Dinner is brought up by a small army of waitstaff. Her Secret Service detail has undoubtedly checked the food, and the agents watch closely as they set the table up in the suite. Once everything is satisfactory, Alicia thanks the staff and slips them a generous tip. The agents leave with the hotel employees, leaving her alone with her husband.

"I would say you look lovely this evening," Brendan says, taking his seat. "But the weight of the world on your shoulders is causing your face to contort—"

"Brendan!"

"You're starting to look like the guy from that Edvard Munch painting."

She wants to be mad, but he's right. Alicia is having a major falling out with the bathroom mirror these days. She doesn't want to even look at herself.

"The cabal cooked up the charges against the vice president-elect. They forced me to ask for his resignation. If I step out of line, they'll compel me to accept it, Kerrigan will be on the street, and they'll install one of their people."

"That sounds about right."

"Andrew hit me with an insult that's still bothering me. He said this is simple math that even an arrogant politician like me could do on my fingers. I…I used to be better at this…smarter. The old me never would have let someone like Cooper or Li get the upper hand."

"You're playing their game, Alicia. Andrew is right in one respect – you can do the math. Only you have never settled for doing simple arithmetic. You do calculus. To change the game, you need to change the math."

Alicia frowns. Brendan makes it sound so easy. Metaphors usually do. It's harder to distill them down to the tactical level. How does one "change the math?" What tactics need to be employed, and what resources are leveraged to do that? What is the risk assessment of your actions? Where is the wargaming of results and consequences? It's not so easy once a plan needs to be put into play. That's why politicians never discuss the details on the campaign trail or during interviews. Yes, it would bore people, but it's also because the devil is in the details.

"Campos is the only reporter I can trust with this."

"Oof," Brendan says, wiping his mouth with a linen napkin. "How did that taste coming out of your mouth?"

"I know how that sounds. The world is upside-down. The woman who I thought was bent on destroying me after Brockhampton has now saved me once and tried a second time on election night."

Alicia hated her for taking down Ethan Harrington, Ryan Baino, and the Safe America Act with them. But, despite the horrible things she said about America's most intrepid journalist, Tierra still warned her not to publicly suspend her campaign in New Hampshire until after the Burgess interview. And she sneaked into her victory speech on election night to warn her about Cooper.

"Maybe Tierra isn't as bad as you thought. I'll even admit that she's a pretty fair journalist. Think about this: If you had known the truth about Ethan Harrington, would you still have worked with him?"

"Hell no. It turns out that he was complicit in the murder of dozens of students."

"Do you think the people were entitled to hear the truth about what really happened that day?"

"Yes."

"Then why are you more pissed at her than yourself? It was dumb luck, Alicia. This country has hundreds, if not thousands, of school shooting victims. You just happened to pick the one who used his victimhood to cover up a crime."

"Whose side are you on?"

The truth hurts. That misstep almost cost Alicia a shot at the presidency. It was dumb luck, but it still smarts.

"Yours, always. But, my love, sometimes you need to hear a different perspective from a voice you trust. Campos was willing to help you. What makes you think she isn't now?"

"I can only hope Moira acted on my note. Even if she did and Tierra agrees to help – and I still think that's a long shot – I can't exactly coordinate plans with her. I can't even leave this hotel without a convoy. Tierra Campos has a better chance of hitching a flight to Mars than setting foot in here with Machiavelli guarding the door. I don't know if it will be enough."

Brendan leans back in his chair. "Well, as first gentleman-elect, I feel compelled to regale you with a story from my youth. Did I ever tell you about my last math tournament?"

"You are such a dork," Alicia moans with a half-smile.

"But a lovable one. It was my senior year at college, and we had lost to Princeton the previous three. We weren't about to make it fourth, so we brought in a ringer. Isaac was a community college transfer of sorts. He technically wasn't eligible to compete…but rules are meant to be broken. This kid could do the craziest problems in his head without breaking a sweat. We won that last math tournament in a walk."

"You cheated."

Brendan shrugs. "If you ain't cheatin', you ain't tryin'."

"Where did that ridiculous saying come from?"

"How would I know? I researched it once, leading me down four rabbit holes. What's it matter? This is politics, and you always say fair fights are for chumps."

"I don't have a ringer to bring into this game."

Brendan leans back in his chair. Alicia knows that smile. It's the same one he uses when he's about to get a ridiculous word score in Scrabble. He's up to something.

"Are you sure about that?"

CHAPTER FIFTY

TIERRA CAMPOS

Wilson Newman's House
Falls Church, Virginia

The basement lounge in Wilson's house has been turned into a pseudo-conference room. The three dominant forces in the alternative media accepted our invitation to this. They all were interested in joining *Front Burner's* initiative to reshape journalism in America. It took some cajoling from Austin, but they agreed to listen to my sales pitch on the opportunity to be a part of something historic.

This will be the single most important presentation I ever give. I need them on this team, or the plan will fail. Those are the stakes. I'm not worried about the integrity of the information we have. Drucker's laptop was a treasure trove of information.

I'm worried about their reaction. The *Front Burner* team has already seen this and is on board. That's easy because they have nothing to lose. These people are different. They have massive numbers of followers and make multi-millions in ad revenue. This could backfire for them spectacularly.

That's why Austin has been gone for so long. He racked up serious credit card bills traveling around the country to persuade them that we aren't baking some crazy conspiracy theory while wearing tin foil hats. I'm suspicious about how he managed it, but he likely used the same charm that lured me to *Front Burner*. Of course, I was desperate then. The alternative media personalities in this room are established household names with millions of followers. He must have been convincing.

The guest of honor is Tom Swim. He hosts the *Let's Go Swimming* channels on several livestream platforms. His array of guests ranges across the political spectrum. It's a unique show to host in a polarized world, but it works. He has millions of followers and subscribers and is America's most influential independent voice.

Radio Free America is fast becoming another heavyweight. Jo Pagano has joined us as the founder because she loved the idea of partnering with *Front Burner*. Technical limitations have stymied their growth, and their moderate and balanced approach to delivering short interviews and news segments has earned them scorn from both extremes of the ideological divide.

Alétheia is Greek for "true to fact." They are the undisputed kings of exposés and documentary videos highlighting corruption, ulterior motives, and conflicts of interest. They aren't broadcasters but have a knack for presenting complex information in meaningful and entertaining ways. Alétheia also holds records for most video viewers on several social media platforms, something that Estevan Cardoso reminds everyone of every chance he gets.

Then there's *TNT*. He's no longer a force on the Internet, but Oliver Jahn started *Tomorrow's New Today* as a basement podcast before he signed a cable deal. His fans are loyal, as I learned all too well, and this is right in his wheelhouse. His partisan bent would actually add legitimacy to the presentation.

We get started, and I begin walking them through the mountain of information, starting with unlocking Isiah's files. That's what allowed us to confirm the identities of Machiavelli, Nietzsche, Robespierre, and Rasputin. We then move on to what we learned about Actyv Private Equity, the S.O.F., and the Keystone Militia. The coup de grace is the information on Ian Drucker's laptop. It's detailed, concise, and damning. There isn't a jury in America that wouldn't lock the four cabal members up and throw away the key.

My presentation lasts for the next three hours. Wilson had the meeting catered, and people get up for food and drinks periodically, still paying rapt attention to the material being presented. Tyler projects the laptop display onto the television and navigates to all the files. When I finish, I wait for a reaction. Three hours is a long time for these personalities not to speak.

"This is the craziest thing I've ever seen," Tom Swim says, shifting in his chair. "And I've seen a lot."

"Welcome to my world. Are you okay, Oliver?"

My former archenemy looks like he ate bad sushi. "I'm gonna throw up."

"Yeah. You get used to that feeling."

"This is amazing work, Tierra," Jo from RFA interjects, "but what do you expect us to do about it?"

"She's right," Estevan says, turning to his peers. "Even if we combine Alétheia's forces with yours, they'll coordinate their denials, and we'll look like fools."

"You're right," I confirm. "Working together, Cooper, Li, Van Herten, and Williams are too strong for us to take head-on. Among the four of them, they have the mainstream media, the DOJ, the executive branch of the government, and outside resources lined up to protect their secrets. They're unstoppable."

"Okay, Suzy Sunshine. If it's hopeless, then why are we here?" Oliver asks.

"Swim, toss me that orange."

The podcaster leans over, picks one from a silver serving tray filled with fruit, and chucks it to me. It's a little harder throw than I expected, but I make a one-handed catch and hold it out for everyone to see.

"This is our enemy."

"A sweet, succulent fruit that's best when fresh-squeezed into a glass?" Oliver asks.

"Close. Tough on the outside and impossible to devour in one bite. Steps need to be taken before it can be enjoyed. First, it needs to be peeled."

I make slices into the orange with a knife I snatch from the table, naming each cut as I do. "*Let's Go Swimming*. RFA. *Tomorrow's News Today*. *Capitol Beat*. Alétheia."

The news influencers and podcasters exchange glances before Tom raises his hand.

"Okay, how do you propose we…slice the orange?"

"We want to take everything you've heard today and divide it up among you. Each will focus on an aspect of the big picture. We don't hit the American people with all of it. We start taking shots at the cabal from different angles, making them think their co-conspirators have leaked damaging information."

"What good will that do?" Jo asks.

"Fracture them," Tyler says.

"I don't see how that's going to happen," Estevan moans, leaning back in his chair.

"Understandable. I didn't either until I figured out why Brian Cooper kept me around. He *needed* me. Brian said something during our meeting that finally registered. That they worked together because their interests were aligned. He used me to safeguard against one of them going rogue."

"That makes sense. After Brockhampton and New Hampshire, people listen to you," Oliver admits.

"You were on the trail, and he could have used you to implicate any dissenters," Tom Swim agrees.

"But wouldn't they just burn the rest of the cabal if that was the case?" Estevan asks.

"I thought of that," I admit. "Cooper is a planner. He must have found a way to insulate the rest of the group from any fallout."

"That's actually brilliant," Jo says.

"It's definitely devious. It also means this isn't really a cabal, at least in the sense we think of it. It's a marriage of convenience."

"They don't trust each other," Wilson says, a grin creasing his lips. "We're going to exploit that."

There isn't a single person in this room who doesn't respect Wilson and his accomplishments. Even Oliver Jahn looks up to the man. His words carry a weight that mine never could. Maybe it will in a few decades, but I don't have his street cred despite everything I have been through and reported on. He is a legend, even in the emerging alternative media.

"Okay, assuming that works, then what?"

I break apart the pieces of the orange. "We do what Napoleon did to his enemies. We divide and conquer."

Josh smiles. He's made countless accidental contributions to my work, including solving the puzzle that unlocked Isiah's files. I'll never live it down and never want to. It also means there will be many more history documentary screenings in my immediate future.

"If they aren't supporting each other, it's harder to defend against us," Logan contributes.

"Exactly. We strike hard and fast after Thanksgiving in a one-night coordinated effort that methodically spells this out for the American people on all our platforms, with each of us contributing."

Oliver rubs his chin. "It would be the story of the century. Bigger than Watergate."

"At what cost, though?" Swim asks. "If we fail, they'll come after all of us. What makes you think they won't join forces again to stop us?"

"The deputy attorney general is the only person who can take direct action against us. He'll be too scared by that point."

"What could Conrad Williams possibly be scared of?" Jo asks.

I smile and nod to the door.

"Her."

CHAPTER FIFTY-ONE

VICTORIA LARSEN

Wilson Newman's House
Falls Church, Virginia

All eyes track to Victoria standing in the doorway. There is a chorus of gasps. All of them have talked at length about the manhunt for who the government calls "the nation's most dangerous terrorist." Now she's standing fifteen feet away from them. In a meeting already full of surprises, they likely didn't see this one coming.

"Well, we're all accessories now," Oliver laments. Mi Sun smacks him on the head from behind. "Ow! I mean that we might as well help since we're likely to go to prison."

"Agent Larsen," Tom interjects, "I have to say, from reading the messages on my live streams, you have a big fanbase out there pulling for you."

"Tom's right. A lot of people aren't buying this 'you're a domestic terrorist' thing."

Victoria nods at Jo. "That's refreshing, and I appreciate the kind words. Fortunately, they aren't the only ones who think that."

Daniel Murphy materializes next to her, eliciting another series of gasps.

"Wait…aren't you…hunting her?"

"Turns out it was more the other way around, Estevan."

"That sounds like an interesting story," Jo surmises.

"And one we're happy to explain to your subscribers when this is over. If we're not dead or imprisoned."

Everyone studies Victoria to see if she's kidding. She isn't.

"Cards are on the table, folks," Tierra says. "What's it going to be?"

"RFA is in," Jo declares. "I don't think this is something we can pass up."

"I'm in, also," Oliver says, causing Tierra to look at him in surprise. "It's not just because Black Widow over there would kill me if I didn't. Although, I'm certain the thought crossed her mind. We all came into this game to make a difference. To present information that the mainstream media wasn't interested in reporting. What bigger story is there?"

"It's compelling," Tom agrees, running his hand over his bald head. "It's terrifying, actually. But I can't be a part of this."

"Why not?" Victoria asks.

Tom stares intently at his hands as he presses them together. "I've spent a decade building my channel. I wasn't given my subscribers and followers – I earned them. If this blows up in our faces, all of that is gone. I can't take the risk."

"Same here," Estevan says. "What Alétheia does is critical to eliminating corruption and the health of our Republic. This isn't our brand of vodka. I'm sorry."

"Don't apologize to me," Tierra says to Tom and Estevan before pointing at the door. "Apologize to Victoria."

"What do you mean?"

"She means that I've risked everything to come this far. We all have, including everyone at *Front Burner*. Our friends are getting shot or locked up. I've been labeled a terrorist, and they manipulated one of the Bureau's best agents to hunt me." The comment causes Murphy to smile. "What are you risking?"

"I don't think that's fair," Estevan whines.

"It's not fair," Murphy chimes in. "None of this is fair – for any of us."

"I have watched all of you since you first started," Olivia says from the far corner, sliding off the stool borrowed from the kitchen. "I've always been a fan. I defend you when people say you're grifters who don't care about truth and are only out to make a buck. Is that true?"

"No, it isn't," Estevan says in an annoyed tone.

"Then prove it."

"It's not that simple."

"It is, Mr. Swim. Remember the ransomware attack on you a few years ago? I knew the kid who did it."

"Who the hell are you?" Swim asks as the skinny white kid watching the show moves off the wall and walks around the sectional.

"His name is Brian," Tierra explains, "but he goes by the handle Dial Pirate."

"Wait…the hacker? The one who doxxed you, Tierra?"

"The very one," Brian says, joining Olivia in the front of the room. "He told me you refused his demand and asked me what he should do. I told him to return control of your files to you because you were a man of integrity who would never back down."

"So what? Do you think I owe you one or something?"

"No, sir," DP says, shaking his head. "I'm just wondering if I was wrong."

Swim recoils like Dial Pirate hit him with an anvil. He takes his reputation very seriously. He is as devoted to his fans as they are to him. His show lacks the usual BS, and he asks his guests questions that are almost as hard as Tierra's. Integrity is everything to him. Despite the angry look on his face, he doesn't offer a retort.

Seconds pass, but it feels much longer than that. The tension in the room adds to the awkwardness, creating a feedback loop. It all comes down to Tom and Estevan. They can move forward without them, but it's not likely to have the desired impact. Everyone needs to be on board for this to have any chance at success.

"Hackers, mavericks, fugitives, adversaries, and icons, all in the same room," Estevan says, looking around. "It's starting to feel like we were brought together for a purpose. This is the *Breakfast Club* of journalism. Screw it. Alétheia is in."

All eyes turn to Tom Swim.

"Okay, okay. I'm in, under one condition. Someone important needs to validate all this. If this becomes our word against theirs, we're going to lose whether this cabal is united or not. Someone with authority has to vouch for our reporting for this to work."

Moira Kinsella has been sitting in the back of the room, absorbing what she sees. Of everyone here, she's the only one not affiliated with law enforcement or the alt-media. As a reporter for a respected news organization, her words carry weight. Victoria doesn't know what took her this long to walk to the front and stand next to Tierra.

"You're one hundred percent right. We do. I think you'll enjoy the surprise I'm arranging for the big finale."

CHAPTER FIFTY-TWO

SSA DANIEL MURPHY

Daniel Murphy's Apartment
Pentagon City, Arlington, Virginia

It's the Sunday before Thanksgiving, and most of America is huddled around their televisions to watch football. It's not something Murphy has had many opportunities to partake in. Work doesn't stop on weekends in his world.

There is a knock at the door, and he mutes the television before letting his colleague in. DeAndre is dressed casual, but his mind is in overdrive. Murphy can see the strain on his face.

"What's so important that you came here on your rare day off?"

"The trail for Larsen has gone ice-cold. The Hoover Building is starting to micromanage the manhunt and question our decisions."

"I know. Conrad Williams read me the riot act because of our lack of progress. It will be okay."

"Can I speak freely?"

"DeAndre, I consider you a trusted colleague more than a subordinate. You don't have to ask to speak your mind."

"All right. You're awfully calm about the higher-ups criticizing our work. You would normally be neurotic about that. What the hell is going on?"

Murphy shrugs. "The Bureau likes results. As long as we get them, the time it takes won't matter in the long run."

The junior agent shakes his head. "Are you sure it isn't more than that?"

"What do you mean?" Murphy asks, retrieving a pair of beers from the refrigerator and popping the caps.

"I mean that none of this makes sense."

"So you've mentioned."

"The attackers armed with MP5s in Boston and D.C. The ones who went after Campos and Seth Chambers. They're ex-Russian Spetznaz employed by a private military company called Voin. That means the attacks are linked, but nobody in the Bureau seems to care. They're treating the incidents like they never happened."

Murphy takes a long swig from the bottle. PMCs have emerged as a valuable tool for a nation protecting its national security interests and executing policy objectives. They have increasingly become a core component in hybrid warfare strategy by complementing or substituting for more overt forms of statecraft. In that way, they aren't unlike colonial powers using privateers to raid shipping lanes or civilian hackers to infiltrate a rival's computer networks.

Voin rose to prominence when the Russian military disintegrated during the Ukraine War. Formed by army generals and Kremlin officials, the group's name inspires fear in enemies and cultural pride for the Russian people. Voin has an elite branch called "Shaska," a single-edged weapon primarily used by Cossacks mounted on their horses. It's certain to conjure up memories of past heroic victories.

"We aren't the only ones after Larsen," Murphy concludes.

"But why? Murphy, you can't be blind to the fact that something else is going on. There's just too much—"

"How long have we worked together, DeAndre?"

"A couple of years, I guess."

"In that time, have I ever given you a reason to question my judgment?"

"Never."

"Until now, right?"

DeAndre lowers his head. Murphy knows how the junior agent feels. He was dressed down by a superior in the same way not long after graduating from Quantico. He feels bad about this, but it's necessary. He needs to know that he can trust Agent Wright. One misstep at this point will lead to disaster.

In a perfect world, this wouldn't be necessary. Murphy would prefer to shield his team from any potential fallout. But DeAndre is smart, efficient, and loyal. He doubts he could keep this a secret from his subordinate, and this plan works better if he's in on it. Thank God Victoria agreed to the tactic.

"I'm going to ask you a question, and I need an honest answer. You've had reservations about this manhunt for a while now. Do you want the truth? Because once I tell you, there's no going back. There are no mulligans. And if you tell a soul, we will all end up in prison or worse."

Wright wears a look of surprise mixed with confusion. "Tell me."

"Victoria Larsen is being hunted because she uncovered evidence that powerful people have formed a cabal that has effectively seized control of the presidency during the next term."

"Wh-what?"

"Yeah, that's what I said," Murphy says, unable to resist a smile. "You may want to sit for this. I needed to."

DeAndre finds a spot on the couch, and Murphy launches into the short version of everything happening and why. The junior agent remains quiet as he processes the information. Or he's speechless. Maybe both.

"That's insane."

"Yeah," Murphy agrees. "It's also the truth. I've seen the evidence, and Williams convinced me through his reaction when I challenged him that it's accurate."

"What are we going to do?"

"There's a group led by Tierra Campos preparing to bring this out of the shadows. In the meantime, we continue our search for Larsen."

"What if we find her?"

Murphy smirks. "We already have."

He nods at the door, and DeAndre cranes his head to see Victoria standing there with her own bottle of beer. His jaw hangs open, and his eyes remain riveted to her as she moves into the living area and collapses into an overstuffed chair. His eyes track back and forth between Daniel and Victoria, likely wondering why they are hanging out like a couple of old college friends.

"He looks like he's seen a ghost," Murphy says, amused.

Victoria forces a smile. "Boo."

CHAPTER FIFTY-THREE

BRIAN COOPER

Cooper Residence
Bethesda, Maryland

It's mid-November. The temperatures are cool, but the coffee is hot. The gas fireplace is more than enough to warm this magnificent study to an appropriate temperature. In every regard, it's a perfect Saturday morning. Except Brian can't figure out why it doesn't feel like one.

He strolls over to the study's sitting area and takes a seat, his eyes locked on the chessboard. The black and white pieces are lined in rows at opposite ends of the board. There are only two sides, not multiple players with different agendas. The rules are defined, and the pieces are predictable. It's such an elegant game, unlike life itself.

Politicians are prominent figures, but political consultants work in the background to support their efforts. In short, men and women like Brian move the pieces around the chessboard. Maybe that's why he was drawn to the game at an early age. He likes the strategy aspect of it. It's also a useful metaphor for many things in the political sphere.

He became a consultant because of a love of politics and because it matched his skillset. Brian has a unique ability to analyze data and trends, just like understanding what an opponent does in a chess match. He instinctively knows how to manage a candidate's public image and offer advice on how to get it to resonate with voters.

Understanding politics is the primary skill for anyone in his line of work. Political operatives are required to guide their candidates and elected officials to decisions that benefit voters and themselves simultaneously. A deep understanding of history, government function, and the strengths and weaknesses of adversaries raises the chances of success.

Much of that insight comes from research and observation. Research helps Brian deeply understand voters and the political landscape. It's more than just surveys. It's an understanding of what drives people. There is an old talking point in the political world surrounding "kitchen table issues." These are the things that really matter to most people. Researching which topics are being discussed over dinner can make or break a candidate or policy initiative in Congress.

Observation helps recognize and adapt to changes in public opinion. Most politicians are already skilled in this. Brian always liked to monitor a politician's blind spot. Alicia Standish had several you could hide an eighteen-wheeler in. Voters expect quick, thoughtful responses from candidates on contentious issues and nationwide events. He prided himself on preparing his employers for the storm ahead. In Alicia's case, he successfully hid the oncoming hurricane from her until it was too late.

And that's his most important skill: problem-solving. Although it was never stated, Brian is certain that's why Actyv recruited him over his peers. His knack for reexamining ideas and making quick changes when challenges arise makes him indispensable for operations like the one he pulled off. The cabal's success hinged on his ability to constantly monitor and update their strategies and tactics. They couldn't have done any of it without him.

All these skills are useful, but none are helping him see what he's missing. Something feels wrong, and he can't put his finger on what. Larsen is still a threat, but she's on the run and can't do much harm. Tierra has Isiah's files and maybe even Drucker's laptop, but she understands the consequences of publishing. His employers at Actyv made sure of that, much to his chagrin. And Machiavelli has Alicia under control. Knowing it would destroy her, she can't resign and won't go public. So, what is it?

It could be his discontent with the guys at Actyv. Going after Tierra and Seth Chambers was a tactical mistake. Even if it had succeeded, it was a professional hit, and those often attract attention. It's better to have Larsen die in a shootout with the FBI and Tierra to either disappear or have a tragic accident than face the publicity of what transpired. The mainstream media has ignored both attacks, but how long can that last?

Brian returns to staring at the chessboard. Moves and countermoves. Offense and defense. It's an elegant game that only works when both players know the rules. It feels like his game's rules are changing. He just needs to figure out how before it's too late.

CHAPTER FIFTY-FOUR

PRESIDENT-ELECT ALICIA STANDISH

Standish Temporary Presidential Transition Headquarters
Hay-Adams Hotel, Washington, D.C.

The fallout from the whistleblowers is taking a toll. Vice President-Elect Kerrigan has been in hiding since their meeting, leaving her transition team to deal with the consequences. She has his resignation letter, although Andrew and Brian Cooper haven't instructed her to accept it.

Brian was truthful about taking a wait-and-see approach. The media are feasting on the story, naturally led by DeAnna Van Herten's network. While she may be enjoying the boost in ratings, it's at the expense of one of her co-conspirators. Machiavelli is frazzled, and he severed the rails that led to this trainwreck. Karma's a bitch.

"That pain-in-the-ass reporter is back," Andrew says, poking his head into her office.

"Which one?" the president-elect moans. "They're all pains in the ass."

"Moira Kinsella. She wants a follow-up to her interview with you and Brendan."

Alarm klaxons sound in Alicia's head. There is only one reason for Moira to return, and she's dying to know if the reporter spoke with Tierra. Unfortunately, Alicia can't sound too anxious to speak to anyone in the media, considering everything happening with Everett. Machiavelli will instantly get suspicious.

"A follow-up on a puff piece?"

"It sounds fishy to me, too. I think Kinsella wants a statement for the record on the VP-elect."

Alicia makes a show of rubbing her temples. "Okay. Let's find out."

Andrew checks his tablet and shakes his head. "You have a very busy schedule today."

"We can spare fifteen minutes. Send Moira in. I want to find out for myself what her intentions are. It's going to be increasingly important to separate our friends from our enemies."

Andrew grimaces before nodding. "Okay."

A staffer shows Moira in, and Alicia rises to shake her hand. Both women sit with the desk between them. This isn't a formal interview with cameras and comfortable chairs. This is the favor of access. With Moira's back to the door and her head blocking Alicia's, Andrew can't easily see either of their faces.

"Thank you for meeting me again on such short notice, Madam President-Elect."

"You picked a very bad day to drop in, Moira. What can I do for you?"

Moira checks over her shoulder and spots Andrew hovering outside the door. "I came across some…interesting information on Friday that I'm hoping you'd be willing to comment on."

"This isn't about the interview?"

"It is, at least indirectly."

Alicia leans forward and interlaces her fingers on the desk. "If this is about Everett Kerrigan, I'll have the Secret Service throw you out on your ass and ensure you don't step foot within a half mile of the White House after the Inauguration."

"I assure you, it's not. That's someone else's story. Are you aware that Colin Bradford is coming to town next week?"

The president-elect cocks her head to the side. This isn't how she expected this conversation to start, not that she expected Moira to outright say she followed the instructions on Alicia's note and met with Tierra Campos.

"No. Why would I care?"

"Tactics and strategies that may help you," the reporter says, measuring her words. "Rumor has it that he's meeting with Republican leadership and plans on asking them to drop the lawsuits in Pennsylvania."

Alicia leans back in her chair. Bringing Colin Bradford into the loop was Brendan's suggestion on date night. She dismissed it as crazy, but it might be the bold move she was looking for. If he's willing to keep an open mind and not make this political. That's a big ask. She wonders if this was Moira's idea or Tierra's, not that it matters.

"That's interesting. I hadn't heard that."

"He claims it's an olive branch."

Andrew perks up as he listens in. Alicia bites her lower lip and nods slowly. She hopes the signal that she's amenable to offering one of her own is received as intended. She shifts her eyes to the door and squints, hoping the reporter understands the tone of this next question.

"Moira, I am very busy. Is there a question you came here to ask?" the president-elect snaps.

The reporter can barely suppress her grin. "Are you amenable to returning the favor?"

"What favor? It was his choice to sue, as is his right. We would have done the same thing if the roles were reversed. That's the process in a close election. Do you expect me to host him for dinner here?"

"No, that would be absurd."

"Completely," Alicia says with a sneer as she winks.

The corner of Moira's mouth curls. "Besides, I doubt the Republican presidential candidate would dare to push through the mob of reporters camped outside."

"Unfortunately, it's what almost every visitor here faces," Alicia laments. "It's *nearly* unavoidable to get an audience with me until the GSA gives us the space we need."

Moira nods at the emphasis she placed on "nearly," getting the gist of the comment. There is a way to sneak Governor Bradford in without being seen by the prying eyes of the American industrial media complex. Explaining how the service entrance works is a problem for another day, as is figuring out how to get her guard dog to gnaw on a different bone for a few hours.

"It would be a nice bipartisan moment," Moira argues.

"And it will never happen. Republicans don't do bipartisanship, so let's move on. The transition team has a lot planned for next week, starting Tuesday, and I need to get to work."

Alicia finishes the sentence with a squint and a slight nod.

"Understood, ma'am. My apologies."

Moira asks her questions, and Alicia replies with curt answers as if annoyed by them. They aren't on camera, and the taped interview will be airing soon enough. Nothing she says will make it into that report, even on deep background. Moira came here on a mission, and she accomplished it. Tierra Campos must have been very compelling. That doesn't surprise her. What does is the idea that Colin Bradford may be open to a meeting. That will be a first in modern American politics.

CHAPTER FIFTY-FIVE

VICTORIA LARSEN

Daniel Murphy's Apartment
Pentagon City, Arlington, Virginia

There is no better hiding spot than this. Pentagon City is less than a mile from the Potomac River and two miles from the National Mall in downtown Washington. It has ample transportation options, including the Blue and Yellow Lines of the Washington Metro, countless hotels, businesses, and residential buildings. It's also where Daniel calls home.

That made it easy for Victoria and Daniel to get here. Keeping her hidden and unrecognizable helps. They are still looking for a blonde, not a redhead walking with the man charged with hunting her down and bringing her to justice. Still, the area is home to thousands of federal employees, agents, and military personnel. The Air Force lieutenant who lives next door tried conversing with Victoria on the elevator.

Daniel insisted that she stay with him. He was right in saying it's the safest place for her. She thinks it's also because he wants to keep an eye on her. That's a sensible precaution. She would be equally insistent if the roles were reversed.

Her host orders a couple of pizzas, which are delivered from a nearby Italian restaurant. Victoria and Daniel avail themselves of the IPAs in his fridge as funny stories are swapped about their exploits in the field. It feels to her like reconnecting with a long-lost colleague, and she almost forgets she's residing at the top of the FBI's Most Wanted list. They've already been having fits of laughter for almost an hour as they reminisce about their days at Quantico.

"Remember the guy who spent two weeks being forced to say, 'I know nothing' like Sergeant Shultz from *Hogan's Heroes*?"

"Oh, my God!" Victoria says, almost snarfing her beer. "I had forgotten about that! It was Alex Crosch. The instructors *hated* him."

"Well, can you blame them? He answered every question that week with, 'I don't know.' You might know this: Who was the woman who tried to bend her shots on the range like the assassins in that ridiculous movie *Wanted*?"

"Okay. First, that movie is one of my guilty pleasures. Second, it was Amanda Zeiss."

"That's right! She hoped everyone would start calling her Fox after Angelina Jolie's character."

"Yeah, so the instructors called her Cathy after Wesley's ex-girlfriend. Ahh, that was priceless. I wasn't sad when they washed her out. She was batshit crazy."

The two share a laugh, and Victoria snatches another slice. If things go wrong, this may be her last pizza for a long time…or ever. She pushes the thought out of her mind.

"I won't say Quantico was fun, but it had its moments."

"What about since then?" Daniel asks. "I know you aren't married. What about boyfriends?"

"I kinda have one."

"Kinda? What happened?"

Victoria eyes him and smirks. "I saved an FBI assault team from getting massacred, shot a wanted fugitive in the head, stole his laptop, and became one myself. You saw him at the 'orange' meeting."

Tierra's presentation to the alt-media has earned that moniker after her impromptu demonstration with the fruit. It has the benefit of being both innocuous and descriptive. Daniel's eyes shift, and he mumbles as he recounts the people there.

"It couldn't be him…it must…Austin Christos? A journalist?"

Victoria shrugs. "It's a strange world we live in. What about you?"

"Nothing quite that dramatic. I was engaged to a wonderful woman named Julia."

"What happened?"

Murphy shrugs. "What always happens in my relationships. I cared more about the job than her, and Julia wanted more than I could offer."

"I know the feeling. It's never too late to get her back."

Daniel grins and takes a swig of his beer. "Oh, it is. She's married with two kids now. He's a soldier in the 25th ID stationed at Schofield Barracks in Hawaii. She's happy, or at least happier than she was with me."

"That's tough. I'm sorry."

"Don't be. I chose this life, the same as you. People don't understand what we do. They see the negative press. They see the politics our superiors play. Nobody takes the time to understand the sacrifice the agents on the ground make."

"All true."

"Can I ask you a question, Vic? Why were you willing to go this far? I mean, duty aside, you're risking everything. Don't say it's for love of country. You've already done enough."

Victoria sets her beer down. "It's for *my* people. Rigo lost his team and got shot at Loughborough. Diego Valez was shot by the S.O.F. with a dozen of his people. Takara Nishimoto and Lance Fuller were murdered. Tierra has been attacked, beaten, shamed, harassed, and her love interest was shot. The list goes on and on."

"And you want revenge."

"I want justice. I want those responsible held accountable. And I don't want the cabal to win. They can't be left to think that the ends justify the means when people's lives are sacrificed to achieve them."

Murphy stares blankly at the pizza. Victoria isn't sure if it's indigestion, indecisiveness over having another slice, or something else. He finally looks at her and frowns as she retrieves her beer.

"I couldn't have done what you did on my own. You're stronger than me. But I will say this: I'm honored to work alongside you to make all that happen," Murphy says, clinking her beer bottle with his. "Do you think Tierra can pull this off?"

"I've been friends with her since Brockhampton. You know what she taught me since then? Never underestimate a pissed-off Latina. She has a gift for timing. I have a feeling that we're about to be treated to a spectacle they will write books and make documentaries about."

CHAPTER FIFTY-SIX

TIERRA CAMPOS

Wilson Newman's House
Falls Church, Virginia

I check my watch and find that it's five minutes to nine. Josh is upstairs with Wilson and Mi Sun, so I seize the opportunity to switch the channel to VHN. I feel dirty watching DeAnna Van Herten's network, but I need to see what Oliver is doing. It's on him to drop the hammer hard.

The momentum has been building. Tom Swim and RFA have done a magnificent job presenting information, but their reach only goes so far. The media isn't covering it, so my anti-cabal has relied on social media to amplify the message. That's working, but it won't be enough to scare Brian Cooper and his cohorts. For that, they need a grand gesture and an assault on the one person I am guessing is the weakest link.

"Welcome to the show where you get *Tomorrow's News Today*. I'm Oliver Jahn, your beacon of light in an otherwise coal-black darkness. Tonight is going to be a different kind of show. Yes, you will still have my devilishly good looks to feast your eyes on, and the broadcast will, naturally, be filled with humor and sarcasm.

"It's different because I'm going to make you think for yourselves. I know it sounds painful, right? I promise it won't be. I'm going to ask questions, and I will leave it to you to figure out the answers. As painful as it will be for me, I will not tell you what I think. Well…maybe once or twice.

"It's an important exercise right now because we live in strange times…I'm not talking chihuahua skateboarding in Times Square strange…but close. It seems like the world isn't what we thought it was. At least what's being presented on this network isn't."

I sink deeper into the couch. Shots fired. Oliver Jahn rarely holds his network accountable for anything. He quickly criticized media outlets during his podcast days, but the fat contract he signed with his first network ended that. It seems he's returning to his roots, much to my surprise.

"I watched the earlier programs today. I know, I know…I was cheating on myself. Here's what I don't understand. The media is covering the manhunt for Victoria Larsen like she was the Boston Marathon bomber. Do you remember that? Two schmucks set off a pair of bombs near the finish line back in April of 2013. They killed three spectators and wounded more than two hundred fifty other people. The manhunt lasted for days and kept Americans riveted to their televisions.

"They're doing the same thing with Victoria Larsen. I understand it's a news story and must be covered, but where is the inquisitiveness? I reviewed more than a week's worth of press conference footage. Do you want to know what question was never asked, much less answered? *Why?*

"Victoria Larsen was lionized as a heroine following Ethan Harrington's arrest in the Brockhampton school massacre and the elimination of the Sword of Freedom in New Hampshire. She's the kind of agent you only see conjured up by Hollywood, and may just as well have walked off the set of *Charlie's Angels.*

"Yet nobody is asking the government why Victoria Larsen is suddenly a domestic terrorist. Why we haven't seen any concrete evidence showing she was working with Ian Drucker and the Keystone Militia. Why would an American hero suddenly turn to the dark side to sabotage an election?

"All good questions, to be sure. Apparently, since nobody else has bothered to ask, I thought of them all by myself. So, I will take all the credit and ask another: Why isn't my network asking those questions?

"VH Media has torn down politicians for less. Our investigative journalists have uncovered national scandals and exposed massive fraud…mostly with Republicans, but that's beside the point. Bureaucrats and politicians who pretend to represent the public are constant targets of our reporting. Yet, somehow, Lisa Ehler, Conrad Williams, and the Department of Justice are now beyond reproach? Should FBI Director Michael Krekstein's word be taken at face value and left unquestioned? Because, Lord knows, there's never been a shady head of the FBI."

There may never be a time that I don't think Oliver is annoying. His presentation style is far different from Wilson's, lacking the professionalism and seriousness that should be inherent in any news broadcast. It is effective, though. He reaches an audience that *Capitol Beat* never would. There is something to be said for that.

"Ladies and gentlemen, this isn't how it works. So, if my network won't do the heavy lifting, I'll do it for them. If Victoria Larsen is guilty of everything they claim she is, she will be imprisoned for it. But what if this is something else? We will dive into the deep end of the pool by exploring these questions and reporting on some juicy tidbits TNT obtained from our sources after this commercial break."

"This is a sight I never expected," Josh says from the bottom of the stairs leading into the finished basement. "The Queen of Pretenders is watching the man who bestowed on her that title."

I mute the television and glare at my boyfriend. I'm still getting used to thinking of him that way.

"Call me that again, and you'll be eating through a straw for the next three months," I warn Josh, only half-playfully.

"You've been hanging around Victoria too long," he says, sitting beside me on the couch. "What did Oliver have to say?"

"All the right things. You know, I wasn't sure he would go through with this. I figured he would stab me in the back the first chance he got."

Josh nods. "Mi Sun said he wouldn't."

"Yes, she did. That doesn't mean I believed her."

I have slowly come to trust the woman, but doubt lingered in the back of my mind. Her departure from *TNT* and hiring at *Front Burner* could have been an elaborate ruse she concocted with Oliver. Allowing him to be involved in unraveling the conspiracy could have monumentally backfired. Those worries have kept me up at night. I'm relieved they are for nothing.

"Do you think this will be enough to drive a wedge in the cabal?"

I shrug. "Who knows? Based on what Brian told me in the park, I'm assuming he wasn't lying about them not being tight. I could also be wrong about why he's keeping me around. I could be wrong about everything."

"I doubt that. You sense things, Tierra. That started way before you realized there was more to Ethan Harrington than people knew. I'm going to bet that you're spot on with your assessment. You need to believe in yourself."

That's never been the easiest thing for me. I shimmy closer to Josh and put my head on his chest. He wraps his good arm around me, seizes the remote in a slick maneuver, and unmutes the television.

"Let's see where Oliver goes from here."

CHAPTER FIFTY-SEVEN

SSA DANIEL MURPHY

FBI Washington Field Office
Washington, D.C.

This is harder than he thought it would be. Searching for wanted criminals is laborious, stressful, and time-consuming. It required sifting through leads, exploring them in detail, and either confirming or dismissing them. The larger the team, the faster the work, but it's still work.

The manhunt is a twenty-four-hour operation. Agents rotate on shifts, and the FBI has pulled manpower in from field offices nationwide to help. All that effort needs to be coordinated, which is why he's still at the office after nine p.m. The constant media scrutiny has ratcheted up the stress of finding a single human being in a sea of over three hundred and forty million.

If conducting a manhunt is difficult, faking one has additional challenges. Daniel knows where Victoria is. She's sitting on his couch watching television and likely raiding his refrigerator. That means he has to pretend to be looking for her without anyone realizing he isn't tackling the manhunt with his usual zeal and insistence on results. And he's not the only one.

Murphy journeys from the war room to another conference room that DeAndre acquired. He expects to find the junior agent engrossed in a game of solitaire or online poker. Instead, he is combing through social media feeds.

"The Internet is blowing up. I didn't expect that," DeAndre says as Murphy enters the room and moves around the table.

"Me neither. I guess the election was a favorite topic while scarfing down Thanksgiving turkey. That's impressive since Americans aren't usually this dialed in."

Social media is an interesting cultural phenomenon. Some Americans live on it, and others want nothing to do with it. It's like having an alternate reality on full display for the world to see. Passive users on any platform make the biggest difference in the numbers and popularity of any given subject. In this case, it seems they are engaging in the subject of this manhunt.

"Why is Oliver Jahn trending?" Murphy asks, leaning in to read the screen.

The two men scan the tweets. "He's asking questions."

"Wow. Oliver is actually questioning whether the DOJ has it wrong about Larsen."

"Even better, he's taking VHN to task for not probing deeper. He's all but insinuating that they're colluding."

Daniel stands erect and crosses his arms. DeAnna Van Herten is going to have kittens when she hears about that. Even alluding to an unholy alliance between her and Williams will land Oliver Jahn in hot water.

"This is the endgame. The podcasters and Oliver have done what they said they would. The only question is whether it will work."

DeAndre leans back. "How are we going to know?"

"We won't."

"Murph, we're the world's leading investigative force. Why can't we put some bodies on Williams or get eyes on Van Herten's house and watch what happens?"

It's not the worst idea, except for the way it is. Murphy and Larsen wargamed that even before Tierra's meeting at Wilson's house. They could use the intelligence, but the risk outweighs the reward.

"What happens if they find out? The FBI has no reason to keep either under surveillance. Even if we had a handful of agents we could trust, we would still risk having the operation blown. Krekstein would can both of us in a heartbeat, and the cabal would learn that we're onto them."

"So, we're going to sit here and play-act until Tuesday?"

"The best we can. Things are going to start getting more desperate after this," Murphy says, pointing to the laptop. "I expect a lot more pressure to deliver results."

"Meaning Larsen's head on a pike."

Murphy nods.

"Then what?"

"I don't know. We'll have to cross that bridge when we get to it. Until then, check the war room and see if the team has any solid leads, and then get them to chase one. We need to keep people busy."

"What if that solid lead points people to your apartment?" DeAndre asks with a smile.

"Then we'll both have much bigger problems tomorrow morning."

CHAPTER FIFTY-EIGHT

BRIAN COOPER

Cooper Residence
Bethesda, Maryland

Oliver Jahn. If there was ever a bigger useful idiot on this planet, finding him would take a decade. The best part is that he was never part of the plan. His going after Campos was a happy accident, and that's why he embraced DeAnna bringing him into the VH Media fold when his contract expired. It just made sense.

Despite his being an affront to journalism, he has a dedicated following. That much was evident when his followers began harassing Tierra and then assaulting her. He can pretend that his words didn't inspire violence, but the world knows better. Yet, his popularity has only soared at his new network, which was exactly what they needed to help set the narrative moving forward.

It's also what makes this broadcast so interesting…and problematic. The "journaltainer" is reporting on the mess in Pennsylvania but is questioning the official narrative instead of advancing it. He's even calling out the coverage of his own network by pointing out things that don't add up.

It continues a trend that began this week with popular podcasts and social media sites doing the same thing, only in different areas. Tom Swim openly pondered why Alicia Standish would name Conrad Williams as attorney general instead of her friend and current AG Lisa Ehler. *Radio Free America* reopened Andrew's promotion to campaign manager after the tragic death of Angela Mays, whose investigation they are challenging. Alétheia released a video with a guy named Strohs, a Keystone Militia member who claimed Victoria Larsen drugged him at a bar and interrogated him for information. None of that makes sense since the government alleges Larsen was *working* with Ian Drucker.

This normally wouldn't be a problem since the reporting isn't seeping into the mainstream media, and only a small percentage pay attention to the alternate media. Now, Oliver Jahn is joining the chorus. That changes things.

Brian's cell phone rings with an unknown number. He already knows who it is.

"Yeah."

"Good evening, Brian," Xinming Qi says, his tone even yet still somehow threatening. "We haven't heard from you in a while and thought it was time to check in."

"Everything is under control."

"Oh, I doubt that. If that were true, I wouldn't see names and events being discussed on the Internet and social media."

"It's nothing of consequence. The nation is still traumatized about the election, and the grifters are doing it for likes and views. Nothing more."

He wishes that were true. While content creators often churn out videos about the issue du jour to increase their channel's visibility, this feels different. He certainly can't say that to his Actyv masters. The less they interfere, the better. Attacking Seth Chambers and Tierra Campos was already a misstep they've been fortunate to cover up.

There is a long silence. Brian can almost imagine Qi using non-verbal communication to get instructions from Garrett and Roman. The three men are in lock-step with whatever they do.

"Very well. You will keep us informed of any developments."

"Of course."

The call disconnects without any additional dialogue. It's a far cry from the hospitality Brian received when he visited their Midtown Manhattan office in the campaign's final days.

His relationship with the powerful New Yorkers is the least of his concerns. That was too easy. Qi was setting him up for an ambush that never materialized. He could pass it off as not wanting to have the conversation over a cell phone, but that only explains some of it. Veiled threats are just as intimidating as overt ones.

That's something for Brian to consider when he isn't mentally spent. He is about to turn up the volume on the television when his phone rings again, and he sees "DVH" pop up on the caller ID. He doesn't bother connecting the call. Whatever she has to say, he doesn't feel like listening tonight.

The ringing stops, and Brian peels his eyes off his computer, expecting to see a notification for a long-winded rant on voicemail. There isn't one. A minute later, a text notification arrives on his screen:

Wolfwood 8pm tomorrow. Be there.

He sets his phone down. There's no getting out of that meeting. It's time for the cabal to have it out. Whatever is going on, it's a threat to all of them, and the stakes are going up. There's a bad moon rising, and he needs to be there when his co-conspirators start howling at it.

CHAPTER FIFTY-NINE

PRESIDENT-ELECT ALICIA STANDISH

Standish Temporary Presidential Transition Headquarters
Hay-Adams Hotel, Washington, D.C.

This is going to work, or it isn't, but it's a chance worth taking. Alicia needs breathing room. If she pulls this off, she will get barely enough to set some wheels in motion. One outcome is better than the other, but the president-elect would settle for any small victories. Unless Andrew sniffs her out or she isn't convincing in selling this crisis. That would be a disaster.

Alicia has barely left the Hay-Adams since arriving here after the election. She's been home all of once and has visited almost nowhere else. She spent Thanksgiving here because the transition is so far behind where it needs to be.

The optics aren't bad. Americans want to think their elected leaders are always hard at work for them, although that's rarely the case. They won't think twice about her bunkering in this high-profile hotel to vet candidates for cabinet and other high-level executive positions. It's what transitions are all about.

But it's stifling, and she needs room to maneuver. Andrew likely knows that. It's why he keeps her schedule full and her travel restricted. He has that power. So long as she makes an appearance in the press room once in a while, nobody will be the wiser. Everyone is still exhausted from the election, and with Thanksgiving finished and Christmas coming, nobody is concerned about how she spends her time.

"I'll make the necessary arrangements. Thanks, Richard," Alicia says, hanging up the phone.

She rises from the chair in her temporary office and stops at the threshold.

"Tanya, can you begin making travel arrangements for me?"

"Where are you going, Madam President-Elect?" the young assistant asks.

"Pennsylvania. I need to meet with the lawyers running point on the lawsuits up there."

"Why would you need to meet with them, ma'am?" Andrew asks, walking over from across the room.

"Because they asked me to. They have new information and want to strategize with me about our response."

"I didn't hear of any new information," Machiavelli says.

"Because you weren't listening in on that call, I suppose," Alicia says, her voice as sweet and innocent as possible. There is little doubt that he has every phone in this office tapped and probably even her personal cell.

"Is this something I should know about?" he asks.

"No, I've got it handled. Please make the arrangements, Tanya. Start with the Secret Service. They'll need to arrange to send an advance team up there."

Alicia notices Andrew clench his jaw. As chief of staff, he has considerable influence. The one thing he doesn't control is the United States Secret Service. When it comes to protecting the president, or in this case, the president-elect, they call the shots. When the president gives an order, they accommodate it to the best of their ability without input or approval from the chief of staff.

"May we talk in your office, ma'am?" Andrew asks.

"Of course."

The line has been cast, and the bait is in the water. Let's see if Machiavelli bites.

"What is this new information?" Andrew asks, although the question sounds more like a demand.

"You tell me."

He grimaces. "I have no idea. I don't have sources or assets in Pennsylvania."

"Does Brian Cooper?" she asks, getting a glare in return. "It's irrelevant. The lawyers received information that the secretary of state may be unduly influenced. Apparently, the man has…unconventional tastes. But you already knew that. The information is slowly leaking, and they believe the GOP will use that to attempt to delay certification until after the Electoral College meets."

"They won't. Everything is on track," Andrew argues.

"Tell the lawyers that."

"I will. You stay here. You have a lot of work to do. I can meet with the legal team and give them the necessary direction."

"No, you won't," Alicia says, planting her hands on her desk and leaning her weight on her arms. "I've already committed, and I'm going. That's the end of it."

Andrew crosses his arms. "You forget how this works."

"Is the plan to keep me barricaded in the White House for four years?"

"When is the meeting?" Andrew asks, ignoring the question. That alone speaks volumes.

"Monday evening with the lawyers, with a follow-up session with the DNC strategists on Tuesday. They expect to have a plan by the end of the day. It's something I need to bless off on."

"And you will, through me," Andrew says. "I will ensure this gets sped up. You remain at the Hay-Adams and conduct your interviews."

"Andrew—"

"It's settled, Madam President-Elect. I will inform Tanya of the change in plans."

Andrew leaves, pulling the door closed behind him. Breathing room. It's one of life's little pleasures.

He will ensure a plan is in place to watch her, but it will be from afar. His power comes from proximity, and he can't wield it from Scranton. That should give her the window to hold the most important meeting of her life.

CHAPTER SIXTY

VICTORIA LARSEN

Warehouse Store
Pentagon City, Virginia

Victoria knows this area well. It's filled with people who work for the federal government in some capacity and is home to countless federal agents from a myriad of three-letter agencies. The police are hypervigilant, knowing that terrorist threats against the citizens and infrastructure in this area are omnipresent.

That makes driving risky. Police presence on the road is ubiquitous, and getting stopped for even a minor traffic infraction would be game over. Most law enforcement are on the alert for her. Rideshares are also risky. Victoria stands out, even when she tries to blend in. She can't risk being recognized and reported by an Uber or Lyft driver. Changing her hair color doesn't change her face.

The only alternative was to hold this meeting within walking distance of Daniel's apartment. The warehouse store at the southern end of the Fashion Centre shopping mall is the best of the available options. It won't have many government employees in it at this time of day, and she will blend in. Mostly.

Victoria arrives early and wanders around, perusing the goods on steel shelving that almost reaches the ceiling. She can't relate to needing two massive jugs of ketchup or a fifty-pound bag of white rice. Bulk shopping makes little sense for a woman who lives alone and is rarely home.

She eyes Imani moving through the store, taking sharp turns and pausing unexpectedly. Victoria scans the store for threats or surveillance. It doesn't appear that Imani is being followed, and nobody appears to track her movements from nearby or afar. Not that anyone has a reason to, but you can't be too careful.

The pair makes eye contact and meanders their way into the clothing section. Victoria is not a shopper. Tierra helped select the two sundresses that make up most of her civilian wardrobe outside of jeans and t-shirts. Victoria stops at a table covered in women's tops, wondering what the allure of shopping is for her gender. Imani comes up alongside her and giggles.

"What's so funny?"

"The sight of you in civilian clothes," Imani says as she stifles another laugh.

"I'm glad you find it entertaining. I think it's sad."

"You're right, it is. But not for the reason you think. You're dressed like a bum and still manage to look amazing. Women must hate you."

Victoria rolls her eyes. She has never been fixated on her appearance. That doesn't mean the rest of the world isn't, women and men included.

"Did you have any issues getting down here?"

"None. I'm ready to go."

"You don't have to do this, Imani."

"Yes, I do," the young agent argues. "Daniel explained the situation to me. You certainly can't show up at Van Herten's house, and he has no reason to. That leaves me. I know the risks, and we've been through this before, so save your breath. I want to help."

"Okay, but we're sending one of Murphy's guys with you."

"I'm a big girl, Vic. I can do this by myself," Imani protests, not hiding the annoyed look on her face.

"I have no doubt, but you showing up alone would look weird. A pair of FBI agents will feel more plausible. This is about optics. It has to look convincing."

Imani nods. She understands the importance of this. It's not an arrest or even a real investigation. It's meant to have a psychological impact and must appear authentic to have the desired results.

"Imani, you'll be on their radar the moment you knock on her door. These are dangerous people. If we fail and they realize this was a ruse, they will put a bullet in you without thinking twice about it."

"I didn't join the Bureau because I fancied a life nestled in bubble wrap. I'll be fine. I'm more concerned about you."

"I can take care of myself."

"I know. That isn't what I was talking about. I'm talking about what happened in Liberty," Imani says, turning slightly so she can see Victoria's reaction. "I know killing Ian Drucker the way it happened is still bothering you."

"I'm slowly coming to peace with shooting him in the back. After the attack at Seth's house and seeing what happened to Tierra, I realized there wasn't any alternative. My focus needs to be on taking down this cabal. I'll deal with the psychological consequences of that journey later."

"You're on your way to that goal," Imani says, changing the subject. "The Internet chatter is ridiculous. I would have thought most people would tune out during the week of Thanksgiving. Instead, it's all that anyone seems to be talking about."

"Let's hope it's enough," Victoria says, dipping her hand in the pocket of her jeans. "Here are your instructions for meeting Agent Wright. Good luck, Imani, and please, be careful."

The two women embrace. Imani is fast becoming like a little sister to Victoria. That's how she regards her. The agent is capable, smart, and has great instincts. That doesn't mean Victoria can easily fight the overwhelming urge to protect her.

"What are you going to be doing?" Imani asks after they separate.

"Rattling some cages. I'll catch up with you on the other side of this."

Victoria leaves the store and heads back toward Daniel's building. It feels weird. She is the most hunted person in America right now, and she's walking down a sidewalk looking like she doesn't have a care in the world. It's an illusion. She has a lot of them as they close in on the endgame.

CHAPTER SIXTY-ONE

BRIAN COOPER

Wolfwood Estate
Vienna, Virginia

Brian steers his car through the gate once it opens. The familiar vehicles are parked in the exact locations in the driveway as last time. A butler wearing the same outfit answers the door before he can ring the bell. That's where the déjà vu ends. Instead of being shown downstairs to a festive atmosphere, Lurch gestures toward the shouting from the sitting room.

There is nothing celebratory about this gathering. There will be no champagne flowing or exaggerated stories about conquered foes. This is open warfare, and Brian is walking straight into the battle.

"Oliver Jahn works for you, DeAnna!" Conrad shouts in his baritone voice from across the room as Brian waits out of sight. "Why are you blaming any of us for his broadcast?"

"Because the information he had didn't come from me! It didn't come from his producers, researchers, or anyone else at VH Media. The information came from one of you, and I want to know why."

"You have some nerve!" Conrad seethes.

"He could have gotten it from Tierra Campos," Andrew offers.

"Are you listening to yourself? Because, if you were, you would understand how insane that sounds. I want answers, and I want them now!"

"This is a fun group," Brian says, entering now that he's determined it's time to intervene.

"About time you got here," Andrew says, shaking his head.

"One would think you'd be acting more urgently," DeAnna piles on. "Unless you disabled your Internet connection, turned off your television, or are responsible for one of these guys leaking information leading one of my employees to attack me."

"You make it sound like you're the only one in the crosshairs, DeAnna," Conrad argues. "Did you watch *Let's Go Swimming* this week? He was all over the FBI and DOJ. He knew things about Ian Drucker that he shouldn't have. I wonder where he got that information."

Conrad turns his head and narrows his eyes at Andrew.

"Whoa. You aren't seriously thinking—"

"That the man who ran the S.O.F. and is the only one who knew that information could be selling me up the river. Yeah, that's exactly what I'm thinking, *Machiavelli.*"

"You're a fool. Why would I give anything to a wanna-be idiot like Tom Swim?"

"You tell me."

"Enough. All of you," Brian interjects. "What the hell is wrong with you guys? Nobody here has any reason to leak anything to Swim, *Radio Free America*, or any other copycat moron using it as clickbait to earn a buck. And as for Oliver Jahn, he's a pain in the ass who adores ratings above everything else. He knew that show would make him go viral. It's partly why you hired him, DeAnna."

"Are you really going to pass this off as a coincidence, Brian?"

"It doesn't matter if it is or isn't. It can't hurt any of us. Start looking three moves ahead. Pennsylvania is about to certify the election. The Electoral College meets in less than two weeks. Once the electors cast their votes, nothing else matters."

DeAnna shakes her head. "For someone who prides himself in seeing the big picture, you're missing what's right in front of you. Someone is undermining me. You may think you're all more important than I am, but mess around and see how wrong you are."

"Is that a threat?" Conrad asks.

"Did I stutter?"

"We all had a role to play," Brian says, trying to regain control of the conversation, but to no avail.

"Do you know how easy it would be to sic the FBI on you, DeAnna? VH Media is a huge company. I'm betting I can find all kinds of fraud if I have agents start poking around."

"They already are!" DeAnna screeches, getting Brian's attention. "A pair of agents showed up at the house this morning. Does that sound like a coincidence?"

"I didn't send them," the deputy AG says.

Denials are tricky things. Most people accused of something they didn't do get irrational and angry. It's a natural reaction to lash out at an unjust charge. People who remain calm may be innocent, but the lack of righteous indignation makes them appear guilty. That's the dilemma Conrad finds himself in. Brian can't imagine that the deputy AG would do something that reckless, but even he wonders if Williams had a hand in these leaks.

"I don't believe you, Conrad. They came here and asked questions about Ian Drucker and Victoria Larsen. Then they asked about my relationship with the DOJ. Not my network's relationship…*mine.*"

"Why would they ask you that?"

"You tell me. You're basically running the show over there, aren't you?"

Conrad looks over at Andrew. "That's the kind of stunt you would pull."

"Yeah, I arranged for a pair of agents who don't report to me to drop in unannounced in my spare time while I'm babysitting Standish."

"If they were agents at all," Conrad muses. "They could have been imposters for all we know. Maybe Machiavelli is trying to keep us in check while he enhances his influence."

"And maybe I'm the second shooter on the grassy knoll, you paranoid imbecile."

"Nobody is trying to enhance their influence!" Brian almost shouts, commanding his co-conspirators' attention.

"Not even you, Brian?" Conrad says, happy to deflect attention from himself. "It just occurred to me that you're the outsider here. The one without any real power. Maybe you're trying to take us down a notch."

Brian purses his lips and strolls closer to the center of the sitting room. "I have the *most* vested interest in our success. I assembled this group because you're all needed to reach our goals. Each of you is valuable and always will be. This isn't over yet."

"It is for me," DeAnna says. "I don't trust any of you."

"Coming from the woman safely ensconced in a Virginia mansion," Andrew says with a sneer. "The rest of us have the most to lose if our actions are ever publicized."

"You should have thought of that before you came after me."

"Nobody is coming after you, DeAnna," Brian says, becoming exasperated. She's like a playlist with one song on repeat. Or a Debbie Gibson song from the '80s. It's the same lyric over and over.

"All evidence to the contrary. You think you have this under control, Brian. You don't. One of these guys is going rogue. Maybe both of them are. Or maybe it's you. Either way, I'm done protecting the lot of you."

Conrad stands and points a finger in the host's face. "If I see one report on VHN with my name in it, you'll find out what someone coming after you really looks like."

The media tycoon doesn't back down. "My lawyers will have a field day with that."

"Is this how you all really want this to end? We are so close to—"

"Shut up, Brian. You and your giant ego made this mess. If the information Tom Swim, RFA, and Alétheia are reporting didn't come from one of us, then it came from Campos because you decided to let her live."

"It's not coming from her," Brian argues reflexively.

"Then, there it is. Nobody's responsible. Isn't that quaint? I want you all out of my house right now."

Two security guards arrive at the door. They aren't acting aggressively or threateningly, but their size alone is intimidating. Both could be linemen for any NFL team.

"You're overreacting, DeAnna."

"And you're proving to be inept, Brian. If you want my continued assistance, you had better show some loyalty and find out who's been leaking information to the alt-media. Until then, I have nothing to say to you."

The trio is shown out of the house. Each peels off to his car and drives off without saying a word. There are no goodbyes or questions about how to fix this. It's almost as if the fracture is a relief.

That's a problem. Brian knew this was a risk but thought he could talk them off the ledge. He was wrong. Instead of listening to reason, they dug in. Publicity was the threat that kept them in line. It's the role he needed Campos to unwittingly play. Now someone is playing that card against him.

The damage can be repaired, although not easily. First, he needs to find out how the alt-media is obtaining its information. Once he knows the source, he can start mending fences. Until then, he has another concern: What Actyv will think when they discover his cabal has just dissolved.

CHAPTER SIXTY-TWO

TIERRA CAMPOS

Wilson Newman's House
Falls Church, Virginia

I would think this is the calm before the storm, but nobody is calm. Brian and Olivia are figuring out how to reliably stream the most important podcast of our lives. It's not beyond the realm of possibilities that the government tries to shut us down. We need contingency plans, then we need backups to those contingencies.

Logan, Tyler, and a smattering of others are still sorting through information. There are a lot of documents, but only a small percentage will make it to the broadcast. The world and law enforcement will want to see the rest of the evidence, which requires databasing, indexing, and securing the records. None of that is quick work.

Naomi is still rallying the troops, and Wilson and Mi Sun are making a food run after spending the day putting together the skeleton outline of the broadcast. That leaves me with little to do but get in people's way. With that in mind, I head to the kitchen and catch Austin sitting in the dining room, scowling as he stares at his laptop.

"Uh-oh. I don't like that look on your face," I say as Austin runs his hands through his hair.

"Yeah. Tom Swim is getting cold feet."

I wish I could say that is surprising. Swim is a good guy and a great podcaster who has built a small empire online. He makes an obscene amount of money through sponsorships and is beholden to nobody. Tom's also an odd duck who marches to the beat of his own drum and can be very difficult to work with.

"That's a huge audience we'd be losing."

"I know, but this was a possibility. Of the three groups, Swim was the most tentative about going through with this. Now they're balking at participating in Tuesday's broadcast and are even on the fence about simulcasting it."

"What's the problem?"

Austin shrugs. "The unknown."

"That's vague," I conclude, pulling out a chair and sitting at the table.

"Your plan is to divide and conquer. If the cabal splinters, maybe we can pull this off. Without them protecting each other, it's easier to make a move. If it backfires, they will circle the wagons and use whatever tools are at their disposal to destroy all of us. VH Media alone could do unspeakable damage to anyone working with us."

"And we have no way to know it's working," I say, getting to the root of the concern.

"It's not like Brian Cooper or the others will issue a press release. Short of tapping their phones or following them, neither of which we could do if we wanted to, we can only *hope* that this is having the desired effect. The cabal could have already disintegrated, or it could be stronger than ever. Tom's concerned that we're rushing ahead without seeing the big picture. He may be right."

"We're out of options, Austin. The Electoral College meets next week, and there is no chance that the Senate won't certify the result in January. That, and Victoria can't run forever. It's now or never."

"I agree. It's just who will be willing to go for the ride. Swim has a lot to lose if this fails."

Now, it's my turn to scowl. "We all have a lot to lose. What will it take for Swim to stay the course?"

"Some sort of confirmation that our plan is working."

He might as well be asking us to count the exact number of stars in our galaxy. There is no chance for us to find that out…unless…there is one person who wants to play more of a role in this endeavor. Maybe it's time to leverage that.

"Then let's get it for him."

"How?"

"Moira Kinsella."

"She's a good reporter, Tierra, but you can't be thinking that she should walk up to one of the co-conspirators and ask."

As entertaining as that would be, it would end in disaster. The four members of the cabal are very different people. They have varied skill sets, backgrounds, and values. It's why Brian struggled so mightily to keep them in line. We have been exploiting those cracks for over a week. Why not target the weakest link in the chain?

"Not at all. Cooper is in the wind, but the other three have jobs. Conrad Williams keeps a schedule, but the DOJ isn't likely to divulge anything. That leaves Andrew Li and DeAnna Van Herten. Moira may be able to get some insights from Standish on her future chief of staff, but I doubt Andrew tells her much about what's going on. That leaves DeAnna."

"Who rarely leaves her estate."

I let the smile march across my lips. "Precisely. The cabal will meet in person to hash this out. She can quietly find out if DeAnna has had any or is expecting guests. VHN leaks like a sieve, and I'm betting her house staff can be paid to talk."

"House staff? Like maids and butlers?"

"Billionaires don't own mansions and then do the chores and cooking themselves. They also have security. Wolfwood Estate has a staff, and I'm willing to bet someone like Moira will know how to get to them. If we can prove the cabal met in person and get at least a description of their emotional state, would that be enough for Swim?"

"It's better than nothing," Austin admits. "Let me make some calls. We're going to make this work, Tierra."

I smile weakly. "I know."

I don't know. I'm putting on a brave face, but completely uncertain this will work. I am focused on success but have convinced myself to go down swinging if we fail.

My phone vibrates, and I check the caller ID before answering. "Hi, Mi Sun."

"Tierra…I…we…."

The upset tone of her voice immediately raises the alarm. Mi Sun is not prone to overreaction or emotional fits.

"What's wrong?"

I hear her fighting to stifle a series of sobs. "It's Wilson…he…."

"He what?" I ask, shifting uncomfortably as a shiver runs down my spine.

"He collapsed. It was so sudden! I'm following the ambulance to the emergency room. You need to get there, fast!"

CHAPTER SIXTY-THREE

SSA DANIEL MURPHY

J. Edgar Hoover Building
Washington, D.C.

FBI Headquarters is situated between 9th and 10th Streets in northwest Washington, D.C., directly across Pennsylvania Avenue from the Department of Justice. Constructed in the 1970s, it was meant to rejuvenate a section of "America's Main Street" that John F. Kennedy once characterized as "ugly." They failed in that mission. The building has been panned by critics since its construction, and that opinion hasn't improved with time, for good reason.

Murphy provides his credentials at the desk and heads to the director's office. The executives, special agents, and professional staff here organize and coordinate global FBI activities. Daniel considers them bureaucrats more interested in playing politics within the Beltway than getting results in the field. It's an opinion shared by most agents who have little use for red tape when their lives are on the line.

Director Krekstein was appointed by the president and confirmed by the Senate several years ago. His term is limited to ten years. Murphy needs to determine whether he should last that long. Under the Constitution, the FBI director can be removed from his position if circumstances warrant that removal. But since 1908, the president has only once removed the head of the FBI from office.

President Bill Clinton dismissed William Sessions as FBI director in 1993 after allegations of Bureau leadership conflicts and misuse of government resources for personal travel. Like with most things in this city, the removal was considered political. This one won't have that stigma.

Murphy doesn't know if Krekstein is actively colluding with Conrad Williams or is just a stooge. As he is let into the director's office, he's about to find out.

"Supervisory Special Agent Murphy…is it possible I misinterpreted the deputy attorney general when he told me you questioned your assignment and challenged him on Victoria Larsen's terrorist designation?"

"No, sir."

"Then I'm sure you have a brilliant explanation for how Victoria Larsen hasn't been taken into custody yet."

"She isn't your typical domestic terrorist," Murphy deadpans.

"You have the resources of the entire FBI at your disposal, Agent Murphy! Nobody on the planet should be able to hide from us this long."

"That would be true if Larsen were a street thug or drug kingpin. It would also be true if she were a criminal mastermind. She's none of those. Victoria Larsen is an agent, which means she knows how we operate. That gives her an advantage. She will be caught, sir, but it will just take time."

Krekstein scowls and leans back slightly as his eyes bore into his subordinate.

"Time is a luxury we don't have. Agent Murphy, you were hand-picked to lead this investigation and manhunt," the director summarizes. "You're capable and driven, yet all I've heard from you are excuses. Couple that with your disrespectful conversation with the man tasked by the AG to administer the FBI, and I can't help but think you may be sandbagging the investigation. Are you?"

"No, sir. We're actively investigating every lead."

"Then why don't I see results?" the director asks, sounding more like he's leveling an accusation. "Victoria Larsen is a direct threat to this country—"

"How?"

"Excuse me?"

"How is she a direct threat? The deputy AG said that there is evidence that she's planning a terrorist attack, but I haven't come across any. I was told it was beyond my purview. Fine. But if this evidence helps me track Larsen down and stop her, I don't understand why it's not being handed to me."

"As was said, it's beyond your purview."

"Have you seen it?"

The director shifts uncomfortably. "You have orders to follow, Agent Murphy. You are to track, locate, and apprehend Victoria Larsen. That is all you need to know, and you have every tool to do so at your disposal. Follow your orders. We will handle the rest."

"Yes, sir."

"Good. I expect reports from you every twelve hours on your progress. Now get out of my office. The next time I see you here, it will be because Larsen is behind bars or dead."

Murphy leaves without acknowledging that directive. The clarity he sought didn't come. Krekstein is toeing the line, but Daniel isn't sure if Williams has cowed him into submission or because he's aligned with the cabal. He thinks it's the former, but there is nothing to back that conclusion.

He only knows Krekstein cannot be trusted so long as he carries Conrad Williams's water. Something needs to be done to show progress. He has an idea, but it's risky and not one that Victoria will like.

CHAPTER SIXTY-FOUR

PRESIDENT-ELECT ALICIA STANDISH

Standish's Hay-Adams Hotel Suite
Washington, D.C.

A Secret Service agent shows Colin Bradford into the suite and shuts the door, leaving the political rivals alone. He looks around at the décor. This has to be more awkward for him than her, and that's saying something. At least she won the election. Or, more accurately, had the result thrown in her direction.

"Thank you for coming, Governor."

"Thank you for the invite, Madam President-Elect," Bradford says, shaking her hand. "I think."

Alicia gives him a quizzical look. "I'm surprised you used that title."

"Let's be honest. My legal challenges aren't going to pan out. There isn't a judge in the country willing to overturn the election result without concrete evidence it's wrong. A lot happened in Pennsylvania, but there's no way to determine the true result."

Alicia nods, knowing why. It's just the way Cooper wanted it.

"When I received your invitation, I figured Andrew Li would greet me. I heard he's running a tight ship around here."

"You have no idea. He traveled to Pennsylvania at the governor's request. Would you like a drink?"

"I may need one. Thank you. I expected to be ushered through the main entrance into one of the conference rooms in front of a horde of camera-wielding reporters. Instead, I was brought in through a service entrance and escorted to your suite."

"Why would you expect a media circus?" the president-elect asks as she fills a couple of crystal tumblers with bourbon from a decanter.

"Ma'am, with all due respect, you invited an opponent who has yet to concede the election to meet with you. It's either in the name of bipartisanship or to show the country you're determined to ensure the outcome is fair. Both of those need media coverage."

"That's an astute conclusion. Only the outcome isn't fair."

"I'm sorry…what?"

Alicia hands him a drink and goes to sit before sticking her index finger up. She walks back over to the cart and retrieves the decanter. She sets it on the small table between them when she returns.

"That's ominous."

"Governor, I'm about to divulge information that only a handful of people know."

"Please, ma'am, this is an informal meeting, and I get the feeling you're about to drop a bomb on me. Please call me Colin. Is this about the Roswell aliens? The JFK assassination?"

"Worse," Alicia says before inhaling sharply. "Andrew Li is Machiavelli."

Bradford stops sipping his drink. "Madam President-Elect, are you saying—"

"Yes, and call me Alicia. Please. Andrew was in charge of the S.O.F. and was responsible for trying to manipulate the Democratic New Hampshire Primary."

"Whoa. That means...."

"Yes, that's exactly what it means. It gets worse. There are four people in a cabal responsible for manipulating the general election. Andrew Li is one, and a man called 'Robespierre' is the second. He happens to be Deputy Attorney General Conrad Williams."

"Who you just named as the incoming AG," Colin says, slowly nodding as he digests that information. "I thought it was weird that you didn't keep Ehler."

"Now you know why. 'Nietzsche' is DeAnna Van Herten, and she's the third member, who helps them establish the media narrative surrounding these events."

Colin leans back in his chair. "That's incredible. How certain are you of this?"

"One hundred percent. There's one more thing, and that's why you're here. The cabal is run by 'Rasputin,' who worked for your campaign. In fact, he *ran* it."

"Brian Cooper?"

Alicia nods. Colin leans forward and steeples his hands in front of his mouth as he stares at the table.

"The events in Pennsylvania were orchestrated to ensure whoever sits in the Oval Office would appear illegitimate. I was their first choice to win because they thought I wanted the presidency so badly that I would play along with their power grab."

"Which you're not."

Alicia shakes her head slowly. "No. Once I take the oath of office, they have all the leverage they need to do anything from start wars to bankrupt companies. The damage could be incalculable, and it would all be on my watch. The moment I open my mouth after the inauguration, my presidency is over."

"And because Brian Cooper is the ringleader, I'm also implicated in the scandal. He could make it look like.... Jesus, who else knows about this?"

"My husband, of course. Tierra Campos, Victoria Larsen, and a few others in their circle. That's it."

"That explains a lot."

Alicia grins. He's been paying attention. The attacks in Boston and against Tierra in Washington didn't get much media attention. The manhunt for America's public enemy number one certainly has. Most people would shrug and accept that Victoria Larsen is a traitorous domestic terrorist and move on. Colin has already looked at the events and determined something isn't right.

"Tierra warned me on Election Night after she snuck into the convention center before my speech. She confronted me right after VHN called the election. She didn't have proof, and I didn't believe her. Victoria Larsen has been trying to gather evidence, and apparently, they have it from Ian Drucker's laptop. They want to go public, and they have my support."

"And you want mine," Colin concludes.

"I'm asking for it, yes. I can show you all the proof if you want to see it. This is an elegant coup, and the American people will be terrified when they learn the truth."

Alicia doesn't bother pointing out the obvious consequence. America is resilient, and its people have always prided themselves in a stable government. Political scandals, unpopular wars, and cultural upheavals have challenged that belief, but the country has always endured. Not this time. Americans have been losing faith in their government for decades. This could be the final nail in the coffin for the Republic.

"You took a huge risk bringing me here to tell me this information. You just beat me in a race for the presidency. We've spent the last five months dragging each other through the mud. What makes you think I won't go public about it?"

Alicia takes a deep breath and nods in understanding of the question. "You know, I was like every other politician who comes to this city. I wanted to be different. But partisan politics eventually sucks everyone in. We stop caring about our constituents and begin worrying more about power, ideology, donations, and our respective parties. It's more about the game than governing. Republican, Democrat, liberal, conservative…we do everything to highlight our differences and maintain the divide because that's how elections are won.

"Then something like this happens that puts it into perspective. Cooper took advantage of hyper-partisan politics. He's still counting on it. The last thing he ever would have expected is my conversing about this with you. Colin, we may have two different visions for America, but I believe we both have the people's interests at heart. Despite the campaign rhetoric, I believe you're a good man who only wants the best for America. I don't know what will happen when this is made public, but it's better for everybody if they see us facing it together before the Electoral College meets."

"Even if it ultimately costs you the presidency?"

"It's not going to be *my* presidency. It'll be Brian Cooper's."

Colin rubs his temples with his left hand. She knows how he feels. Alicia has been nursing a stress headache since meeting the cabal after the election when they informed her of her new reality. The governor drains the rest of his bourbon. She thinks he's about to get up and storm out when he wiggles the empty tumbler.

"Okay. Other than pouring us some refills, what do you want to do?"

CHAPTER SIXTY-FIVE

TIERRA CAMPOS

Seven Corners Memorial Teaching Hospital
Seven Corners, Virginia

Seven Corners is a Fairfax County commercial area with a Falls Church mailing address that doesn't fall within its city limits. The area got its name from the intersection of Leesburg Pike, Arlington Boulevard, Sleepy Hollow Road, and Hillwood Avenue. The junction of these three state roads and one U.S. route once created seven corners before the intersection was reengineered to ease traffic congestion.

The area also has the Memorial Teaching Hospital, one of the country's top ten medical instructional institutions. I don't give a damn about that so long as Wilson receives expert care. While a teaching hospital may sound like gambling with inexperienced doctors and nurses, they are at least passionate and attentive.

I burst onto the floor before the elevator doors fully open, and I dart past the nurses' station. They all raise their heads to watch me, but none protest or reprimand me for sprinting in the corridor. So much for being attentive.

Josh is behind me, struggling to keep up. I slow when I reach the door to the room I was given at the reception desk, rounding the corner and bursting in like I'm on a SWAT team. Mi Sun is standing there, and the force of my entrance causes her to take a step or two back.

I stop and stare at her. Her cheeks are wet with tears, and her eyes are red and bloodshot. She rushes over and hugs me hard. I don't dwell on who this is and how I wouldn't have shed a tear three months ago if she had been hit by a bus. Despite my earlier reservations over her loyalty, she's a member of the *Front Burner* family now.

"You guys are acting like I'm dead or something," Wilson muses from his bed.

Josh walks over and shakes his hand while Mi Sun and I release the embrace. "That hospital gown suits you. Mine had polka dots."

Wilson scoffs before smirking.

"You gave us quite a scare, old man," I say, trying to get him to smile as I move to his bedside.

"Hey there, missy, watch it with the 'old' stuff. I'm as fit as a fiddle."

"You just had a heart attack!" Mi Sun screeches.

"It was a minor myocardial infarction."

"Otherwise known as a *heart attack*," I clarify. "You're lucky to be alive."

Wilson waves a dismissive hand. "It takes more than that to kill me."

A lot is said about generational differences. Wilson may be a much-maligned Boomer, but there are things about his generation that mine can appreciate. He's tough and as stubborn as a mule. That can have its advantages.

"Well, your diet is about to change dramatically," Mi Sun informs him. "I'll do the shopping for you if I have to. Plenty of heart-healthy foods and salads. If something kills you, it won't be your heart because of a bad diet."

"No, having to eat salads might kill me, though."

I pull up a chair and kiss his hand. Tears begin rolling down my face as Josh touches my shoulder supportively. I haven't known Wilson for all that long, but he's like a father figure to me. I can't bear the thought of losing him.

"I'm fine, Tierra."

"I know. I just…When Mi Sun called, I thought someone had tried to kill you. I couldn't…if something happened to you…."

"But it didn't. Nobody tried to kill me, and no one's after me. It's okay."

"It's not okay, Wilson. They came after me, and they shot Josh. They're chasing Victoria. It's not unreasonable to think everyone I know is in peril. It will be worse if the cabal takes power."

"Then we make sure they don't," Wilson says. "That's the whole point."

"It's a risk," I mutter. "We might not win."

"Tierra, listen to me. Life is about risk. It doesn't mean someone should waste their life by being reckless. But if safety is your only goal, then you aren't really living."

"This is different."

"Yes, it is. Just like soldiers and firefighters, we're fighting for something bigger than us. This is about serving. I, for one, am happy to do it, even if it costs me my life. That's what sacrifice is."

I never thought of it that way. This has been personal for a long time. It was made doubly so when I learned that Brian Cooper was the puppet master. Sometimes I forget that the American people have a stake in the outcome. If this cabal is exposed too late, the truth could lead to the collapse of the American government.

"How long are you going to be in here?"

"According to the doctor, at least a couple of days," Mi Sun answers. "They want to run more tests and observe him for a few days."

"Okay," I say, drying my cheeks. "Oliver will take care of the podcast. You need to heal up."

"Not a chance."

"Not negotiable. You're no good to us dead, Wilson. You will abide by the doctor's orders," Mi Sun says.

"And no escape plans," I add before he can protest. "And don't harass the nurses."

Wilson frowns. "You two are determined to take all the joy out of my life, aren't you?"

I smile and let out a nervous laugh. Mi Sun joins me. We will have to rethink the broadcast, but that's for another time. Most of *Front Burner* will be on their way to see their colleague. We can at least rejoice that he managed to slip through Death's grasp. I can only hope that trend continues.

CHAPTER SIXTY-SIX

BRIAN COOPER

Cooper Residence
Bethesda, Maryland

It's been a hectic twenty-four hours. For Brian's new plan to succeed, countless requirements must be satisfied, which takes time to plan and execute. Fortunately, he still has some left. The sand in the hourglass is losing its battle with gravity, but plenty of grains still need to make the final journey. The hard part is mental. It's tough initiating an elaborate plan that he hopes he never needs.

The dissolution of the agreement that had brought each of them to the threshold of success is an unwanted and unexpected development. Brian is optimistic they will return to the fold, out of necessity more than any other reason. Each player has their own strengths. They each had a role to play. That doesn't end just because the election is over.

This is the equivalent of walking the last half mile of the marathon. The hard part is over. There is no reason not to finish strong unless some affliction or impairment forces you to pull back. Nobody he's working with has that excuse.

That's what makes these reports making their way around the podcast and alternative media circles so disconcerting. Brian doesn't know where they're coming from. The origin can't be Campos pushing Isiah Burgess's files or anything Victoria Larsen may have retrieved off Ian Drucker's laptop. The reporting is too vague and speculative. Any of that information must have more detail than the reports are divulging.

Campos could be playing a game with them by letting information leach into the public sphere. She's wily enough to pull that off. But *Front Burner* has no relationship with Tom Swim or *Radio Free America*. They are competitors. And there is no way she would ever leak information to Oliver Jahn. That's a non-starter.

It's more likely that DeAnna, Conrad, and Andrew are leaking information about each other. It started with one, and the rest was retaliation, just like they accused each other of. That's a problem. It means the situation could worsen to the point where somebody outside his control decides to investigate. There are dozens of state attorneys general eager to make a name for themselves who would salivate over putting these pieces together.

Brian steers his car into the driveway and kills the engine. He locks it using the fob before striding up to the portico and punching in the code that opens the front door. The house is still, not that anything otherwise is expected. He should change into something more comfortable, but his mind is racing. Tonight is the kind of night when he needs to let it do its thing.

The consultant turns left and enters the study. He's about to flip on the light when the desk light switches on. A man is seated at the desk with his feet propped up, and seeing him takes three years off Brian's life. He holds his hand over his thumping heart as he recovers from the shock, and that's when he notices the gun in the man's hand.

"This is a nice weapon, Brian," the Russian says with a healthy accent, admiring the sleek lines the forged steel makes. "You need a refresher course on gun safety. A desk drawer is not the same as a safe."

"Who are you?"

"Anatoly Morozov. Please, do something cliché and ask who I work for."

Brian doesn't need to. He flips on the light and moves deeper into the study. He was sent here by Actyv, which means he isn't here to kill Brian. Yet.

"How did you get in?"

Anatoly laughs. "Our employer owns this house, Mr. Cooper. Who do you think uses it when you aren't? I'm the one who picked the front door code."

"The guest room is made up if you want it. There is no room service, and I ain't Mary Poppins."

Anatoly laughs. "They told me you were quick-witted. Here I am with your gun, and you think this is business as usual. It isn't."

"Let me guess: Roman saw the reports and thought there was trouble with my operation. He sent you here to extract information and ensure I understand that if things go south, there are fates worse than death if I decide to roll over on them."

"Very sharp conclusion, Brian. They also said you were a smart one."

"Not my first rodeo," Brian admits, causing the Russian to cock his head. "It's an expression."

"Ah."

The Russian stands and smooths out his suit jacket. He gracefully moves around the desk, taking time to run the finger of his left hand over the smooth, lacquered wood. Brian is keenly aware that he's casually holding the gun in his right hand. It dangles at his side like it's an extension of his body. In all likelihood, it is. The man is comfortable and confident.

"Our employers need not worry, Anatoly. I have experienced setbacks throughout this process and always found a way to deliver the results they were looking for. This is no different. They understand the risk-reward proposition. It would be imprudent of them to believe I can't be trusted to complete what I set out to do."

The Russian smiles. "In my homeland, we also have an expression: *Yazyk harasho padvyeshen.* It means your tongue is well-hung. You use eloquent words, mister political advisor. They must work well on weaker men who wear suits and attend meetings all day. They are meaningless to men who favor results over assurances. As you are about to learn."

Anatoly raises the weapon and points it at Brian's forehead. Before the consultant can react, he moves his finger to the trigger and squeezes. The trigger bar pulls back the Glock's firing pin, and the connector guides the trigger pin downward. The firing pin is freed to strike the primer. There is a click, and then nothing. There are no cartridges loaded in the weapon.

"Phew," Anatoly says, setting the gun down on the desk. "I couldn't remember if I ejected the chambered round. That would have been embarrassing."

Few things rattle Brian. This does. He stares at the man sheepishly as the enforcer starts past Brian in the middle of the study before stopping abruptly.

"I am told you are a good employee. You have delivered for our employer, but there is no resting on one's laurels with them. You must keep delivering. If you have problems, solve them. If not, the next time we meet will be under much less agreeable circumstances. Do you understand?"

"I do."

"*Khorosho.*"

Anatoly pats Brian on the shoulder and shows himself out, even locking the door behind him. No car was in the drive, so he must have parked down the street. Brian doesn't bother checking to ensure the Russian left. He will be true to his word and only return if Brian fails.

His legs feel like jelly, so he eases into one of the chairs and stares at the chessboard. Another countermove. Too much is happening, and he's losing control of the situation. He can't sit back and hope things work out. It's time to take action.

CHAPTER SIXTY-SEVEN

VICTORIA LARSEN

Constitution Avenue
Washington, D.C.

Victoria walks down the sidewalk like she doesn't have a care in the world again. To the average person, she's just another one of the city's thousands of visitors taking a Monday sunset stroll in the nation's capital. The FBI agent has never done theater, but it's incredible acting. Her carefree constitutional is an illusion. She carries an enormous amount of stress in her shoulders and lower back, causing them to ache.

As a wanted domestic terrorist and fugitive, it's insane that she's ambling down a sidewalk two blocks from the seat of executive power. Machiavelli, who is likely with the president-elect at the Hay-Adams, is three blocks behind her. Robespierre, who's in his office at Justice, is a block ahead. Talk about wandering into the dragon's den.

Her phone vibrates, and she taps on one of her earbuds. "Yeah."

"Vic, where are you?" Daniel asks.

"I just crossed 12th Street and am coming up behind the natural history museum."

"Okay, we're in position on 14th near the Department of Agriculture. Imani is on the call with us. She's standing by on 4th near Independence."

"Lucky me. This is the stupidest plan I've ever heard of, Murph."

She can almost hear him chuckle. "Hey, you wanted to shake things up."

There's no arguing that. The first part of the plan was to divide the cabal. Once isolated, the second part is meant to instill a little fear in the cabal. Imani is taking care of DeAnna Van Herten. Victoria's job is to rattle Andrew Li and Conrad Williams. Unfortunately, no plan ever survives first contact with Daniel Murphy. He hijacked it and came up with this potential disaster.

"That doesn't mean I want to get caught. Or shot at. Or killed."

"If it makes you feel any better, we don't want that either," Imani says.

"It doesn't. I get Imani, but you used to be by the book, Daniel. What happened?"

"I've been hanging around you for a couple of weeks. Look, you said that we need to keep the cabal's eyes off Tierra Campos, and I need to show progress in catching you to ensure that happens. This plan should accomplish both goals."

Victoria shakes her head. "It's dumb."

"Says the woman who got rolled out of a hotel in a suitcase during the Brockhampton investigation," Murphy argues.

Victoria smiles. She had almost forgotten about that. When the Massachusetts State Police obtained an arrest warrant for her justified shooting of a thug during the riot that ensued after the governor's assassination, Tierra and Austin snuck her out of their hotel in an oversized duffle bag. It worked, but it isn't one of her fondest memories.

"That was evading capture. This is inviting it. Do you have any idea how many laws we're breaking with this stunt?"

"Are you seriously worried about that now?" Imani asks. "You drugged a civilian, interrogated him, and left him handcuffed around a tree in Pennsylvania."

"Then you stole a vehicle and snuck into a militia compound without a warrant."

"You handcuffed a campus policeman to your car in Boston after shooting at him."

"I get the point," Victoria says, interrupting her colleagues' back-and-forth recap of her numerous transgressions.

"Absolute effing legend," she hears DeAndre muse.

"I'm happy you guys are having fun with this. You forget that I also shot Ian Drucker in the back in cold blood."

"We didn't forget," Imani explains. "We're jealous. You're the one beating yourself up over it."

"Actually, I'm jealous of everything she's done," Agent Wright says.

"You're a gangster at heart, DeAndre. It's showtime, Vic. Ready?"

She looks around. "No."

"I'll take that as a yes. DeAndre, make the call, and be convincing."

Murphy flips the strobes and siren on and mashes the Crown Victoria's accelerator to the floorboard.

"This is Special Agent DeAndre Wright with actionable intelligence on a credible threat to the deputy attorney general. Victoria Larsen was spotted on Constitution Avenue, two blocks from the Justice Department. I need tactical teams and a Metro Police SWAT unit sent to that area immediately."

"There she is!" Murphy shouts for the benefit of the field office dispatcher DeAndre is talking to. "Here we come, Vic."

"Yeah, I heard you from the other side of the Mall and heard Wright's report," Victoria says, spotting the car as it screams toward her before skidding to a stop forty feet away. Here goes nothing.

Victoria starts to run up the avenue, away from Murphy and Wright.

"Victoria Larsen! Freeze, federal agents!"

Life is a funny thing. Every day since fleeing that Pennsylvania lumber mill, she's imagined this could happen. With their resources and excellent agents, the FBI would catch up to her eventually. Never could she dream it would go down this way.

CHAPTER SIXTY-EIGHT

PRESIDENT-ELECT ALICIA STANDISH

Standish's Hay-Adams Hotel Suite
Washington, D.C.

Colin has incredible mental focus. Alicia threw a lot of information at him, and to his credit, he processed, analyzed, and drew conclusions based on it without even needing a break. A month ago, Alicia couldn't stomach the idea of paying the man a compliment. He was an enemy that needed vanquishing.

She's certain he feels the same way. Yet here they are, contemplating the ramifications of the most devastating scandal in American history. They will have one chance to mitigate the damage if the people are willing to listen to their pleas. Americans are fickle. They can be disengaged and apathetic, but once their mind is made up during a scandal, most don't budge.

That's what makes the *Capitol Beat* broadcast so important. Tierra knows that she has to stick the landing. If it's handled wrongly, or she doesn't convince her viewers that this cabal is an actual entity, the damage will be catastrophic. That's her cross to bear. Alicia is concerned about what happens if she succeeds. The man sitting on the sofa across from her may be the key.

"Are you okay?"

"Uh, yeah. Honestly, I want you to be lying to me."

Alicia stares at her hands as she wrings them. "Governor, I wish this were some kind of political ploy to embarrass you and the Republicans. Believe me, I'd sleep better at night. What are your thoughts?"

"Centered around what will happen when this goes public. Americans…I don't know how much more they can endure. Ethan Harrington was bad…no offense."

He didn't mean it as a dig. His face changed the moment the name left his mouth. He's right in that the Ethan fiasco did enormous damage to the public trust.

"None taken," Alicia assures him.

"Then New Hampshire and Pennsylvania…the reaction to this information could be disastrous. There may be rioting…states could even try to secede from the Union."

"Whatever happens can't be any worse than having an unelected political consultant extorting the president of the United States."

Alicia has been numb since learning that Tierra Campos's warning in Boston wasn't a ploy to deprive her of the presidency. She is caught in the middle of a coup. They are calling the shots, and the decisions she gets to make on her own are out of their good graces. It's extortion, and that's not a word she ever wants to get comfortable using.

"I'm not so sure about that. There will be endless questions about how this was allowed to happen. It will destroy the FBI and the DOJ. And that's before we start figuring out what to do next. Everyone will want to take advantage of this."

"That's how we got into this mess in the first place," Alicia concludes. "We were so busy beating each other over the head that we missed some powerful people using the chaos to their advantage."

Colin shakes his head. "There's always been contention between political parties. It's why they exist. But when did this become so toxic? When did we let our differences define us instead of only having issues we disagreed on?"

"I was pondering that a few nights ago. I'm not sure. I think it's been happening for a while."

This situation is as bad as it gets, but that's not what's troubling her opponent. He's seen the information and is disgusted about what's happening. This is something else.

"The Republicans are going to be desperate to use this. Monica Stengel's job as head of the RNC is in jeopardy. She'll be out for blood."

"Even if the cabal manipulated both of us?"

Colin looks up and frowns. "Yeah, because you won."

"Cooper told me I was the preferred winner because they thought I would be easier to control. He never thought I would be willing to give up the White House once I got elected. On the other hand, you were a bigger question mark…apparently."

"That's why you reached out to me," the governor says, now understanding why Alicia brought him here. "You figured that if they had reservations about my playing along, there must be a reason."

The corner of Alicia's mouth curls. "I've been searching for any way to undermine this cabal from the moment I learned it was real. They don't have many tells. That was one of them."

"It doesn't solve our problem with my party."

"Or mine. The Democrats are going to label this a right-wing conspiracy. It doesn't matter that most of them are registered in my party. They want to hang onto the White House at all costs. It's two Supreme Court justices, hundreds of lower court appointments, and we get to set the national narrative for four years. The DNC isn't going to want to give that up."

"And while our parties argue back and forth and dozens of lawsuits are filed, the nation won't have a leader. The Electoral College could pick someone else. The Senate may not play ball during the certification. It will become a constitutional crisis that could spell the end of the United States."

"Especially with the media involved. They will stoke the fires and further divide the people in the name of ratings and readership. If we are lucky enough not to end up in a civil war, we will still lose whatever faith the people have left in our ability to govern."

"Now you sound like a Republican."

Alicia chuckles. "The right doesn't have a monopoly on thinking the government is broken. We just differ on why and what to do about it."

She gave him an opening for a partisan attack. At a minimum, she half-expected a snide retort about him being right and her wrong. She gets neither. This isn't the campaign trail, where such barbs are exchanged daily. Governor Bradford is in problem-solving mode.

"There are a thousand holes in this plan you have."

"I know. So does Tierra Campos. But if we wait to get our ducks in a row, we'll never get across the street. Sometimes you gather what you have and make a run for it."

"Then we had better get busy," Colin says, sitting a little straighter. "Because if this plays out the way I think it will, we may be the only two people who can stave off disaster."

CHAPTER SIXTY-NINE

TIERRA CAMPOS

Lincoln Memorial
Washington, D.C.

Josh and I exit the Foggy Bottom metro station and head south for the fifteen-minute walk to the Lincoln Memorial. I'm relieved that there were no issues on the ride here. I haven't had the best of luck on the metro in recent months, so my best friend decided to tag along. Or is he my boyfriend now? I guess we should work that out at some point.

Both of us have been here countless times before. I filed countless reports from the steps of this marble monument as a human interest reporter for WWDC News. It's the one monument in Washington that always has people around. The prominent location at the western edge of the National Mall, with its commanding view up to the U.S. Capitol, makes it a must-see destination.

The temperatures aren't mild but aren't cold either. It isn't peak tourist season, but a small army of tourists wielding backpacks and cameras is catching the sunset over the nation's capital. I'm beginning to think I have post-traumatic stress disorder. I don't like public places. I never feel safe outside the confines of a familiar space. The attack at Josh's even shattered that illusion of safety. I'm not sure I can relax until this is over.

I lean against one of the ionic columns and stare at the Washington Monument reflecting pool while Josh lurks nearby. My head is on a swivel, and I spot Lisa Ehler approaching from the left before climbing the stairs. She stops next to me and assumes the same leaning pose I have against the pillar.

"I was surprised to hear from you," I say without greeting.

"Not as surprised as I am to reach out. Moira Kinsella dropped into my office and suggested I talk to you. She can be…convincing."

"Did she explain what's happening?"

"She gave me the highlights," the AG says. "It's more than a little tough to believe. We're talking about four people essentially seizing American executive power. In most circles, that's called a coup."

"That's exactly what this is." I reach into my pocket, pull out a thumb drive, and hold it up. "All the documents we have are loaded on this. Most originate from Isiah Burgess's files and Ian Drucker's personal laptop liberated during the FBI's assault on the Keystone Militia compound."

"And you're handing it to me?"

"A copy of it, yes. We're maintaining the originals in a safe location."

"Where?" the attorney general asks.

"In a safe location," I repeat, determined not to give that piece of information away. I won't even say the dark web or online. It can't be risked.

Lisa Ehler stares at the drive for a moment before pocketing it. Her face changes. Curiosity has been replaced by something that seems more…reticent.

"Ma'am, the president-elect intended to keep you as attorney general."

"That's not what Alicia told me in Cambridge. She said she wanted to go in a 'different direction.'"

"That wasn't Alicia Standish talking. It was Brian Cooper. He instructed her to appoint Williams to head the DOJ, and Andrew Li is ensuring you carry out the order."

"Is that on here?"

"No, but it's not hard to figure out why Brian Cooper would want Conrad as AG instead of you. He was a key player in this, and that's his reward. By taking over your job, Williams has control of the country's premier law enforcement agency. As AG, he determines what is investigated and prosecuted and what isn't. That limits the cabal's exposure."

"I'm a lawyer, Miss Campos. Logic is not proof, no matter how good it sounds."

I nod. "Okay, then why else would Alicia do that? You've been friends with her for years, and by all accounts, you are capable at your job. Please let me know if you can think of a better reason she would betray you."

Lisa focuses on a man who trips climbing the stairs to his wife's and children's amusement. Tierra smiles at the sight. They are just having a good time, completely oblivious to what is happening in the political world around them. They don't know how lucky they are.

"Do you enjoy sunsets?" the AG asks.

"I'm from Arizona. There is nothing like a desert sunset's violets, pinks, and reds. I'll take that over this any day."

Lisa smiles weakly. "I like walking the National Mall when I need a break. I would bring Conrad along to yell at him once in a while. We've never gotten along that well. He was always too ambitious for my tastes."

"I can see that," I say, otherwise at a loss for words. I don't know Conrad like I do Brian Cooper.

Lisa removes the thumb drive from her pocket and holds it in her palm. "I don't know if I can do anything with this."

"I'm not asking you to. I am providing the attorney general of the United States with evidence of subversive activities directed against this government. What you do with that information is up to you. Just know that if you move forward, or if Williams and Cooper even think you have that information, your life is in danger. They have killed for far less."

"This will destroy Alicia," Lisa laments.

"Maybe. It will be worse if the president-elect doesn't come forward. Best case, she gets impeached when the truth finally comes out. Worst case, Brian Cooper has carte blanche to do whatever he wants. I'm not a politician, but I think this is the best option for everyone, including the American people. They deserve to know the truth."

"Tell me something," Lisa says, turning to face me. "How do I know this isn't something you ginned up to stick it to the president-elect? You don't exactly have a warm relationship with Alicia Standish."

"You don't," I answer honestly, "and nothing I can say will convince you. You need to make up your own mind. That evidence should help. Good luck, Madam Attorney General."

There is nothing more to say. I have no idea if Lisa Ehler is willing to help, but it would be a coup of my own if she is in our corner. Williams may be in line to take her job, but he doesn't have it yet. For once, the light I see at the end of this tunnel might not be the train bearing down on me.

I nod at Josh, and he joins me as we descend the stairs and traverse the plaza toward Lincoln Memorial Circle and sirens begin wailing farther up the Mall. I can see the flashing strobes converging on the area from all directions. Lisa is going to have a crappy commute back to the office.

CHAPTER SEVENTY

SSA DANIEL MURPHY

Constitution Avenue
Washington, D.C.

Victoria may be a wanted terrorist, but she has the easy part of this charade. She's a crack shot, and they gave her the perfect target to hit. Murphy's career will be over if an errant shot hits a pedestrian, regardless of what happens to the cabal.

She turns, pulls her weapon, and fires three rounds into the windshield of their Crown Vic. Murphy and Wright duck behind their doors. Daniel pops up, draws a bead on Victoria, checks the backdrop to ensure it's clear of fleeing civilians on the sidewalk, and then shifts his weapon slightly to the right. He squeezes the trigger twice, putting two rounds into the trunk of a car parked along the curb.

Victoria returns fire, hitting the radiator and causing it to hiss steam. DeAndre fires at her, putting the rounds into the same car. Some insurance adjuster is going to have something to say about that. Hopefully, the owner can bill the Bureau for the damage. They can afford it.

Murphy watches their quarry bolt up the sidewalk and veer right before he nods at his partner.

"Shots fired! Shots Fired!" he screams into his cell phone. "Suspect engaged near the Department of Justice. Larsen is heading toward the Museum of Natural History. We need backup! Now!"

They begin to pursue when they hear another shot. After a wary glance at each other, they pick up the pace as they race down the driveway running along the museum's east side. The downward slope mimics that of the 9th Street Expressway as it heads for the tunnel that bisects the Mall.

The two men pull up in a small parking area for museum employees. It's mostly empty except for some white vans parked along the embankment that rises to the street above.

"Where'd she go?" DeAndre asks.

"Check the vans."

Murphy moves toward the building, sweeping his weapon back and forth. He hears the shrill screech of an interior alarm before seeing that a service entrance door has been forced open. He suppresses a smile. That woman is always thinking ahead.

"Wright! Get over here!"

The junior agent hustles over and inspects the door. He then glances up and spots the shattered camera in the corner.

"Did she shoot out that camera?"

"Looks like it," Murphy confirms.

"The Smithsonian is so going to bill her for that when this is over," DeAndre says with a grin before pulling out his phone. "Suspect may have entered the museum. The alarm has been tripped. When can we expect the SWAT team?"

Murphy moves away from the alarm, his weapon still out. "Vic, where are you? Please say you're not inside the museum."

"I'm going for a jog. Why do you think I was dressed in workout clothes?"

"How the hell did you get out of this parking area?"

"The stairwell that leads up to Madison Drive. How else?"

Murphy walks along the wall that separates the parking area from the street above. He didn't even see the concrete stairs sunken into the embankment. He must be slipping. There's an almost completely unnecessary crosswalk leading from the museum straight to it.

"Are you okay?"

"I fell in behind a small group of other joggers who were conveniently heading in my direction, so I am for now."

Murphy chuckles. "You'll fit right in with that fanny pack you're wearing."

Victoria scoffs. "At least you're smart enough to say that *after* I had the chance to shoot at you."

"Damn straight. Police units are arriving in force, and SWAT will be here any minute. Your diversion should pin them here, but a perimeter will go up. Get out of the district as fast as you can. Contact me when you rendezvous with Imani."

"Wilco," Victoria says, short for "will comply." She's not even out of breath from her run across the Mall.

"I have to go," Murphy informs her before ending the call as a police lieutenant approaches him.

"What's the situation?" the man barks.

"We got into a shootout with Victoria Larsen after receiving actionable intelligence that she planned to assassinate the deputy attorney general. She fled this way and appears to have taken refuge in the museum. A door has been forced open, and the alarm was tripped."

"The museum is closed, so the building should be empty."

"Yeah, but it's big, and it will be a bitch finding her in there. We need teams covering every exit. How many men can you muster?"

"Hundreds, if we need to."

"We need to. I have a SWAT team on the way. The FBI can clear the building, but I need you to set up checkpoints in the entire area."

"Why? She's in the museum."

"Until I find her snuggled up with a wooly mammoth, I'm not assuming that. We need contingency plans. This is the first fix we've had on Larsen since Boston, and I'm not about to let her slip through our fingers due to a lack of imagination."

"Let me get this straight," the lieutenant protests. "You want us to lock down the National Mall?"

"I want you to set up posts at major intersections and get a good look at anyone and everyone walking, driving, or having a beer south of Madison Drive down to the Potomac."

"I need to call this in."

"Do what you need to, but every second you delay increases the chances that a known terrorist walks free in this city."

The word "terrorist" always has the desired psychological impact. The lieutenant gets on his radio as Murphy eyes the SWAT vehicle coming down the access road. This area will be swarming with officers, federal agents, and reporters with cameras in a matter of minutes. It will make for a long night, but it should buy Tierra and Victoria the time they need to make the magic happen. At least, Murphy hopes so.

CHAPTER SEVENTY-ONE

BRIAN COOPER

The Washington Monument
Washington, D.C.

More sirens scream in the distance as Brian walks along the path from the Lincoln Memorial to the stone obelisk rising in the middle of the National Mall. George Washington's military and political leadership were indispensable to the United States' founding. He drew raw troops from thirteen divergent colonies as commander of the Continental Army and turned them into a force that outlasted Britain's superior professional army. As the first president, his leadership set the standard for his successors.

The Washington Monument towers above the city that bears his name. It serves as a reminder of George Washington's greatness, even if Brian finds it dull and uninspiring compared to the majesty of the Lincoln and Jefferson Memorials. But as tour guides like to posit to tourists, the monument, like the man, stands in no one's shadow.

Brian won't stand in anyone's shadow, either. He never had aspirations for the presidency, so he hijacked it ahead of the coming global transformation. The end of World War II ushered in the Cold War, and that superpower rivalry gave birth to globalization. Now that the system is morphing into something new and unique, Brian wants to be positioned to shape the new world order alongside his overlords from Actyv Private Equity. He just has to finish this first, which is proving easier said than done.

A lone figure stands beside the monument staring at the White House gleaming under lights in the distance. He doesn't turn as Brian comes alongside him.

"Did you bring your doohickey?" Andrew asks.

"I never leave home without it," Brian relays, feeling in his pocket for the toy the NSA gave him to deter eavesdroppers.

"Good. Williams is failing all of us."

Brian sighs loudly. "Tell me you didn't drag me down here to whine about that."

"I didn't," Machiavelli says, shaking his head as more sirens screech in the distance. "It sounds like all hell is breaking loose tonight."

"Apparently. What do you want, Andrew?"

"Standish is up to something."

"You're not naïve enough to believe she would assent to our demands without a fight. You wanted the responsibility of being her chief of staff. It's your job to watch her. Conrad and DeAnna would contend that you're failing. Now, you're admitting it."

"I have control of her," Andrew says through clenched teeth. "I only said she was up to something."

"What do you need me for?"

"To handle Campos."

"Andrew, I'm not going another twelve rounds with you," Brian says evenly. He's not about to let Machiavelli provoke him into an admission of his own. "That's being taken care of. What else?"

"A cease-fire between us."

"You have a funny way of asking for one."

"None of this was possible without the risks we took. DeAnna crafted the media narrative, and Conrad kept the FBI off our backs, but we made this happen. *We* did. I will be the chief of staff, but I need you around to watch my back."

"Because you don't trust the others?"

Andrew scoffs. "Do you? We've had the most to lose throughout this. It's always been our asses on the line. You can't effectively control Standish without me, and I can't effectively do it without you. That's worth something."

Brian inhales deeply before letting the air slip from his lungs. Andrew is right. It is worth something. Without someone inside, he won't have the control over Standish he needs. She will be free to devise plans to slip out of his yoke. For better or worse, the man for the job is Andrew.

"Yes, it is. What's your plan?"

"I'm going to force her to accept the VP-elect's resignation. I don't trust Kerrigan…or her. She needs to know that resigning the presidency isn't a viable option to thwart our control. If anything, it will enhance it."

Brian has never given that tactic good odds. Alicia Standish eyed the Oval Office like a fat kid ogling a dessert tray. After winning the election, he could never devise a scenario that she would be willing to give power to her running mate. First, she's too much of a narcissist. Second, her relationship with Everett Kerrigan is professional, not friendly. He was brought in to help her win the upper Midwest and for no other reason.

"Okay. That's always been your call."

"Will you be choosing the replacement?"

"There are three chosen candidates. One is head and shoulders above the rest, with the other two as backups. I can get the ball moving. When is this happening?"

"As soon as you can arrange the leak of the information I am framing him with. Once that hits the media cycle, Standish will issue a public statement and have a press conference to announce that she accepts his letter of resignation for the good of the country."

"I'll make it happen. Anything else?"

"Yeah, don't screw me on this," Andrew says, facing Brian for the first time.

"It wasn't my idea to dissolve our group. I could say the same thing."

Brian is not about to have this conversation. Working with Andrew may be a necessary evil, but that doesn't mean he needs to prolong the agony. Rasputin sets off back toward the Lincoln Memorial, his mind already racing ahead to plot what must be done to complete the frame. Andrew is still with the program, and that simplifies things. Despite the detour, everything is still going according to plan.

CHAPTER SEVENTY-TWO

VICTORIA LARSEN

Constitution Avenue
Washington, D.C.

Victoria follows the joggers as they cross the National Mall. She's close enough to look like part of the small group without being so close that they wonder what she's doing. Since listening to music is almost a requirement while running, she could have her earbuds in and converse with Daniel and Imani without anyone being the wiser.

Her fellow runners make a right turn in front of the Smithsonian Castle and follow the outermost gravel path toward the Lincoln Memorial. Victoria veers onto the grounds and heads to the dimly lit gardens in the rear. That's when she slows to a stroll and goes into lost tourist mode.

The castle is the Smithsonian's first and oldest building. It's also one of Victoria's favorites. The building is constructed of red sandstone in a combination of late Romanesque and early Gothic styles. It was originally cut off from downtown Washington, D.C. by a canal upon its completion. The city has changed a lot since then.

The gates to the Enid Haupt Garden are still open, and it's a nice shortcut to Independence Avenue. Victoria picks up her pace slightly. She walks past the horticultural beds toward the Museum of African Art and the gate that leads out of the grounds.

"Imani, are you close?"

"I'm rolling up now."

"I'll be on the sidewalk in thirty seconds."

"Freeze!" a voice commands as a flashlight clicks on and shines directly in her face.

Maybe longer, the agent thinks as she does as directed. Victoria doesn't shield her eyes from the light. It could be considered aggressive, and this guy could be jumpy, considering there was a shootout in front of the DOJ.

She recognizes the patrolman's utility belt and catches the light glint off a gold badge when he steps closer. Victoria curses Murphy under her breath. Of all the dumb luck – she escapes a shootout to get caught here.

"Damn, it is you. Victoria Larsen. I almost didn't recognize you with the red hair. You look like Black Widow."

Victoria clenches her jaw. The first thing she will do when this is over is color her hair blonde again.

"Domestic terrorist and wanted fugitive, at your service," she says with a slight bow.

The cop doesn't move. She thinks about going for her gun before he reaches for his radio, but it's tucked in the fanny pack. He's not about to let her dig through that. Even if she could pull it, what good is it? She's not about to shoot a cop. All she can do is hope Imani is in a position to somehow intervene.

"Are you alone?" he asks.

"It's been that way for a while, unfortunately."

He looks around the area to see if he can catch movement. There won't be any.

"I thought I heard you talking to somebody. You armed?"

Victoria nods down at the small pack on her hip. "Of course. I was just in a shootout with Special Agent Daniel Murphy and his partner on Constitution."

"I heard. Was anyone hurt?"

"No. I'm one of the good terrorists. Look, it's already been a long night, and the sun is barely down. You know who I am and what I'm accused of. Arrest me and get it over with."

Imani isn't talking. Hopefully, she got the message that there's a problem and is silent while crafting a rescue plan. She will need it if she doesn't want to ride out the rest of the fight against the cabal in a jail cell.

"Pssh," the officer says, holstering his weapon. "Not a chance."

It takes a lot to surprise Victoria. She's seen a lot of things in her life, but never once has she heard of a police officer confronting a terrorist, fugitive, and likely suspect in a shooting a quarter-mile away and then holstering his weapon. He should be holding her at gunpoint as he radios for a small army to take her into custody.

Instead, he stands there with his arms resting on the bulkiest parts of his utility belt. Victoria wants to ask if this is a joke. It has to be.

"What are you doing?"

"What does it look like? I'm pretending that I never saw you."

"Why?"

The man smiles. He looks up at the reddish walls of the castle that look more brown in the dim lighting.

"I love this job. I get to walk the National Mall every day and help visitors feel safe. My brother and I are third-generation law enforcement. I followed in my father's and grandfather's footsteps and joined the Metro P.D. My brother took a different route and went to Quantico. He's in the FBI."

It's a partial explanation for his actions but not a complete one. Plenty of FBI agents thought she was a maverick who flouted the rules and deserved to be kicked out of the Bureau before all this happened. Now, most of them think she's a terrorist who belongs behind bars.

"Here in D.C.?"

The officer shakes his head. "Philadelphia field office's SWAT team."

The reality of what that statement means settles in and causes her to shiver. Of all the gin joints in all the towns in all the world, she runs into the brother of a man storming the lumber mill. It explains his nonchalant reaction to catching her.

"He was on the Keystone Militia raid up in Liberty."

"I spent an hour at Thanksgiving listening to him explain how you saved his team's collective asses that night. The lights, the mill starting, the premature detonation of the anti-personnel mines…he's convinced you were responsible for that. Is it true?"

Victoria nods. "I saw the map in Ian Drucker's bunker and knew they were walking into an ambush. I did what I could do to throw a wrench in the militia's defense plan before anyone got hurt or killed."

"It worked," the officer admits. "He knew those bastards were lying. My brother swore repeatedly that it was you and you were being railroaded by the Bureau for some reason. I'm glad to hear he was right. He'd disown me if I arrested you now, so get out of here before any of my colleagues show up."

Victoria nods, not wanting any further banter to cause the officer to change his mind. She hurries in the direction of the gate leading to Independence Avenue.

"Agent Larsen?" She stops and turns. "Thank you."

"For what?"

"It's what my brother would want me to tell you. When we exchange presents on Christmas morning, my gift to him is getting to relay his and his family's gratitude for saving his life."

"What's your name?"

"Sergeant Chris Burns. My brother is Special Agent Kyle Burns."

"You and your brother stay safe. And check the Internet tomorrow night. You'll find out precisely why they're after me."

"Can't wait," he says with a smile.

Victoria heads out the gate, knowing that if she were a cat, she would have just burned another of her nine lives. She can't have that many left.

Imani is waiting as Victoria reaches the sidewalk on Independence Avenue. She climbs into the vehicle, and the young agent slams the car into drive and heads down the Avenue.

"You were breaking up a little on the line. Who were you talking to?"

"Metro P.D.," Victoria deadpans.

"What?"

"It's okay. He's a big fan. Do you happen to know Kyle Burns?"

Imani's head snaps to face her. "Absolutely. Really good guy. Why?"

"That was his brother."

"I'm taking you to Vegas when this is over," Imani says with a smile as she guides the vehicle off the curb. "Maybe your luck will rub off on me."

Victoria settles in and looks out the window. She's going to owe her guardian angel a case of scotch. This plan was reckless, but Murphy was right – it will have the desired effect. He will remain in charge of the manhunt, and media and law enforcement eyes should stay off Tierra for as long as this shootout is a story. There are twenty-four hours to go, and the clock is ticking. One way or another, she can't wait for this journey to end.

CHAPTER SEVENTY-THREE

PRESIDENT-ELECT ALICIA STANDISH

Standish's Hay-Adams Hotel Suite
Washington, D.C.

The lead agent tells Alicia that her guest is on the way up. The president-elect wonders if her detail is curious about the recent cloak-and-dagger happenings at the Hay-Adams. Probably not. These agents have been in the service for a while and have probably seen a little of everything.

The doors swing open, and Lisa Ehler is escorted in by a second Secret Service agent. She nods, and the pair of agents leaves, closing the door behind them. Lisa watches them before turning back to face her former friend.

"Hello, Lisa. Thank you for coming."

"I didn't want to, but—" The attorney general stops short when the governor and Republican presidential candidate rises from the sofa. "Okay, I…Governor Bradford?"

"Surprise," Colin sings out.

Lisa begins looking around the suite and then up at the ceiling. Alicia tracks her eyes around the room and crinkles her brow, wondering if the attorney general is searching for hidden video equipment like this is a bad *Candid Camera* episode.

"What are you looking for?"

"The Four Horsemen of the Apocalypse. The end times must be near. After that election, you are the last two people I expected to see occupying the same room."

"With good reason," Colin says, gesturing toward the adjacent sofa. "You're going to want to sit down for this next part."

"So, Campos was telling the truth?" Lisa asks as she obliges. Alicia joins the pair in the sitting area.

"Unfortunately. Tierra showed you the evidence?" Alicia asks.

"She handed it to me on a thumb drive. I only got through a quarter of it before I shut down the computer in disgust. It was enough. I just wasn't sure if it was true or something Campos manufactured."

"It's all true. Remember when I told you in Cambridge that you were being replaced because I wanted to go in a different direction? I was lying. I've been under the control of Brian Cooper, Andrew Li, Conrad Williams, and DeAnna Van Herten. They have been forcing me to select certain cabinet positions. Williams wanted yours."

"It's a coup, Madam Attorney General," the governor clarifies. "And it's real."

"This is insane," Lisa gasps, leaning deeper into her chair.

"If it makes you feel any better," Colin interjects, "I had the same reaction when the president-elect informed me."

"Does the president know?"

Alicia shakes her head. "Not yet. This is the part you don't know. *TNT*, *Capitol Beat*, *Let's Go Swimming*, *Radio Free America*, and Alétheia are doing a joint podcast tonight. They are putting together a broadcast to spell this out for the American people. He'll find out then."

"No, no, no. I can't keep this from the president. He will fire me if I let him get blindsided by a potential coup in this country. You would expect the same notice."

She's right. The president of the United States makes dozens of critical decisions every day. The chief executive needs timely, accurate information to do the job effectively. The federal government is structured to provide data to support those conclusions. Surprises are the mortal enemy of rational planning and coherent decision-making.

"Then tell him, but it has to be right before they go live. We don't know who else Cooper could have sway over. They will move mountains to find a way to shut that broadcast down. That can't be permitted to happen."

"It's not inconceivable that Cooper's reach extends into the White House. He ran my campaign and had Andrew Li installed to run the other. He's an infiltration expert capable of leveraging people from the inside."

"Alicia—"

"This is the way it has to be, Lisa. I took a chance by having Moira reach out to you. Tierra took a bigger one handing you a copy of the evidence. We're trusting you with this information."

She cocks her head. "Why?"

The president-elect glances at the governor before leaning forward. "Because we need your help. Victoria Larsen is planning on taking this information to the FBI."

"What? She's a fugitive that we declared a domestic terrorist. Special Agent Murphy will arrest her the moment she shows her face."

Colin smirks. "Actually, Agent Murphy has been working with Larsen for a couple of weeks now."

"What?" Lisa asks, her head jerking over to the governor. "How? Why?"

"He was shown the same information you were and had a change of heart."

Lisa lets out a nervous chuckle and massages her temples. That has to be a first for the Bureau. In the extensive litany of investigations and manhunts, it would be a challenge to recall a single one where an agent was working with the subject being hunted.

"The world's gone mad. Krekstein will never go along with this."

"He will if you intervene," Colin notes.

"Lisa, you are still the AG. You run the Department of Justice, and the Bureau works for you. Williams may have coopted your authority, but it's your show. You can get a warrant and have the FBI take down this cabal. Even a fraction of the information we showed you is enough grounds."

The AG runs her hand over her hair. "You know, I've seen a lot of things in politics in my time here in Washington. Crazy things. This tops them all."

Colin chuckles. "We couldn't agree more."

"Lisa, the country is going to erupt when this goes public," the president-elect declares. "We need to take the cabal down as soon as it does. They can't be roaming freely around the countryside once America hears this. This coup must be quashed, and its ringleaders neutralized to instill some confidence in the people."

"What will the two of you be doing when this broadcast happens?"

"We have something special planned."

"Okay. Walk me through everything you know. If I'm going to partake in this insanity by going to a judge, I might as well try to sound more informed than crazy when I do."

CHAPTER SEVENTY-FOUR

SSA DANIEL MURPHY

Martin Luther King, Jr. Memorial
Washington, D.C.

Located in West Potomac Park at 1964 Independence Avenue, S.W., referencing the year the Civil Rights Act of 1964 became law, the Martin Luther King, Jr. Memorial honors the Baptist minister and his social activist legacy in the struggle for freedom, equality, and justice. It's the first to honor an African American on the National Mall and is a serene place to contemplate his non-violent philosophy.

A lot of thought went into making each part of the memorial significant and symbolic. A Stone of Hope surges forward from the looming Mountain of Despair to serve as the memorial's focal point. There are countless quotes etched into the walls, and this one references a line in one of King's speeches: "With this faith, we will be able to hew out of the mountain of despair a stone of hope." There, the likeness of Dr. King captures him in a moment of determined and resolute thought.

Daniel has always loved the monuments on the National Mall, and this one honoring MLK, Jr. is a long-overdue honor. He never thought he would be holding a meeting with the director of the FBI here. That's what offices are for, and the head of the FBI rarely has meet-and-greets with field agents.

"Will he show?" DeAndre asks, admiring the beauty of the place in the waning minutes of sunlight.

"He'll be here."

"Great. Why does this feel like the end of my brilliant career?"

Daniel grins. "Doing the right thing often feels that way. Just ask Victoria."

DeAndre scowls and looks like he's about to reply when Director Krekstein strides through the entrance in the Mountain of Despair and approaches them. He looks annoyed and in a hurry. Daniel straightens. If the director thinks he's in a bad mood now, wait a few minutes.

"I have an office, you know," Krekstein barks.

"I'm aware, sir."

"Then you've taken leave of your senses. Why are you here meeting with me when you should be scouring this city for Victoria Larsen? You had her in your sights and let her slip through your fingers. I am still waiting to hear how she managed to escape a locked museum that had every exit covered three minutes after she entered. I'll chalk that up to gross incompetence, but I'm betting she's still lying low in the city. She's probably not far from here."

"You have no idea how right you are, sir."

Murphy nods at DeAndre, who whistles like he's signaling some ranch hands to supper. Victoria and Imani appear from behind the wooded island to the northeast. Krekstein's eyes grow wide when he sees her walking straight at him.

"What the hell is this? Why aren't you arresting her?"

"Because he's seen the evidence behind what I'm about to tell you, Director," Victoria says as she walks. "You're being manipulated by a cabal that has seized the presidency of the United States."

Daniel smirks. The woman is as subtle as a chainsaw.

"That's ludicrous! Alicia Standish…arrest her, Special Agent Murphy! That's an order!"

"The president-elect isn't a member of the conspiracy, Director. She's the victim of it. Give me a chance to explain."

"Wait…the shootout…you staged it!"

"Yes, we did," Murphy admits, surprised that Krekstein quickly connected the dots.

"You…you're a traitor who will be drummed out of the Bureau. And I'm not giving you anything other than a one-way ticket to the deepest hole I can throw you in, Larsen," the director says, pointing at her. "You're a terrorist, an affront to the Bureau, and a disgrace to this country!"

"Do you really think that, or are you repeating Conrad Williams's words?"

Victoria thinks she knows the answers to that. None of the evidence she found, nor what Tierra retrieved from Isiah, implicates the FBI director in the cabal. He's likely a useful idiot to Williams, who put himself into a position to leverage when needed. The same can be said for Vice Admiral Davis Mullin of the NSA. It might not save either of their careers when this is over, but at least they'll avoid prison.

"Are you saying I'm not capable of independent thought?" Krekstein asks, his hands balling into fists like he's ready to knock Victoria down and drag her to prison.

"No, but you're basing your conclusion on incomplete evidence and what the deputy attorney general wants you to believe. Unless Murphy is wrong and you are working with him to usurp executive power."

"You've all gone mad. There is a federal warrant for your arrest. I am going to ensure that warrant is executed. And you three," the director says, pointing at Murphy, Bangura, and Wright. "You are going to be suspended pending an investigation."

"Yeah, none of that is going to happen," Victoria says.

Krekstein looks like he's having a stroke. "I'm not about to stand here and listen to this. If you're here to shoot me, Larsen, do it. But I am *not* going to throw in with a terrorist. I work for Conrad Williams, and I—"

"Actually, Michael, you work for me," a voice announces behind the director.

He turns to see Attorney General Lisa Ehler standing at the Mountain of Despair with her arms crossed.

CHAPTER SEVENTY-FIVE

TIERRA CAMPOS

Wilson Newman's House
Falls Church, Virginia

Falls Church is about to become the new epicenter of American alternative media. It would be easy to dismiss that as irrelevant. After all, the public has dismissed the impact of podcasts and news videos for almost a decade. The mainstream media gets to set the narrative. DeAnna Van Herten believes she's the arbiter of what's newsworthy and what isn't. She's about to find out how wrong she is.

The combined viewership of *Capitol Beat*, TNT, *Let's Go Swimming*, RFA, and Alétheia videos is astounding. It more than triples the ratings of the best primetime cable news channel show. I expect that this broadcast will set records. At least, I hope it does.

This isn't going to be done at Wilson's dining room table. The team has made multiple trips to big box hardware stores for lumber, paint, and accent lighting to convert Wilson's basement into a studio. Alétheia handled most of the audio-visual components and lighting since our office is still locked, courtesy of the FBI. It's impressive how fast this is coming together.

Every room on the main level has a purpose in planning for tonight's broadcast. Sheets of printer paper labeled with a Sharpie and taped to the door jambs indicate the function of each. We have video editing, copywriting, and production planning. The broadcast will be divided into segments called blocks, and coordinating graphics, videos, and lead-ins is a dance with many partners. It's dynamic and stressful, yet everyone here is having the time of their lives.

Everyone except me. I have no role here outside of trying to be helpful. Unfortunately, I find myself just getting in the way. Brian, Olivia, and the staff from Alétheia have the technical aspects of the podcast covered. Oliver is reviewing the flow of the broadcast with Mi Sun and Austin. Logan is fact-checking, and Tyler is busy overseeing set construction with Jerome, who is surprisingly a good carpenter.

Naomi is building the social media setup in the far corner, with some assistance from repurposed *Front Burner* staff who have only a loose understanding of what we're presenting. There is less for me to do down here than upstairs, so I decide it's time to make for the stairs and head outside for a walk to clear my head. I don't make it halfway across his finished basement when the silver-haired owner of Chateau Newman appears in the doorway.

"My housekeeper is going to make voodoo dolls of all of you when she sees this mess," Wilson says from the doorway.

"Wilson! What do you think you're doing?" I ask, storming over. "You should be in the hospital!"

"Oh, Tierra, if you think I'm missing this, you hit your head on something."

"Wilson—"

"No arguments. I'm not skipping the most important broadcast I'll ever make. And it's my house."

I made my point, so I reach up and give my mentor a hug. "I'm glad you're here."

"Thank God! I didn't really want the responsibility of doing this myself," Oliver says, coming down the stairs. "I heard you returned to the castle, Wilson. It's good to see you up and about."

"Thank you. It was just a minor cardiac event."

I scoff.

"Since you're back, do you want to take over the anchor desk?" Oliver asks, cocking a thumb over his shoulder. "I can help fill in, but this might be better coming from—"

"No," Wilson declares emphatically. "We should do this together. Me and you, side-by-side."

"Are you serious?"

It wasn't the bemoaning question asked to a dentist when you're told you need a root canal. Instead, Oliver's buoyant reaction was akin to the response when you won an all-expense paid trip to Bora Bora for a month. He looks like a kid on Christmas morning.

"Absolutely. There's plenty of room on that backdrop for both the *Capitol Beat* and *TNT* logos. We are about to do something epic. So, let's be epic. Besides, Mi Sun knows our styles and can help make this a podcast for the ages."

Mi Sun rubs her hands together and grins ear-to-ear. It looks like she's getting her wish. She loves working with Oliver and Wilson for different reasons. Now she gets to team up with both of them.

Tyler walks over, removing paint from his hands with a rag as he joins the gaggle at the bottom of the stairs.

"I love what you guys have done with the place, Ty."

"We'll clean it up, Wilson. I promise."

"Nah. I like it this way. This house has never felt more…alive. All right, everybody. We have a show to put together. Let's get to it."

Austin sidles up next to me. He wasn't here for the attack on me and the arrest, and he still feels guilty about his absence. It's not his fault – he had an important job and wasn't even on this side of the country when it happened. That isn't stopping him from running a low profile around me.

"I never expected to see those two have a conversation, much less plan to work together."

"I think people would universally agree."

"It ought to drive even more numbers. People will tune in to see them reciting the U.S. tax code, much less pulling back the covers on a national conspiracy."

It's true. Wilson Newman and Oliver Jahn are journalism's version of *The Odd Couple*. Their styles are different, although ironically, each often strives to be more like the other. Mi Sun had Wilson injecting humor into *Capitol Beat* before the shutdown, and Oliver's broadcasts became more solemn and serious.

"I'm starting to think we live in the matrix. It's good to have you back here. Is everything set with Tom and Jo?"

"Moira worked her magic. They're enthusiastically on board. Dial Pirate has already patched into *Let's Go Swimming* and *Radio Free America*. They will simulcast the livestream until we throw the broadcast over to Tom. He's giddy about being a part of this now."

"That's a relief."

"RFA is lining up guests for interviews to discuss the fallout. The good ones will be packaged into videos and released on social media, YouTube, Rumble, and others to amplify the message. Alétheia is helping with our video packages using information Logan is feeding them. This is really coming together."

"That's good because I feel useless."

"Why don't you join the broadcast?"

"Too many chefs in the kitchen. Wilson and Oliver have it covered."

It's a weak argument. This has been my story from the beginning, and both men would gladly step aside to let me break the news to the American people. Only, I don't want to. Not this time.

"Well, you've done enough. It's time for the rest of us to pick up the ball and run with it. Just kick back and enjoy the moment."

Austin rubs the top of my arm before moving back to work with the gang from Alétheia. Kick back. It's good advice, but I'm not sure I can. There is so much riding on this that sitting on the sidelines makes me feel like I'm letting everyone down.

There is one thing I can do, but nobody will like it. That means I can't ask for help getting the information I need. With nothing but time until the show starts, I grab my laptop and try to find a quiet part of the house. Everyone has their role, and I have one task left that deserves to be handled personally.

CHAPTER SEVENTY-SIX

BRIAN COOPER

Cooper Residence
Bethesda, Maryland

Brian leans back in his chair in the study and rubs his eyes. They're red and bleary from staring at the screen for the past couple of hours. He has always been intuitive, requiring research to confirm his feelings before turning them into actions. That's what he's facing now.

He isn't much of a *Star Wars* fan, especially when it comes to the newest movies. It's a personal preference. The original trilogy was amazing, despite space operas not being his chosen genre. What he loved about the concept was that the Jedi could feel when things were wrong. He didn't care much for the reasons behind the ability, only that he could relate to the feeling.

Obi-Wan Kenobi sensed the destruction of Alderaan and commented, "I felt a great disturbance in the Force, as if millions of voices suddenly cried out in terror and were suddenly silenced." Brian hasn't sensed terror, but he's noticed the sudden silence. It's almost deafening for those who pay attention.

Podcasters are shameless self-promoters. It comes with gaining the subscribers and viewers a channel needs to thrive in the algorithm. Creators will use any opportunity to shill for sponsors or plead for people to follow them. Most use short promotional videos and social media posts to remind people about their upcoming shows.

The die-hards will always tune in for their fix, but special events are constantly plugged to draw as many eyes as possible. Even on slow news days, marketing efforts are relentless. This is anything but a slow news day, and that's the problem.

Stalwarts like Tom Swim and *Radio Free America* have been uncharacteristically silent. Oliver Jahn has also taken an unexpected leave of absence from VHN. None of that should be concerning. None of those people work together. But they have never all gone silent simultaneously, and that's a red flag.

Worse, Victoria Larsen is in Washington. The sirens he heard while walking up the National Mall were for her. She was nearly caught, but *nearly* isn't good enough. She should have been eliminated months ago. The rogue agent has now made her way home, and her proximity is alarming. The president-elect is here. All four members of Cooper's cabal are within a fifteen-minute drive. Worst of all, Tierra Campos is still in town despite his warning.

The intrepid journalist should have taken his advice and gotten out while she could. That means she either didn't take his threat seriously or is up to something. It could involve *Let's Go Swimming* and *RFA*, but that would be a stretch. Still, his gut is telling him that something is wrong. He listens to that. Larsen has multiple targets she can set her sights on. So does Campos.

Williams, Li, and Van Herten being at each other's throats coincided with an uptick in media reports about them. Is that a coincidence? Oliver Jahn was involved. *RFA* and Tom Swim were in on it, and even Alétheia released videos on the subject. Despite dismissing it, Brian thought it felt like a coordinated effort at the time. The improbable now feels plausible or even likely.

Brian rubs his chin. His original assumption that the other players tried to one-up each other for leverage was logical. Now that they have nearly reached their goal, the person with the most influence will be best suited to shape national events. The easiest way to gain influence is to reduce other people's ability to wield theirs. Now, he's convinced there is more to it.

He stretches his arms and cracks his knuckles, then returns his hand to the mouse and opens his email. He composes a quick message to one of his few contacts for this address:

Possible compromise that threatens objective. Team needed for remediation.

Satisfied that the email will get the required attention, he clicks send. Brian doesn't expect immediate help but should expect something. As was said, investments are meant to be protected. That means it's time for him to do the same. He needs to say goodbye to his leverage. He's done everything he could do to keep her alive. He warned her to leave town and escape with her life. It's a shame that he was ignored.

She's been doxed, survived a riot, was publicly humiliated, fired several times, financially ruined, and cheated certain death at the hands of a gunman in her high school and Russian commandos at an apartment. It was a nice run, but it's over. Fate always intervenes, and now it has determined that Tierra Campos must die.

CHAPTER SEVENTY-SEVEN

VICTORIA LARSEN

Martin Luther King, Jr. Memorial
Washington, D.C.

Krekstein turns his back to Victoria to face the head of the Justice Department. It's too bad. The agent would love to see the look on his face. The attorney general walks over to them, nodding at the four agents before turning her attention to her FBI director.

"Director, it turns out that the man you're taking orders from is the terrorist. The deputy attorney general is involved in what can only be called a coup."

"That's not...not possible," Krekstein stammers.

"Unfortunately, it's not only possible – it's a fact. There isn't a grand jury in the country that wouldn't indict Williams with a fraction of the evidence I've seen. He aligned himself with Brian Cooper, Andrew Li, and DeAnna Van Herten to extort the future president of the United States. They won't succeed only because of these four agents...and Tierra Campos."

"That's absurd! I...I need to see that evidence."

"Collect yourself, Director. You don't *need* to see anything. I'm still the attorney general of the United States of America, and I'm instructing you to act on this."

Ehler dips into her coat pocket and produces a tri-folded piece of paper. She hands it to her subordinate and waits patiently while he scans it.

"An arrest warrant for Conrad Williams?"

"Signed by a federal judge an hour ago. I have three similar warrants for the other co-conspirators. They will all be executed in the next hour, and we are going to the DOJ to handle Williams personally. You're going to join us."

"Why? We have teams that—"

"Because I'm not entirely convinced you aren't involved, Michael."

The director recoils like he just stumbled upon a rattlesnake. Before coming here, Victoria was laying three-to-one odds that Michael Krekstein was involved in this. He was too willing to do Robespierre's bidding.

Now, she's not so sure. His reaction to the AG's accusation can't be faked. It was the shock only an innocent man could muster. Victoria steals a glance at Murphy, who raises his eyebrows. He noticed it, too.

"What?"

"I finally had the chance to review the evidence against Agent Larsen. To call it speculative would be generous. A stacked court in some backwater banana republic would have a hard time being convinced. Did you ever question what Conrad Williams was telling you, Director? Or did you not care?"

"The evidence was sound!" Krekstein argues.

Ehler shakes her head. "It was only presented to look that way. A careful study of the evidence by a competent law enforcement professional would have raised serious red flags. You missed all of them, assuming you bothered looking at all. That's either dereliction of duty, sheer stupidity, or something more nefarious. By the end of the night, we'll find out which."

"She's a fugitive, ma'am," the FBI director screeches, pointing at his agent.

"Not anymore. I had the judge rescind the warrant on Victoria Larsen. She's on our team, Michael. The question is, are you?"

That's the second shot the AG fired across his bow. Krekstein glares at Daniel and DeAndre, likely wondering why his two agents didn't give him a heads-up about this ambush. The short answer is he never would have believed it. This conversation would be going differently had his boss not materialized at the entrance to the memorial to set him straight.

"You were played, Director, the same as I was. It took Victoria ambushing me in my hotel room and showing me the evidence to see that."

"I had nothing to do with whatever Conrad Williams was into. I only followed his instructions, assuming they were coming from you."

Politics sucks. The FBI director isn't a law enforcement position as much as a political appointment. Most served as attorneys in civilian law firms or as federal and state prosecutors. Precious few of them rose through the ranks and earned the title. The director needs to know how to play the political game to survive. Agents just want to lock bad guys up.

"For your sake, Director Krekstein, I hope that's true. I have vehicles waiting for us at the entrance. Let's go to the office and arrest Conrad Williams."

The group heads back up the path toward Independence Avenue. Victoria hangs back with Ehler. "Thank you for coming, Madam Attorney General. Moira Kinsella said you would be coming, but I wasn't sure you'd make it."

"Victoria, after everything you've been through, you can call me Lisa now and forever. We'll have a long conversation about this when it's over, but we have work to do. This coup is going to end, but that isn't good enough. I want to see every member of this cabal in leg irons on the news tomorrow. That is what America will demand, and by God, we're going to deliver it."

CHAPTER SEVENTY-EIGHT

TIERRA CAMPOS

Wilson Newman's Makeshift Podcast Studio
Falls Church, Virginia

I look around the rooms at the determined faces. It's showtime. I wasn't alive in 1969 when Apollo 11 left Earth atop a Saturn V rocket. The men at Kennedy Space Center and Mission Control in Houston must have looked the same as my colleagues. They are filled with steely resolve, but there is an underlying nervousness and anxiety. All the plans and preparations come down to this.

A thousand things could still go wrong. An FBI team could storm in and pull the plug. We could lose electrical power or our Internet connection. Despite all the contingency plans, the things we haven't considered scare me the most.

I move to the corner and stare at the monitors. *Capitol Beat* and *TNT* have countdowns on the sites. *Let's Go Swimming* has a special banner announcing something newsworthy that subscribers will want to tune in to. The combined count of those waiting is already approaching a million viewers. Once this rocket leaves the pad, that number will soar into the stratosphere.

The anchor desk is the only spot in the house with no apparent anxiety. Wilson Newman has done this thousands of times before. Oliver Jahn is a rookie by comparison, but he is most comfortable with a camera pointed at him. Old school and new school are meeting, and everyone can't wait. We have all worked so hard for this moment.

"Okay, heads-up, everyone," Mi Sun says when the timer reaches ten seconds. She gives the count beginning at five and goes silent at three, just like on television. The studio lights come up, and the background dims. Suddenly, this no longer looks like Wilson's basement.

A clever mash-up of the old *TNT* and *Capitol Beat* openings plays. Alétheia had to have put that together. I could park myself in front of Garage Band or Adobe Premiere Pro for a month and not come up with something half that slick.

"It is Tuesday, November 28th, I am Wilson Newman, and this isn't only *Capitol Beat*," the anchor says, gesturing to his counterpart. "I have a very special guest beside me tonight."

"One that almost any person watching this broadcast would never expect you to be sitting next to," Oliver Jahn interjects. "I'm the co-host who will help you drink from the fountain of information we are about to provide, which will not only prove to be *Tomorrow's News Today*, but will likely dominate headlines for the next month."

I was wondering how they were going to handle the intro. Both men have unique introductions to their shows that are highly recognizable. That they worked it out seamlessly and without ego is a testament to the criticality of nailing tonight's broadcast.

"We are joined tonight by Tom Swim of *Let's Go Swimming*, *Radio Free America*, and Alétheia to bring you the most shocking scandal in American history."

"For once, that isn't hyperbole coming from Oliver," Wilson says, folding his hands on the desk. "It's not sensationalism or clickbait. What we are about to tell you this evening is verifiable truth. It's not a conspiracy that fills information voids with made-up nonsense. We have evidence and testimonials. We will even have a couple of special guests join us to verify this information."

"I have teamed up with Wilson and our partners because what we are about to tell you isn't partisan. It isn't ideological. It is about an actual threat to our Republic. So, what is this about?"

"Ladies and gentlemen, the presidency of the United States is on the verge of being hijacked," Wilson states in a grave tone. "That sounds crazy, but everything that has happened since the New Hampshire Democratic Primary is an orchestrated extortion attempt against President-Elect Alicia Standish. A small group of powerful people has used the divide in this country to manufacture an electoral crisis by interfering with an election. The events in Pennsylvania are the culmination of those efforts."

"The code names of the conspirators are Machiavelli, Robespierre, Nietzsche, and Rasputin," Oliver continues, as I see Mi Sun ready the first of the graphics packages. "Machiavelli was identified as Isiah Burgess during the *Capitol Beat* interview at Granite State University, but that was erroneous. We learned the conspirators' names through an investigation by Tierra Campos of *Front Burner* and wrongfully accused domestic terrorist Special Agent Victoria Larsen of the Federal Bureau of Investigation. Don't worry—we'll get to that part later.

"The conspirators are Andrew Li, Standish campaign manager and future White House chief of staff; Conrad Williams, current deputy attorney general and future attorney general of the United States; and DeAnna Van Herten, the billionaire mogul and head of VH Media. Yes, the owner of my network has been plotting to take control of our country."

The faces of the three people show up on the screen. There is a pause to let the viewers digest what they were just told. Then the camera focuses on Wilson.

"The ringleader is Brian Cooper, former chief of staff to Senator Standish, political consultant, and campaign manager for Colin Bradford, Governor of North Carolina and the Republican nominee for president."

I close my eyes as a wave of relief washes over me. It's out there. Millions have heard the names. I feel myself breathe for the first time since they started.

"We will start tonight with the executive summary – what happened and how we got here," Oliver says as the camera switches to show the two of them. "Before we walk you through this critical information, know that law enforcement has already been alerted and is acting on this information. This is not something we are presenting for the first time. The authorities are involved and will help bring the members of this coup to justice."

Wilson looks down for a moment before turning his attention to the camera. "That's a word I never thought I would be uttering when talking about this country. America has witnessed horrible incidents before, but this was a *actual* attempt to circumvent governmental authority in this country without any of us knowing."

"Through intimidation and threatening to release misinformation, Brian Cooper and his co-conspirators are forcing the president-elect to make decisions benefitting them, not the people of this great nation. How did it get this far? Let's start with the events immediately following the New Hampshire Primary."

Oliver sets the stage, and he and Wilson begin to methodically walk everyone through the search for Isiah Burgess's files. That's when some of the first evidence begins appearing on screen. There will always be doubters, but we have a plan for that. With the broadcast off the ground, the rest of this is old news.

The evidence will be sent in chunks to mainstream media outlets after it is presented here. Alétheia already produced videos to help walk audiences through the finer points of what's being presented. Everyone is still on guard for the unexpected, but there is a collective sigh of relief that the show is off to a good start.

"The hard part is over," Austin whispers in my ear after stopping beside me. "Oliver and Wilson have good chemistry, and the technology is cooperating. You should be elated, so why do you look like someone shot your dog?"

I don't expect anyone to understand, with the possible exception of Victoria. For the people here, presenting this information to the world is the culmination of their mission. It's more than that to me. It's personal.

"Austin, can you do me a favor? Have Josh call me in fifteen minutes."

"Call you? Where are you going?"

I smile weakly. "To get some air."

I don't like lying to him, but he isn't going to want to hear the truth, and I don't want anyone to try stopping me from what has to be done. I walk upstairs, grab Wilson's keys, and climb into his car for the longest drive of my life.

CHAPTER SEVENTY-NINE

PRESIDENT-ELECT ALICIA STANDISH

Standish's Hay-Adams Hotel Suite
Washington, D.C.

It took three trips for the young man *Front Burner* sent over to bring the needed equipment to Alicia's suite. He introduced himself as Brian and immediately got to work. If he was remotely curious about why Alicia and Colin were occupying the same room, he didn't show it. He was either briefed ahead of time or has a remarkable lack of curiosity.

He also doesn't seem intimidated by power. He made eye contact when he introduced himself. His handshake was firm, if not strong. There was no sputtering in his language nor fawning over meeting the future president of the United States. For all intents and purposes, he was completely indifferent to the powerful duo in this room. Alicia finds it almost refreshing.

"I bet you never thought you'd find yourself doing this," the governor observes as he watches Brian work.

A smile creases his lips as he fine-tunes the camera angle. "That's a very safe assumption, sir."

"I hope sneaking you through the service entrance wasn't too off-putting," the president-elect says as she watches him connect cables.

"I've done far worse, ma'am."

"That sounds like a story."

"Not one I want to tell the government," Brian says with a smile as he adjusts the LED lighting kit he brought along. "Although that's the least of my transgressions."

"Do you work for *Front Burner?*"

"I'm a contractor of sorts."

"You're very good. What do you usually do?"

Brian stops and thinks about it for a moment. "Financial transactions. Recently, I've gotten into data management. You should be all set. Let's see if we can make a good connection."

Mi Sun comes on with a smile and a wave. He can hear Wilson and Oliver talking in the background.

"Hey, DP."

"How do I look?"

"Like you haven't seen the sun in ten years."

"Good. Then the color is perfect. Madam President-Elect…Governor…" Brian says, offering their chairs. "They're all yours, Mi Sun."

"Good evening, President-Elect Standish. Thank you for joining us. Same to you, Governor Bradford. My name is Ahn Mi Sun. I work for *Front Burner* and Oliver Jahn."

"Both of them?"

She grins. "It's complicated. You're both experts at being on television, so you won't need much of a refresher. Just remember to maintain eye contact with the camera. This isn't a speech or press briefing. There is only one camera angle on this podcast. If you look around, you'll appear shifty and untrustworthy."

"Good tip," the governor says.

"You'll both do fine. Brian is there in case any technical hiccups occur during the broadcast."

"There won't be any," he reassures. "The wi-fi here is solid."

"You're thirty seconds out. Stand by."

"We have already presented a lot of information this evening, and there is more to come," Wilson assures the audience. "But we aren't expecting you to take our word for it. What we're reporting is too serious for you to accept as true on faith alone. So, Oliver is right. We need someone who can corroborate this information."

"How many people are watching this, Brian?" the governor asks, turning his head to face Brian. He isn't used to doing podcasts.

Brian points at the screen. "Over two million and climbing fast, if you combine the numbers from Swim's show and *Radio Free America*. It's being simulcast, and they bring in a lot of viewers. The numbers will continue to climb as word spreads."

The governor and Alicia exchange a look. They could have only dreamed of this audience on the campaign trail. Politicians have no problem talking. The issue in politics is getting a captive audience to listen.

"Many of you are going to think what you are about to see is a deep fake. I assure you, it isn't. From the Hay-Adams Hotel in Washington, D.C., please welcome to *TNT* and *Capitol Beat* President-Elect Alicia Standish and Republican candidate for president from the State of North Carolina, Governor Colin Bradford. Thank you both for joining us this evening."

"Thank you for having us, Oliver," Alicia says.

"And thank you as well, Wilson," the governor adds.

"I'm not sure if you're aware, but we have presented a lot of information tonight. We understand that you have received a copy of all this evidence and had a chance to evaluate it. What are your thoughts, Madam President-Elect?"

"We've been watching," Alicia says, "and can tell you, without reservation, that everything you presented on your broadcast is one hundred percent accurate. Brian Cooper led a cabal that included my campaign manager, the deputy attorney general of the United States, and media mogul DeAnna Van Herten to seize the reins of government power for themselves."

"Governor, you ran against the president-elect and lost. It was a bitter fight that's still contested because of what happened in Pennsylvania. What did you think when you heard this news?"

"I was as shocked as I believe most Americans are tonight."

"I can imagine," Oliver says. "Only this is something I never would have believed. Instead of screaming about unfairness and trying to overturn the result, you are sitting with your opponent at the Hay-Adams."

"I am."

"Why? Explain it to our audience because they aren't going to understand that."

"What is happening transcends party politics. For as much as we make about the ideological divide between the left and right, we are all Americans. The future of our Republic is in jeopardy. The president-elect and I may have different political stances on issues, but we agree wholeheartedly on one thing – our nation comes first."

"If I may," Alicia chimes in. "Governor Bradford has shown incredible courage being here. He could have made this political. As my opponent in the last election, the governor could have seized this opportunity to deepen the divide. Instead, he chose to sit with me this evening, and I'm incredibly grateful for his support as we rise to meet the challenges that will ensue."

Colin nods graciously.

"Ma'am, we have discussed the cabal at length already. One of the questions all Americans will want to know is when you first learned about this."

Alicia takes a deep breath. "The cabal confronted me two days after the election, but that only confirmed what I was already told. Tierra Campos warned me at the Boston Convention Center minutes before I gave my victory speech."

"And you didn't tell anyone after either of those revelations?"

Alicia hangs her head for a moment before looking back at the camera.

"I don't think that was a reasonable expectation at the time. Who would have believed President-Elect Standish? The very premise of a coup in this country is unthinkable. I know I wouldn't have accepted such an outlandish accusation without proof. The people would have demanded it, and hearing none, things would have gotten political. To expose this cabal and its attempted coup, we needed the evidence that Tierra Campos and Victoria Larsen have worked so hard to provide."

Alicia stares at the governor. It was a gracious save from her Republican opponent. It's easy to be jaded in today's society, especially while working in this town. Republicans and Democrats are conditioned to hate each other as sworn enemies. The art of compromise vanished long ago. All that exists is winning or losing a generations-old blood feud over the soul of America.

But here he is, doing the opposite. Reaching out to him was an act of desperation but the right thing to do. If they can find common ground on this, maybe there are opportunities to do so in the future. If nothing else, this interview won't be as devastating as Alicia once thought.

CHAPTER EIGHTY

SSA DANIEL MURPHY

U.S. Department of Justice
Washington, D.C.

Victoria stares out the window at the looming façade. Before the construction of this building, the U.S. Department of Justice occupied a succession of temporary spaces in governmental and private office buildings. With its limestone exterior, red-tile roof, and classically inspired colonnades, this structure became the department's permanent home in 1935. It contains over one million square feet of space on the prominent trapezoidal lot bounded by Constitution and Pennsylvania Avenues and Ninth and Tenth Streets.

The attorney general's driver is waved through the security checkpoint and parks in the central courtyard. Like most Federal Triangle buildings, the DOJ was designed with interior courtyards to provide ventilation and natural light. The vehicular access allows the easy reception of VIPs and high-ranking government officials inside a secure perimeter.

Ehler exits and stares at her building while everyone departs their vehicles.

"How do you want to play this, ma'am?" Murphy asks.

"I'm going to walk up there and jam my authority down Williams's throat."

"That sounds like a good plan, but what about me? The moment I walk in there, ten guys will tackle me."

"The warrant was rescinded, Victoria."

"Yes, ma'am," Murphy interjects, "but with due respect, this is the federal government. We have to assume not everyone got the memo on such short notice."

"Agent Larsen will be walking in with the attorney general and the director of the FBI. Nobody will tackle her. Come on."

It doesn't quite play out that easily. Victoria has the most recognizable face in the FBI, and not only because of her beauty. The attorney general manages to get the security detail at the door to stand down, instructing them to call their superiors to validate that there is no longer a federal warrant for Larsen.

DeAndre remains behind to ensure compliance and greet the FBI tactical team that's ten minutes out. The director also instructs him to contact the CIMC to inform all FBI agents to stand down in arresting Victoria Larsen.

With that business handled, the five of them ride the elevator up and navigate the corridors to Conrad's office. They file in, finding him glued to the podcast playing on his computer. He only stands when he sees his boss enter. His demeanor changes when Victoria walks in behind Murphy. That has to be a development he didn't expect.

"What the hell is this?"

"You've been a bad boy, Conrad," Lisa says, wagging her finger.

"And you're consorting with a known terrorist."

"Not according to a federal judge, I'm not. I am in the presence of one, though."

The AG pulls out the arrest warrant and slaps it on his desk. He doesn't bother to look at it. He already knows what it says.

"What fresh excuse do you have now, Robespierre?" Lisa asks, folding her arms.

The moniker doesn't faze her deputy. He remains calm and collected as he taps the mute button on the podcast. His eyes shift to the director.

"You should have picked your people better, Michael. You said you had this under control."

All eyes turn to the wide-eyed head of the FBI.

"Everything I did was on your instructions, Conrad. *Yours.* Don't try to assign blame to me. Had I known what you were up to, I would have arrested you myself."

Conrad laughs. "You're a politician, Krekstein. You couldn't handcuff your wife to a bedpost without first watching a 'how-to' video. I'm sure these fine agents want to believe you're just a useful idiot. I suppose that's why the president put you in charge of the FBI."

"Screw you, Williams," Michael mutters.

"And you…you just won't die," he says, pointing at Victoria.

The corner of her mouth curls. "Maybe you should have picked *your* people better."

Conrad smirks. "Touché. Are you going to read me my rights? I'm sure you've been dreaming about that."

"No," Ehler interjects. "We're going to question you first, and you're going to talk. No lawyer and no right to remain silent. You're familiar with the public safety exception to Miranda v. Arizona. If you're not, you're about to be."

"There is no public safety threat."

"You tried to hijack the presidency. You coerced the president-elect to get yourself named attorney general in the Standish Administration. One of your co-conspirators is in line to be the White House chief of staff. A first-year law student could argue that you're the country's number one threat to public safety."

"The game's over, Conrad," Murphy declares. "Your co-conspirators are all being arrested. The American public knows the truth. You're a traitor."

Williams doesn't lash out. He isn't sweating or acting nervous. Instead, his smug smile broadens when he folds his arms across his chest.

CHAPTER EIGHTY-ONE

VICTORIA LARSEN

Conrad Williams's U.S. Department of Justice Office
Washington, D.C.

There's an old adage that you should never corner a wounded animal. That's what Lisa has done. She could provide Conrad an off-ramp, like immunity for his testimony against his co-conspirators. But this is the AG's show, and Victoria doesn't think she's about to do that. For her, this is about betrayal, and betrayal is among the most personal of crimes.

"You guys think you have it all figured out, don't you? You have no idea how wrong you are."

"Why don't you enlighten us, Mr. Williams?" Lisa asks. "We just heard the president-elect of the United States and the man she ran against confirm every iota of the story. Are you seriously going to plead innocence and accuse the leaders of both major parties of lying?"

"Yes, because she is!" Williams exclaims, his brow beginning to form beads of sweat on it. "Alicia Standish knew everything they were up to. She had Brian Cooper installed with Bradford so she could win the election."

"That's funny," Murphy says. "Tavern Wench seems to say otherwise."

The deputy attorney general's eyes grow wide in surprise. There's no way he saw that coming even knowing Larson had the laptop.

"That's right, Conrad," Victoria says. "You made a huge mistake in trusting Ian Drucker. He was a contemptible human being, but he wasn't stupid. He kept notes on every conversation you had and every order you issued. That includes screenshots of your chat conversations in *Knights of the Crusade*. I think he was right in claiming that the game sucked. You were right, too – it was an effective way to communicate. Of course, you forgot there are four easy ways to screen capture in Microsoft Windows. Ducker used Alt + Printscreen, in case you are wondering."

"None of that will stand up in court," he smugly argues.

"On its own, you're probably right," the AG says. "Have you not been listening to Oliver Jahn or seen the evidence he and Wilson Newman are presenting?"

"Lies and fabrications."

"What do you think my testimony will be?"

Ehler's question gets Conrad's attention. He thrusts his chin out defiantly. "You can't prove anything. I am not Robespierre."

"Will your co-conspirators confirm that?" Victoria asks. "You must have a lot of faith that none of them will turn to save their own skin. I mean, this cabal of yours is rock-solid, right?"

"Let's stop wasting time and find out who cuts a deal with prosecutors first," Ehler says, gesturing at her former deputy. "Agent Larsen, will you do the honors?"

At no time in recorded American history has someone who rocketed to the top of the most wanted list ever legally slapped handcuffs on the man who was spearheading the manhunt. She and Daniel will add this to the list of things they laugh about someday. Right now, she's worried about impropriety. It shouldn't be her who does this, just in case it freaks the prosecutors out.

Williams eyes her hard. "I'll tell you what…let's not find out."

He slides some papers over and snatches the gun hiding under them. Murphy and Victoria spring into action as he brings his weapon to bear. The first shot is aimed in the direction of Lisa Ehler. Murphy lunges and tackles her to the ground as the round is fired.

The director stands like a statue, helpless to stop what comes next. William's next shot catches him square in the chest. Victoria is determined to not let there be a third trigger pull.

She pulls her weapon from its holster and squeezes the trigger three times in quick succession. The bullets all strike Conrad in the center of his chest, their force pushing him to the back wall. He slides down it and collapses to the ground.

Victoria rushes over and secures the weapon. She tucks it behind her back and squats for a better look at the deputy attorney general. There is no need to check for a pulse. His lifeless eyes are still open and staring at the ground.

"Clear!"

"That's good," Murphy says, on his hands and knees. "Because I could use some help over here once you call this in."

Victoria snatches the phone from Williams's desk and hits zero for the DOJ switchboard. "Shots fired. Deputy AG's office. We need an ambulance immediately."

"I can't believe that bastard shot me," Ehler moans. "How did he get a gun in here?"

"A conversation you'll have with security later, I'm sure," Murphy says, applying pressure to her shoulder. "Now stop moving. I don't want you to lose more blood than you already have."

Victoria moves around the desk to check on the FBI director. The bullet caught him in the head. She doesn't need to check for a pulse but does anyway. There isn't one. Krekstein dealt with the devil, and the devil cashed in.

"Krekstein's dead," she announces.

Four men barge in with their guns drawn. They fan out in the room and see Murphy tending to the AG and Victoria lamenting the death of the FBI director. They can also see Williams's corpse on the floor behind his desk.

"Easy, fellas," Victoria says, standing. "It's over."

CHAPTER EIGHTY-TWO

BRIAN COOPER

Cooper Residence
Bethesda, Maryland

Brian sets the bottle of wine down and settles into the high-backed leather executive chair. At least it will take them some time to find him here. He knew the game was up the moment he saw Wilson Newman sitting next to Oliver Jahn on a podcast. There is only one reason those two heavyweights would be in the same room: to break the news on an epic scale. Events only snowballed from there when Williams and Li made their panicked calls.

In the pantheon of busy news nights, this will rank somewhere between the Kennedy assassination and the 9/11 terror attacks. It only took about fifteen minutes for cable news broadcasts to pick up the information the joint *Capitol Beat-TNT* broadcast was announcing. From there, the networks broke into regular programming with special coverage.

That's only the mainstream media. Many Americans are watching events unfold live on their computers and mobile phones. The number of viewers on Oliver Jahn's podcast will break records. It goes up by triple digits every few seconds as word spreads nationwide.

Their podcast is being simulcast on two other sites – *Let's Go Swimming* with Tom Swim's almost two million subscribers and *Radio Free America*, with its loyal social media following. He can imagine the number of people watching is approaching three million and climbing. It will lead every news broadcast for the next few weeks.

The only thing left is waiting for the inevitable call from New York. He's surprised he hasn't gotten it already. The suspense is killing him, and he stares at the device, willing it to ring. Still nothing. Brian has many gifts, but being a psychic isn't one.

All he could do was anticipate. Moves and countermoves. That is the real meaning of life, at least his. And Brian was good at it. Nobody else could have gotten as far as he did. He had to adapt to circumstances on countless occasions. Like Murphy's Law, no part of this plan ever survived first contact with the enemy intact.

But that's what Brian thrives at. It was what made him a great political consultant. He could take any negative and turn it into a positive. If only his co-conspirators could have been on the same page. That's the tragedy in this. They stopped running when they saw the finish line.

Brian jumps when his phone finally rings. He answers the call and places the device to his ear.

"You're watching?"

"Most of America will be by the end of the night," Garrett says, this tone even and unflustered.

"We were so close."

"You were. You did good work for us, Brian. Excellent work, actually. It's a shame to see it end this way. The possibilities of what we could have done with Standish under our control were endless."

"Will this change your plans?"

"Alterations will be made, but contingencies have always existed. Your success was never guaranteed, so this doesn't materially change anything."

Brian's brow crinkles. "I'm not sure I understand. You lost control of the White House. How could that not change anything?"

"I don't expect you to understand. You are fighting a single battle. We are worried about the entire theater of operations. We got what we needed. It's not ideal, but we can make it work."

Brian has always wondered what the endgame is for the trio at Actyv Private Equity. It's far more than controlling the president of the United States, and that thought is disturbing. He has pieces of the puzzle but hasn't been able to put them together. He never wanted to jeopardize their business relationship by getting caught digging too deep.

"I hope you'll continue using my services in that war. I need a lift out of Washington first. Can you send your private jet to get me?"

There's a long silence on the other end. Brian needs to confirm that the connection is still active. Maybe Garrett is consulting with Roman and Qi. Maybe he's deciding for himself. Either way, it shouldn't require this much contemplation.

"I'm sorry, Brian. I don't think that would be in our best interests. We can't be linked to you after this."

The political consultant frowns. He wishes he were surprised, but he knew in his heart they wouldn't come to his rescue, despite promises to the contrary. He already has his final salvo loaded to get Garrett to change his mind.

"I will be pressed to talk by the feds. They will dangle all kinds of deals in front of me. What do you think will happen when I end up in custody?"

"A tragic accident."

Brian closes his eyes. "After everything, that's how it's going to be?"

"You sent an email asking for a team. One is being sent, just not for Tierra Campos. You knew this was a possibility when you embarked on your assignment. We made that very clear. You were close, as you stated. But close and successful are two different measures, and there are consequences to failure. That is a fact of life. Goodbye, Brian."

The call ends, and Brian sets the burner phone down. He was a patsy. A disposable asset, much like Marx, Vassyl, Ian, and the Keystone Militia were. He was used in the same manner. As infuriating as that is, the kicker is that he didn't see it sooner.

"Okay," he mumbles, moving windows around the dual displays attached to his laptop before opening a second browser window. He opens the webmail account for an address he hasn't used in years. He never thought he would again but hung onto it in case of an emergency. This qualifies.

He types a series of sentences, inserts the text from a stored file, and smiles. One last grand mystery for her to solve. She's going to love that.

Brian spent weeks setting this up. It was the culmination of years of travel and developing an overseas network of associates and contacts that he could rely on in a pinch. It's all very unnecessary. That's the beauty of it.

In a few clicks, he schedules the email to be sent at the appropriate time and engages the encryption on the device. The NSA will need ten thousand years to brute force the device open. He and his associates will be long dead before they uncover its contents. In that way, he's at least smarter than Ian Drucker was.

Brian focuses on the muted television as Oliver Jahn and Wilson Newman prattle on in their podcast. The media is reporting live from Wolfwood Estate, where DeAnna Van Herten is being dragged out of her mansion in cuffs. She will lawyer up and may even talk, but probably not. The trio in New York will see to that.

He turns the bottle of wine on his desk and reads the label. This was his victory dance, a drink that would be enjoyed the evening after the inauguration. Now, it's his swan song. Brian uses the automatic corkscrew to open the bottle. He sets it down to let it breathe when he hears a noise in the driveway. It's almost time.

CHAPTER EIGHTY-THREE
TIERRA CAMPOS

Cooper Residence
Bethesda, Maryland

I pull into the driveway and shut off the engine. The house is mostly dark except for a few lights on the first floor. The floodlight over the garage switches off after having detected the motion of my vehicle as I parked. Nobody is sneaking up on this place.

"I'm here."

"You don't need to do this, Tierra. Let law enforcement handle it. Please," Josh pleads over the car's speakers.

I want to take the advice but can't. This has always been about Brian and me – the game he was playing that I wasn't clued in on. We'll meet as equal players for the first time in our long relationship since Brockhampton. He needs to know that. I need to show him.

"I'll call you when it's over."

Josh sighs. "Okay. Good luck, Tierra. Happy hunting."

I end the call and climb out of the car, closing the door and checking to ensure the device isn't still paired to the car. I hit the record button and place the phone in my pocket. He might still have his personal jammer, but there's no harm in trying to get a record of whatever happens.

I take a deep breath. I've already come this far and need to see it through. I didn't spend time researching Actyv's property holdings and identifying this house to chicken out now. Cooper wasn't easy to find. Brian gave up his apartment when he went to work for Bradford and spent the last months of the campaign residing in hotel rooms. This was my best shot, and I guessed right when I saw his car parked in the driveway.

The house is gorgeous, but I don't expect anything less in this area. Bethesda is one of the wealthiest suburbs in the D.C. metro area. It's brick and stone, with a two-car garage turned ninety degrees from the front of the house. The large front door, big windows, and old-school copper gutters running down the façade enhance the appeal. This place must easily run at least two-and-a-half million dollars. More than Cooper can afford.

I should ring the bell, but I'm not going to. I want the element of surprise. The front door isn't locked, so I open it without announcing myself and step in.

Wilson's voice is coming from the other room. And then I hear Oliver Jahn. Like many Americans at this point, Cooper is watching his downfall live. Good. That will be less for me to explain.

There's no point in sneaking around. My heels click on the hardwood floors as I pass through the foyer and enter the study through the open door. It's a beautiful room, complete with filled bookshelves, an oak desk, and a sitting area with leather chairs. It looks like something out of the game of Clue.

Brian looks up at me as he uncorks a bottle of wine. "Tierra! You made it! I didn't think you were coming."

"I didn't realize you were expecting me."

"Oh, please. You're a reporter. And a damn good one. You need answers to your questions, and this is how you get them."

"I see you're keeping up on current events," I say, gesturing at the television.

He glances over at the cable news channel showing the police response outside the Department of Justice. The chyron reads, "Deputy AG Conrad Williams Killed in Shootout."

"You know me. I like to stay informed," Brian says, punching the mute button on his computer and silencing Oliver Jahn mid-sentence.

"So do I. I won't stay long. Just tell me why, Brian. Why do this?"

The political operative presses his lips together and shakes his head. "I'm a lousy host. I just opened this nice bottle of wine I've been saving for a special occasion. Will you have a glass with me?"

"Is it laced with hemlock?"

He rubs his chin. "I'm not sure I would even know where to find hemlock."

"It's a highly toxic plant that's a member of the carrot family and grows wildly in most states."

My college botany course is paying off. Hemlock is commonly mistaken for wild parsnip or parsley and is fatal if ingested. Every part of the plant is poisonous, including the seeds, root, stem, leaves, and fruit. The ancient Greeks used hemlock to execute criminals or political prisoners, with Socrates being the most notable example. That's why I took an interest in it. It's about the only thing I remember from that class.

"Interesting. No, the wine isn't poisoned. Come, sit down. Let's have a glass while we enjoy one final chess game."

Brian moves over to the sitting area, but I don't budge. He stops and looks at me.

"Are you really going to make me plead with you?"

Against my better judgment, I join him on the opposing chair. A beautiful ebony and ivory chessboard with hand-crafted pieces rests on a coffee table between us. Brian hands me my glass and sets his down before pulling a pistol from a concealed holster in the small of his back. He sets it on the small table next to his chair.

CHAPTER EIGHTY-FOUR

PRESIDENT-ELECT ALICIA STANDISH

Standish's Hay-Adams Hotel Suite
Washington, D.C.

Most Americans have no idea how scripted interviews typically are. When politicians, celebrities, and other figures are interviewed, there is almost always an agreed-upon set of questions and topics. *Capitol Beat* was different, which is why it was such a powerful force in Washington.

Alicia and Colin both lean back and exhale when their podcast interview concludes. It was exhilarating. The questions were tough but fair. Oliver and Wilson didn't gang up on them, mostly because their answers were honest and transparent. At least, that's what the president-elect attributes it to.

Brian walks over and silently disconnects the camera. He gives a thumbs-up to them to acknowledge it's no longer capable of recording. Alicia checks the number of viewers. It's massive. The comments are scrolling so fast that she can't read any of them before the text is pushed off the screen. Most of them seem to be positive, looking at the emojis they include.

"How'd we do?" the governor of North Carolina asks their tech.

"I'm no expert," Brian says, "but I thought it was honest."

"You're not an expert in honesty?" Alicia says, a wry smile crossing her lips.

Brian returns the grin. "I think you did very well under difficult circumstances. I'm going to start breaking the setup down. Is that okay?"

"Do what you need to. And thank you."

Alicia and Colin stand and move away to give Brian some room to work. They are amped up and have a lot of nervous energy as they position themselves to see the television. Cable news is in an uproar.

There is a knock at the door, and an agent allows a staffer to enter. "Ma'am? The phones downstairs are ringing off the hook."

"I bet," Alicia says. "Accept no interview requests. There is no additional statement to make at this time. Just keep a log of who called."

"Yes, ma'am."

The heads of Alicia's and Colin's details enter as the staffer leaves. They know each other but probably never thought they would be working together in such proximity after receiving their assignments four months ago. The thought almost causes her to smile. It's been a week of firsts.

"The FBI is on its way. They should be here any moment."

Alicia nods. "And Andrew Li?"

"He arrived about fifteen minutes ago, ma'am. We have an agent babysitting him in one of the small meeting rooms."

"I want to be there for his arrest."

"That's not a good—"

"Between the FBI and Secret Service, there will be more guns downstairs than phones. I'm safer here than most Americans. Let's go."

The agents don't look thrilled with the decision but don't protest. Colin falls in behind her as they walk to the elevator.

"Crimson and Cardinal are moving to the lobby," an agent whispers into his sleeve mic.

"Cardinal?" Alicia asks her former opponent as they board the elevator.

He shrugs. "State bird of North Carolina. It's also the codename of a high-placed CIA asset that Jack Ryan needs to extract from Moscow in the Tom Clancy novel *Cardinal of the Kremlin*. I prefer to think of it that way."

Alicia smiles at the reference as they reach the ground floor and walk to the transition area. A dozen armed FBI agents wear their trademark windbreakers. Another half-dozen in tactical gear wait near the entrance. They came loaded for bear.

A man in a suit strides over under the watchful eye of the Secret Service detail. "Madam President-Elect, we have a warrant for Andrew Li's arrest."

"Good. Take these gentlemen to him," Alicia commands her detail.

A staffer spins in her chair, an alarmed look on her face. "Andrew left. He's not in the conference room."

"Are you sure?" the lead FBI agent asks.

"Positive. I saw him walk out about five minutes ago."

Alicia looks at her lead agent and notices the look of concern. "There was no report."

All hell breaks loose. The Secret Service rushes to the conference room door with several FBI agents in tow. Alicia cranes her head to see if she can spot anything. With weapons out, they burst into the room. Andrew isn't there, but the agent watching him is sprawled on the floor in a pool of blood.

"Agent down, Hay-Adams!" the head of her detail barks into his mic as a pair of FBI agents rushes in to administer aid. "Lock down the hotel. I want the footage from every camera in this hotel scanned starting fifteen minutes ago. In five, I need to know where Andrew Li went."

"Ma'am, sir, you need to come with me. Right now!" Colin's lead agent orders them.

The FBI team isn't sitting on the sidelines for this. They spring into action, moving outside to secure the door and form a perimeter around the building. Pandemonium reigns as orders are barked and staffers are ushered out. The only sound Alicia hears is the constant ringing of phones until they reach the elevator surrounded by a half-dozen agents.

The suite is already being searched when Alicia and Colin return upstairs. A guard is perpetually posted at her door, so the odds of Andrew waiting in there with a gun or explosive vest are zero. Still, the Secret Service has procedures, including checking any space their charges will be in, just in case. Brian is already gone, as is the podcast equipment. They likely helped him pack before ushering him out of the hotel.

Alicia knows that Andrew's evading arrest will contemplate things. The American public needs to know that this cabal has been neutralized. There will be seeds of doubt that feed constant conspiracy theories until he is found. That's a problem for authorities to solve. She and Colin will have plenty of others to worry about.

The lead agents take one more look around and nod at each other. Her agent brings his sleeve up to his mouth.

"Crimson and Cardinal are secure."

CHAPTER EIGHTY-FIVE

VICTORIA LARSEN

U.S. Department of Justice
Washington, D.C.

The courtyard in the DOJ building will never be confused for a botanical garden, but it is serene. The respite from the chaos happening beyond these walls is welcome. Victoria doesn't need breaking news alerts to know the nation is panicked. The broadcast is being covered on every news station and network. At this point, she'd be surprised if the Discovery Channel hasn't coopted their regular programming.

Even VH Media is showing footage of DeAnna Van Herten's arrest. You know you've lost control when the anchors you pay handsome sums to are narrating your perp walk. It's priceless. After all these months, they can finally declare victory.

"You look like you could use this," DeAndre says, handing her a steaming cup of coffee that she graciously accepts.

"Did you raid the breakroom?"

DeAndre scoffs. "It's the least the DOJ can do."

"How's the AG?"

"Ehler's being loaded in an ambulance. She's going to need surgery but should be fine, at least physically. She's pretty pissed about getting shot and may need a few anger management classes when she gets discharged."

Victoria nods. The AG didn't deserve that bullet. She stepped up in a city where people rarely do the right thing. There was no way any of them could have expected that Williams would be armed. Or maybe they should have. Not that it matters. What's done is done.

"Can I be honest with you about something?" the junior agent asks.

"Sure."

"I never thought you were involved with anything they said you were. I even told Murphy as much. I didn't have the strength to fight for you more aggressively. I owe you an apology."

Victoria shakes her head. "No, you don't."

"You're going to get one anyway. I don't know how you found the strength to do the things you did these past few weeks. You had to know the odds were stacked against you. You did them anyway, and I couldn't muster the courage to disagree with my boss."

"Our situations were different, Agent Wright. You only *suspected* I wasn't involved. I knew the unequivocal truth about the cabal."

"Still…what you've accomplished is nothing short of amazing."

"Don't inflate her ego any more than you already have," Murphy says with a smile as he walks toward the vehicle. "So, Black Widow, your work here is done, and you're a sovereign citizen who's not being hunted by your government for a change. Do you have a place I can drop you off?"

Victoria brushes her hair back. There is still plenty of red in it, and now she fears one of Miranda's favorite monikers will stick. She likes it better than Queen V, but still. She would never consider herself an Avenger.

"Wilson Newman's house. I need to see Tierra. Can you take me to Falls Church?"

Murphy nods at the Suburban. "Hop in. DeAndre can handle things here. It's all yours, buddy. Make me proud."

His subordinate nods, and they climb in. Murphy points the vehicle at the access gate, and they're waved through. Not that they get far. A Metro police cruiser pulls up and blocks their path as uniformed officers surround them with their weapons drawn and pointed at the vehicle.

"Victoria Larsen! Step out of the vehicle with your hands up!"

"You *have got* to be kidding me."

Murphy rolls down his window. "What the hell is this?"

"Step out of the vehicle, sir."

"I don't think so. I'm a federal agent on official business," he says, showing the unmistakable badge hanging around his neck.

"Good for you. There's a federal warrant for Victoria Larsen's arrest. It looks to me like you're aiding and abetting."

Victoria's door opens, and she keeps her hands at shoulder level. She signals that she's going to unfasten her seatbelt and does so slowly. She complies with the officer's order to exit the vehicle. There is no winning this argument.

A federal judge issues warrants authorizing law enforcement to arrest someone charged with or suspected of being involved in a federal crime. Only a marshal or authorized officer may execute the warrant anywhere within the jurisdiction of the United States or where federal statutes permit. It takes a while for the dogs to be called off.

"A judge rescinded the warrant hours ago at the attorney general's request."

"I haven't been notified of that," the officer argues.

"I just told you."

"That's not good enough. I'm bringing Larsen in. If the warrant was terminated, as you suggest, she'll be free in no time."

"Not good enough, tough guy. Show her the warrant. Do it now."

"It will be shown to her at booking."

The arresting official must show the defendant the arrest warrant, or if it is not available at the time of the arrest, inform the defendant of its existence and provide it upon request as quickly as possible. This officer knows the law.

"I'm not letting you take her into custody," Murphy barks as Victoria is relieved of her weapon and patted down. "Do you have any idea what just happened here?"

"Get in our way, and you're obstructing justice. You fancy FBI types know what that means."

"It's okay, Murph," Victoria says, not resisting as she's handcuffed. "I've done this before."

"It's not okay!"

"It will all get sorted out. In the meantime, release Rigo, his father, and Miranda. And make sure Seth Chambers is cleared of wrongdoing."

"Victoria—"

"Murphy, please. Take care of them. I'll be fine."

Daniel watches as Victoria is placed into a cruiser. This is ridiculous. Angry, he stops back into the courtyard to find DeAndre. His night just got longer.

CHAPTER EIGHTY-SIX

SSA DANIEL MURPHY

U.S. Department of Justice
Washington, D.C.

Murphy hangs up with the Boston field office. That was the last call he needed to make to fulfill Victoria's wishes. Fifteen minutes have passed, and he still hasn't found DeAndre. The senior agent finally catches up to him with a pair of EMTs wheeling the director's body out of the building.

The courtyard provides some privacy. The streets around the Department of Justice are choked with media and curious onlookers. Camera lighting on the sidewalks provides more illumination than streetlights. Videos of the FBI director in a body bag and being hauled off in an ambulance would dominate headlines for a week if it weren't already a big news night.

"Hey, boss," DeAndre says. "What are you doing back here?"

Murphy launches into the short version of the story that still takes three minutes. DeAndre shakes his head.

"Don't we all play for the same team?"

"You know better. What do you have?"

"Agent Bangura phoned while I was upstairs. DeAnna Van Herten is in custody."

Washington, D.C. may have the largest density of media on the planet, but even they have limited resources. With so many elements of this story to cover, he wonders how much attention that arrest will get.

"Will we see footage of that on the news, too?"

"Are you kidding? The media beat Bangura to Wolfwood Estate. Even Alétheia was camped outside the gate when she arrived. They filmed her being escorted out in 8K, Full Ultra HD. Watching that perp walk is going to be wildly entertaining."

"What about Cooper?"

"Agents from the D.C. field office just tracked him down and are en route to his location. I had CPB flag his passport, and I notified local airports. A BOLO went out to local law enforcement in case he tries to flee."

"He won't try to escape by car. A flight to a non-extradition country is more likely. Have Customs and Border Patrol closely monitor charter flights. I want every private jet between Baltimore and Richmond checked before departing overseas."

"Roger that. I'll get on it," DeAndre says before stopping. "This is going to be messy, isn't it?"

"A cabal seized power over the Executive Branch. People will be scared, and scared people do stupid things."

"What do you think the government is going to do?"

That is the question. If it's handled well, legacies will be built. Rudy Giuliani became "America's Mayor" due to his handling of the attack on the World Trade Center in 2001. On the other hand, revolutions have started for less than this. Murphy hopes it doesn't come to that.

"They're politicians. Odds are they'll find a way to make it worse."

"What are we going to do?"

The FBI has been much maligned over the past decade. Countless blunders by the Hoover Building have caused all manner of angst in the Bureau's ranks. They may have redeemed themselves tonight, at least to some degree. As for what happens next – that's anyone's guess.

"I think we've done enough for the country tonight. I'm going to get Larsen out of jail."

"Boss, the judge may not have filed the order rescinding the warrant. You'll need Ehler or Krekstein to help. He's dead, and she'll be in surgery for the next few hours. What can you do?"

"Whatever I need to," Murphy decrees. "I'll break her out of D.C. Jail if I have to, but Victoria isn't spending a night there after what she did for this country."

"You know, I think she wore off on you," DeAndre calls out as Murphy walks away. "You've gone full beast mode. I like it!"

Murphy smiles. Maybe he's right. It's long overdue.

CHAPTER EIGHTY-SEVEN

TIERRA CAMPOS

Cooper Residence
Bethesda, Maryland

My eyes linger on the gun too long. Brian notices my stare and tracks them there before turning his head back to face me. He's expressionless. There is no anger, sorrow, or even angst. I refocus my eyes on the board, content that there's no point in dwelling on things I can't control.

"It looks like you already started a game," I observe, staring at the pieces already moved around in a game that appears to be about twenty moves old.

"Ah, not really. I was working on a new strategy."

"You need one."

Brian winces. "Ouch. Shots fired."

"Is this what all this was to you? A game?"

Brian leans back, crosses his legs, and sips his wine. "That's what life is. Moves and countermoves. Some people win. Others lose. It's harsh, but it's reality."

"Your reality was stressful. It caused pain, and it was deadly."

"And that is how the world has worked since cavemen were beating each other with clubs," Brian says, rubbing his chin. "You know, something just dawned on me. This feels a little like Professor Moriarty and Sherlock Holmes facing off at the end of *A Game of Shadows*. Did you see the movie?"

"I did. Only I can't play chess without looking at the board, and Moriarty didn't know he was beaten until the end of the match. You already know you lost."

"Aw, come on, Tierra. You're intent on stealing my fun, aren't you?" Brian says, reaching forward to move the pieces into their starting positions.

"Don't bother resetting the board, Brian. Our game has already been played."

He stops and stares at me. "How so?"

"First, you sacrificed Dylan Spencer up in New Hampshire," I say, picking up a black pawn. "I still am not entirely sure why, but it was your opening move."

I toss the black pawn into the center of the study.

"I don't count Frederick Lamm. He was collateral damage in the arsons. But then the S.O.F. tried to kill Wilson and Olivia. Luckily, they escaped death," I say, moving a white pawn and bishop to safety. "The attack was too aggressive. It exposed the S.O.F., and they were taken out by a successful counterattack. Marx…Sartre…Trotsky."

I remove a black rook and two pawns as I recite their names. Each piece sails across the room, to Brian's amusement. I select a white knight and hold it over the board.

"The assault on their safehouse wounded several New Hampshire State Troopers, including Diego Valez. He was out of the game. Drucker then took out Takara Nashimoto and Lance Fuller to get to Victoria."

I set the knight down and flick two white rooks off the board with my index finger.

"Your trap was set. Vassyl Strachenko was a few moves away from checkmate in Loughborough. It was a brilliant strategy. Rigoberto Benitez's team was taken out along with the FBI assault force," I moan, removing all the white pawns except one. "Of course, Vassyl and his guys weren't supposed to die in the process."

I collect the black knight and two rooks, and toss them over my shoulder. Brian nods and finishes his wine before pouring himself another glass.

"And then there was Angela Mays."

The world only just found out about that. Brian confirmed it in our meeting at Dupont Circle, but I had no proof until Victoria accessed Ian's laptop. His journal contained a detailed account of her murder. It was damning evidence.

"Oliver and Wilson did a great job of explaining that, from what I saw," Brian admits.

I remove another white bishop. It was the only way Andrew Li could play a bigger part in the campaign, but even Brian admitted it wasn't necessary. I lay this one down next to the board respectfully.

"And then there was the Keystone Militia."

"Yeah, that went all sorts of wrong," Brian admits. "I didn't expect the FBI to make the connection to them that quickly. None of them needed to die."

"The three ex-cons at the print shop would disagree, but they can have that argument in hell. Don't pretend that you didn't view them as expendable."

I swipe all the black pawns off the board for dramatic effect.

"Their loss didn't matter," I conclude. "You already accomplished what you needed to. The election was tainted. What really went wrong was losing Ian Drucker."

I remove the black queen and hold it in front of him.

Brian frowns. "Oh, I don't think that's the piece I would assign him, but okay."

"He *was* your queen. He was mobile and deadly. Your mistake was leaving him exposed for too long. But his loss didn't matter, either. We've been on the defensive since the election, and you still had plenty of strong pieces to take us out one-by-one. Miranda, Imani, Rigo, Seth Chambers...."

Pieces fly off the board in quick succession. A bishop, rook, and a pair of pawns all arc gracefully through the air before clanking on the hardwood floor.

"And you had me cornered," I say, tapping the queen. "I had no moves left to make. You made sure of that."

"I would absolutely assign you that piece. Does that make Victoria Larsen the king? Or is it Alicia Standish?"

"Standish wasn't a piece. She was the *prize*. Victoria Larsen was the one you needed to take out. You knew that. The game would have been over if Strachenko, Drucker, or Marx had done their jobs and eliminated her. It's why Conrad Williams has moved mountains since to catch her."

"That's very true. Poor dead bastard."

"Speaking of dead," I say, removing a black bishop. "Or arrested. Or on the run, from what I heard."

I remove the other black bishop and a knight representing Nietzsche and Machiavelli.

"Your plan was brilliant, Brian, but you never counted on the one pawn we had left making it to the back line. Tom Swim, *RFA*, Alétheia, and the remnants of *Front Burner*. The alt-media."

Pawns are the only chess piece that can't move backward. So, when a pawn reaches the eighth rank of the chessboard, where the opposing king starts, the player gets the chance to replace it with either a queen, knight, rook, or bishop of the same color in a 'pawn promotion.'

"Don't forget Oliver Jahn. You really need to explain how you managed to bury the hatchet with him."

I grin. "The enemy of your enemy is your friend."

"Fair enough."

I clear the board of all the pieces except for the black king and the white queen. Nobody else matters. Not Victoria, Wilson, Oliver Jahn, or even *Front Burner*. I lean forward and stare directly into Brian's eyes.

"That leads us to right here…right now. Me and you. The decisive endgame."

I nod over at the gun resting on the table.

"What's your move?"

CHAPTER EIGHTY-EIGHT

BRIAN COOPER

Cooper Residence
Bethesda, Maryland

It's amazing how the most important of life's lessons came during a chess game in Union Square. Brian thinks back to the words Abe said to him at that table. "True freedom is laying your king down before someone does it for you." It was the best foreshadowing he's ever heard.

Brian grabs the top of his king and topples it. He reaches over to the table next to his chair and picks up the handgun. He studies its shape and feels its weight in his hand. The steel feels cool against his skin. Brian has never been a fan of guns but understands their appeal.

"Have you ever noticed how many movies end like this? The good guy confronts the bad guy, who proceeds to spill all the details about his devious plan before the movie ends. Is life like that, or is it lazy screenwriting?"

Tierra presses her lips together. "Both. Audiences want answers because it's in people's nature to want answers. The struggle needs to have context and meaning. Most of all, they want to know how the story ends. It gives them closure."

"Is that why you came tonight?"

"Yes and no. I believe the story never ends. It's why history repeats itself."

Brian shakes his head. "That's not true. History doesn't repeat itself, but the themes in history do. That's why there will always be wars, corruption, and exploitation…the quest for power and money is a propelling force."

"Which were you after? Power or money?"

"So, you do want the meaning behind all this?"

"The journalist in me does, but I came here to thank you."

He lifts his head in shock. That's not what Brian expected her to say. Then again, she has always been unpredictable. It's another thing he admires about her.

"Thank me for what?"

Tierra fidgets in her chair. "We've come a long way since meeting on the U.S.S. Constitution when I was a scared former D.C. human interests reporter who stumbled upon a national scandal. So much has happened since then. I could have easily let things destroy me. Instead, they made me stronger. You made me stronger."

"I've always loved your perseverance," Brian says, offering a weak smile as he fiddles with the gun. "So many others would have quit."

"Good. Then you won't be offended if I ask you why again."

"Asking questions is what you do. I'm a political operative. I've made a career of dodging them. It's just another game we all play. Will you be disappointed if I don't answer?"

"I'm used to living with unanswered questions. Some of them I answer myself. Like why you kept me around."

"I know. And you managed to destroy me because you did. Then you put your life in grave danger by coming here tonight. You had to have known that. And still, you came. Is the answer to the question really that important to you?"

"Yes. I want to know why a man as brilliant as you chose this route. Why did you hijack the presidency instead of helping a deserving candidate win it? Everyone will want to know."

"The answers to the world's most important questions cannot be conveyed to the inquisitive but only learned for themselves. Instruction is a means of education, but not of understanding."

Tierra crinkles her brow. "John Stuart Mill?"

"Nah. A great American philosopher said it: Brian Cooper."

The line causes his guest to smile as they both turn their heads at the sound of approaching sirens.

"It appears our time is up."

Tierra rises and nods. "It is. Good luck, Brian."

She rises, turns her back to him, and starts for the study door.

"You know that I can't leave things like this."

Tierra freezes in place but doesn't turn to face him. "Like I said, Brian, it's your move."

"Yeah, I guess it is. May God forgive me."

He points his gun at Tierra's back and holds it there. His jaw tightens as the weight causes his arm muscles to tense. Gravity fights to drag the weapon to the ground. He won't cede that battle. It's the last victory he cherishes before putting the muzzle against the roof of his mouth and pulling the trigger.

CHAPTER EIGHTY-NINE

PRESIDENT-ELECT ALICIA STANDISH

Standish's Hay-Adams Hotel Suite
Washington, D.C.

The Secret Service trail Alicia as she makes her way up to the suite. When she reaches the door, they open it for her and enter first. That will take some getting used to for her. The lead agent nods at her and then exits the room.

The briefing downstairs was short and filled with more assurances than information. It was meant for Alicia as the president-elect, so Colin was asked to remain in the suite. At least he's making himself comfortable.

"Any news on Andrew Li?" the governor asks without looking at Alicia.

"No, he's gone. The Secret Service has assured me that the building is secure, so at a minimum, we aren't trapped here. Where are we?"

"Wilson and Oliver are taking a break," Colin says from the sofa.

"And hopefully taking something to ease the swelling in their throats. They've been at it for hours. I almost lost my voice a dozen times on the campaign trail, and Wilson has more than a few years on me."

"Ditto, on both accounts. Tom Swim has taken over the broadcast from his podcast studio. The views are off the charts."

Alicia sits on the opposite sofa. She stares at the television where the podcast is being screencast from the nearby laptop. "You have to hand Tierra and *Front Burner* credit. Tom Swim has brought being a maverick loner to new heights. I never would have thought he'd cooperate. What about the mainstream news networks?"

"My phone is blowing up with alerts. It's breaking news on every network. Cable has been following it closely from the beginning. Networks broke into programming right as we went on."

"Millions of Americans have learned the truth tonight. Now all that remains to be settled is what happens next." Alicia notices Colin lower his head. "What?"

"Honestly, I feel like an idiot. I can't tell you how many times Cooper told me that you were dangerous and couldn't be allowed to win the White House. And then, this…."

"Well, I'm joining you in the corner with a dunce cap on. I hired Andrew Li, not realizing he was the man who sabotaged my campaign in the first place. The important thing is that we wised up before the real damage could be done."

Colin nods. "What does it look like downstairs?"

"Chaos. Phones are ringing off the hook. There are so many people outside the hotel that they had to block off the street."

"I bet."

The Secret Service is going to earn their paychecks tonight. They undoubtedly called the D.C. Metro Police to help control the growing crowd outside the Hay-Adams and hunt for Andrew Li. Lafayette Park is ground zero for the assembly. The concern is them getting violent. So far, there has been no indication that rioting is planned. If history has taught Alicia anything, it's a conflagration capable of consuming everything is always triggered by a single spark.

"Have I thanked you for this, Colin?"

He smiles. "You have."

"I'm doing it again. I don't know what is going to happen, but…I'm not sure I could have done this without your support."

"You could have," the governor admits. "I have no doubt about that. You know that the leadership of both parties is going to scream at us. I know my side will want to make political hay out of this. We're supposed to be blood enemies, and I'm supposed to contest your win, not help you fight off a coup."

"I'm sure my side will flay me for even thinking about working with you. Even when the nation's fate is at stake, we aren't allowed to be seen working together to govern and solve problems. It's the world we live in now."

"It's not the world I want to be a part of. If there was ever a moment in the past quarter century that we should be uniting, it's now. This is the greatest test our government has faced since the Civil War."

America has been through the fire before. The attack on Pearl Harbor that dragged the nation into World War II, and the terrorist attacks on 9/11 shook the country to its foundation. The Watergate scandal rattled faith in the presidency. The countless scandals since then undermined the belief that the elected leaders were acting on the people's behalf.

This is different. What Brian Cooper and his cohorts did was more than influence an election. It was a power grab that put him in a position to subvert the will of the people and control the highest elected office in the land. What little confidence the public has left in the government was shattered tonight. It falls to Alicia and Colin to restore it, at least to some degree.

"I didn't want any leaks, so I didn't mention our meeting to anyone, including my wife. She learned it when the rest of the country did. She's flying to Washington to ensure I didn't lose my mind."

Alicia laughs. "My husband is already somewhere over Connecticut on a flight out of Logan."

"This is going to be a fun one to explain to them."

"They'll understand. Everyone else should, too, and I'm beginning to not care what my party says."

"You know, we are technically the leaders of our two parties."

"Yes, that's true. What are you suggesting?"

A grin creeps across Colin's lips. "We lead."

Hail to the Chief starts playing from Alicia's coat pocket. Her calls are silenced, except a special rule is in place for this one. When this number calls, she had better pick up.

"That's a tad presumptive."

Alicia gives him an amused look and shows him the screen. It has one word: POTUS.

"Yes?" Alicia asks before pausing for a moment. "Yes, Mr. President. Yes. Of course. Okay. Right away."

Colin stands and retrieves his jacket. "Let me guess. We're taking a walk across Lafayette Park."

"Close," Alicia says, smoothing hers out. "He's sending his limo. He wants the two of us standing in the Oval Office in fifteen minutes."

TWO DAYS LATER

CHAPTER NINETY

VICTORIA LARSEN

The Legislator Regency Hotel
Washington, D.C.

There are hotels, then there are luxury hotels. And then there is The Legislator Regency. Its only rival in the district is the Hay-Adams, whose reputation was built on the prestige of its location. This hotel, a stone's throw from the marble halls of the Capitol, is the new gold standard for a luxurious stay in D.C.

The architect did a masterful job designing the building. To avoid detracting from the beauty of the white marble Capitol and Supreme Court building, the façade is modeled after the neo-gothic style of the House and Senate office buildings. The inside is a different story. They kept an Italian marble quarry very busy.

Victoria is starting to feel like a celebrity. The bellman looked like he wanted to take a selfie with her, and clerks at the front desk gawked as she walked through the lobby. The upside to all the attention is that she'll never again be asked to do undercover investigative work, not that she ever has or will even remain in the Bureau to get that assignment.

She reaches the elevator and punches the button for one of the upper floors. It will be a short ride. Structures in D.C. are not tall, thanks to the one hundred thirteen-year-old Height Act that limits most buildings to thirteen stories to protect the capital's skyline. This hotel is only ten.

A quick knock on the door creates a stir Victoria can hear on the other side. She's nervous about this. So much has happened, and she can't anticipate the response. The question is answered when the big man opens the door, and his face lights up.

"Victoria!" Seth Chambers screeches as he moves in and hugs her.

"How are you, Seth?"

"I'll live, thanks to you."

"Well, technically, if it wasn't for me, you wouldn't have had heavily armed Spetznaz commandos show up at your house."

The detective playfully rubs his chin. "That's true. I guess you owe me another one."

They share a laugh as Victoria enters the suite. It's almost over-the-top in its décor and appointments. Victoria had always known The Legislator had a reputation for luxury, but this is borderline ridiculous.

"This is swanky."

"It's the least they can do."

"Sorry I haven't had the chance to check in on you sooner. I…."

Her voice trails off, and Seth grins. "No apologies, Victoria. You've had a few other things to deal with, not that being a federal fugitive and being arrested are legitimate excuses."

"You're enjoying this, aren't you?"

"Immensely."

"Are you all set for tonight?"

He nods over at the bedroom. "I already have my best suit laid out. What about you? Please tell me you aren't thinking about ditching this?"

"I wouldn't miss it."

"With everything happening, the government is taking its eye off the ball. Cooper and Williams are dead, Andrew Li is missing, and DeAnna Van Herten is cooling her heels in a jail cell. The problem is they aren't the only perpetrators of this coup."

"You mean Actyv."

"The story isn't fully written, Victoria. They're the dangerous ones."

"They're finance weenies, Seth."

"You know better. Cooper and friends hired thugs to do their dirty work. Assassins, militia…not once did they enlist resources from a private military company. That came from somewhere else, and Actyv is my bet."

"Do you have proof?"

"I have intuition. My Spidey senses are tingling."

If most other people had said that, Victoria wouldn't give it a second thought. But Seth is a good man and a great detective. He listens to his inner voice, which makes him great at his job. If something is bothering him, there's a reason for it. She's about to respond when there's a noise behind her.

"So, I finally get to meet the woman who keeps getting my husband shot at."

Shauna Chambers is standing in the open doorway to the bedroom. She's short in stature but well-dressed and lovely. She looks angry at seeing the former agent talking to her husband, but she smiles broadly and hugs Victoria when she reaches her.

"You're even more beautiful in person than you are on television. If I were a jealous woman, that would be concerning. Fortunately, Seth knows the consequences of infidelity."

Victoria turns to her friend. "Shauna said she would cut my balls off and run them through a blender. I'd like to think she's bluffing, but she probably isn't."

"I believe it. It's nice to finally meet you, Shauna."

"Likewise."

"I'm sorry for constantly putting Seth in harm's way. It was never my intention to make life so dangerous for him."

"I knew who Seth was before I married him and wouldn't change a thing. Being a cop's wife isn't much different from being the wife of a combat soldier. The qualities that attract us to our men are the same ones that terrify us about what could happen to them. Sometimes, Seth can be a complete moron, but he's always been my hero."

That sounds familiar. Austin is the same way. He can be infuriating in the things he says and does, but he also has a good heart. Austin makes mistakes but owns them. And he's honest. Those are qualities that Victoria has never historically found in the men she's dated. That's why she had all but given up on it.

"I hope I no longer need to put him in danger."

"That doesn't mean he won't find it on his own," Shauna muses.

The women talk, mostly about Seth, with him standing there wincing when another knock at the door commands their attention. The detective checks the peephole and opens the door, revealing a man in a suit and wearing a blue windbreaker with gold lettering.

"I'm sorry, we're closed for business."

"Is Special Agent Victoria Larsen here?" the man asks without cracking a smile.

"Your colleagues are all business, Victoria."

"Former colleagues. I'm no longer in the Bureau, Agent…."

"Ross. I was sent here by Daniel Murphy and Imani Bangura. There's something they *need* you to see."

His placing emphasis on "need" is not an accident. He was instructed to do that, probably by Imani. Victoria may have known Daniel longer, but Imani knows her better. Still, she needs to be done with this life. Whatever problem they have is for them to figure out. She's done her part.

"I think I'll pass, Agent Ross. Thank you. Have a pleasant day."

The agent doesn't move. "I know you've been through a lot, ma'am, but I think you should take their offer."

"Why?"

"Closure."

It's a lame argument, but there is something about the look on his face that gives Victoria a moment of pause. It's a mix of surprise and…satisfaction. Victoria turns to Seth, who looks like he's doing his own analysis.

"You should go, Vic. Shauna and I are going to stroll around the National Mall anyway. We'll catch up with you later."

"Okay, lead the way, Agent Ross."

Victoria really doesn't want to go. The last thing she wants is for Daniel to think he can whistle and she'll come running. But something happened, and the word "closure" piqued her curiosity. She can spare a little time to satisfy it.

CHAPTER NINETY-ONE

SSA DANIEL MURPHY

Tidal Basin
Washington, D.C.

The Tidal Basin is a happening place right now. The walkway along the water is packed with D.C. Metro police and agents searching for clues about their latest discovery. Daniel doesn't join in. They aren't going to find anything in this part of West Potomac Park.

Murphy loves this part of the city, despite it being a premiere tourist destination. The one hundred-seven acre, ten-foot-deep body of water's shore is home to the Jefferson, Martin Luther King, Jr., FDR, George Mason, and John Paul Jones Memorials. It's also the home of the Floral Library, the Japanese Pagoda, and the Japanese Lantern, all accessible via the Tidal Basin Loop Trail.

"She's here," Imani says, spotting the car they dispatched for Victoria.

He watches the driver pull in and find a spot behind a half-dozen other Crown Vics, Suburbans, and police squad cars. She exits the vehicle and surveys the scene, spotting Murphy and Imani staring at her from the concrete walkway along the basin.

"If you're going to drag me down to the Tidal Basin, you should at least do it during cherry blossom season."

Murphy smirks. This area is associated with Washington's Cherry Blossom Festival, which occurs each spring when the trees bloom with pink and white flowers. The city is never prettier than at that time.

"I wasn't sure you would come."

"You really need to stop underestimating me," Victoria says, smiling as the two shake hands.

Imani doesn't settle for a handshake. The two women hug.

"All right. You got me here. By the looks of this mess, whatever you found has a lot of interest."

"Yeah, you're going to want to see this."

The trio walks over to a single body bag on the walkway, guarded by an agent and some uniformed police.

"I'm on suspension from the Bureau. I can't investigate anything. What do you want me to do?"

"Get some closure, as I'm sure Agent Ross told you."

Murphy nods at the cops, and one of them unzips the body bag.

"He was found this morning by a pair of joggers. The coroner says he's been in the water for less than a day. We don't think he was killed here. Whoever dumped him knew the body would be found quickly. Before you ask, we have positive identification."

Victoria squats to study the bloated corpse. She doesn't need fingerprints to know that it's Andrew Li. Life can change quickly. A couple of days ago, he was on the verge of becoming the White House chief of staff. Now he's dead. There is something very Machiavellian about that change in fortune.

"They didn't waste time, did they? Cause of death?"

"Single gunshot wound from a small caliber weapon to the back of the head. It killed him instantly."

Victoria stands. "Professional hit."

"It looks that way," Imani says. "Victoria, someone is cleaning up their mess. You know who."

"Actyv Private Equity. Except good luck proving that. I hope you have a close eye on DeAnna Van Herten."

"We do, but she doesn't like her accommodations, so that's being used as leverage to get her to talk."

"Is she?" Daniel shakes his head. "Well, you two will figure it out."

Victoria takes one more look at Machiavelli as they zip the body bag up. That chapter in her life is complete. He was responsible for the socialists in the Sword of Freedom and Ian Drucker. They attacked Wilson Newman and Olivia in New Hampshire. To her, seeing Andrew Li's body is like watching the Wicked Witch of the West melt in *The Wizard of Oz*. Wearing a hint of a smile, Victoria nods at the agents and turns to walk back to the car.

"Where are you going?" Imani asks.

"Capitol Hill. Then I'm going to find a nice beach to lie on. I don't care if I have to swim there."

"What if we need you?"

"You never have before, Murph. Imani is the most capable agent you will ever work with. Trust me, you'll be fine, provided you manage to pry her out of Pennsylvania."

Victoria starts walking again.

"There are still bad people out there, Vic," Murphy calls out.

"There always are."

The pair watches Victoria walk through the grass back to the car. She doesn't look back and shows no interest in anything happening around her. It's not a good sign.

"Do you think she's going to come back to the Bureau?"

Imani stares at her new boss. "After all this, would you?"

"I never in a million years thought I would hear myself say this, but we need Victoria Larsen. Someone killed Andrew Li, and I'm with you that the trail leads back to Actyv Private Equity. There are still dark forces at work. We may have stopped the immediate threat, but I have a bad feeling that the worst may be yet to come."

CHAPTER NINETY-TWO

TIERRA CAMPOS

U.S. House of Representatives Reception Room
Washington, D.C.

It's the who's who of American politics in the Capitol today. Every legislator who is physically able to attend is in the building. There are cabinet secretaries, members of the military, foreign dignitaries, and bureaucrats. And then there is us.

Everyone associated with the broadcast that is breaking video records is here. We were supposed to gather in Statuary Hall, but with so many people milling around the Capitol, they moved us to the Reception Room adjacent to the House Chamber. *Front Burner* employees are joined by Oliver Jahn, Ahn Mi Sun, Tom Swim, Jo Pagano, and Estevan Cardoso and their team members. The mood isn't celebratory, given the gravity of the moment, but it is polite and uplifting. They all know they were a part of something special.

My eyes continue to move around the room. Seth Chambers and his wife are talking to Rigo Benitez and his father. Dial Pirate and Olivia are in the corner with Logan, Tyler, and Jerome. I bet DP never thought he'd be the guest of honor in Congress. He definitely never thought he would end up in a budding relationship with a woman like Olivia. It will be interesting to see where that goes and whether he gives up hacking to do something more productive for society. I'm betting that he does.

The only ones not attending are Daniel Murphy and Imani Bangura. They declined the invite after Andrew Li's body was found. Duty comes first, and they will see plenty of future accolades. The nation is lionizing Murphy for his intuition and courage, and Bangura is regarded as the next Victoria Larsen.

"I overheard the Capitol Police say they are on the way into the building," Josh says, joining me at my side.

Victoria smirks when she sees him gently place his hand on my back. We haven't had a chance to catch up, and I'm sure she wants the details about how that happened. She'll get them because it will be the perfect time for me to remind her that she owes Austin a date before taking off to some desolate Caribbean beach.

Colin Bradford arrives first. He makes it a point to greet everyone in the room. Politicians have a social stamina that I could never match. His words are warm, appreciative, and, most of all, genuine. I chat amiably with the other guests while watching him work the room. I don't know what Bradford's future has in store for him, but I doubt he will retreat from the national stage anytime soon.

The president-elect arrives with her Secret Service detail. She is equally engaging and social. She owes a lot to the people here but cuts her greetings short by excusing herself to walk over to Victoria and me. This isn't the first time we have met face-to-face. Some of those were more contentious than others. This is different.

"Special Agent Larsen. I saw you at Granite State University in New Hampshire during the *Capitol Beat* broadcast, but I don't believe we've ever been formally introduced. I'm Alicia Standish."

"It's nice to meet you, ma'am," Victoria says, shaking her hand. "You should know that I'm no longer a federal agent."

The president-elect smiles. "We'll see about that. If I have my way, not only will you remain with the Bureau, but I'm going to build a statue of you."

"If you do, make sure she's riding a horse," Rigo says, smiling before introducing himself.

"How's Lisa Ehler doing?" Victoria asks.

"She's still in the hospital. She sent her regards and asked me to apologize again for what Conrad Williams put you through. I expect her to reach out to you and Agent Murphy once she's back on her feet."

Victoria nods, and Alicia turns to me.

"Tierra, I owe you an apology. I should have listened to you in Boston."

"Yes, ma'am, you should have. Unfortunately, that wasn't reasonable, given our history. If our roles were reversed, I would have done the same thing you did. It was worth the try."

"And I'm thankful you did. You've proven me wrong several times now. I thought you were another partisan hack out to get me. Instead, you may be the most honorable journalist I have ever met."

Now, it's my turn to smile. "Remember that when you start casting bronze statues. Madam president-elect, there will always be some tension between us. That's the media's true role – to challenge those in power on behalf of the people. To make them answer difficult questions."

"I look forward to it. As bad as this attempted coup was, it may help redefine priorities in this city. If I have one when this ends, my administration will always work to benefit the people. That's my pledge."

"Let's hope that philosophy takes root."

"I'm going to do my best to help," Colin says, arriving next to his former opponent. "The partisan bickering has gotten out of hand. We may not agree on issues, but that doesn't mean civility should be lost. That almost cost us everything. We owe you a debt."

"Repay it for us by doing the right thing – whatever the people decide that thing is."

The White House chief of staff enters the room and beelines for the president-elect. I've never had the pleasure of meeting the man, but he comes across as all business.

"Excuse me all," Robert Ackerman says. "Ma'am, the chamber is being called to order. The president will arrive during your remarks and address Congress once you've concluded. He will then meet you and the governor back at the White House."

"Thank you, Robert."

"We should say a few words to everyone here," Colin says after Ackerman departs. "We won't get another chance."

The room falls silent as they ask for everyone's attention. "Thanks to all of you for being here," the president-elect opens. "The nation owes you a debt that may never be repaid. Tierra and Victoria may be getting much of the public credit for taking down this cabal, but they are the first to share it with each one of you."

"The president-elect and I asked you here because you are now a part of American history. You should witness firsthand what happens next."

I don't hear anything after that. Instead, I move to a spot along the wall with Josh. I know Standish and Bradford are thankful, but we don't even understand the consequences of what was done. We may have thwarted a coup, but the specter of what comes next is haunting me.

"What do we do now?" I whisper to my new boyfriend.

"We find our seats."

"No, I mean tomorrow or next week…when life returns to normal."

Josh shakes his head. "What is normal, exactly? I'm not sure we've brought the true villains to justice. There's more work to be done. Even with the cabal defeated, plenty of people are working to destroy this country. Someone needs to report the news to the people so they can make educated decisions."

"You sound like you want a job."

Josh shrugs. "We could commute together. Besides, I need something to look forward to just in case life with you gets dull and mundane."

I reward him with a playful slap on the chest, carefully avoiding his wounded shoulder. Josh is right. This has always been my fight, and it may not be over. There are more threads to pull, starting with Actyv Private Equity. The crisis is over, but the war may still be raging out of sight. Something tells me that we aren't out of danger yet.

CHAPTER NINETY-THREE

PRESIDENT-ELECT ALICIA STANDISH

U.S. House of Representatives Chamber
Washington, D.C.

Alicia isn't overly familiar with this end of the Capitol. She was in the Senate, and although she attended State of the Union addresses and joint sessions of Congress here, she could almost count those instances on two hands. Meetings with House members were conducted in their offices. She had no reason to visit this side of the building.

When she entered this chamber, she always imagined strolling down the aisle to thunderous applause before one of her addresses. Well, applause from her party and a polite golf clap from the Republicans. The greeting at the onset of the address is typically the only bipartisan moment during recent speeches.

As an elected officer of the House of Representatives, the sergeant at arms is the chief law enforcement and protocol officer of the House of Representatives. The man currently holding the position is responsible for maintaining order in the chamber, reviewing and implementing safety and security measures, and coordinating extensively with the U.S. Capitol Police. The American public only recognizes the individual who announces the arrival of the chief executive with the line, "Mister Speaker, the president of the United States."

Alicia is announced, followed by Governor Bradford. Everyone rises, but there is no applause. That's what makes this so eerie. There isn't even a cough or sneeze as the unlikely duo strides down the center aisle to the rostrum. The gravity of this moment in American history precludes the typical political theatrics and showmanship.

The president-elect takes her position at the lectern, Governor Bradford by her side. There are two sets of microphones set up, and the pair decided ahead of time who would say what. Being brave in front of a computer while speaking to a camera during a podcast is easy. Now, Bradford is facing his Republican colleagues, who are irate over his cooperation. The Democrats are hardly enthusiastic about how she's handling this crisis.

Given the political realities of their situation, Alicia thought that determining the message could be contentious. She was wrong. It wasn't. Her cooperation with the governor has been the easiest part of this whole ordeal.

"Mister Vice-President, Mister Speaker, and distinguished members of Congress, Governor Bradford and I thank you for your invitation to address the American people on this inauspicious occasion. Our political system has been framed for generations as left versus right, Republican versus Democrat. We find any reason to fight among ourselves over issues both serious and trivial. Our discourse is far from civil, and the rancor has spilled from this building's marble halls to the public forum. Our cooperation is ignored while our arguments are amplified to an increasingly bitter and disenfranchised nation.

"Instead of finding common ground to unite us, we have let the divide grow. We target our opponents and treat them like enemies on a battlefield. Our rhetoric has become a toxic manifesto that has inspired violence, deepened mistrust, and caused the people to lose faith in their government and country."

Alicia stares at the five hundred thirty-five legislators crammed in seats on the floor. One or two may be missing, but most are present for this address. She moves her eyes up and scans the gallery above. It's full as well. Most are dignitaries and high-level bureaucrats wanting to be here for a part of history. There may not have been a more important speech in this room since Franklin Delano Roosevelt asked for a declaration of war against the Empire of Japan following the attack on Pearl Harbor. This may also be a day that lives in infamy.

"The events that transpired during and after this past election, as outlined for the American people on Tuesday, should give us all a moment of pause. Our division and hatred for those who don't share our views allowed our real enemy to exploit our weaknesses. They meant to usurp our democratic ideals and position themselves to cause real harm. America, for all her warts and blemishes, is still the best system devised by man. While our nation has committed terrible sins that we are not proud of, the American people should never lose sight of how far we have come."

Alicia doesn't expect applause and is surprised when a pair of congressmen, one from each party, starts clapping. Slowly, others join in. It's not enthusiastic applause, but she'll take it. The fact that it's coming from both sides of the oft-divided chamber is a victory in itself.

"The news reports presented on podcasts around the country are true. *Front Burner's* subsequent reporting, as Mark Swim, *Radio Free America,* and Alétheia echoed, is accurate. The election was tainted, even if the Pennsylvania results were accurate. My position as president-elect was compromised. Powerful forces attempted to hijack the presidency, and they almost succeeded."

Alicia turns her head to glance at the governor. She doesn't think he will betray her, but the risk of that happening isn't zero. She's grown to respect him, even if she thinks his views on issues are wrong. That doesn't mean he hasn't been playing along to set up a political ambush in front of Congress and the American people. There is no doubt that members of his party have been advocating that.

"I stand here with President-Elect Standish as a testament to our promise for transparency to the American people. This is a time for reconciliation and working toward a common goal to preserve our Union. Never before in our nation's more than two hundred fifty-year history have we faced such a daunting challenge to our existence. This threat did not come from Nazi fascists in Germany or Soviet nuclear weapons in the Cold War. It came from our own countrymen.

"Brian Cooper. Andrew Li. DeAnna Van Herten. Conrad Williams. These four people conspired to influence an election and use that leverage to control our land's most powerful executive office. They threatened to destroy the integrity of the presidency. They killed to achieve their objective. They were thwarted only through the dedication of some of America's finest alternative media sources, journalist Tierra Campos, and Special Agent Victoria Larsen of the Federal Bureau of Investigation."

Another polite applause erupts, but this time it gets louder and becomes a standing ovation. Alicia and Colin join in as she stares at the two women in the gallery. They are surrounded by the remarkable people she met before the speech. The country owes them a great deal. Getting an acknowledgment from this chamber is the least this government can do.

"I am standing before you today because of President-Elect Standish's transparency. She has asked me to help determine the path forward following this attempted coup. Despite our political differences and personal ambivalence following a brutal campaign, she will get it.

"This is not a time for politicking or using blame to curry favor with voters. My campaign was equally compromised, and it just as easily could have been me who was forced to make the difficult choices President-Elect Standish was faced with. I am here to offer you a challenge. Will we rise to the moment and overcome this attempt to subvert the notion of democratically elected representation, or are we content to let our divisions be our guiding ideology? That is one of the decisions that face this legislative body today."

"We, as a nation, and you as a Congress, must determine our path forward," Alicia says, picking up the plea. "The circumstances in which we find ourselves are unprecedented. So must be our leadership. Not for party or ideology. But for America. The people of this great nation must be our first and only concern during this difficult period. May God bless you as we steer this nation toward a more perfect Union, and may God bless the United States of America."

Alicia nods at Colin, and the pair makes their way off the lectern to another polite applause. The president will follow and outline his plans for a path forward out of this mess. Congress can either accept or reject that. The Supreme Court will likely also get involved as lawsuits are inevitable. The road ahead will not be easy, but every journey begins with a single step. Alicia Standish took hers by putting her best foot forward. Whatever happens next is out of her hands.

TWO WEEKS LATER

EPILOGUE

VICTORIA LARSEN

Sunset Beach Resort
Providenciales, Turks & Caicos

Grace Bay's seven-and-a-half-mile stretch of soft white sand and beautiful turquoise water makes it Victoria's favorite place on Earth. She closes her eyes and feels the gentle caress of the breeze and the sun's warmth beating on her face. She digs her toes in the powdery sand, thankful for her being here and not in a jail cell.

Victoria didn't think she'd ever see the Caribbean again. She wasn't sure if she would ever see a beach again. Prisoners don't get seaside field trips, especially to islands as magical as Turks and Caicos. She had nearly lost hope of escaping that fate. Nearly.

The FBI quickly dismissed all warrants against her, thanks to Attorney General Lisa Ehler. Still, she half expected a SWAT team to show up at the airport when she checked into her flight. Instead, she was greeted with a smile and best wishes for a happy vacation. That's exactly what she plans on having.

"You're going to burn."

A figure stands between her and the sun, casting a shadow over her. He's silhouetted, so she can't immediately see who it is. An eerie feeling of déjà vu washes over her. It's the same movie as the last time she was here, only different.

"Are you offering to slather lotion on me to earn my gratitude?"

"If all goes well," Austin says, sitting in the lounge chair alongside hers. "In case I haven't mentioned it before, this was a truly excellent idea."

"I couldn't agree more. I plan on enjoying every last moment until reality sets in."

"We go home?"

Victoria shakes her head. "We get handed the bill."

Austin waves a dismissive hand. "We can always wash dishes."

"You know, I was lying in this spot the last time I was here. It's when Rigo showed up to lure me back to the Bureau."

Austin checks over his shoulder. "He's not here now. You're in the clear."

"Thank you for making sure. It's been a long road since then."

"For both of us."

A waiter comes up to take their drink orders. Laha is Tibetan and has been with the resort forever. The story about how he got here was interesting, not that Victoria was paying rapt attention. She couldn't wrap her mind around the difference in climate between Nepal and Turks and Caicos. It would be hard to find a more extreme difference on the planet. How does he even explain that back home when he visits?

"What do you think I should do?"

Austin closes his eyes and exhales. "Put lotion on and enjoy the view."

"I did, and I am. I mean, about going back to the Bureau?"

"You said no work talk."

"I'm sorry. I guess it was unavoidable."

Austin shifts onto his side and watches her. Normally, she would get self-conscious and then aggravated at letting someone make her feel that way. But it's different with Austin. He's different, and she finds herself perfectly at ease.

"You know, a wise woman once gave me some advice about you. She told me you're a violently independent woman with confidence and smarts in spades. That it's what makes you a great agent and that I need to respect your space. I plan on heeding that advice."

Victoria smiles. She works in a male-dominated field and has always had more male friends than women. That changed the moment she met a gun-shy journalist in a Boston hotel room. Tierra is a true friend. She also has a way with words.

"Would you be okay with it if I did?"

"I would worry like a 1940s housewife waiting for her husband to come home from the war. I have never thought that a job defines who someone is. I'm a journalist, but that's what I do, not who I am. It's different with you. You have found your dream occupation because it's ingrained in your soul. It's who you are, and I really like who you are."

Victoria stares out at the water. The truth is, she can't imagine doing anything else. She's tried to walk away before and couldn't. She's been arrested twice in the performance of her duties and watched friends get injured or die. She was chased by the very government she worked for. If she returns, does she expect the next time to be any different?

"I could always work for *Front Burner.*"

"Journalists don't carry guns," Austin says with a smirk.

"Maybe they should start. I could be a trailblazer. A new standard for the investigative arm of America's resurgent news organization."

"Tierra would love the idea."

Her gun charge was dropped as well. The D.C. Metro Police didn't like the idea, but they liked the idea of crossing the DOJ even less. A school shooting survivor taking out a pair of former Russian Spetznaz commandos will make a great part of her next Peabody acceptance speech. That will likely make three. Not bad for a girl who once reported on the squirrels running around the National Mall for WWDC News.

"Would you be open to the idea of me working there?"

"Would you be comfortable doing anything other than saving the country?"

Victoria shakes her head. "I didn't set out to do that."

"The great ones never ask for glory – it's thrust upon them. America has never needed people like you more. Lord knows that the Bureau needs more agents willing to do the right thing no matter what. I would love to have you at *Front Burner*, but I'm not sure you can ever quit doing what you were born to do. You can only take breaks."

Victoria has always avoided serious relationships because she found the experience stifling. The men always seemed to want to make the decisions for her. For the longest time, she thought the entire gender was like that. Austin isn't. It doesn't mean he's a pushover, whipped, or indecisive. He just respects her enough to make her own choices.

"You're not making this easy."

"I'm a man. Get used to it."

She smiles. "I plan to."

Victoria wraps her towel around his head and pulls his lips to hers. Choices about her future can wait. This is a time to get lost in the present. They kiss, slow and soft and then more passionate. Austin's a very good kisser. At this time, in this place, with this man, everything is perfect.

EPILOGUE

TIERRA CAMPOS

Front Burner Washington Headquarters
Washington, D.C.

The lobby isn't a hive of activity, but it also no longer feels like an abandoned shopping mall. People have come and gone in the time I've been waiting down here. Staffing a business takes time, and *Front Burner's* online media presence and current business model make it even more complicated. That doesn't mean there aren't support service needs to fill. Among the first hires have been in advertising, IT, legal, accounting, and copyediting. They've ramped up quickly.

One thing Naomi quickly contracted was the front desk staff. Absent anyone to stop them, too many people wandered into the office. Some were looking for jobs, and others wanted to verbally berate us. A group of tourists even came in looking for selfies with the staff. It's been weird. It's also a physical security issue that needed to be remedied.

I decided to meet our newest employee in the lobby. We already have a badge printed out and waiting for him, but I felt I needed to do this. The two weeks since we broke up what the mainstream media calls the "most serious coup in American history" has been a wild ride. This is the cherry on top of that sundae.

"He's here," Marci says from behind the desk.

I turn and walk over to the new arrival as he enters, meeting him in the center of the lobby. He stops and looks around. Of all the places Oliver Jahn thought he would land after leaving VHN, this has to rank at the bottom of the list.

"Okay. Not that I'm ungrateful, but does this feel as weird for you as it does me?"

I shrug. "Life is unpredictable."

"Tierra, we have a…history. Are you sure you're okay with this?"

That's the same question I've been asking myself. It doesn't have an easy answer. Oliver Jahn made my life miserable. His words motivated his followers to chase me on a boardwalk and later put me in the hospital. He was despicable and deplorable. I have more reason to hate him than anyone.

"Follow me. I have something to show you."

Oliver tucks in behind me, scanning his badge at the gate after I do. We take the elevator up to the floor below my office. It's not as empty as it once was when virtual tumbleweeds were drifting between the cubicles. It's one of our many changes.

"You know, I'd be lying if I denied having dreams about burning this place to the ground."

"That's okay. I've spent countless days imagining throwing you out of one of these windows just to watch your head explode on the sidewalk. And that was among the quicker deaths I envisioned for you."

"I bet. I know Mi Sun never apologized to you for…well…."

"No, she didn't."

Oliver gently grabs my arm, stopping me between rows of cubicles.

"Before you walk me over to what I'm certain is an empty elevator shaft to push me down, I want to. I'm sorry, Tierra, for everything."

I lower my eyes as I process his words. They were sincere, not a perfunctory mea culpa without meaning or emotion behind them. I never expected to get one.

"I appreciate it…I do…but an apology isn't a magic wand you can wave to make everything all right. I'm learning to trust you, Oliver. Maybe even like you a little. But the damage won't be undone overnight."

"Then why am I here? *Front Burner* was under no obligation to hire me, and I'm certain Naomi wouldn't have over your objections."

I take a deep breath and exhale slowly. "I was resentful when Mi Sun showed up here. But she's been nothing short of amazing. After working with her, I realized that I can dwell in the past, but it will be like swimming with lead weights on my ankles. I don't want to live like that, and instead, I choose to look toward the future. After everything I've been through, it's the only path worth following."

"I understand."

"I have a question for you. You were making millions, and we're not paying you anything approaching that. I know other networks were floating you big offers to be their flagship show. Why join us?"

"Because I realized something when Wilson and I explained all this to the world. I really want to do the *news*. I was happy for the first time in…well, as long as I can remember. Nothing beats my old podcast days. Mi Sun and I were working in the corner of my basement to put on a good show and inform our audience. There were no ratings to worry about or network executives to please. It was just us."

I can't suppress a smile. "Then I think you're going to like this."

"What are you showing me?" he asks as we cover the distance to a pair of freshly painted double doors labeled "Studio Two."

"This."

I swing open one of the doors to his new podcast studio. It's small and cozy compared to the *TNT* set he's grown accustomed to. It's also decorated as close to his old basement studio as we could possibly make it.

There are some modern touches. A small control room off to the side will handle camera angles and audio mixing. The lighting is far better. There are some other neat technologies, but the look and feel are basically the same.

"Whoa," Oliver says, looking around while his jaw hangs open. "How did you…?"

"Mi Sun showed us pictures, and we pulled up some of your old podcasts for inspiration. We gave the design ideas to the contractor along with the first deposit. She oversaw their work, and voilà! The rest, as they say, is history."

Oliver runs a finger along the anchor desk. He almost looks like he's about to cry.

"Tierra, you guys were bankrupt five minutes ago. Why did you spend your resources on this?"

"Like I said, Oliver, we're looking to the future."

"I…I don't know what to say."

"Oliver Jahn is at a loss for words? That's a first," Mi Sun observes as she walks in and immediately hugs her old boss.

Wilson is leaning against the door jamb. Mi Sun is fast becoming like a second daughter to him. That makes me the older sister. The more time I spend with her, the more I'm okay with that.

"I don't hear screaming," Naomi says, carrying a tray of coffees. "That's good. I half expected to see Tierra gutting you with a Swiss Army knife."

"I wore body armor, just in case," Oliver says with a smile.

"Welcome to *Front Burner.*"

The studio begins to fill. Tyler and Logan come in, followed by Olivia and Dial Pirate, who are holding hands. They make the cutest, if not oddest, couple. Josh arrives and sets another tray of coffee on the anchor desk before standing next to me and sliding his arm around my waist.

I'm still getting used to being in a relationship with him. It's been great, but it is an adjustment. We've been friends for so long that we're both careful about the next steps. It will be a journey, but one I'm looking forward to.

Jerome is the last to arrive, having just arrived back in Washington. Everyone is here except Austin, who is in the Caribbean on an important assignment. Outside of Josh and me, there have never been two people on Earth I've wished to find happiness together more than him and Victoria. They deserve it.

"I'm sure that most of you have a bottle of something stashed in the bottom drawer of your desks," Naomi says, spot on in that assessment. "But I refuse to start drinking this early in the morning, so java will have to do."

Naomi distributes the coffee. I've had my issues with her, but she is a good leader. No task, no matter how mundane, is beneath her. That's the way to build the right culture here.

"What are we toasting to?" Logan asks after everyone gets a cup and peels the plastic lids back.

"I thought it was bad luck to toast without booze," Tyler observes.

"I think we're beyond superstitions in this place," Wilson says to universal agreement.

"Let's toast to new beginnings," Naomi says, getting approving nods. "We have all been through a lot. Some more than others. But each of us brings to the table unique perspectives. That will fuel *Front Burner* for years to come while we report the *actual* news in this country. The good and the bad, free from bias and agendas. It's going to be hard, but most worthy causes are. We may even fail. But I promise you, the people in this room are the brightest light for journalism in America. It's time to show the country what it looks like."

"Hear, hear," a chorus of voices chimes out.

"Cheers!" a few say enthusiastically as we tap cups. It doesn't have the charm of clinking crystal champagne flutes, but it will suffice.

The room breaks out into side conversations. Everyone offers Oliver Jahn their congratulations and shakes his hand. I stand off to the side and take it all in. We've all come a long way. Old enemies have become new friends as tattered relationships have been repaired while new ones are formed.

It's the way life should be. I'm fully aware there are people out there plotting our demise. There are still conspirators who need to be dealt with. That's for another day. I allow myself the broadest smile I have worn since childhood. This is the best I have felt in a long time.

ACKNOWLEDGMENTS

It's been quite a ride. Victoria and Tierra have been two of my favorite characters to write about because they had very different paths in life. Each grew as this story arc unfolded. Tierra became tougher and put her past behind her. Victoria became a little softer and learned to let people in. The long character development that spans novels is the most rewarding for me.

Is that it for them now that we have reached the decisive endgame? Don't count on it. There is still more story to tell, so count on a sequel trilogy coming. Until then, I sincerely hope you found this ending satisfying. I toyed with not putting the two epilogues at the end of the story, but I thought it was worth conveying the light at the end of the tunnel that both women longed for.

This is a difficult genre to write in the modern age. That's a reason I appreciate all the readers who take a chance on picking up one of my novels. Nobody wants to be preached to, and that has permeated many forms of entertainment since the turn of the century. I convey messages in my writing but try to be even and balanced in my approach. Thank you for trusting me with your precious time to allow me to tell you a story. That's the best reward for an author.

In the information technology world, unexplained problems are called "gremlins." Mike Waitz of Sticks and Stones Editing and I experienced that when it was time to begin the edit of *Decisive Endgame*. Emails weren't being delivered, and weeks were lost. He had to push hard to meet the deadline, and I appreciate his diligent effort to finish. I get to work with some great people in bringing these novels to you, and he is absolutely one of them. That's the nicest thing you'll ever see me write about an editor.

Another is Dave at JD&J Design. Creating a book cover can be stressful for an author, as it's the first thing a reader sees. It must convey a message, and Dave does a fantastic job putting together excellent covers based on often incoherent guidance.

Michele, the love of my life and travel partner, is along for the ride, as my readers are. She gets the director's cut version as she endures countless sessions of me working through scenes, plotlines, and book ideas. Too often, she needs to pause the television to find out what I'm laughing at as I write and rewrite. I crack myself up, and she always needs to know why. Sometimes she regrets asking. Life as an author's wife can be challenging.

To Meg, for whom this book is dedicated, thank you for your stories. I know I make your job seem sexier than it is. The FBI has been getting dumped on for a while now, but the leadership is often to blame for that. The rank and file are professionals just trying to do unforgiving and unappreciated jobs who deserve more credit and praise than they will ever be given.

The other half of the dedication was for a friend and brother-in-arms who sadly passed away last Christmas Eve. I had the pleasure of serving with some great men and women during my military service. Like all of us, Ted Chambers was flawed, but he was a good friend who spent most of his adult life serving our nation. If the last name looks familiar, he was the inspiration behind Massachusetts State Police detective Seth Chambers. May he finally rest in peace.

Family is important, and I cherish mine. My mother, Nancy, has some reading to catch up on. My sister and brother-in-law do as well. My nephew only gets a pass because he hasn't started school yet. They are always there to support me, and it is always appreciated.

ABOUT THE AUTHOR

Mikael Carlson is the award-winning author of the novel *The iCandidate* and the Michael Bennit Series of political dramas. He also has written two other ongoing series: Tierra Campos Thrillers and Watchtower Thrillers. His newest series, America, Inc., is a retelling of the futuristic dystopian Black Swan Saga that serves as a cautionary tale of life in a world following a global economic collapse.

A retired veteran of the Rhode Island Army National Guard and United States Army, he deployed twice in support of military operations during the Global War on Terror. Mikael has served in the field artillery, infantry, and in support of special operations units during his career on active duty at Fort Bragg and in the Army National Guard.

A proud U.S. Army Paratrooper, he conducted over fifty airborne operations following the completion of jump school at Fort Benning in 1998. Since then, he has trained with the militaries of countless foreign nations.

Mikael earned a Master of Arts in American History in 2010 and graduated with a B.S. in International Business from Marist College in 1996.

He was raised in New Milford, Connecticut, and currently lives in nearby Danbury.